NEXT GIRL ON THE LIST

MCRYAN MYSTERY SERIES

ROGER STELLJES

NEXT GIRL ON THE LIST By Roger Stelljes

Never miss a new release again, join the new release list at www. RogerStelljes.com

ISBN 978-0-9835758-7-0 (ebook)

ISBN 978-1-6534266-1-4 (paperback)

First edition November 10, 2016

ACKNOWLEDGMENTS

To Scott Crossman – golf partner and book critic.
Thanks for helping to make it all happen.

1

"I'M SOMEONE WHO IS ONCE AGAIN GOING TO CHANGE THE TRAJECTORY OF YOUR LIFE."

WASHINGTON, DC

The man peeked through the vertical blinds and could see the first flecks of daylight elevating over the rooftops of the two-story brownstones across the street. Not a window was illuminated anywhere along the street on a sleepy early April Sunday morning.

It was time to finish.

The dead body laid in a naked pose, staged in the center of the living room, displayed under the light from the swing arm of a reading lamp.

He'd killed her seven hours ago. The formula—the seduction and the deception, even these four years later—still worked, and the exhilarating sensation he'd felt as the life drained from her body was just as he'd remembered it.

That gave him the excitement he craved.

After the excitement of the kill, it was then time to quietly and methodically create his work of art. If killing was the excitement, the art was his passion.

It had taken great patience to arrange the display of her body with the proper detail, her body placed face down on the floor and her arms extended left and right as required by the masterpiece he was emulating. It had taken him more than an hour to run the small string of beaded pearls through her hair, which he'd needed to painstakingly and methodically style from an awkward angle as her body laid still and lifeless on the floor. In his final analysis, he'd concluded that her hair color was a shade of brown lighter than perfection, but it was close enough. However, if there were some slight qualms about the lightness of her hair color, he had absolutely none with regard to the quality of her body. It was perfect. The width of her hips and softness of her flesh was ideal; from that standpoint, she perfectly fit his vision of what he wanted to do.

Once her body was displayed just as he wanted, he then screwed the ornate gold frame into the narrow panels of the hardwood floor. Her name wasn't Grace, but she was an incredible likeness to the body in the masterpiece laid beneath her.

That was the conclusion he reached as he snapped his photographs.

He only took photographs of the first victim, so as to properly motivate those he was challenging. The final photo he selected would be his calling card, a dramatic showpiece to start matters with the proper intensity.

Picking up the camera once again, he brought it up to his eye, focused the lens with his left hand and then snapped three more pictures, checked the display screen to assess the quality and then snapped two more photos. He checked and evaluated the pictures before deciding to snap yet two more. All eight pictures were seriously considered, clicking the back and forth arrow buttons. Eventually, he narrowed it down, clicking between two pictures taken from the left side of her body, which in his critical analysis better exhibited her and the lovely softness of her features. There were two specific pictures that really captured the essence of what he wanted, and with that, he was finished.

The last item on the checklist was to set the little black timer. The countdown, which started the first quarter of the game, was always the last item on the mental to-do list. Checking his watch, he set the timer and watched it start its countdown. He then switched off the reading lamp and returned it to its resting place amongst a stack of books surrounding a reading chair to the left of the front picture window.

It was time to leave.

At the front door, his gloved hand on the knob, he stopped and glanced back and took one last lingering look at Lisa. She was such a lovely woman, shy and reserved, unconfident and unsure, yet gracious and polite, so wanting to have a relationship and to have it with him. He had truly enjoyed her company over the past weeks, discussing their mutual interests, their favorite paintings and artists. She had a nice and quite underrated selection of pieces haphazardly displayed throughout her cramped and extremely cluttered townhouse, even remakes of a couple of his favorites.

In some ways, having to do what he did left him feeling a bit melancholy. To do what he must, he had to take the life of someone who shared his love and passion for the arts. The saving grace in his mind was that developing that fondness for the victims, knowing, appreciating and understanding them to the degree he did, served as motivation and significantly enhanced the quality of his performance and staging. The victims were what they often admired, the subject of work of a brilliant and renowned artist. After he brutally squeezed the last breaths of life out of a victim, in some ways he felt as if he was apologizing by treating their body, their corpse, with such great and gentle care. It was his aspiration that each victim would be the prime focus of the piece of fine art they were meant to embody. Over time, as he honed his craft, each detail became more refined and each scene became more elaborate and astonishing. It made his early work look almost crude in comparison.

At the front door, he prepared to leave. He slid a stocking cap onto his head, pulled the hood on his black sweatshirt up over the cap and then slung his backpack over his shoulder.

This was a time of maximum peril. Peering out the front door peephole, he saw nobody on the street and therefore no threats to identify him. Exhaling, he opened the door just a crack, scrutinizing every aspect of the street; first left, then right and then back to the left again. There was no one about. Quietly and quickly, he slipped out the front door, pulled it shut and then locked the deadbolt with her key. He casually walked down the steps and the short front walk, constantly checking left and right as he made his way to the Honda Civic. Within twenty seconds, he drove away.

Thirteen hours later, with the sun nearly down as the clock approached 7:00 p.m., he slithered down the narrow crevice of an alley, holding close to the sides, staying in the shadows of the small garages and uneven privacy fences. He reached the intended garage and secured the plastic bag with the note and picture to the garage door handle and then as quickly as he'd arrived, he disappeared.

Now there was but one thing left to do.

~

Mac stuffed the last of the dishes into the dishwasher while his redheaded fiancée, White House Deputy Director of Communications Sally Kennedy, finished up hand washing the large serving plates in the sink.

They would be married in six weeks. The wedding would be a small, intimate affair with their family and closest friends at a private estate overlooking the Chesapeake Bay.

He could hardly wait for it to arrive.

All the planning was done, the wedding dress bought and fitted, the bridesmaids' dresses were set, the tuxedos sized and rented, the menu selected, the invitations sent and the responses received. His close family and friends were all making the trek from Minnesota and he couldn't wait to see and spend time with them. All they needed was to get to the date.

A few of those that would also be wedding guests—their DC friends, as they called them—were now grabbing a fresh beer or glass of wine and making their way from the kitchen and into the living room. He checked his watch again, as he had every thirty seconds for what seemed like the last hour. He silently admonished himself: *Mac McRyan, time does not go faster when you do that. If anything, it drags.*

"Get in here, you two," Dara Wire yelled from the living room. "It's starting in a minute."

"Your public awaits," Sally teased as she lightly cupped his face with her right hand and pecked his lips. They each grabbed fresh beers out of the cooler and made their way into the living room and over to the couch in front of the flat screen that hung over the fireplace.

"Nervous?" Sally asked loudly, holding his hand.

"Not as much as you," Mac replied with a rueful smile. "I can only imagine the political ramifications if I blew this."

The group erupted in laughter; Sally's friends from the White House staff numbered many in the room.

"It'll be fine," Wire added. "I'm sure I covered for you."

The iconic stopwatch of *60 Minutes* appeared on the screen. Veteran correspondent Steve Kroft introduced the segment, the book's flag-draped cover in the story background along with head-shot renderings of Wire and Mac.

"It all started with the murder of a political blogger in an out-of-the-way motel in St. Paul, Minnesota," Kroft started. "Mere days later, that murder, and the resulting investigation, hit at the very foundations of this country's electoral system. This is the story of that investigation told from the perspective of its two investigators, Mac McRyan and Dara Wire."

When Mac and Dara agreed to write a book about their investigation of a series of murders in the days and weeks prior to the last presidential election, an investigation that revealed that the Vice President's campaign had rigged voting machines in three vital states, they thought it would be of some mild interest to the public, although Mac was dubious.

"I'll do it. I have the time and it will be an interesting experience. But when the book finally comes out it will be eighteen months after the election. In this day and age, that's like forever. The public will have long moved on."

It took less than a week to prove Mac wrong.

Mac and Wire were educated, talented and intelligent, but writers they were not. Ellen Paulson, an accomplished and award-winning author who'd written both fiction and non-fiction, was hired to assist them. Paulson was perfect for the project and did something special with all the material Mac and Wire provided over hours and hours of interviews reviewing the course and scope of the investigation. The publisher thought so too and engaged in a large promotional campaign. The book opened in the top ten of the *New York Times* Best Seller list and was climbing. It was an instant hit, was all the rage on the political talk shows and now their publisher and agent were fielding calls from movie producers.

"You can't be serious," was Mac's flabbergasted response when the book agent called them. "They want to make a movie out of this?"

"Are you kidding me? Mac, it reads like a movie script," their agent replied excitedly. "A damn good one, and the best part is, it's a true story. This is the real deal. People eat that stuff up. Car chases, shootouts, conspiracies related to the highest office in the land. This screams movie."

"I want Angelina Jolie to play me," was Wire's thrilled reply, and then to Mac, she said, "Would you just lighten up and enjoy the ride? What actor is in his mid-thirties, six-foot plus, has blond hair, is marginally attractive and has a huge dimple chin? That's who we need to play you."

"Nobody has a chin like this, so I guess they won't be able to cast for the role," Mac replied derisively. For some reason, he wasn't excited to see his likeness on screen.

"Fat chance," Wire answered, shaking her head at her friend. "Man, you have got to get over the sourpuss routine on this. Lighten up, for cripes' sake. *This is awesome!*"

"Well, Mac, maybe this will make you happy," their agent offered. "You two have already *easily* covered your advances. The royalty checks are coming, and they won't be little. So sit back, enjoy it and start thinking about what you'll wear to the movie premiere."

This didn't mean everyone loved the book.

While Wire, their literary agent, their publisher and those around them were reveling in the attention, Mac knew there was a price to be paid. The entire time he was working on the book, he knew where he was most vulnerable, and that was in the arena he hated the most —politics.

Mac had never felt like he showed any political favoritism what-soever when investigating the case. He pursued the facts and the evidence wherever they led. There was no disputing what he and Wire found and who was responsible for the murders or trying to fix the election. However, when it came to politics, people often liked to focus on the *process* rather than the *result*.

In running the case, it was Mac who let Wire join the investiga-tion, and she was working for the Vice President's opponent. He kept Judge Dixon in the loop and accessed some of his resources. The Judge was running Governor Thomson's campaign. Sally worked for Judge Dixon at the time and now worked for him and President Thomson at the White House. So while Mac felt like he played the investigation straight, he was left wide open to charges of political bias. The supporters of the Vice President and his party, the ones *not* implicated in the scandal, were more than happy to point that out, and were doing so repeatedly to anyone who would listen. Of course, in response, representatives of the President's party were using the book as a proxy to launch counterattacks, which in the end put him, as the lead investigator, in everyone's political crosshairs.

"Don't worry about it," Sally said, unworried. "Besides, contro-versy means clicks, interest and increased sales. Laugh all the way to the bank."

Mac wasn't laughing.

Prideful, he didn't like his credibility being attacked, and in the first week the book was on the market, it was attacked, *repeatedly*. To some, he'd engaged in a political witch hunt on behalf of Judge Dixon, the man who would become President and his soon-to-be wife.

"Then go on the offensive," Sally had argued, going into her communications director mode. "You're not talking. You're saying no to every interview request. So in the absence of you speaking up for yourself people will wonder whether there's anything to all this bullshit people are slinging. *Fight back.* The media wants to talk to you. So talk."

Mac and Wire had spoken very little to the media, even with the book's immediate success. As cops, they had a natural skepticism of the media, the gotcha questions and the short interview segments where it could prove difficult to defend yourself, or your comments or answers were taken out of context.

Then, not long after Sally's pep talk, *60 Minutes* called.

In return for the exclusive interview, the producer promised a lengthened segment to take a deep and objective dive into the investigation.

They were both still leery, but then Mac said, "It is *60 Minutes*. They aren't infallible, but they are—"

"The gold standard," Wire answered, finishing the thought. "If you can't trust *60 Minutes*, who can you trust?"

"I think we need to do this," was Mac's ultimate conclusion.

Now they were watching the segment.

All in all, they were happy with how it turned out. Steve Kroft was a pro and asked Mac some hard but fair questions, particularly about the involvement of Judge Dixon.

"You can understand how people might claim bias," Kroft suggested. "You can understand how some people would say it affected how you approached the investigation."

"I can," Mac answered, nodding his head. "I guess all I can do is say two things in reply. One, once I realized what this case might be about from a political standpoint, knowing the election was just days away, I needed to find the answers as quickly as possible. I didn't want to find the answers two days *after* the election—just think of *that* scenario. It would have made 2000 look like a picnic. So to avoid that, I needed resources, and Judge Dixon had immediate access to those, so I took his assistance for one night. It was a shortcut. I allowed Dara Wire to join the investigation despite what people see as a conflict. She's a damn good investigator, was offering to help and I needed help at that moment, but to let her tag along was, I'll admit, not the usual protocol. So people may question me and how I went about things, but my second point is what you don't hear, Steve. You don't hear our critics questioning *what* we found. They question the *how* but not the *what*. People can question me and my integrity all they want, but the final results speak for themselves, and nobody, not even the people questioning me and my conduct of the investigation, can question the guilt of those involved. If I have to take some heat for *how* I got the job done, I can live with that because in the end, justice was done. We. Got. It. Right."

"Great answer, Mac," Wire said, making a toast with her beer.

"It's the truth."

"Even Kroft liked that answer," Sally added, patting Mac on the knee happily.

The segment ended with Kroft asking Mac, "So how has this changed your life?"

Mac laughed, lightly shaking his head. "Man, where do I even start? It's changed everything. I was a St. Paul police detective, very happy with my fairly anonymous life. Now I'm living in Washington, DC. I have a best seller to my name. I've had the privilege of working on a few cases I'd have never seen otherwise, all because of who I now know. I'm here with you on *60 Minutes*. None of this was on my life radar. I couldn't even have imagined it. The case"—he shook his head— "the case has completely changed the trajectory of my life. And I suppose a lot of other lives too."

The segment ended.

The room erupted in conversation, smiles, laughter and toasts. Mac and Wire were relieved. They'd both felt good about how the interviews went, but until you saw the finished product, how they arranged it, what they left in, what they cut out, you just never knew.

"You did great, babe," Sally beamed and then pecked him on the lips. "I'm so proud of you."

"That was great," Wire said as she gave him a high five.

"What a relief," Mac answered, finally feeling like he could breathe.

Their house phone rang.

"Excuse me," he said to Wire. He slowly worked his way across the living room to the phone. He smiled at the room filled with laughter as he picked up the phone on the fourth ring. "Hello?"

"Is this Mac McRyan?"

"Yes, it is. Who's this?" he asked lightly, covering his right ear, trying to keep out the noise of the chatter in the room.

"I'm someone who is once again going to change the trajectory of your life."

"Excuse me?" Mac asked, immediately on guard. It was in the tone of the caller, almost sinister in nature. And it wasn't the caller's real voice. It was being disguised. "Who the hell is this?"

Sally approached, seeing the sudden change of his expression.

"It's game time, Mr. McRyan. Is Ms. Wire there with you?"

Mac scanned the room to find her. "She is."

"Oh, so much the better," the caller replied. The voice might have been disguised, but you couldn't hide the taunting and dark nature of it. "Are you two ready to play?"

"Play what?" Mac asked while finally catching Wire's attention, urgently waving for her to approach. "What game are you talking about?"

"You are now on the clock, Mr. McRyan. And you don't have a moment to waste."

"Clock?" Mac asked as he walked into the kitchen and away from the crowd. Wire and Sally were on his heels, confused and alarmed, having heard the strained tone of Mac's voice and seen the concerned look on his face. "Did you say clock?" he asked.

"Yes. The countdown has begun."

"Countdown? Who the hell are you?" Mac asked, but something he read many years ago had him wondering if he already knew, and he instantly dreaded the thought of it.

"I left you a little present," the voice taunted. "You'll find it hanging on your garage door. Once you find it, you'll know what to do and then ... our game can begin."

"Hello? Hello?" Mac asked urgently, but the line was now dead. "Shit."

"What is it?" Sally asked.

"Mac, talk to me," Dara asked, concerned. "Who was that?"

"I don't know, someone ... something bad, I think. Something very, very bad." Mac explained the call quickly while he took out his keys, opened a kitchen cabinet over the refrigerator, reached up high and extracted a silver metal box. He unlocked the box and resting inside were two 9mm Glocks. He handed one to Wire, who instinctively checked the magazine and then slammed it back in. Mac did the same, chambered a round and then grabbed two flashlights from the same cabinet, as well as a pair of rubber gloves.

"Where are you going?" Sally asked.

"To see what is hanging on the garage door," Mac replied, moving toward the back door. Wire followed close behind, pulling her long black hair into a tight ponytail.

"Shouldn't you call the police?" Sally suggested worriedly.

"We are the police," Mac answered grimly as he handed a flashlight to Wire and said, "Cover me."

"Let's go," Wire answered, ready.

He opened the back door and slowly walked down the steps, the flashlight in his left hand crossed underneath his right hand holding the gun, slowly and methodically scanning the small backyard, side to side and up and down. Wire covered him from behind as he approached the back of the garage and then the small gate in the privacy fence to the left. He flipped up the gate latch and pulled it open while Wire covered him from the corner of the garage.

Mac looked back to Wire, who nodded for him to go.

He guardedly slipped through the door and then turned right, facing the front of the garage, and pointed the flashlight at the garage door.

Attached to the decorative handle was a large clear plastic Ziploc storage bag. The bag contained a note and a picture. The picture was of a larger woman, naked, lying over what looked like a portrait of some kind. The note read:

Dear Mac and Dara,

Lisa White lives on 11th Street NW in Washington DC. She's number one. At the address, I've left you a hint for number two, and a timer counting down to when I shall kill her. As Sherlock Holmes often said: "Come, Watson, come. The game is afoot." I wish you good luck.

Rubens

"Oh my God," Wire gasped.

"He's back," Mac muttered as he re-read the handwritten note.

The trajectory of their lives was indeed about to change.

2

"BY MY COUNT, THAT'S WEDNESDAY NIGHT, 9:00 P.M."

"*J* *esus!* Is it required that if you drive a Subaru, you have to slow everyone else down?" Wire barked as she speedily passed a green Forester rolling along five miles an hour below the posted limit.

While Wire aggressively negotiated the traffic, Mac went into investigation mode and thought to make two immediate phone calls.

The first was to Metropolitan Police Department of the District of Columbia (MPD) homicide detective Lincoln Coolidge. Coolidge was one of the best on the DC force and a man they both knew well and knew they could work with. Mac hurriedly explained what he had.

"Rubens, really? He's back?"

"Looks like it."

Coolidge didn't hesitate. "I'm out the door now."

Mac's second call was to FBI Director Mitchell. Not many people had the director's cell number, but Mac did. If it was Rubens, the FBI would have to be involved and nobody could get the gears of the FBI running more quickly than its director.

"Mac, I'm on my way, but at that scene, you're FBI," Mitchell ordered.

"Is she still alive?" Wire asked as she veered wildly around a Honda Accord, who honked in annoyance as they passed.

Mac shook his head. "She doesn't look alive on the photo. If this is him, she's dead. *Long* dead."

"What do you know about Rubens?" Wire asked worriedly.

"He started, I think, ten years ago and killed four women in Boston. Then he hit Chicago a few years later and then Los Angeles, I want to say … maybe four years ago. He killed four women in Chicago and then four more in Los Angeles. He calls himself Rubens after a famous painter and his victims are much like the voluptuous women in the artist's paintings."

"Voluptuous?"

"I think today's descriptive term would be plus-sized. If I recall, the women are often described as Rubenesque."

"This is unbelievable."

"No, what's unbelievable is he thinks it's a game: four women, four quarters, a timer counting down to the next victim with a winner at the end—either him or us. That's what we're in for here. You should have heard him on the phone. I don't care that the voice was disguised, it was freakin' eerie. He was on a high, getting off on it."

"You seem to know a lot about him," Wire suggested as she honked at the white Camry in front to move to the right lane.

Mac shook his head, "No more than what I remember reading from when he was killing in Los Angeles. I was a pretty new detective at the time, solved a few cases and felt like I was hot shit and all, sitting there reading the news accounts thinking it might be really cool to go after someone like him."

"What do you think now?"

"Now I know better," Mac replied as Wire turned a hard left onto NW 11th. "If this is him, be ready to be consumed by this," he counseled. "He's going to taunt and haunt us. That's what he does. He was already doing it to me. We're going to get to our victim and there's going to be a timer, counting down to his next victim. Supposedly, he leaves a clue or clues behind that identify the next victim but for the detectives in the other cases before us, it's been like deciphering

Zodiac's Code. I don't think it's ever been cracked, or if it has, never in time." Mac scratched his head, dreading what was to come. "There have been books written about him, I think," he added. "It's a big media circus for two or three weeks every time he strikes. And then, when it's over, *poof*—he's gone."

"And now he's here in DC."

"Sure seems that way."

"Did we bring this on ourselves?" Wire asked.

"You mean *60 Minutes*. *Electing to Murder*. The Reaper case."

"Yeah, is he here because of all of that?"

"I don't know," Mac answered. "It might just be a convenient coincidence. If his past is any indication, he's been here a long time planning. We're involved because we're the flavor of the month. If we don't show up, he probably picks on someone like Coolidge or someone from the Bureau."

Lisa White's townhouse was set mid-block on 11th Street NW, on the west side between Columbia Road and Irving Street. Patrol units already on the scene flooded the front with light. Mac and Wire exited the Range Rover and quickly strode up to the front of the house.

"Are you two McRyan and Wire?" one of the uniforms asked.

"Yes," Mac answered.

"Coolidge says it's your show. He's on his way."

Mac took a look at the two-story townhouse and quickly walked up the steps, still wearing the white rubber gloves. He carefully tried the door, but it was locked. He peered in the side window to the right of the door but couldn't see inside. As he evaluated his options for entry, Coolidge arrived.

"Mac, is it him? Is it really him?" Coolidge asked, jogging up the sidewalk in black jeans, a black t-shirt and black leather jacket looking like *Shaft*.

"We'll find out soon enough, Linc, but I think so," Mac replied, thinking back to the phone conversation and its authenticity. "The voice was masked but the cadence, the words and the tone—"

"All said it was him," Coolidge finished.

Mac nodded slowly and then said quietly, "It was—creepy."

"You want to go in?"

"Yes." Mac turned back to the door and looked at the side window. He wanted to preserve the door for prints on the extremely long odds that the killer actually left them, so he took a chance. He pulled his Glock out from his waistline, flipped the butt end and hammered the glass to the right of the door. The glass shattered and created a jagged hole just large enough for him to carefully slide his right arm through to reach the deadbolt and twist it open. He cautiously pulled his arm back out and opened the door.

"Wire and I, Linc and two men." Mac led them inside.

Straight ahead were a set of narrow steep steps up to the second story. Coolidge and two patrol officers went up with flashlights and guns drawn.

"I'll take the back," Wire said quietly as she went straight ahead, down the dark hallway leading past the steps toward the back of the townhouse.

Mac went sharp right, into the living room, and his flashlight immediately caught a long mirror in the corner of the living room near the curtains to the front picture window. In the bottom of the mirror's reflection was a naked body lying on the floor, and resting above the body, striking in the darkness of the room, were the red block numbers of a timer counting down.

Mac rotated left and held his flashlight high over the body of the victim, which was placed on top of what looked like a large portrait underneath the corpse as if it were a rug. To add illumination, he turned on a reading lamp in the corner of the room.

With the light, he could better see the full exhibition of what Rubens left behind. "Sweet Jesus," he muttered under his breath.

In the portrait, there were three naked women, one in the middle with her back to the viewer, then one to the left and one to the right. The three women all had wide hips, large thighs, soft stomachs and large breasts, and visually they formed something of a circle.

Lisa White was staged lying face down over the pose of the woman in what would be the middle of the portrait. Her head was turned slightly to the left so that you could make out the soft profile of that side of her face. Her right arm was stretched out from her shoulder so as to look as if it were placed gently over the shoulder of the woman to the right in the portrait. White's left arm was extended to look as if it were wrapped around the upper waist and just under the right breast of the woman on the left. Around the perimeter of the portrait, screwed into the floor, was a large, ornate gold picture frame.

Mac approached White, crouched down and gently reached to check for a pulse on her left wrist. There was none and he could feel that rigor had set in. She'd been dead for some time.

"Oh my," Dara gasped quietly as she stepped into the living room.

"Oh my, is right," Mac muttered as he stood up and swiftly worked his phone, typing in a Google search for *Rubens* and *portrait*. Fifteen seconds later he had his answer. "The portrait is *The Three Graces*."

"This is?" Wire asked, gesturing to the floor.

"Yes, crude as it may be," Mac replied as he showed Wire the photo on his phone.

"That's definitely it."

Mac crouched back down and examined what Rubens the killer had done with Lisa White. The way White was staged gave the whole portrait a haunting three-dimensional look. The whole morbid display, especially with the frame, took up a significant portion of the floor of the small, narrow living room.

"This had to have taken him a lot of time," Mac muttered as he stood up and folded his arms across his chest, taking in the detail of the scene.

Coolidge came into the living room. "It's all clear—whoa," the detective said, stepping back in shock.

"Seriously disturbing is what it is," Wire replied.

"And I suspect we now know how our other two victims will be posed," Mac suggested. "I bet in the next two murders he has planned we'll find the other two Graces. And," Mac turned to his right towards the timer, "we have our time window."

Sitting on the ledge of a set of vertical built-in shelves was a timer, black with red digital numbers, counting down. The current count was 69:18:24: sixty-nine hours, eighteen minutes, twenty-four seconds.

"That puts the next murder in three days," Coolidge stated.

Mac sighed as he set the countdown on his phone. "By my count, that's Wednesday night, 9:00 p.m."

3

"THERE ARE MORE PICTURES IN THIS HOUSE THAN THE LOUVRE."

M PD as well as FBI forensics teams arrived on the scene along with the Chief Medical Examiner for the District. With the living room getting crowded, Mac, Wire and Coolidge removed themselves out to the front lawn. They were quickly joined by Alonzo Weathers, the Chief of Police for the Metropolitan Police Department of the District of Columbia and FBI Director Thomas Mitchell, who arrived later, having driven himself to the scene.

Mac explained the phone call he'd received and the scene they'd found inside.

Mitchell and Weathers quickly made their way inside the house to take their own look. At the front door of the townhouse to the left of White's, two uniform officers were talking to a smallish man dressed in a white golf shirt and pressed khakis. Mac and Wire made their way up the steps to join in. One of the officers introduced them to White's neighbor, a diminutive man in a navy blue sweater vest named Casey Schmidt.

"What happened to Ms. White?" the neighbor asked Mac.

"That's what we're trying to figure out."

"Is she dead?"

"I'm afraid so," Mac answered regretfully, "And it appears she's been dead many hours, Mr. Schmidt. Did you see anything out of the ordinary around her townhouse today?"

"No, sir," Schmidt answered, shaking his head vigorously. "I didn't see anything at all and I was around pretty much all day."

"How about last night?"

Schmidt shook his head again. "Nothing that I remember, sir."

"Any noises?" Mac inquired, thinking of the frame screwed into the floor. "Say, like a power drill or a hammer, anything like that?"

"No, no, sir."

"Any screams, shouts, loud noises?"

"No, not that I heard," Schmidt replied. "It was real quiet, kind of like it always is."

"Always is?" Wire asked. "What do you mean?"

"Ms. White, she was a quiet lady."

"Did you know her well?"

The neighbor shook his head. "No, not really other than to say hello, good morning and have the occasional chat here on the stoop or over the fence out back, stuff like that. She was pleasant and all, very polite and respectful, but kept pretty much to herself."

"Any boyfriends, things like that?" Mac asked.

"I didn't know her *that* well, so I don't really know," Schmidt answered. "I don't ever recall noticing any gentlemen callers coming around for her. That's not to say that there weren't, I just don't remember any."

"How about lady friends? Any of those ever come around?"

"What kind of lady friends?" Schmidt asked with raised eyebrows.

"Any kind," Mac pressed.

"Not many of those that I remember either."

"Tell me more about her," Mac asked. "What was she like?"

"There's not much to tell, sir. She was quiet, very reserved but a nice, courteous neighbor." Schmidt looked off in the distance for a moment. "She liked books—I saw her carrying books many times. And I know she enjoyed painting. When the weather is nice in the spring and fall, she was often out painting in her little garden in the back. I know she liked flowers, she has a number of planters out back and the two on the front stoop that she was constantly tending to."

"How about a job? What did she do?" Wire asked, taking notes.

"She worked over at Georgetown University. I think she was some sort of administrator there." The neighbor thought for another moment and then shook his head. "That's about all I know."

There would be more to be learned about Lisa White, but for now, this gave them a little insight. Mac and Wire descended the steps of Schmidt's townhouse just as Director Mitchell and Chief Weathers descended down the steps of White's.

"If this is Rubens, and I think it is," Mitchell started, "this is number one. He has three more planned."

"Three more?" Weathers asked, concerned.

The director nodded. "He generally kills four women of Rubenesque body type then disappears, or at least that has been the M.O. so far when he went on his three other sprees." Then Mitchell turned to Mac. "I assume you saw the timer?"

"We calculate that to be Wednesday night, 9:00 p.m.," Mac answered, showing the countdown on his phone.

"That's what I thought too," the director answered, then tacked in a different direction. "He called you?"

"Yes." Mac related the phone call.

"He's going to keep calling you," the director stated. "That's part of his routine. The other times he found one cop to call, torment and ridicule. This time, that looks like it's going to be you, Mac."

"Yes, sir."

"You ready for it?"

"Do I have a choice?"

"No, no, you don't," the director answered candidly. "So let's get to it. How do you want to handle this?"

Mac looked to Wire who replied, "How about like we did last time?"

"That works," Mac answered quickly.

"What does that mean?" Chief Weathers asked.

"We run it like the Reaper case. The FBI and your people, Alonzo, run a normal investigation, I put a special agent in charge to run it from the FBI side, give it a face, and you have your man," Mitchell answered. "At the same time, Mac and Wire run their own investigation off to the side and coordinate with the agent in charge. There are two investigations, but when push comes to shove, Mac is in charge." The director glanced back to Mac. "Will Galloway work?"

"Yes, sir," Mac answered.

Mac and Wire worked with Senior Special Agent Don Galloway on the Reaper case. Galloway would be comfortable with the command structure, had a deft touch with the media and was an administrative wizard. With him handling all of that, Mac could just concentrate on the case. He could completely focus on Rubens.

"Okay, then there is one other person we will call in—an FBI Consultant named April Greene who works with the Bureau's Behavioral Analysis Unit. She's written numerous books on serial killers, including two on Rubens. She consults with us on cases that interest her. I'm pretty sure the return of Rubens will get her in the mood to help out."

"I think we'll need all the help we can possibly get," Mac answered. He had a friend on the FBI side in Galloway; he wanted one on the city side as well. He looked to Chief Weathers. "Chief, if I might, can I suggest—" Mac shook his head. "Wait, strike that. Can I make a request you put Coolidge in charge on your side? I know Lincoln—we've worked informally together. He's a really good cop."

Weathers nodded. "Done. Lincoln is one of the best I got."

"It's settled, then," Mitchell stated. Then he looked to Mac. "What's your first move?"

Mac looked to Wire. "Thoughts?"

She looked down at her watch and then back toward White's townhouse. "For tonight I think we need to go back inside and take a longer look around," Dara replied. "He leaves a clue about his next victim, right?"

"Yes," Director Mitchell answered. "But I have to caution you, it's never been figured out ahead of time."

"Which is why we can't bank on that," Mac replied. "So, Director, first thing in the morning we're going to need to see everything there is on this Rubens character. All the way back to the beginning," he added. "Unless we catch a lucky break, the way we'll catch him is to try to understand him, how he operates and how he identifies his victims."

"I'll make sure that gets done. Did he call you on your home phone or cell?" Mitchell asked.

"Home."

"We'll get it monitored," Mitchell answered as they all looked out to the street. While the police had taped off a wide area, the onlookers were gathering and media was on the scene, lights glaring, cameras rolling and pictures being snapped. The little confab they were all having was undoubtedly already on film and being reported.

"And here I thought I was done with the media," Mac moaned.

"Chief Weathers and I will handle this tonight," Mitchell stated. "You two start working."

Mac and Wire hurried back inside White's.

"I'll go upstairs and look around. Who knows," Wire mused with a wry smile as she reached for the stairway banister, "maybe she wrote down the killer's name."

"Right."

"Hey, a girl can hope."

Mac went back into the living room. The medical examiner was evaluating the body and she looked up to see Mac.

"Time of death?" Mac asked.

"Preliminarily, based on body temperature and the amount of rigor, I'd say between eighteen and twenty-two hours ago, so last night between eight and midnight," the medical examiner replied.

"How did he do it?"

The doctor pointed with her right index finger at White's neck. Mac couldn't see it in the dim light of earlier, but now with the body fully illuminated with portable lights he could see the bruising around her throat and neck.

Mac crouched down next to the medical examiner.

"It looks like he strangled her, both hands," the doctor stated clinically. "Just basically choked the life out of her. At least that's my initial thought as I look at this. I'll know for sure once I get back and examine her at the morgue, but that's my early unofficial diagnosis."

"Well, if you need any help on this, ask," Mac counseled. "The FBI and MPD are working together on this one."

"No lack of resources then."

"No," Mac answered. "If there is something you need, ask—you'll get it. This case is high priority. Everything will be fast-tracked."

"Good to know."

Mac looked down to White one more time and something about the cause of death raised a question in his mind. *How does he get up so close and personal without making a sound?* The neighbor was home all night and didn't hear a thing.

Unable to solve that problem at the moment, he proceeded to walk around the small living room area of the townhouse, which was stuffed with a mismatched assortment of furniture. There was an oversized loveseat, two tall, soft chairs covered in a different and dated green, orange and purple floral fabric, four small end tables— two round, two square—a narrow but newer Talisman coffee table and three ornate lamps all with a different styled shade. All of the furniture was pushed to the sides of the room so that the killer could display White's body in the center of the room.

The neighbor was right about Lisa White's love of books. White was definitely a zealous collector. The built-in bookshelves were stuffed with a mixture of hardcover and paperback books organized in no particular fashion. Mac enjoyed the peace of reading when he had the time. While he took in the occasional mystery, his interests trended more toward non-fiction historical books and autobiographies, and he was particularly drawn to anything about World War II.

Lisa White's tastes were far broader than his and her shelves were chock full of the works of the great authors. With just a quick inspection, Mac found the works of Hemingway, Salinger, Steinbeck, Dickens, Austen, Orwell, Chaucer, Hawthorne, Tolstoy, Dostoyevsky, Poe, Conan Doyle, and the list went on. She must have been a rare bookstore's dream customer. It was an impressive collection that had obviously taken years to assemble. And the collection wasn't limited to the classics. Intermixed with the classics were hundreds of fiction books containing a mixture of young adult, romances, mysteries and thrillers from all of the big names and far more from writers with which he was unfamiliar. It reminded him of *Once Upon a Crime*, the great little mystery bookstore back in Minneapolis that he occasionally frequented when looking for a mystery or thriller for himself or more likely for Sally, who loved nothing more than to escape the stress of her job by curling up with a good mystery and a glass of wine.

As he moved around the room, he approached the small table in the corner, a table that didn't appear to have been moved. On the table was a tall stack of books, topped by *Go Set a Watchman*. Mac sighed as he carefully flipped open the cover and read the inside flap of the book jacket. He couldn't bring himself to read the new Harper Lee book. *To Kill a Mockingbird* was the best book he'd ever read, one of the few he'd ever read more than once. It was a masterpiece. He thought Atticus Finch was the most honorable fictional character he'd ever read. He didn't want the new book to do anything to ruin his admiration for Atticus Finch or for Harper Lee. However, as he soaked in the vibe of the townhouse and his impression of White's life, he sensed she spent many of her off hours in one of the soft chairs of the house reading.

He turned back to the room and what drew his attention next was the vast collection of artwork. Well, at least some of it was artwork. In the living room, as well as the dining room and even the small segment of the hallway he could see leading back to the kitchen, the walls were covered nearly floor to ceiling with framed pictures, portraits and framed movie posters of all sizes. It did not appear that Lisa White believed in leaving empty wall space. She may have liked to paint but it was clear she had no interest in painting walls.

As he began to slowly scan the walls, there were recognizable prints of Picasso, da Vinci, Michelangelo, Rembrandt, Caravaggio to go with some popular American portraits from Jackson Pollock, Andy Warhol and John Singer Sargent, along with many other paintings from artists he'd never heard of all oddly mixed in with posters from some older movies he'd never seen, although he did recognize the faces of Audrey Hepburn and Humphrey Bogart in one of them. If there was a small piece of empty wall space, it appeared that White filled it with a small painting or framed picture of some kind. He'd seen this type of decorating on maybe one wall in a house, like a collage, often on the wall of a long stairway, but not on what seemed like *every* wall of the house.

Another thing he noticed was that Lisa White was also proud of her own work.

There were several of her paintings, watercolors and oils interspersed with all of the other artwork, pictures and posters. He was sure there would be more upstairs. As he followed the hallway into the back of the townhouse, he found a small room off the side of the kitchen where he found her painting supplies, easels, brushes, paint tubes, smocks and the like.

As he continued to examine the paintings and posters, he eventually made his way back to the living room when he found it placed between pieces from Picasso and Michelangelo: a singular painting from Rubens.

The painting wasn't *The Three Graces* but instead *The Judgment of Paris*, as Mac learned, returning to his earlier Internet search of Rubens paintings. The same women from *The Three Graces* were used but in a different fashion and there were additional small naked children and two men added to the scene. It hung to the left of where White's body lay, oddly displayed amongst not only the Michelangelo and Picasso, but also a series of classic movie posters for *North by Northwest, On the Waterfront* and side-by-side copies of *Breakfast at Tiffany's* and *Sabrina*.

"There are more pictures in this house than the Louvre," Wire remarked seriously.

"And more books than the Library of Congress," Mac replied.

"You should see upstairs. There are shelves full of books up there, and then more stacks on the floors."

Coolidge came inside. "It's a zoo out there. Cameras, reporters, microphones and questions nobody would ever answer. Why do the television reporters throw out questions like that?"

"Why do dogs bark?" Wire retorted.

Mac looked around the room and then down to the dead body of Lisa White still lying on the floor. He'd done enough looking around; it was time to do some speculating and detecting. "So the medical examiner says time of death was sometime between eight and midnight last night. She says White was likely strangled with the killer's bare hands. So how did it go down? How did he kill her?"

"In this case, does it matter?" Wire asked.

Mac nodded. "Every answer you get tells you something."

"Well then, I'd say it's hard to know," Wire replied, inspecting the room in her own right. Then back to Mac, "You're the savvy homicide detective."

"And this isn't your first murder scene, Special Agent Wire, so detect. What do you see?"

"I'm sure the furniture was not arranged in this fashion. If there was a struggle, there isn't a sign of it or if there was, he probably cleaned it up. I mean, was she even killed in this room?"

"I'd bet on that," Coolidge suggested. "Or at least she was killed on this level."

"Why?" Wire asked. "How can you know?"

"I can't know for sure, but—"

"But what?"

"Well," Coolidge hesitated. "She was—big."

"Don't you mean plus-sized?" Wire shot quickly back with a gleam in her eye, looking over to Mac, a knowing wink toward their earlier conversation.

Mac piled on, "Yeah, Linc. Have a little respect. I mean *Sports Illustrated* just put a beautiful plus-sized model on the cover of the Swimsuit Issue. Get with the lingo."

"Uh...uh... yeah, sorry," Coolidge replied sheepishly.

"Voluptuous works too. That's how the women in Rubens works are described," Wire continued.

"Or so Google told you," Coolidge replied sarcastically, recovering quickly, giving a dig of his own. "The point is, however, that given her plus-sized, voluptuous nature, the killer probably didn't move her very far." Coolidge scratched the back of his head. "But that's as far as I can get."

"But that does tell us something, maybe. Ms. White is a larger woman but I'm also betting she was fairly strong. So our guy is also very strong or ..."

Coolidge's eyes lit up. "Or he drugged her."

"In fact, I'll bet we'll find he uses drugs regularly," Mac answered, nodding. "That would allow him to get his hands around her throat and choke her without any ruckus." He thought about it for a second. "That makes some intuitive sense as well. The neighbor next door doesn't remember hearing anything. If there was a fight, he might have heard something."

"If he put his hands on her, then maybe we get his prints, then?" Wire offered hopefully.

Mac thought for a second then shook his head. "We can hope, and the medical examiner will check, but I really doubt it. If our speculation is correct and he drugged her, then as she's falling into the drugged state he has time to pull on gloves so that he leaves no prints behind."

"But he could have left them elsewhere," Wire replied.

"He could have," Coolidge agreed. "But if time of death is right he may have had all night to wipe the place down, removing any of his prints."

"And," Wire nodded, picking up the thought, "if he planned it out this much, he then kept really good track of anything he might have touched, and—"

"Wiped them away," Mac finished. "All the same, forensics will print the whole place. The autopsy will give us a better idea if our suspicions are correct. Of more importance at the moment is to get an idea of what she was doing in the days before her death. We need people interviewing her friends, co-workers, family, other neighbors and anyone else who had any contact with White in the last month at least, if not longer. Was there someone new in her life? If so, did anyone see him? Did anyone get a name? How did he pick Lisa White? Why did he pick Lisa White? Linc, I need your people working the street on that. If anyone finds something, I want to know."

"Consider it done."

"We're not doing that?" Wire asked.

"We're not doing as much of that," Mac answered. "At least yet."

"What are we doing, then?"

"Learning about our killer," Mac replied. "First thing in the morning, we're going to get to know everything there is to know about the killer, Rubens."

Wire dropped Mac off a little before 1:00 a.m.

He pushed his way in the front door to find an agent sitting with a laptop hooked into the house phone. Sally came down the steps in her robe to find him.

"You should be sleeping," Mac said, concerned.

"With all of this going on? *Right*."

"Sorry."

"Not your fault. So is it the guy? Is it this Rubens?"

"Yes," Mac replied as he headed into the kitchen. He grabbed a beer and the pasta salad leftovers and sat down at the eating nook.

"So what happens next?"

"I report to the Washington Field Office first thing in the morning and go to work."

"For how long?"

Mac suddenly realized where part of Sally's concern rested. Sally understood what he did from time to time: the cases, the hunt, the search and his tendency to go all in on it. As a former prosecutor, she knew how important that was. But, they were getting married in six weeks. Was he going to be tied up in an investigation all that time? Was it going to interrupt all of that?

"I don't know how long, Sally. My recall on this guy is he hangs around for a few weeks, kills the four women in rapid succession and then disappears."

"But you don't know that."

He reached for her hand. "I'm going to be at our wedding. This is not going to get in the way of that, the honeymoon, anything. I won't let that happen."

"What if this Rubens doesn't leave you a choice?"

The phone rang.

It was late.

Mac immediately went to the living room and to the house phone the agent was sitting by. "I don't have to tell you that the longer he stays on the better."

Mac nodded as he picked up the receiver. "Hello."

"Home so soon?" It was him, the masked taunting voice. It was Rubens.

"I was anticipating your call."

The voice laughed. "Well, if you did, then score one for Mac McRyan. Is it okay that I call you Mac?"

"If that works for you, it works for me."

"Good. Quite the work of art, wasn't it?"

"Oh, quite," Mac replied casually, wanting to talk to him, get a feel for him. "Lisa White is just the first of *The Three Graces* you're going to kill, isn't she?"

"Mac, I so love that painting. The use of color is magnificent. There's the paleness of the Graces' bodies contrasted against the darker ornate background and then that blast of dark blue over the left Grace's head just explodes onto the canvas. It's that blue that drew me to that painting. It was one of his later works but in my opinion, one of his best. I simply felt compelled to honor it here in our nation's capital."

"So is this how this is going to go now? You're going to start calling me for these little chats?"

"From time to time. Opponents must talk in a game like this. But look, I know you want this call to last but it's not going to happen. All I want for now is your cell phone number."

Mac gave him the number. "Aren't you worried we'll trace you?"

"Not tonight."

The line went dead.

The FBI agent was on the phone, and then covered the mouthpiece and reported. "We had to triangulate it. The call was coming from southwest of Baltimore, up where Interstates 95, 895 and 195 all weave together. He was moving and I suspect it was a drop phone. He probably pitched it out the window the second he was done." The agent got back on the phone. A search would be made for the cellular device.

While the agent did that, Mac listened to the playback of the call with Sally listening in.

"Is he crazy?" Sally asked.

"Psychopath," Mac answered. "But, as I'm sure I'll learn in the morning, a very smart one." He played it back one more time, thought about calling Wire and then decided it could wait. There was nothing more that could be done tonight. He reached for Sally's hand. "Come on, let's go to bed."

"How can you possibly sleep?"

"Because I have to," he answered wearily.

Upstairs they quickly and quietly went through the mechanics of getting ready for bed. Sally got into bed first and Mac followed a few minutes later, first setting his alarm for 5:30 a.m. before extinguishing the lamp on his nightstand and laying his head back on the pillow. He stared at the ceiling, the case disturbingly running through his head as he tried to settle his mind.

"Mac?"

"Yeah, babe."

"Catch the bastard."

4

"WHAT'S A GUNNER?"

M ac was up and out of the townhouse by 5:55 a.m., a light mist of rain falling, making for a cool and damp morning. Along the way, he stopped at Starbucks for a large coffee and breakfast sandwich. He pulled into the FBI field office parking ramp, drove underneath the building and slotted his SUV to the right of a bland, brown four-door Taurus. He unfolded his wiry, athletic six-foot-one-inch frame out of his BMW X5 while Wire pulled in right beside him. They were inside the FBI DC field office by 6:15 a.m. Special Agent Grace Delmonico, a friend of theirs who they worked the Reaper case with almost a year ago now, was inside awaiting their arrival in the elevator lobby.

"Special Agent Gracie Delmonico, we ride again," Mac greeted, extending his hand.

"Good to see you, Mac," she answered, taking it. "I really wish it were under different circumstances."

"Have you been up all night?" Dara asked, giving their friend a quick hug.

"Galloway and I both were, pulling things together," Grace replied tiredly as the three of them exited the elevator and walked back to an expansive conference room. "Galloway went home but will be back.

He scheduled a meeting for 9:00 a.m. to get the whole team together. In the meantime, we've pulled the FBI files on Rubens as you requested," Delmonico stated, waving her arm toward the conference table. On the long narrow table were stacks of investigative files, as well as a series of banker boxes and a small stack of hardcover books, not to mention laptops and other materials Mac had requested.

"Wow, this is a lot of stuff to try to get through," Wire sighed worriedly.

"And there will be more, a lot more. So let me tell you what is here," Delmonico suggested as she walked along the left side of the conference table. "First, these red folders contain an overall summary of Rubens, the victims and the investigations. It's the ten-thousand-foot read. I'd start there."

Grace moved down the table. "These twelve tall stacks of brown expandable folders are the FBI's individual files on Rubens. In the stacks of folders are all the paperwork, notes, interviews and reports for the twelve prior victims. The banker boxes that are behind the stacks of folders are where you'll find the physical evidence, pictures and anything else relevant from the crime scenes. The small brown file at the end is what we have on Lisa White thus far. It isn't much but I'm sure that will change throughout the day as more data is collected, we interact with MPD and get the medical examiner's report."

Delmonico walked around the end of the table. "On the other side of the table here are more banker boxes. These sets of boxes contain copies of the investigative files from Boston, Chicago and Los Angeles police that the Bureau has a copy of. We've already heard from the Chicago and Boston police, telling us if we need anything else to call. I'm sure we'll hear from L.A. as well. It's still pretty early out there but these are complete copies of each police department's files on Rubens."

"Is this all available electronically?" Wire asked.

"You'll be able to remote into the case management system."

"What's with the books?" Mac asked, noticing the stack at the end of the table.

"Those are all of the books written about Rubens," Delmonico replied. "Two of them are from the FBI's April Greene."

"We heard about her last night," Wire said.

"She's a profiler from the Behavioral Analysis Unit down at Quantico, or at least she used to be. I think she's a consultant now. She's writing books and traveling the country speaking and consulting on cases, but she'll be around for this, I'm sure. Rubens kind of made her."

"That's what the director said last night," Mac noted, flipping over one of the books to see the picture of Greene on the back and read the book jacket description of her background.

"Anyway, at last count, she's written six books on criminal psychology. With regard to Rubens, her two books are titled *The Homicidal Artist* and *Inside the Mind of Rubens*. There are a few others that have been written—two of particular interest are the ones written by Hugo Ridge."

"Who's he?" Wire asked, lingering over the picture of Ridge on the back of one of the books.

"He was a crime reporter for the *Boston Herald* when Rubens started ten years ago. His reporting on the murders was picked up nationally and he made a name for himself. By the time Rubens reappeared in Chicago four years later, Ridge was writing crime features for *World News Magazine* and he covered the murders in Chicago and turned it all into a bestselling book."

"Really?" Wire asked.

"Yeah," Delmonico replied. "You two should appreciate that. By the way, I thought you were both really good on *60 Minutes*."

"Thanks, I thought it went well," Wire replied. "I'm not so sure about him though," she said, throwing a thumb in Mac's direction.

"It went fine. Unfortunately, I got to enjoy that it was over for all of five minutes before Rubens called."

"Well, on that front," Delmonico transitioned, "Ridge's first book was simply called *Rubens*. Four years ago when Rubens popped up in Los Angeles, Ridge covered it again for *World* and turned it into a follow-up book titled *The Killing Game*. That one won him a Pulitzer."

"Catchy title," Mac suggested, ignoring the book and scanning the markings on the banker boxes.

"It is," Delmonico replied, and then sighed. "As much as it pains the Bureau to admit it, Ridge's books were good, contained a great deal of detail and added some keen insight, and while they were non-fiction, they read a little like a novel. In fact, he's started writing novels and he's doing quite well."

"What would you read?" Wire asked Grace.

Delmonico shrugged. "Probably April Greene's."

"Why do you say that?" Mac asked.

"Greene's books are more the bricks and mortar of what makes Rubens tick, the profile of him, who she thinks he is at least psychologically as compared to other killers she's studied, of which she's also written extensively. It's really the other books from which she's gotten rich which have led to the speaking and lecturing and so forth. She pops up on CNN and FOX News from time to time when there is a big murder case, a serial killer or a particularly brutal homicide somewhere in the country that garners interest, and she provides insight on what motivates the killer and what not. The books on Rubens are a heavier read because she gets pretty deep into the weeds on him."

"And Hugo Ridge's books?" Wire asked.

"I'd say they're probably more for entertainment. His books are more about the victims, the designs of the crime scenes and how Rubens taunts the police, the more sensational aspects of the cases," Delmonico replied with a yawn. "Give a look if you want—you might get some insight, especially if you want background in three hundred pages or less."

Mac snorted his skepticism as he flipped open the top of a banker box.

Wire detected his cynicism. "You know, you wrote a non-fiction account of an investigation."

"Yup, and it'll be coming to a theatre near you soon," Mac dead-panned. "However, I seriously doubt our book will ever end up in an FBI investigative file, nor should it." He sensed her disapproval and glanced over in her direction. "Your interest wouldn't have anything to do with the dust jacket picture, now would it?"

"Oh, now you question my integrity."

"No," Mac replied, not looking up. "Simply your taste."

"Sometimes you can be such an incredible asshole."

"So Sally tells me."

"Maybe I should question her taste," Wire needled.

"You wouldn't be the first."

"In any event," Delmonico stated, getting them back on track. "This is pretty much everything. Meeting at 9:00 a.m. Until then—" She waved to the table with an exhausted smile. "Enjoy."

Delmonico peeled out of the conference room and Mac and Wire looked over the table of information. They both grabbed a summary file, sat down and started getting educated.

The summary report was thirty-six pages in length. It started with a short rundown of all twelve victims over the ten years from victim number one, Nicole Franzen, staged in the pose of Aphrodite in the Rubens painting *The Judgment of Paris*. She was strangled, very similar to how he imagined Lisa White had been strangled. However, there was no clock and no clue left behind; those elements apparently came later on. The last victim four years ago in Los Angeles was Ronda Hollister, a sculptor, who was drugged and then smothered. She was posed like the woman in the portrait *Leda and the Swan*, as a dead swan was found at the scene. However, before Rubens was able to finish his masterpiece completely, the police somehow got a lead that Hollister was the next victim. It was the closest the police had ever come, missing Rubens by mere minutes. How they learned about Hollister was something Mac was keen to find out.

He read through the full summary once and then went back over some parts of it again, while Wire started flipping through some of the individual case files.

Finished, Mac dropped the folder onto the table. He took a sip of his now lukewarm coffee and leaned back in his chair with his hands clasped behind his head and closed his eyes.

After a minute or two, Wire broke the silence. "Thoughts?"

"Twelve prior victims," Mac replied. "And the one thing that really sticks out to me is there isn't any sort of consistent useful description of our killer. In Boston, they had one guy they thought was the killer. He lived in the same building as the first victim and then was seen on video within five blocks of victim number two in the hours after she was killed. They apprehended the suspect, but then victim number three was killed while he was in custody and number four was killed while he was under police surveillance. He wasn't the guy and other than that, Boston PD had nothing.

"In Chicago, there were vague descriptions of a man ranging from five-foot-seven to as tall as six-foot-two. One pegged the man as having short brown hair and a different witness for another victim said she thought the new man in her life had longish gray hair down to his shoulders. The summary suggests that the descriptions were likely not of the killer but simply people who'd been in the vicinity of the victims in the day or two before the murders. None of the victim's friends, co-workers or family members ever actually met the man in their victim's life, although in almost all cases people thought there was someone new.

"In the series of Los Angeles murders, there were varying descriptions of new paramours: one with a dark beard who was of stocky build, another with black hair and a dark mustache, and still a fourth that had him as a thinnish blond with longer, almost surfer-like hair. There is no consistency to height, weight, hair color or appearance. Again, no friend, family member or co-worker ever met a boyfriend of the victim so again, the descriptions, to the extent they exist, are worthless."

"I saw that," Wire answered.

"Of course, as the summary indicates, we don't even know if the descriptions we have are really of *our* guy. These were all descriptions from a distance of men a witness thought they saw with or near the victim."

"Could just be random or it could be that he's always changing his look."

"The forensics report section references hair fibers that were collected at three of the murder scenes, two in Chicago and one in Los Angeles. The fibers are fake and probably from wigs of some kind, so he's changing his look," Mac continued. "It's not that hard if you have the right supplies and have some skill, which our guy clearly does. He spends months, maybe years, setting up these killings."

"This April Greene seems to think he spends a long time seeking out his victims," Wire added. "He knows them very well by the time he meets them."

"All of which allows this guy to get close to them. Rubens knows what kind of men they would be most attracted to and which buttons to push to get the women to go for him. I bet he spends a lot of time hunting for possibilities. Once he's assessed the field, he assembles a list and uses some process to whittle it down to four. Then, the targets set, Rubens moves in all Rico Suave-like, and they melt because he pushes all of their buttons. He gets them to let their guard down and he strikes. Usually, it is in the victim's apartment, although he used an abandoned building once. His most common method is strangling eight times with his hands, including last night. He's also smothered two women and used a nylon rope once. He's also used a bat, and most gruesomely he used a knitting needle, sticking it right into the victim's ear and into her brain."

"We have no consistent description of the killer and no consistent method of killing. What is consistent?"

"The victims. He has a very *distinct* type. They are all, as the summary report suggests, Rubenesque."

"Plus-sized women," Wire noted.

"Correct, but that's not all," Mac continued. "The victims are not just voluptuous. They are also women who appear to be shy, reserved, introverted and overlooked. Nobody ever notices them. You can see it in the summary—these women had few friends that could provide background. They all were employed yet at work, they had few *close* friends. As for the victims that did have some good friends?" He shrugged. "It would appear that those people knew very little about a man in their friend's life, although they suspected something was up."

"A woman has a certain glow, a way about her, when she has a man in her life," Dara noted.

"Yes, she does," Mac agreed. "And for a few of the victims, their friends knew of a new man but there's never a name and none of the victim's friends ever actually met the man. Not once."

"His type is Rubenesque, but also working class," Dara observed, flipping back into the summary again. "Not necessarily blue collar—actually more white collar, but worker bee types. Three were administrative assistants of some kind, two were legal assistants at large law firms, one worked at a veterinary clinic and another at a library."

"Right," Mac nodded. "Another two worked at museums, one at a sewing store, another was a bookkeeper for a small chain of greeting card stores. All honest and decent jobs and the victims were quiet, dependable employees. So why that kind of employee, why that kind of woman?"

Dara sat back in her chair and kicked her feet up. "Because any woman who could handle a blue collar working environment is not the quiet and meek type. She's tough and doesn't put up with any shit."

"There are lots of women like that in white collar jobs too. Take you, for example."

"Yes, but take me for example. There is no way in hell this killer would approach me. I'm confident, outgoing, mildly attractive and—"

"Definitely not Rubenesque."

"That's right, but there are lots of very attractive, confident, incredibly successful, self-assured women who are what people consider voluptuous. And you know what, lots of men like a little junk in the trunk. Did I ever tell you that I actually had a man suggest to me one time at a party that I was too bony for him?"

"No way," Mac replied in disbelief.

"Way. We're having a nice conversation, he's a good-looking guy and I was getting mildly interested, and then he just blurts out, 'You know, you have kind of a boney ass.' Can you believe that? Do I look too bony to you?"

Dara was trim, in excellent shape, attractive and he suspected just a little freaky. Were it not for Sally, he'd have rushed Wire off somewhere for a long weekend to find out just how freaky. But one thing Dara wasn't, was bony. She was a strong, tall, athletic, full-bodied tough woman who wasn't to be trifled with under any circumstances. "No, Dara. As a man very much in love and looking forward to being married in a matter of weeks, I can say without being a pig that among your many very attractive physical features you have a very superb, non-bony ass."

"Thanks."

"Don't mention it. Now, leaving the topic of your exquisite ass and getting back to our

victims—"

"They were not confident women, at least not outwardly. All evidence says they were loners who worked and then all of them engaged in singular pursuits, such as books, painting, sculpture, gardening, pets, knitting, the kinds of things you can do by yourself for hours on end."

"And those were the kinds of women he focused on, lonely women of a particular physical makeup who were introverted and had few close friends. They wouldn't have friends to warn them off of the guy, to get spooked by the guy," Mac deduced and an investigative strategy started forming in his head with regard to Lisa White. "It looks like Lisa White fits this profile to a tee so we're going to go through her life with a fine-tooth comb. We have to try and put ourselves in Rubens' head. Where would he have first noticed her? Where could he have observed her in action for long enough periods of time so that he could get a sense that she fit his profile?"

"Would it take that long?" Dara asked. "I mean, he's probably good enough to spot them from a mile away. Would he really need that much time?"

"Yes, yes he would," a pixie of a woman in what looked to be her mid-forties with a stylish blonde bob haircut and wearing a sharp black pantsuit said from the doorway.

"And you are?" Mac asked with a raised left eyebrow.

"April Greene," Wire finished, holding up the book at the other end of the table.

Quick introductions were exchanged.

"So why would he need a lot of time?" Dara asked.

"Because to get as close as he did to kill them, to get into their apartment, townhouse or house, he had to have spent time with them. He got to know them to the point that they let their walls down and let him into their lives. Any two-bit killer can attack a woman in an empty parking lot. It takes someone entirely different to do what Rubens is doing."

Wire understood, nodding. "But to kill like this, and to make it into a masterpiece, you have to get close."

"Very close, if not intimate," Greene added. "And that's what Rubens does. He breaks down those walls and these women let him in."

"They don't see it coming?"

Greene shook her head. "No, they don't. I guarantee you, when he kills them, they are sitting there wondering how did this happen? They know him, trust him and have absolutely no fear of him. Then boom, they're dead."

"You wrote the book, tell us more about him," Mac asked.

"My read on him is that the man we call Rubens is a white Caucasian male of average weight, height and looks, such that you'd probably hardly ever notice him."

"Why do you say that?" Wire asked.

"Because nobody ever really notices him," Greene answered.

"No solid description," Mac added. "He blends in."

"Exactly," Greene agreed. "Part of that comes from the fact that he has thought everything through. He is very intelligent and I think he is probably highly educated and well read. His victims are smart, intelligent people interested in literature, the arts, wine and culture in general. That says to me to operate so easily and effectively with these women, he has those interests and in my experience, people with those interests are characteristically highly educated. And not only is he smart, brilliant really, he also possesses an almost pathological need to constantly demonstrate that brilliance. Hence, the phone calls and taunting, which he's already started with you. Am I right?" she asked Mac.

"Yes, twice."

Greene nodded. "Rubens is smart, wicked smart. He knows it, he wants *you* to know it and he wants to dominate, intimidate and frustrate you with that intelligence. That, more than anything, is what seems to drive him, at least in my view."

"In other words, a gunner," Mac suggested.

"That term works," Greene agreed. "That term works really well because he always wants people to know how smart he is. He needs to validate that intelligence. Just like a gunner does."

"Gunner?" Wire asked. "What's a gunner?"

"We used the term in law school," Mac answered. "It applied to the people who always talked in class, who raised their hands constantly and wanted to argue with the professors and generally thought of themselves as lawyers, not law students. They were the ones who never stopped talking about how late they studied and how hard they worked. Gunners were the ones who hogged the professor's office hours so they could try to discuss arcane and irrelevant legal issues in the cases we were reading. Typically, they were pretty smart people. However, they were often people so socially unaware and awkward that they would have made lousy lawyers. There were exceptions, of course. The valedictorian of my law school class was a gunner. He was ridiculously smart, annoyingly smug when correctly answering professors' questions and begrudgingly I'll admit has become one hell of a lawyer. But overall, in my time in school, he was the exception to the gunner rule. Gunners were most often people who were book smart but had no street smarts, and you can't be a good lawyer without both."

"Such as?" Greene asked, not as a question, but to drive the conversation; she could tell Mac had an example to share.

"There was one guy in my class who was a clerk for a district court judge in law school," Mac explained. "When he graduated law school, he clerked for another year then ran for election as a judge. He was out of law school one year, had been nothing more than a law clerk and he thought he was qualified to be a judge. Needless to say, he lost. But it hasn't deterred him. He's run for a judgeship every two years ever since. He's still a law clerk ten years later. His career is in the dumpster and sadly, he's turned into something of a laughing-stock. He had a modicum of book smarts but absolutely zero street smarts. There were plenty of people that were clueless like that in law school. We generally made fun of them behind their backs and played Gunner Bingo with their names."

"Gunner Bingo?" Wire and Greene asked in unison.

"Yeah," Mac replied, surprised. "Don't tell me you two have never heard of this."

"Gunner, yes. Gunner Bingo, no," Greene replied. "Tell me."

"It was simple, really. We put the Gunner names on a miniature bingo card and crossed their names off as they asked questions. Then if you got five in a row you had a—"

"Bingo," Wire said, laughing. "That is so awesome."

"The winner didn't have to pay for beer or pizza after class."

"I suspect Rubens was a gunner," Greene noted. "I bet he was mocked like that, or perceived it as mocking. He may not have recognized the mocking at first. In fact, he probably would have thought he was doing what he needed to do to fit in and earn respect in the environment he was in. However, to others, those very actions would have been perceived as gunner-like. As a result, he needs to constantly tell you how smart he is. He wants to measure up."

"That's what these classmates were like in law school. They always wanted you to think they were so smart."

"Because perhaps they felt inadequate?" Wire asked.

"Maybe," Mac answered.

"How about Rubens? Does he feel inadequate?" Wire inquired.

"Probably," Greene replied. "His behavior suggests to me an upbringing, a school experience or probably even later a professional experience where he never quite seemed to measure up somehow. Maybe it was to his parents, maybe it was as compared to a sibling or classmates, and maybe it was someone or many someones in his professional life, but I've listened to replays of his conversations with the police in Boston, Chicago and LA and you can hear it in his voice, the chip placed firmly on the shoulder. This is his chance to get society back."

"You say professional and you say he's well educated," Mac stated. "What kind of professional? What kind of education?"

"That's a good question," Greene replied. "I've studied him for the better part of ten years and I'm not sure. There is nothing in the manner he kills the women, or in how he speaks when he calls, that tells us definitively what his background is or was. Whether it was business, law, science, medical, I've really never been able to figure that out."

"I've seen evidence that he uses drugs on the victim, so the background could be medical," Wire suggested.

"Maybe," Greene answered. "But keep in mind he drugs them with a roofie. You don't need a medical background to administer a roofie—you need sleight of hand."

"Are we talking college graduate or maybe post-college?" Mac asked.

"I'd say post-college," Greene answered. "He really profiles as quite intelligent."

"MD, PhD, JD, Masters, something like that?"

"Yes, I suspect so."

"How can you know that for sure?" Wire asked.

"I can't. Profiling a killer before they are caught is to a certain degree a process of educated guesses," Greene replied honestly. "But when I look at the varied backgrounds of all of his victims and their education levels, the victims were all well-educated, college degrees at a minimum. He seems to easily move in their worlds, talks their language and engages with them on the things that interest them most. It's like I said, to get the victims to let down their guards to such a degree, to kill them in their homes, to kill them in ways they don't see coming, in a place where they feel secure, he's had to have been able to talk about whatever it is the victim was interested in. Books, art, culture, politics, entertainment, whatever their thing is. He knows this stuff. You could maybe fake it for one date but everything says he would have needed several dates with these victims and you just can't keep a charade up for that long. It's the only way I can explain him time after time getting as close to these women as he does. It's because he can talk the talk and walk the walk in a way that is interesting to these women."

"However, unlike my gunner example," Mac stated, "not only does Rubens have the education, he seems to have some street smarts."

"Certainly enough to have eluded us for ten years," Greene agreed.

"It's like he knows our playbook," Mac offered.

"Are you saying he's a cop?" Wire asked.

"No, not necessarily," Mac answered. "It's just that he seems to know how we're going to investigate these cases. You could learn a lot of this through education, research, searching the Internet or watching the literally dozens of criminal investigation shows on television. It's clear that he knows that the longer we have to work a crime scene, interview witnesses, collect evidence, use the media, conduct surveillance, look at surveillance video, run cell phone records, the more likely it is the killer will be caught, especially a serial, because they usually keep going *until* they are caught. So what does he do? He compresses the time period of the investigation down to a few weeks. He applies all kinds of pressure with a countdown and phone calls making it a race against time, and most importantly he has the discipline to play his game, take the win, leave and then go into hibernation for a while. That takes a special kind of discipline and control."

"What does that tell you?" Greene asked.

"It's as much about the game to him as the killing," Mac answered. "The preparation, the anticipation, the set-up and the time it takes to do that, that's almost more important than the act of killing itself."

"So the killing is just one step?" Wire asked.

"Yeah, it's a component, an act," Mac replied. "It might not be total bloodlust, although deep down you have to have the thirst to kill. But as much as it's about that, it appears that it's more about winning and beating everyone. On the call I had with him, he talked of the game, the clock and asked was I ready to play."

"You're right about that," Greene added. "I think when he first killed it was about killing, but over time, I think I've come to your conclusion, Mr. McRyan. It's become more about proving he's better than everyone, especially the police, and right now, especially you two. He called you and asked for Wire. You two are as much his target as any woman he will kill. You two are who he is playing the game against."

"Why is that?" Wire asked. "Why us?"

"You two are the biggest game in town," Greene answered. "Mr. McRyan, you were a hockey player, were you not?"

"I was."

"Didn't you always want a shot at number one?"

"You bet."

"Ms. Wire, you worked organized crime cases for the Bureau years ago. Did you ever not want to go after the Don?"

"No, it was always all about getting the top man."

"It's the same with Rubens, I think. He wants to take on number one and right now, you two are the best game in town. You're number one. That's who he wants to play the game against."

"Then I better play the game too," Mac answered while asking himself the key question. How exactly should he play the game?

5

"A LITTLE BIT OF LUCK AND A LITTLE BIT OF OBSESSION."

The questions of "how" gnawed at Mac all day.

It started with the 9:00 a.m. meeting called by Galloway. The Senior Agent was the official lead on the investigation but everyone understood that it was Mac and Wire's case, with Mac as lead. With that, Mac's initial impulse was to jump right into the investigation and hit the bricks. He operated on the theory that you lead from in front, not from a desk. To solve a case, you had to be out beating the bushes, making moves and finding evidence. However, the sheer volume of the information on this case and the other jurisdictions both current and past that were involved caused him to put the brakes on his instincts. He didn't know why, but something in the back of his mind told him not to.

So for now, he chose to sit still and give orders.

"Detective Coolidge, you're the lead for the Metropolitan Police Department," Mac suggested. "This is your town. I want you and your guys hitting the streets around White's townhouse. I want you talking to her colleagues at work and any family she has. I'm betting Lisa White had someone new in her life."

"If she did, we'll find out. Do you think it'll be that easy though?"

"No," Wire answered.

"Tell me why."

"Because Mac and I read through the summary of all the past cases, and we've never had a consistent description of Rubens. In fact, we don't ever have a witness who met the man in the victim's life. Nevertheless, we need to know if there was someone new."

"And when and where he came into her life, if at all possible," Mac added. "Linc, he hunts these victims, probably for a long time so it wouldn't be within the last couple of weeks. It might have been a month or two back that he first showed up, maybe more."

"We need to go back awhile then?" Linc asked.

"That's our thought," Mac replied and then looked to Galloway. "Don, while Linc's people are hitting the street seeing if there was someone new, I want the Bureau going through her financials, her computer at work, at home and anything electronic on her. If the guy came into her life, when, where and what she was spending her money on may give us some insight as to when he did."

"I'll coordinate that," Delmonico replied.

"Forensics is still working the townhouse?" Mac asked Galloway.

"They're still there," Galloway replied. "I have an agent overseeing that and all the analysis is on the fast track."

"And the autopsy?" Wire asked.

"Should have it by the end of the day," Galloway answered. "We are offering any and all assistance to the Chief Medical Examiner."

That was a start. The meeting broke up.

"So what are we doing?" Wire asked Mac.

"Learning more about Rubens from the people who've gone up against him."

The first video conference of the day was with Gavin Sullivan, retired, formerly of the Boston Police Homicide Unit. "Every time this son of a bitch surfaces I'm taken back to ten years ago."

Sullivan was at Boston Police headquarters with the Rubens case file in front of him. "I had a good career," he said to Mac and Wire. "I did a lot of good and carry few regrets, but this one? This one stays with me. The faces of those four women stay with me. I bet I take this file out once a month and look it over."

"I suspect even more often when he surfaces," Wire suggested.

"You got that right, Ms. Wire," Sullivan answered.

Sullivan ran through the investigation, victim by victim. "The murders took place over a period of five weeks. The first victim, Nicole Franzen, was murdered in her apartment just north of downtown."

"But no countdown, I noticed?" Mac asked.

"No. That came later with the third victim."

"What do you make of that?" Mac asked.

"The FBI profiler, April Greene. Have you met her?"

"We have."

"Very sharp lady, even back then before she became kind of famous," Sullivan stated. "As I recall, she thought it was a reflection of how he was figuring out the process and was getting more confident and cocky as he went along," Sullivan answered.

"Yeah, like killing victim number three while you had a suspect in custody," Wire noted.

"Correct, ma'am. That was his big *fuck you* to us. We take our guy into custody and then I get the call from him, from Rubens. He tells me I've got the wrong guy, that we're nowhere on the case and that in twenty-four hours I'll have another victim."

"Did you take it seriously when he called?" Mac asked.

"Officially, of course," Sullivan replied and then they heard a sigh. "Unofficially, I'm sorry to say we thought the call was bullshit because the guy we had in custody looked good for it."

"But then you had a third victim."

"Yes, twenty-four hours later, just like he said. Susanna O'Dwyer was a larger woman, a woman that was Rubenesque, I guess. Hell, there's a phrase I never thought I'd utter. In any event, she was posed like the woman depicted in the painting titled *Susanna and the Elders*."

"Tell me about the scene," Wire said, looking at a copy of the file on the murder of O'Dwyer.

"He was sending a message with that one. It was a brutal murder. He hit her in the head with a wooden baseball bat. And that wasn't the worst of it. Not only did we, as it turned out, have the wrong man, but he left that damn countdown clock behind, giving us five days. Then he called me and said I had one more shot at catching him and he was leaving a clue behind that told us who the victim was. I'll be damned if the bastard didn't kill Regina Dyson right on time and then call me to tell me about it."

"And then he was gone," Mac stated.

"And then he was gone."

"So what was the last clue?" Mac asked, the crime scene photos for the fourth victim in front of him.

"Vacuum cleaners," Sullivan replied. "There was an old Regina vacuum cleaner sitting right next to a new Dyson. You'll see it in the crime scene photos—those two vacuums are in half the pictures. Can you believe that shit? I'm supposed to figure out my victim is Regina Dyson because there are two vacuum cleaners sitting side-by-side." The retired detective disgustedly shook his head. "No way."

In the early afternoon, Chicago detectives Vic Wirtz and Paul Trazinski were on video conference. Wirtz was the lead and Trazinski was his partner when Rubens made his way to Chicago three years after Boston. Like Sullivan, Wirtz ran them through the entirety of the investigation.

"It was a tighter timeline than in Boston," Wirtz recounted. "Three weeks and two days and then he was gone."

"He announced his presence on the first victim, I see," Wire stated.

"He sure did. From what I've gathered from the news reports this morning, it was a similar scene to what you two found. The victim, Stella Krazny, was staged like a Rubens painting. In our case, it was *Het Pelsken*. He staged it right down to the fur coat wrapped around her and staged the body in the bathroom, right by the bathtub since the portrait was of Rubens' wife wrapping herself in the fur after getting out of the bath. And he left a note saying he was in Chicago and that Ms. Krazny was first."

"And the clock and the clue?" Mac asked.

"Indeed," Trazinski replied. "And the media spectacle."

"I assume Ridge is who you're referring to?" Wire inquired.

"Him and all of the others. Ridge was on it pretty quickly. But the cable networks got onto it some, our papers and media got onto it big time. It was an intense three weeks."

"Tell me about the clues," Mac asked.

"We could never figure them out until after we found the victims, and in a couple of cases, it took a day or two after. For example, the second victim was a woman named Allison Cole Wheatfield. We found her dead in an abandoned office building on the second floor after he called it in. The clue about her that he left at Stella Krazny's was a small portrait of a Kansas wheat field hanging over the toilet that was painted by an A. Cole, which was Allison Cole."

"So you needed to put together the wheat field with Allison Cole. That's tough," Mac remarked.

"The clues were beyond obscure," Trazinski replied.

"To me, it was almost like they weren't real clues," Wirtz added. "They're really intended to torture you and make you waste your time trying to figure them out. The clue is there but good luck figuring it out. He's just jerking you around. After the fourth victim when he left Chicago I went back to the last victim's house and stared at the clue."

"Is this the one for Joan Loch?" Mac asked, flipping to that part of the Chicago file.

"That's the one," Wirtz replied. "The clue was a combination of a painting of Joan of Arc and the picture of Loch Lomond from Scotland. They were hanging side-by-side on the wall about five feet from the body of the victim. The wall and those two pictures hanging on it were in half of the crime scene photos, but ..."

"But?" Wire asked.

"The clue was wasted on me and Trazinski," Wirtz stated. "I didn't know much about either Joan of Arc or Loch Lomond."

"We've talked about this case over beer for years. We'd have never figured it out. We're street cops, detectives. We understand greed, sex, money, revenge, the typical motives for murder. This?" Trazinski angrily shook his head and smirked. "This was something we couldn't comprehend. The FBI helped. There was a profiler, a woman. What was her name?"

"April Greene," Wire suggested.

"That's the one. She had some thoughts about Rubens, who he was and how he hunted. She tried to help but to no avail," Trazinski confirmed.

"The case will haunt me as long as I live," Wirtz added. "It was the only time in my career where I felt completely inadequate to the task."

Trazinski concurred. "I was just happy when the guy and everything that comes with him left town. Sometimes you just have to acknowledge that crazy wins."

In the late afternoon, they got on a video conference with Sam Walker, the lead detective with LAPD who handled Rubens four years ago in Los Angeles.

For twenty-four days, Rubens terrorized Walker and his colleagues.

"I'd handled five other serial cases, four before this one and one after," Walker stated confidently. "We get a fair amount of them out here, but this one? This one was unlike anything else."

"The media pressure?" Wire asked.

"To be honest, it wasn't that so much," Walker answered. "There was lots of that for sure but we get lots of media attention out here. I've handled a couple of other high-profile cases, got a taste of the O.J. case, so that media element didn't really bother me."

"What did?" Mac asked.

"Rubens. He was ... so different from anything I'd ever run across. Have you two investigated a serial case before?"

"Kind of," Wire answered. "You probably heard about the Reaper case a year ago."

"I did," Walker answered. "But he wasn't really a serial, was he?"

"No, he wasn't. He was a grieving brother avenging his sister's death," Mac answered. "I got involved on the tail end of a serial case years ago in St. Paul, although that ended up tied into another investigation I was working."

"So you've had a taste," Walker replied. "Most serials tend to be pretty smart with an IQ of maybe bright normal. I think this guy is different. I think Rubens is way beyond that."

"I've been thinking the same thing. He has to be, the way he gets into these women's worlds and talks their language," Mac replied.

"That's what I thought too," Walker answered, nodding. "Most serials, while bright, are not overly educated. Rubens is different in that regard. He is educated and highly intelligent on many levels. I also got the sense that, unlike most serial killers, he didn't come from a broken home, nor was he abused as a child, either physically or sexually."

"Because it's not manifested in how he treats the victims," Mac answered.

"That was my impression," Walker answered. "April Greene, whom I'm sure you've met already, agreed with that assessment. There is no sex with the victim, at least when he murders them. If anything, odd as it sounds, since he's killed them he then treats them with great care, staging them like works of art."

"So the killing is ... just an act," Mac suggested.

"It's just one part of the work of art," Walker nodded. "The killing, that isn't what necessarily empowers him."

"No. The power comes from dominating the whole game, from seducing the women and then the game of cat and mouse with us," Mac answered. "That's what he really gets off on. If it was the killing, there wouldn't be the need for the clues, the clocks, the taunts and all of that."

Walker nodded his agreement. "I'll tell you what—the son of a gun was fascinating to go after. If I didn't have a stack of files three feet high, I'd jump on a plane and come help you. I'd love another shot at catching him."

"It looks like you almost did catch him," Wire asked. "In the file, it says you got to the last victim just minutes after she died. How did you get so close?"

"We solved the clue," Walker answered.

"How?"

"A little bit of luck and a little bit of obsession. We were getting nowhere. The pressure on us was immense, that damn ticking clock just staring us in the face all the time. What we were doing wasn't working so I changed it up. I went back to the apartment of the third victim, Leslie Merchant. I locked myself in there for nearly fifteen hours. My phone is ringing, the clock is running, the media is going crazy and I just ignored it all and holed up at the crime scene. I had to see if I could find it, the clue, the connection to the last victim. Now Leslie Merchant wasn't a hoarder, but she had a pretty healthy shopping addiction. She had money, a combination of being an only child who inherited a fair sum from her parents and having a good-paying job at Universal Pictures. I think she filled her free time spending money and buying things. Her apartment was a treasure trove. It was full of pictures, posters, books, bobbles, electronic equipment, furniture and clothes. Oh man, did she love clothes, and she made Imelda Marcos look like she had only a couple pairs of shoes."

"The perfect environment for him to hide the clue," Mac replied. "I'm looking at the same kind of scene right now. Pictures, portraits and books galore."

"That's right, Agent McRyan. I went to her apartment at 6:00 a.m., knowing our deadline was 9:00 p.m. that night. I just sat there just looking around for combinations on the walls and on the shelves."

"What triggered it?"

"I had the police radio on in case a call came in. The media knew when the deadline was. So people were calling in all kinds of tips, all of which were meaningless, except one. Literally a minute after 9:00 p.m., a tip came in that Ronda Hollister, a woman who hadn't missed a day of work or ever even been late for work in fifteen years, hadn't showed for work that day, wasn't answering the phone and this person thought she fit the profile."

"So? How did you make the connection?" Wire asked.

"The album cover for the *Help Me Rhonda* single framed on the wall," Mac exclaimed, staring at a crime scene photo. "It was framed on the wall. And sitting right underneath it was—"

"A Hollister shopping bag. I'd looked at that area a number of times while I'd been there and the minute I heard the name Ronda Hollister—"

"You knew."

"I knew. We were in her apartment at 9:17 p.m. I think we missed her death and him by mere minutes. He didn't leave the masterpiece behind. We found the dead swan for *Leda and the Swan* on the floor next to the body that was lying on a red tablecloth. That was the only time he didn't get to stage things perfectly. He was forced to leave before he wanted to—I guess he heard us coming. I put the whole area on lockdown around her house and I mean lockdown. Twelve-block radius. We searched every house, apartment, store, warehouse, business, bus, dog house, tree house and every vehicle in the area but came up empty. I got a call later that night from Rubens congratulating me on coming so close. That was the last I ever heard from him."

6

"ELEANOR ROOSEVELT, SHE WAS QUITE A HISTORICAL FIGURE."

Rubens sat up in his small bed, drinking a cup of espresso while he took in the morning news reports, his reappearance appropriately taking its place as the news lead. He was quite satisfied with how things had started. The local media was in full frenzy and the national media and the cable networks in particular, were devoting significant time to his reappearance. He'd even seen the first pseudo psychological expert resurface and get some air time. You had to love the twenty-four-hour news cycle.

By 9:30 a.m., he was out of bed and glancing out the window of the small apartment that overlooked East Capitol Street and the Anacostia River farther in the distance to the west. East Capitol Street was a main thoroughfare into the city from the east.

It had started.

He was energized to have the shackles off, to have his plan in motion and to be operating again. There was nothing like it.

Once showered and dressed, he made himself another cup of espresso, poured it into a cheap travel mug and was out the door and settled behind the wheel of his non-descript, three-year-old black Honda Civic. The mid-morning was cool and damp, a light coating of moisture on the streets from the misty rain now dissipating as he pulled out of the parking lot behind the apartment building.

Extra caution was required now that he had begun.

He diligently watched his rearview mirror and inventoried the vehicles in front and behind him as he drove west across the Whitney Young Memorial Bridge and started working his way towards southeast DC.

This wasn't the shortest or quickest route to the office; it was just one of *many* possibilities. The quickest way would have easily been south on the Anacostia Freeway and then west over the 11th Street Bridge. However, even before the game started he'd taken precautions, never driving to the office the same way two days in a row, never wearing the same clothing or arriving at the same time. No patterns, no consistencies and no reliability. He didn't want anyone to remember or notice him. If someone did engage him, he wasn't unfriendly by any means for that *would be* memorable and noticeable. But he didn't go out of his way to talk to people that he didn't need to talk to. It was his goal to not register with anyone. He wanted to be anonymous, someone nobody would give a second thought to if they saw him. What he strove for was to be totally common-looking, of average height and weight, wearing standard clothes, driving a normal, compact fuel-efficient car and engaging in unremarkable behavior. When it was all said and done, he didn't want anyone wondering where he went or what happened to him. He didn't want anyone to remember him at all. People were to never know that Rubens had been in their midst.

That was the discipline that was required.

One slip could end it all.

So there were no friends for the sake of having friends.

No contact was initiated with anyone unless they proved useful for a reason.

It was all about the mission, playing the game and winning it.

For those reasons, the apartment was rented eleven months ago under one name. The car was purchased two years ago under another name and the office was leased for six months under yet a third identity. That was one thing he had an abundance of —identities. When it was all over, he'd walk away from the apartment and office, both leases expiring at the end of April. The car would be dumped for cash, if it was safe to do so, or just simply dumped, left parked on a side street with the keys in the ignition, if need be.

At the end of April, he'd take another long vacation for a year or two and simply disappear.

That was what he'd done previously.

After Boston ten years ago, he made his way to London and traveled across Europe for a number of months before settling in Paris and finding work at the Louvre. It was two years before the States called him back.

When Chicago was finished, he left the country and traveled to Australia and toured the country before settling in Melbourne for six months, picking up work at an art gallery. It was another two years before he was back and settled in Los Angeles.

After the rush of Los Angeles, he'd slipped out of the United States and meandered his way to Argentina staying in Buenos Aires for six months before spending a year in Rio and making decent money as a street painter and artist, a trade he'd first learned in Paris and had been working on ever since. A trade that proved useful in seducing Lisa White.

Those trips were always the way to cleanse any possible trail of him. He left the country on one passport and returned on another. It was those many identities that allowed him to easily do it, the one benefit of his previous profession, the access to identities and personal records. Those identities and a good contact in New York City who flew way under the radar, accepted only cash in small denominations and who could create any sort of needed fake identification from the original identity. She was expensive but well worth the price while also exceedingly discreet and caring not the least about what he needed the identities for.

She allowed him to cover his tracks.

That was the discipline of this.

Discipline and keeping tightly to his timeline.

To do that, he needed to keep his lunch date.

That was his thought as he arrived at the office twenty minutes later. The small office was located in the basement level of a well-past-its-prime, dingy two-story office building filled with small obscure businesses. While not necessarily caring who was in the building, when he first toured it and saw the people hanging around it, he suspected that not all businesses located therein were fully law-abiding. That was good, he thought. This way people kept to them-selves and weren't nosy about what business their neighbor was engaged in. As a consequence, given the clientele and condition of the building, the owner was more than happy to agree to a six-month lease, especially for the extremely difficult-to-lease lower level space. With six months' rent paid in cash, he took the keys and had seen the owner just once since. It was the perfect set-up, an office in a building where everybody minded their own business. Even better was the back entrance into the office located down a set of narrow steps from the alley. He could come and go unseen.

The small office was split in two, a narrow rectangular reception area in the front and then a square office in the back. There was no receptionist to sit up front. No need, really; there wasn't a phone line that he'd activated, nor was there any business that was being conducted. In the back office, there was a closet where he stored his various clothing selections. To the right of the closet door rested a tall, locked metal cabinet. He opened the cabinet doors and stored inside were the various wigs, beards, mustaches, glasses, contact lenses, wrist watches, bracelets and rings that he needed. There was also another box filled with burner phones ready for use and then to be discarded. Finally, on the top shelf was the bottle of Rohypnol pills.

It was time to get ready for her.

Audrey kept checking her watch, waiting for lunchtime. When her computer clock turned over to 12:00, she bolted from her desk. She was pleased the morning rains had moved on and some warm spring air was sweeping into DC. The rain, followed by the sun, would accelerate the blooming of the cherry blossoms on the Mall.

It had been six weeks and she hadn't felt so alive in years, perhaps as many as ten years ... the ten years since she'd escaped her ex-husband.

It had been an awful and eventually abusive marriage.

It started as mental abuse. There were the constant putdowns about how she looked, what she weighed and what interested her. She didn't want to sit in front of the television and watch football all day on the weekend, nor did she want to be at his beck and call to fetch him beer and snacks. "Then what the hell are you good for?" he'd say.

A few years into the marriage she was constantly asking herself what she was thinking when she married the lout. It was probably that there weren't any other options presenting themselves at the time. She was approaching thirty years old, there had been few men to show interest, and while he was an over-the-road trucker, a bit crude and drank more than she liked, he showed up and seemed to offer the possibility of a future. That was despite the fact that he was the complete and total opposite of her. He didn't like art, museums, books or culture. "But opposites attract, right?" she said to one of her skeptical friends.

She took the plunge.

Her friends were right to be skeptical.

The marriage fizzled quickly. He was just mean and at the end, she could barely stand being around him. Finally, one morning, after he left for a four-day trip, she moved out.

That was not the end of it.

How dare she leave him and embarrass him? Who did she think she was? How could a woman who looked like she did think she could possibly walk away from him?

She refused to come back.

"Oh really?" he answered at the hotel room door before he stepped inside, slammed it closed and beat her. He practically dragged her and her suitcase out of the hotel, back to their house where he proceeded to continue the beating. And it continued for three weeks on end until she was calling in sick to work, no longer able to hide the bruises.

She had no family of her own left, having been an only child and her parents were long deceased. Finally, she hid at a friend's house for a few days, got herself together, found a family lawyer who helped her with the police and then through a difficult divorce. Her ex-husband did not go quietly. There was a restraining order in place, but she didn't perceive him as restrained.

When it was over, when the lawyer put the final decree in her hands, he had advice for her. "I've taken the measure of him. I've seen it before and I don't think he's going to stop."

"What should I do?"

"The only thing I think you can do. Leave Tacoma and get as far away from here as you can."

A week later she moved to Washington DC and in the ten years since she'd rebuilt her life.

For those long ten years, she'd essentially ignored men, in part because she was healing and in part because they didn't often pay attention to her anyway. But now that had changed.

"Hi, James," she waved to the gray-bearded gentlemen in the black sport coat and gray slacks looking at the panels of the Vietnam Memorial.

"Hello, Audrey," he answered happily, taking her hands in his and leaning in to kiss her, which she happily accepted. "You look so lovely."

Audrey blushed. She'd worn a light blue sleeveless spring dress under her navy blue blazer and wedge sandals that made her a little taller. "You're so kind."

"So, how long do you have?"

"I have to be back at 2:00 p.m.," Audrey replied.

"Only two hours?" Rubens replied with concern. "Then, my dear, we best make good use of our time together. Please, start by showing me the panel for your uncle." Audrey's uncle was on panel nine of the memorial. From the panel, they made their way along the mall, talking and enjoying the sun.

He'd identified Audrey nine months ago while walking the Smithsonian Museum of American Art over the lunch hour. She seemed like a possibility; with the wide hips and the large breasts, she had the look. The woman was the right type physically. But she had to be the right type mentally and that was always a little harder to determine.

So what made a woman right?

A woman had to be right physically. She had to fit the look of a Rubens woman.

Then the woman had to be a loner.

The target couldn't have a big social circle because once you started becoming close, when things seemed to be getting serious, when a woman started to feel a man might be important in their life, then they had friends and family they wanted to introduce you to. Friends and family created witnesses, someone who could and would point a finger if a friend came up dead. No, if that happened, if he ended up meeting friends and family he simply walked away cold.

That happened once in a while, including twice in DC.

He couldn't risk it, so no matter how perfect the woman might have been, if there was a potential witness he just walked away.

If she was to be perfect, she had to have interests he was well-versed in. What he was doing he couldn't fake, so their interests had to align.

As he'd followed Audrey in the early days, she often walked the many Smithsonian museums, frequented bookstores and enjoyed art galleries. She bought her groceries from a small store on the corner near her townhouse and cooked her meals nightly, often while sipping wine. When he observed her at night, she often sat at home reading books or watching movies. She was a woman with few friends or social acquaintances who liked the arts and lived alone and fit the physical profile.

Audrey was right in his wheelhouse.

Finally, the woman had to be interested in men—*romantically* interested. He didn't want overly eager or experienced women. Rather he wanted shy, reserved women who were somewhat inexperienced with men and just a bit slow to trust, if not just slightly skeptical of his initial overture. It was their trust he needed and wanted to earn. He wanted them to invite him in, to start to take him into their lives and to let their guard down. That was what made the hunt all the more invigorating.

That was also why he initially walked away from Audrey.

In conducting his Internet research on Audrey, he found the police records of the domestic abuse and record of the divorce back in the state of Washington. He surmised she would be very leery of men and that she would be difficult to get close enough to.

He figured it would take a lot of work.

He decided to pass.

So he did. He moved on to other potential women.

Then one day two months later he was in a bookstore when Audrey walked in. Not only that, she came down the American History aisle, the aisle he was standing in. He was holding a book about FDR while discreetly scouting Lisa White twenty feet away. Audrey, as it turned out, was interested in a book about Eleanor Roosevelt.

He took a shot.

"She was an amazing lady," he said.

"Excuse me?" she asked, surprised.

"Eleanor Roosevelt, she was quite a historical figure."

"Oh my... oh yes... yes, she was," Audrey replied awkwardly.

He pressed on. "I was at the Smithsonian National Air and Space Museum and saw a photo of her in a plane flown by a black pilot in 1940. It gave me a greater appreciation of her. At that point in our history, for the First Lady to take a ride in a plane piloted by an African American, that sent a very powerful, powerful message. It's why I was looking at this book on FDR. This book goes into quite a bit of detail about her relationship with the President."

"You're so right," she replied a little more warmly.

The Smithsonian mention and a knowledgeable comment on Eleanor Roosevelt and suddenly he was in.

That was six weeks ago.

It took a while to get her to open up but kindness and a gentle, mild approach had slowly melted the wall she had up. There was dinner at her townhouse two weeks ago. She let him kiss her for the first time ten days ago and again when they met for a quiet dinner five days later.

"I was so happy to see you today," Audrey said as their lunch date came to an end. "And I am so excited that you can come over on Wednesday night."

"I wouldn't miss it."

7

"IF THAT'S WHAT YOU HAVE TO DO, THEN BY GOD, YOU DO IT."

M ac sat back in his chair, arms behind his head and took in the contents of the whiteboard... or in reality, whiteboards, plural.

It had been a long day.

There had been the introduction to Rubens in the morning, the digestion of the FBI summaries, the meetings with the FBI team lead by Galloway and Delmonico. Then in the afternoon were the lengthy video conferences with Boston, Chicago and Los Angeles that lasted into the early evening. By the time those were complete, Coolidge and his people were off in the streets with their updates.

The day had been an onslaught of information.

He'd felt overloaded as it was all coming at him.

That was why he used the whiteboards.

He was a visual person and learner. The greatest thing for him academically in college and law school was PowerPoint. When teachers put everything up for him to see he could just soak it in. As a good student, he undertook the tried and true steps for academic success. He went to every class, completed every reading assignment and took copious notes in class. Despite all of that, it was always best when he could just see it up on a chalkboard, whiteboard or screen and see everything laid out in front of him. He simply learned and retained information better that way.

That was what he was doing as the clock approached midnight, sitting with Wire and Coolidge, soaking it all in.

It was really the first time with the case that he'd been able to do it.

"Tell me about Lisa White again," Mac asked Coolidge.

"Lisa White was forty-one years old. She's lived in DC for fifteen years," Coolidge stated, sitting back in a chair of his own, sipping from a bottle of water. "She was originally a native of Greensboro, North Carolina."

"Does she have family?" Wire asked.

Linc shook his head. "Not much. Her parents are long deceased. She has a sister who lives in Durango, Colorado with whom she wasn't close. They hadn't spoken in probably a year. They were ten years apart in age and never bonded, according to the sister."

"What about her social circle here?"

"It doesn't seem to have been terribly big. We went through her cell phone records and there weren't many calls to speak of. There was one woman who turned up a few times but it turns out it was who White purchased her painting supplies from. They weren't close. We're still looking deeper into the phone records to see if anything pops. That includes calls to the work phone."

"How about work? What did they say there?" Wire asked.

"I went with one of my guys and we interviewed everyone Lisa White worked with at Georgetown. She worked as an administrator in the admissions department."

"What did you learn?" Mac asked, having pushed himself out of his chair and now standing at the whiteboard, his back to Coolidge.

"Lisa White was a model employee. Superbly reliable, almost never missed work and had seven weeks of unused vacation. Yet..."

"Yet?" Mac asked, turning, looking back to Linc.

"It's as if they didn't know her."

"How is that possible?" Wire asked.

"According to the staff, White was quiet, kept to herself and wasn't one to share much about her life. She showed up on time, worked diligently, did her job quietly and effectively and then when the day was over she went home. Everyone there liked her, said she was pleasant to be around and talk to, but nobody really *knew* her. Lisa White never went out for a drink with anyone there. Not one person there had ever been invited to her house nor had she ever accepted an invite to any of theirs. She was often a no-show at the office holiday party and if she did show, she didn't stay long."

"In other words a total loner and introvert who loved to paint, tend to her plants and read books," Wire suggested.

"Pretty much. However, they did say she seemed a little different recently."

"Let me guess, someone new in her life?" Mac suggested.

"They think there might have been because she seemed to have been happier as of late. She was dressing a little nicer with newer, more flattering clothes. There was a new, more updated hairstyle and light applications of makeup. She'd even mentioned something about dieting, which was something she'd never said before. There were more smiles and she was even engaging more with some of her co-workers."

"As if she was a little more confident?" Mac speculated.

"She had the glow," Wire added.

"Yes," Linc replied, gesturing to Wire. "Two women she worked with said exactly that. She had a glow and that suggested to them, at least, that she had someone in her life."

"Did anyone ask her?" Mac prompted.

Coolidge shook his head. "Another woman, Lynette Waller, who works in admissions did ask her what had changed, that she seemed different in a really good way. She tried to get her to open up but Waller said 'that just wasn't Lisa.' She said White didn't really say— she just said she decided to make some changes in her life. So while White never admitted it, this Lynette and a few other folks thought she had met someone."

"So there should be some evidence of that," Wire mused.

"Maybe, maybe not," Mac replied. "Our guy hasn't been caught over his ten-year run. Why? He leaves no trace behind. No descriptions, no names and little to no forensic evidence—and the evidence we do find, like evidence of using a roofie, he doesn't care about. Even more importantly he is a predator, an expert on preying on women," Mac answered. "And not just any kind of woman, either."

"Meaning?" Wire asked.

"I've been reading through the case files on these murders going all the way back to Boston. These women are pretty much all alike."

"Yeah, Rubenesque," Coolidge and Wire responded in unison.

"They're more than just that," Mac answered. "He requires the physical appearance to be right for sure but he goes deeper, much deeper than that. Wire and I talked about it this morning. It's *who* they are. They're all introverts—shy, reserved, whatever term you want to use, those are the kinds of women he targets. These are women who are not prone to trusting men, or even women for that matter. They don't open up to anyone. Yet what is scary is that our guy—"

"Gets them to open up somehow," Wire answered. "Mac, that takes patience and time. It's not a one-week kind of thing."

"No, it's a week after week after week kind of thing," Mac answered and then looked back to the whiteboard, taking in the information not only on White, but on all of the victims. He started nodding.

"What?" Wire asked.

"We have to go really deep on Lisa White," Mac replied and then went for a phone, "Don, good, you're still here. Can you step in here?"

A minute later, a yawning Senior Agent Galloway stepped into the conference room.

"Where are we at on Lisa White's financial history?" Mac asked.

Galloway handed a sheath of papers to Mac as he took a drink from his Diet Coke. "That's all her financial information."

"Credit card history?"

"Last page. She has a Visa. She pays it monthly. In addition to the Visa, you'll see she has over $20,000 cash actually in the bank and another $50,000 in a tax-free fund that she could draw down if needed—kind of a Suze Orman emergency fund. She was putting the maximum into her retirement account and had a little over $400,000 put away. For what it's worth, she was in really good financial shape."

Where she was recently spending her money was of interest to Mac. With Wire and Coolidge looking over his shoulder, Mac scanned through her credit card history of the last four months. There were a lot of charges for stores in DC and the surrounding area. "Don, what kind of personnel resources do we have?"

"Depends. What are you thinking?"

Mac held up the credit card statements. "I'm thinking we need to go to every store she's charged at in the last, say, four months. We need to go through her calendar, anything that tracks where she's been. Somewhere Rubens interacts with her along the way. April Greene thinks Rubens is highly educated, has interests in the arts. So did Lisa White. As I look at her financials, there are bookstores, paint stores and museums. For example, the Smithsonian is on here twice. So where would he be most likely to find Lisa White?"

"At a place of their mutual interest," Galloway answered.

"Correct, a place where she and he would *both* be comfortable. We need to see if we can find him by looking at where Lisa White was spending her time. We need security camera footage of the time of every purchase to see if anyone is with her. We need to show Lisa White's picture at these places, especially the bookstores. She bought books seemingly by the truckload, but it looks like she was buying them at small mom and pop stores. I see only a few chain store purchases and not many Internet purchases either."

"The little bookstores might not have much for surveillance," Coolidge noted.

"True," Mac responded. "But in turn, they know their customers, especially someone who is in the store often. So maybe, just maybe, they saw someone with Lisa White."

"It might have registered with someone at the store if she was there and a man was with her," Wire noted, nodding.

"Or talking to her," Coolidge added and then offered, "I can probably get some people to help. The stores must know her a little. We need to talk to them all."

Galloway looked over the list. "That's good, Detective Coolidge. This is a lot to cover in a short period of time. I'll have to liaison with other local law enforcement and get you some help."

"Good," Mac answered, "but let's try to get detectives on it if at all possible, Don. I love the men in uniform, but detectives will have a better feel for this."

"Understood," Galloway responded. "I'll get it started. We'll be on it tomorrow."

After Galloway left, Mac stepped back to the whiteboard, scanning the evidence, the facts, the information.

"What else?" Wire asked. "What else are we going to do? I mean, this might not work."

"No, it might not, at least not yet," Mac replied. "You have to give it time."

"Give it time? We're on a clock. How can you give it time?"

Mac started to respond and then stopped. One thing that he was thinking about all day was the how. How to find Rubens? How to get to him? He thought back to his discussions with Boston, Chicago and Los Angeles, what he'd heard and the investigative approaches they'd taken. All of the men were good detectives who for the most part were overwhelmed by the case, maybe with the exception of Sam Walker in Los Angeles. Mac liked Walker. The man was real police, a pro, and Mac saw a lot of himself in Walker. Walker came close on the last victim because instead of chasing the case, he stopped looking at the clock, ignored his phone and just focused on the last clue. Mac could hear it in Walker's voice. If he could go back and do it again, he'd have done that sooner. Maybe Mac needed to learn that lesson and play the game differently.

"Mac, how can we just give it time?" Wire persisted.

"It's a game, Dara. Not for you and I, but for Rubens. Think about the profile April Greene gave us this morning. To Rubens, this is a game. It has a beginning and it has an end and we play up to four. Everyone who has gone up against him has played the game on

Rubens' terms, chasing to the next victim, sweating the clock, the pressure, the phone calls and ultimately the failure. I'm not going to play it that way."

"But the women? The victims?"

"The way I look at it is I have three more to play with."

"You have three more ... to play with?" Wire looked at her partner as if he'd lost his mind. "Mac, you're playing with the women's lives."

"No," Mac answered, shaking his head. "No, no, no. Rubens is."

"Yeah, and that sick bastard is going to kill another woman on Wednesday if we don't stop him."

Mac nodded. "That's exactly how he wants you to think of this."

"Because that's exactly what this is," Wire replied. "We have to find him."

"I don't think we can," Mac answered. "Not before Thursday, not unless we get very lucky somehow. Victim number two is as good as already dead."

"You're giving up already?" Wire looked to Coolidge, completely dismayed. "Is he really saying this?"

"Yes, but ... I think I get why," Coolidge replied and then looked to Mac. "The long game?"

"Yup."

"So you just let the next victim die?" Dara persisted, not yet buying in.

"I'm not going to just let the next victim die, Dara. Come on, you know me better than that. Rubens is already getting to you—"

"Isn't he getting to you?" she pressed.

Mac sat down in a chair. "This morning he was. I could feel my chest tightening because I was sitting around reading files and I wasn't out pounding the pavement, looking for leads, sweating witnesses and doing what I'd normally do with a homicide investigation because in your usual homicide the first forty-eight hours are the key."

"What changed?" she asked.

"The conference calls with Boston, Chicago and Los Angeles. By the end of those it had dawned on me."

"What?"

"Let me use a track metaphor. Boston, Chicago and Los Angeles treated the case as a sprint, like you want to treat it, like I would usually treat it. They scrambled like mad to find the next victim and that plays right into Rubens' hands. That is exactly what he wants, and he throws gas on the fire with the calls, the countdown and the clues."

"So, what, you sit back and watch?"

"No. But I'm thinking of this case as a marathon and we're just a little over five miles in. Rubens is way ahead right now but with twenty-one plus miles to go, we've got time to catch up. We have to play to our strengths."

"Which are —" The look that washed across her face told Mac she was starting to get it. "The resources of the FBI."

"The resources of DC. The resources of Boston, Chicago and Los Angeles. And the media as well. They can be an ally in this if used right. This isn't just you and me against him. He wants you and me to think of it that way, but it's not. It's everyone we have at our disposal. We need to let the mass of resources work to our advantage. We need to collect as much information as possible. We need to figure Rubens out, Dara. There has to be a way to catch him. I think to do that we need to understand how he makes his moves so that we can antici-pate them when we get to the end."

"If we chase him from victim to victim, we'll end up like all the others, having failed."

"I want the last book written on Rubens to be how we nailed the prick. To do that I think we need to play this differently than others have. In the short term, we've got Galloway doing his thing and Linc is doing his thing with his people and maybe we get lucky before Thursday. So in that sense we play it like a normal case. But you and I," Mac shook his head, "we're not going to play it that way. The next victim is chosen, that plan is already in action and Rubens is already closing the noose. If I put everything into chasing just that—"

"We just fall further behind," Dara finished. "Still, I don't like just sitting around looking at this whiteboard."

"For now," Mac replied, "that's exactly what we're going to do until we understand Rubens better. If we're going to stop him before he leaves DC, if we're going to stop him for good, we have to think about this like he does. It's a game. Before we can make a move on him, we have to understand him better. In the meantime, we may have to be willing to sacrifice another victim to figure out the game, to figure out Rubens and to catch him once and for all."

∾

When he got home, he spent five minutes vomiting in the small bathroom off to the side of the kitchen. When he exited the bathroom, wiping his mouth with the back of his hand, a robed Sally was waiting for him.

"Are you okay?"

"Just something I ate," Mac replied lamely as he went to the refrigerator and reached inside for a bottle of water.

"Really?" she remarked skeptically.

"You know, on a case like this—cold pizza, sandwiches sitting out, bad takeout—"

"And a clock counting down to another victim," she finished, taking the measure of him. She always seemed to know what he was thinking. It scared him sometimes how perceptive she could be. Sally wasn't buying the food poisoning bit. "It's bad, isn't it?"

He shrugged.

"I know you don't watch the news but it was the lead on the cable networks, the nightly news and the local news. It's all over the web. This author, what's his name?"

"Hugo Ridge."

"Yeah, he's been on a lot already. Apparently, he wrote two books on this guy."

"They're part of the FBI file on Rubens. His books and two by a woman named April Greene who is helping. I have one of her books in my backpack."

"Anyway, it's wall-to-wall coverage. Are you guys anywhere?"

Mac shook his head. "Not yet, but ... it's early."

"There's more to this than that," Sally pressed. "How bad is it really?"

Mac tipped his head toward the bathroom. "That kind of answers the question, don't you think?"

"I've never seen a case get to you like that, though," she replied with concern. "What's so special about this one?"

"Because of what I think we have to do." He relayed his conversation with Wire. "I got her to my way of thinking eventually but the idea of ... just letting a woman ... die so I can learn more because it's a fucking game to this asshole—" His voice trailed off as he leaned forward over the center island, looking down at his bottle of water and shaking his head. He technically said he had three more lives to play with like it was a new set of downs in football. He actually said that. It shocked him that he could be that cold and calculating. Was he as cold and calculating as the killer? Did he have to be to catch him?

After a moment, he took a long drink from the bottle of water and tried to clear his head. "God, I hope I'm doing the right thing." He took another drink of water, a long gulp and looked over to Sally. She was the best sounding board he had. She was wicked smart and he trusted her judgment. "Am I doing the right thing?"

"Do you believe this is what you have to do?"

He nodded. "I think so."

Sally thought for a moment and then nodded slowly. "If I've learned anything working in the White House the last two years, it's that you do whatever you have to do to win."

"Just win."

"That's right," Sally replied, coming around the island, tipping his chin up and softly cupping his face in her hands. She looked him in the eye. "If this is what you have to do, then by God, you do it."

8

"I'M THINKING … RULES."

TUESDAY NIGHT, 6:00 P.M.

"Twenty-eight hours to go," Wire sighed as she looked at her watch while lying on the old orange waiting room-like couch, resting for a moment.

Mac forbade a countdown clock in the room. They all knew the deadline, and it didn't need to be constantly staring them in the face. But it didn't matter. The countdown was everywhere. He couldn't help but look at his watch from time to time. Every clock in the hallway or the one in the break room always caught his attention. People were in and out of the room all day and they were either reporting the time or checking their own watches or cell phones.

It reminded him of the movie *High Noon*. The movie viewer always knew how much closer to high noon Gary Cooper was getting because in every scene there was a clock in the background, sometimes ticking, sometimes silent but there was always a clock in view. No character ever mentioned how much time was left. You just knew. It was ever present, ticking away hour by hour, minute by minute, second by second.

It was that way now.

That time was passing was palpable.

The only way to block it out was to keep working.

He turned his attention back to the whiteboards.

The two-wheeled boards to the left of the main whiteboard mounted on the wall were the Lisa White murder boards. The one farthest to the left contained a summary of everything they'd learned about Lisa White the person. The other whiteboard was for the crime scene itself. They'd spent much of the last day working on the far left board. The focus was her phones, financials and retracing her steps in her final months.

Like many people these days, she did not have a house phone, only a cell phone. The key time period appeared to be the last six weeks, but the odd part was that it was her work phone and not her cell phone that revealed the contact. The records to her office phone at Georgetown University over the last six weeks revealed eight calls from an unidentified number, which they found to be a pay-as-you-go phone, better known as a burner phone. The problem, of course, was *it was* a burner phone. There was no identification attached to the phone's number.

"That's our guy for sure," Wire said earlier, reviewing the calls. "There is no way he gets that close to her without some phone time. But why call her only at work?"

"She wouldn't identify the caller at work," Mac answered. "If he calls her on her cell, there is a chance she adds him as a contact. If she does that, it gives us a name, a number, something to trace."

"But if he's calling at work, she is at least less likely to do that."

"Correct."

They thought that in all his time spent in her townhouse after he'd killed her perhaps he'd deleted his contact name from her phone. The phone had been checked and nothing was changed or deleted from it in the hours before or after her death late on Saturday night.

An effort was made to call the burner but to no avail. It most likely had been disposed of or destroyed. A trace on the number revealed it was purchased a year ago at a convenience store in New Jersey, paid with cash. The store actually had surveillance footage of the day of the sale. The phones looked to have been sold to two young men, one Caucasian and the other perhaps Hispanic. Unfortunately, neither the store owner nor any of his employees recognized the men making the purchase.

"Tells you how long he's been planning," Mac replied. "Bought the phone a year ago and used proxies to do it."

"Still, you'd figure that at some point a contact would be put into a phone if he's calling them," Wire suggested. "At least one of the victims maybe did that."

"We should review that. I'll have Delmonico get on it," Mac offered. "However, even if a contact was entered, do we really think he'd actually give them a real name to go from? A name to which there was actually an identity on record somewhere that was really his?" He shook his head. "I highly doubt it. He's way too careful."

Detectives and agents were still tracking down all of her financial transactions of the last four months. They were going to each store from which White made a purchase, talking to anyone working that day, showing White's picture and collecting surveillance footage if it existed. Earlier in the day, Mac had looked through the surveillance video highlights collated thus far. Nothing probative had yet come to light. Problem was that, despite what you would see on television, surveillance footage was not always of high quality and tended to focus on specific areas of a store, especially a larger one. There were plenty of nooks and crannies that someone could hide or walk in that would allow someone to avoid high visibility on a surveillance system, particularly if you were being careful to avoid any exposure. However, it still had to be done. There were more stores to be checked and footage to be collected. They were getting to it as quickly as possible.

The middle whiteboard was for the murder scene at White's house. Mac peered at it from time to time, seeing if he could discern what the hidden clue might be.

It was there.

Somewhere in the mass of books, pictures, paintings and bobbles rested the clue to their next victim.

Given the time of death until the time of the call, Rubens likely had hours in her townhouse to set it up. Agents were taking turns at White's looking at everything that was packed into her cramped townhouse, trying to see if they could discern any pattern or find a name to check. If they came up with a name, they ran it through the DMV database and checked the photos. Thus far, ten names had been checked. Four of the women were married, three were high school students, one was a college student and two currently resided in nursing homes. None of the women fit the Rubens profile.

Mac already decided what he would do tomorrow as the clock ticked, and that was go back to White's and take his crack at it.

For tonight he was focused on the main whiteboard, the one dedicated to Rubens. There were pictures of the twelve prior victims, a new picture for Lisa White, as well as pictures for the clues for each victim.

Under the heading of "Victims," Mac wrote out all of the traits of the women. The characteristics were important, as was the method. It took Rubens time to get close to the women. The phone records showed eight calls from the suspected burner phone over a six-week period of time. He was slow, methodical and careful.

"If it's six weeks, shouldn't we just look at the last two months of financials?" Dara asked.

"Maybe," Mac replied. "But I'm betting he had his eyes on Lisa White long before two months ago."

"Scouting her?"

"And others," Mac answered. "He purchased the burner phone a year ago. So at least a year ago he was in the planning stages. Then he had to find four women that fit his criteria that he could woo. I mean, think about that for a second."

"Wooing four women?"

"Yeah. You ever woo multiple men at one time?"

"I've been wooed by multiple men at once," she replied with a bright smile.

"You're just so impressed with yourself, aren't you?" Mac mocked. "But seriously?"

"Yes, I've dated multiple men at the same or similar time," Wire answered. "It's actually kind of a pain. I like it better when there is only one in the picture."

"Anyone in the picture now?"

"No," she answered quickly and with a hint of annoyance.

"None of my business anyway," Mac replied. "But think about our guy—he's wooing four, if not more, women at the same time."

"That's a lot of work."

"Dating or a date takes what, a few hours at a time? If they go well, maybe there is a second date. If not, you move on. But our guy, he can't just move on very often. He needs four women that fit his profile and he needs them to fit into a pretty specific window of time that works for him. That's a pretty tight needle to thread. That takes work, balancing, discipline and a ... method." Mac took a good long look at the board.

"What are you thinking?" Dara asked.

"I'm thinking ... rules."

"Rules?"

"Yeah, rules. What are his dating rules? You have dating rules, right?"

"You mean, like no kiss on the first date?" Wire responded. "Although that's such a lame rule."

"I agree," Mac answered. "But I had rules or guidelines or deal breakers, whatever you call them. You had them. I had them. Most everyone has them. So he must have them too."

"Rules he would follow so ..." She thought about it. "That he doesn't raise suspicion or—"

"Get caught," Mac replied. "Or make his prey suspicious."

"She has to fit the criteria, right?" Dara suggested. "All of the criteria you have up on the board."

"Yes, but what are the other rules?" Mac asked.

"Well, nobody has ever given us a good description of Rubens."

"Because nobody has ever seen him because... if they do..."

"He abandons them," Wire surmised, her eyebrows raised in interest. "Nobody else sees him and meets. That's the rule. So if he gets introduced to friends or family, he what? Just walks away."

"He has to. Because if he then kills the woman, especially when she's killed the way Rubens killed her, the first suspect would, of course, be the boyfriend."

"So that's a rule. What do we do with it?"

"Hmpf." Mac scratched the back of his head. "I'm not sure. It seems like there might be something there to use. I have to think about that." He made some notes on the whiteboard. "What other rules?"

"If they're dating, they have to go places."

"Not necessarily," Mac replied. "They could just meet at her place."

"No," Wire replied, shaking her head. "No, no, no, silly boy. If I'm dating a guy, he's taking me out. Dinner, drinks, movies, we're going out."

"Okay," Mac answered. "So bars and restaurants?"

"Perhaps," Wire replied. "But our victims aren't the barhopping type. They're the books, art, museum and gardening types."

"You're probably right, although I've never met a woman who didn't like a good meal and a glass of wine at a nice restaurant," Mac answered. "It's in a woman's DNA. It's certainly in Sally's and we've established it's in yours as well. But if he did take a woman to a restaurant it's most likely going to be a smaller, quieter place."

Wire started flipping through the financials for White. "I don't see a lot of restaurant activity. I see takeout, but not restaurants."

"He's paying," Mac replied and frowned. "If you're right and there are dates, he's paying and it's in his interest to pay. If she pays, that leaves a financial record. No. He's paying and he's probably paying with cash."

"Because," Wire continued, "you can't trace cash."

"So no friends and family, that's a deal breaker. There are probably dates that he's paying cash on, so that there's no financial record. What else?"

"Do they ever go to *his* place?" Wire asked.

"Good question," Mac replied in thought, scratching the side of his face. "I kind of doubt it. That would be risky and I don't think he'd take that kind of risk. Lisa White's picture is plastered all over the news now. So if anyone ever remembered seeing her at *his* place, the jig would be up. But it does beg a different question."

"Which is?"

"He's been here a year, right?"

"Or so we think."

"Where did he come from?" Mac reached for the phone.

A minute later Galloway came in. "What's up?"

"When Rubens was operating in Chicago and later Los Angeles, did the Bureau ever run a search cross-referencing people establishing residences in all three cities, Boston, Chicago and LA in the relevant time periods?"

"Like someone moving from Boston to Chicago and then LA?"

"Yeah."

"I believe so and it came up empty."

"We need to do it again or restart whatever was done before. This guy is using a fake identity—in fact, probably multiple fake identities. He has to be."

"Especially after Boston," Dara added.

"Right," Mac replied, snapping his fingers. "So have our guys throw Boston out and instead run it Chicago to LA to DC. See if anything pops. Heck, let's run down anyone who pops in two of the three. Cast a wide net."

"That's apt to be a lot of people if you broaden it to that degree," Galloway warned.

"It creates a possible pool if we ever do get a name," Mac replied. "Plus, all the names you find you can run against criminal records, employment histories, financial transactions, vehicle history. Our guy moves to these cities and he sets up shop for a long time. He must have a home, an apartment or a townhouse that he's renting with a lease expiring probably at the end of April. Is there any way to search leases expiring at the end of April?"

"Not sure the degree to which there would be a database of something like that," Galloway answered. "I can look into it but we'd more likely have to start calling every apartment complex in the area, assuming he's renting an apartment. He could be renting a house. It could be impossible."

"Give it some thought," Mac answered. "He's living somewhere and there has to be a record of it. Rubens probably is driving, so he has a driver's license. Maybe it's a fake or maybe there's a DMV record under the fake identity, who knows. We need to run it against any leasing records, against anyone who's moved here from Chicago or Los Angeles in the last seven years."

"Okay," Galloway sighed. "It's all a long shot."

"Right now, yes, it is," Mac replied. "But as we get more information we're set up to run it and maybe something pops. By the way, I caught your little press briefing earlier. Great job with the media. Thanks for keeping them off our backs."

"No problem, although Mac, they're asking for you. They know you and Dara are on the case. They know he called you."

Mac sighed but then after a second nodded. "Well, that could prove useful when the time comes."

Galloway, the master of administration and media, went off to take care of his latest massive task.

It was approaching 8:00 p.m.

"You know what I need?" Mac groaned, stretching his arms over his head.

"A burger and a beer," Dara answered hopefully.

"See, this is why we're partners."

They wanted to get out and stretch their legs, so they snuck out the side of the building and walked.

It was a pleasant evening. Spring was rolling in. The night was warmer and they could feel a hint of humidity as they walked the four blocks to The Fillmore.

Historians did not regard the thirteenth President of the United States, Millard Fillmore, as a particularly successful one, so the name was a perfect fit for a dive bar. But it was a good dive bar with burgers, sandwiches and a long selection of tap beers, including many local microbrews. They grabbed a back booth and quickly ordered.

Mac took a long drag of his Port City Wit, one of his new favorite local beers, closed his eyes and exhaled at the brief moment away from the case. "That feels good."

"Agreed," Wire replied as she took a second small pull from her glass.

They chatted about anything but the case.

"So is Sally freaking out about this case ruining the wedding?"

"Naturally. I told her if Rubens held to form, this would be all over, one way or the other, long before the wedding."

Wire nodded. "Have you seen her dress?"

"No," Mac answered, shaking his head. "Why would I want to ruin the surprise?"

His partner smiled. "Oh my, she is going to be beautiful."

"*That* will not be a surprise. I don't know how she couldn't look amazing."

"You're so whipped—it's really kind of pathetic."

With their burger baskets finished, Mac and Wire weren't ready to head back just yet. They ordered coffee, expecting to work for several more hours. Instead, the waitress came back with two more beers. "From the gentleman sitting at the bar."

Mac and Wire both looked over to the bar and immediately recognized their benefactor sitting on a bar stool, smiling.

Hugo Ridge.

"Figures he'd show up sooner or later," Mac muttered.

The author was certainly dressed to fit the image. Tall and slender with three-day-old stubble and his hair stylishly askew, Ridge was attired in tight-fitting blue jeans to go with a brown tweed coat and black button down collar dress shirt. He approached the table with a beer of his own. "Could I join you for a few minutes?" he asked politely.

"Sure," Wire answered immediately, sliding over so he could sit next to her.

"What, no television appearances tonight?" Mac asked sardonically while nevertheless taking a long drink from his new and free beer.

"Already did my duty," Ridge replied. "This is hell for you two, but I'm not afraid to say that for me it's a pretty good deal."

"That's kind of callous, don't you think?" Mac asked.

"Nah, it's America. We're all trying to make a buck. Publicity is good for book sales, both future and past," Ridge answered, unoffended, and then added a zinger of his own. "It's not like your book sales will be hurt by recent events."

"That's probably true," Mac conceded. "So what can we do for you, Mr. Ridge?"

"Start by calling me Hugo."

"Okay, Hugo, what do you want?"

"Is he always this standoffish?" Ridge asked with a smile, nodding toward Mac but looking to his right to Wire.

"Yeah, pretty much."

"How are you two holding up?" the author asked. "I mean the clock is kind of..."

"Winding down," Wire finished. "It is what it is."

"You're not feeling the pressure?"

"Is the Pope Catholic?" Mac replied honestly. "You can't help but feel it."

"No, I know you can't. I've followed Rubens for ten years now and I've seen the impact on the people he torments. Although, I must say I do think this time he has taken on his toughest adversaries."

"What makes you say that?" Wire asked, curious.

"Let's take the guy who led the case in Boston." Ridge shook his head. "I covered Gavin Sullivan for a few years when I had the crime beat for the *Herald*. He was a good man, a respected detective, but he didn't really grasp what he was dealing with until it was too late. In Chicago, those guys were earnest street cops but they couldn't think at Rubens' level. They got absolutely nowhere, were out of their league and I don't think Rubens even broke a sweat there. He just toyed with those two. In LA, Sam Walker was an impressive guy. Now he knew how to run a case. After I met him the first time, I thought there was a decent chance he'd catch Rubens. So did April Greene. And Walker got close, or at least as close as anyone has gotten. You two, however, with the cases you've handled, are at a different level."

"How so?" Mac inquired.

"You're a known commodity, for one. People have heard of you. Heck, you were just on *60 Minutes*."

"Jealous?" Wire teased.

"A little. I've never been on *60 Minutes*," Ridge replied with a smile. "I've spent more time on the *Times* best sellers list though."

"Congratulations. What makes you think we're so much more formidable?" Mac inquired impatiently.

"You both have dealt with pressure and I'm not blowing smoke— you two are pretty smart. I mean, look at your backgrounds." Ridge had done his homework. He'd studied their careers, reciting facts and figures. "Michael Mackenzie McRyan here was a highly decorated St. Paul homicide detective, a fourth-generation cop, a member of St. Paul's first family. Before that, he graduated from William Mitchell College of Law, *magna cum laude* and before that, with equally high honors, from the University of Minnesota where he was also captain of the national championship hockey team. You married once, then divorced and will in just a few short weeks, marry the lovely Ms. Sally Kennedy, White House Deputy Director of Communications. All in all, a pretty damn impressive background, especially for someone in his mid-thirties."

Ridge turned to Dara.

"Ms. Wire, you attended the University of Virginia, graduating with highest honors and eschewed a chance to immediately enroll in the UVA law school to go work for the FBI. You used those hauntingly beautiful dark features to first work undercover and then later run operations designed to take a bite out of organized crime along the Eastern Seaboard, with a particular focus on New York City. You rose quickly through the Bureau but then abruptly departed after having rearranged the facial features of Donald Chandler Jr., the former Vice President's son, I might add, for naming one of your informants who shortly thereafter met his unfortunate demise at the hands of the mob. You now quietly own a thriving private security consulting business and, like your good friend across the table, occasionally lend your investigative talents to the Bureau."

Ridge, very pleased with himself, took a drink from his beer. "Needless to say, at least on paper you two are a much higher caliber adversary for him."

"Not that it has done much good thus far," Wire blurted out and Mac shot her a peeved glance.

Ridge noticed the look and turned to Wire, the more willing of the two to talk. "Have you made any progress?" Ridge asked.

"We're working on it," Dara answered, clamming up.

"That I know to be true. I've been trying to get some time with you two but you've locked yourselves inside the field office and I haven't yet figured out how to slither my way in there, at least not yet. When you two walked out I decided to follow and take a chance."

"Now that you have, any insight you care to share with us?" Mac asked.

"About Rubens?"

"Yeah," Mac answered. "I've been engrossed in evidence and FBI data, so I haven't had time to absorb the undoubtedly keen insight you have in your books."

Ridge smirked but plowed ahead. "Answer me this: what are you two focusing on right now?"

"How he picks the victims," Wire replied, receiving another look from Mac. "Lighten up, Francis. What can it hurt to ask?" she scolded.

"Yeah, Francis, what can it hurt to ask?" Ridge added teasingly.

"Probably plenty," Mac answered tersely, glowering at Wire. "But since one of us has opened the door, how does he pick the women?"

"It's interesting," Ridge began. "When Rubens first started I didn't think that would be that hard a thing for him. This will sound crass but these are not women who are overly attractive, at least as how you and I might look at them, Mac."

"Don't assume I'm as shallow as you."

"Oh yeah, I forgot, Sally Kennedy is *totally* Rubenesque," Ridge mocked in reply. "Anyway, I thought at least at first that he'd probably just go up and talk to them and it wouldn't take much to get them to come his way."

"What changed your mind?" Wire asked.

"When I followed the story to Chicago, I was able to really get good access to the case and I was allowed to even sit down with April Greene, who is very smart by the way. She helped me with this part and explained that these women are actually much harder to get close to. Rubens' victims end up being shy, introverted and slow, very slow to trust. In many cases, they are socially awkward and in a few cases, people described them as a little nutty. These are not women accustomed to a man taking interest in them so, while perhaps excited at the thought of a man's interest, they are nevertheless wary of them and naturally suspicious. These are women who might ask themselves the question, 'Why would this guy be interested in me?' As a result of all of that scar tissue, it would take some time to break down their walls. They don't have a big circle of friends and family. They are basically lonely and somewhat unapproachable people."

"Which is important from a witness standpoint," Wire suggested.

"I think so," Ridge answered. "So, in reality, these are not overly easy women to find. You have to really work at it."

"So how does he find them?" Mac asked. He thought he knew the answer but wanted Ridge's take. Author or not, Ridge had ten years of hunting Rubens and Mac had two days. His perspective, while annoying, wasn't without merit.

"He scouts, follows and gets to know them long before he ever meets them. If I had to guess, he's been in DC a year if not more and he's spent that time scouting. I think women who fit his criteria are found at bookstores, museums, art galleries and even pet stores. Lots of these women have pets, usually cats, although I think two of them had birds."

"Hmpf," Mac snorted. "I hadn't noticed the pet angle yet, that's a new piece. But not dogs though. Dogs make noise and they'll fight back."

"But cats don't and they won't attack someone attacking their owner. They'll hide," Ridge answered. "But if you look at your victims, I bet half of them had cats. I wondered if maybe he met them at pet stores or something. Not sure if anyone has looked into that."

"Odd place to meet people," Wire suggested.

"He may not *meet* them there," Mac answered.

"That's right, he just *identifies* them there," Ridge added. "At least that's one thought I have."

"We'll pay some attention to pet stores as we go back into the financials on these women," Mac noted.

"Yeah, that might help," Ridge answered. "In general pet stores, museums, bookstores, whatever, I think he identifies the women at these kinds of places months before he actually starts pursuing them. He follows and researches them so that when he does approach, he gives himself the best chance of success."

"Because he needs to find at least four that fit his criteria. Four that he then has to get close to," Wire followed.

"Yes, close, but not *too* close. He has to get close yet keep some distance."

"Because he has to juggle four of them," Wire stated, taking a drink of her beer. "Mac and I were just talking about that."

"Exactly," Ridge answered with a big smile and looked to Mac. "I remember one time when I had three women on the line and..." he started but then drew a raised eyebrow look from Wire. "A story for another time, maybe. In any event, he wants to get close to these women, but not so close that it turns into a full on relationship. There would be evidence of that left behind, and to my knowledge, the investigators have never found a useful name anywhere identifying a man in these women's lives."

"So he slowly gets friendly and they slowly become interested. He's wooing them but it's not a full-on relationship per se," Mac followed the line of thinking.

"Yeah," Ridge answered. "I'd be surprised if he's ever slept with any of the victims. I think the autopsies have tried to determine that and to my knowledge, there has never been evidence of sex, at least as part of the murders. Now, a date or two before he kills them?" The author shrugged. "He's a guy. Who knows, if she's offering, he might be accepting."

Mac nodded and looked at his watch and then to Wire. "We should get going here in a minute. But if you'll excuse me first." The two of them watched as Mac headed back to the restroom.

"He's not the trusting type, is he?" Ridge stated. "I mean, he talked a little there."

"He loathes... no, that's the wrong word. Let's just say he has a very healthy skepticism of and not much trust in the media," Wire replied.

Ridge turned towards her. "You seem a little *less* skeptical."

"Only a little," Wire enigmatically smiled in reply.

The author slipped a business card out of the pocket of his suit coat. "Well then, Special Agent Wire, perhaps if you'd like to grab a drink without Captain Skeptical around."

"I don't know," Wire started, but she did take the card.

"The case, it's hectic, I know," Ridge answered with a smile. "Trust me, I know. But I'm going to be hanging around. I find the matchup between you two and Rubens far too interesting to miss. On top of that, I like to commiserate and I love and totally respect off the record talk, not to mention local microbrews. So if you need a break, give me a call."

"I'll think about it."

Mac came back to the table, everyone said goodnight and Mac and Wire started the walk back.

Two blocks from the bar Mac blurted, "So, did you give him your number?"

"No," Wire smiled. "I don't give out my digits nearly that easy, so he gave me his." She held up the business card.

"Just be careful," Mac counseled. "He's looking for another book out of this and ..."

"And what?"

"He's a player and you're not unattractive. You do the math."

"Aren't you getting married to a woman that arose out of mixing business and pleasure?"

"Yes, but that's different."

"How exactly?" Wire stopped, hands on hips, staring him down.

"Sally and I were on the same side."

"Ridge is not the enemy."

"He's sure as hell not an ally," Mac retorted as his cell phone rang.

They both instinctively stopped and checked their watches. There was only a number on the screen, no name. "I wonder," Mac muttered and then answered, "McRyan."

"Maaaaacccc," the masked voice greeted. "How is it going? Are you wilting under the strain?"

Mac quickly looked around and saw they were alone on the sidewalk, two blocks from the field office. He put it on speaker. "I'm fine, really. I'm getting into the case and learning about all of your fucked-up behavior."

"Do you talk to your mom with that mouth, Mac?"

"No, I only talk this way to murderous assholes."

"Asshole—so crude a term and one that I'd warn you I don't like hearing."

"I'll keep that in mind," Mac replied derisively but checked his watch. This call was being traced.

"Mac, don't ruin our relationship. Keep that talk up and I'll call your partner instead."

"I'd be delighted to hear from you," Wire blurted. "Although, fair warning, I can be a lot saltier than him."

"Your partner must be rubbing off on you then," Rubens replied. "Is that all he's doing with you, by the way? You two make such a lovely couple."

"He wishes," Dara answered, checking her own watch.

"Ouch," Mac mouthed back.

"Well, I just wanted to check in with you two now that we're under twenty-four hours from my next work of art. Happy hunting."

"Wait, wait, wait," Mac pleaded. "Hold on. I want to ask a question."

"Mac, Mac, Mac, I'm not going to stay on the line. I'm not going to make it easy for you."

"Why Rubens?" Mac asked. "What is so great about Peter Paul Rubens? That's what I want to know. I mean, he had talent but—"

"Mac. That's a very interesting question. Maybe another time. Good night and good luck."

The line went dead.

They both took off at a sprint for the field office. Less than a minute later, breathing heavily, they were ducking back into the same side door from which they escaped. As they burst inside, Galloway and Delmonico were walking quickly toward them.

"Where?" Mac asked, still panting.

"He was northeast of the city, up north in College Park in the area of the University of Maryland. We're flooding the area but..."

"Don't hold our breath," Mac answered, shaking his head.

"We don't know what to look for beyond probably a white male and even that's a guess. Plus, we couldn't really get a fix on him in that short a period of time from the burner phone. You know the area. Well populated, lots of streets and traffic. But we have roadblocks going up, we're searching vehicles, you never know."

Did he stay on the phone too long with McRyan? Did that last question on Rubens allow the FBI to get a fix on him?

Rubens had been waiting ten minutes in the line of cars, the police lights ahead, stopping vehicles, checking identification, shining flashlights inside. He was startled by the comprehensive nature of the search. Could they possibly know what they were looking for? They were taking their time with each vehicle, opening hatchbacks, popping trunks and were unconcerned about how long it was taking. He could feel his hands starting to sweat as he gripped the steering wheel and his heart was beginning to race.

Eventually, it was his turn as he pulled slowly forward and powered down the driver side window. "Good evening, officer."

"Good evening, sir," the uniformed officer replied as his partner walked around to the passenger side of the car, scanning the interior of the vehicle with his flashlight. "Can I see your driver's license and registration, please?"

"Yes, sir." He reached into his pocket, pulled out his money clip, took out his license and handed it to the officer.

"Mr. Miller, I show your address as down in DC. What brings you up to College Park this evening?"

"I was at an art exhibition at the college," Rubens replied truthfully. He had in fact been through an exhibition and took in a presentation.

"Do you have a ticket stub from the event?" the officer asked.

"Yes, yes, I do." Rubens reached inside his pocket and pulled out the stub and handed it to the officer. "Why are you stopping vehicles?"

"I'm not at liberty to say," the officer replied, looking at the ticket stub while the other officer continued to scan the interior of the vehicle with his flashlight. "Do you have a cell phone, sir?"

"I do," Rubens replied as he reached for the iPhone resting in the cup holder and held it up.

"If you don't mind, please show me your recent calls."

"Yes, sir." He did as instructed.

The officer quickly examined the phone's screen and then handed it back. "Please pop your trunk."

"Yes, officer," he replied as he reached down to the left of his seat for the latch. The trunk popped open. He looked up into the rearview mirror to see the stream of light from the flashlight scanning the trunk, which the patrol officer's partner would find to be empty.

"It's clear," the partner confirmed.

"Okay," the officer replied and looked down into the car. "Very well, sir, thank you for your cooperation. You can go. Enjoy your evening."

"Thank you."

As he pulled away, Rubens took a look in the rearview mirror and exhaled a small sigh of relief.

Two hours later, the search was over.

"Nothing. Sorry, Mac," Galloway reported glumly, Delmonico at his side. The two of them both looked exhausted.

"We did what we could with what we had, which was really nothing," Mac replied with a tinge of bitterness. "There's nothing more to be done tonight. Go home. Both of you go home and get some sleep."

"But ..." Delmonico started.

"But nothing," Mac answered. "Come in first thing in the morning, fresh. Tomorrow will be a long day."

Neither of them protested further. They both turned and left.

Mac walked to the whiteboard and grabbed a black marker.

"What are you thinking?" Wire asked.

"I'm thinking I'm going to go home as well," Mac answered but he wrote a question on the whiteboard that he hadn't seen answered anywhere. *Why Peter Paul Rubens?*

9

"I DON'T FEEL HELPLESS."

Mac awoke at 5:30 with Sally and acted as if it was a normal morning. He got up and made them a breakfast of poached eggs, adding some sliced fruit, coffee and wheat toast. It was a healthy breakfast, both of them trying to stay fit and trim for the wedding. Besides eating healthy, Sally kept trim with yoga every day over her lunch hour. Mac did it with running and going to the club three days a week.

Per usual, she was down to the kitchen and ready by six.

"Do you think you have any chance of stopping him today?"

"You never know," he answered. "But I'm realistic. I think this thing has to play out longer for us to have a chance."

"Is everyone else on board with that?"

"Those that matter understand what I'm thinking."

She quickly devoured her breakfast and coffee, kissed him twice as she always did and was out the door to the White House, where she liked to be before 7:00 a.m. each morning.

To keep it normal, he followed her right out the back door and went for a short run, three miles; a quick, fast, hard loop through Georgetown, right under twenty minutes. It was just enough to break a good sweat, get his heart rate up, the blood flowing and his mind working. After a quick shower, he dressed in faded blue jeans, a gold University of Minnesota t-shirt and black quarter zip sweater and a pair of all black Nikes. He slung his backpack over his shoulder and was out the door. He stopped at Starbucks for a large coffee of his own plus a coffee traveler and cups, along with croissants for the patrol unit that was stationed in front of Lisa White's townhouse. Ten minutes later, shortly before 8:00 a.m., he cut the seal on the door of the crime scene.

Inside he shut the door softly and took in the emptiness.

Everything was still in the townhouse, the books, the pictures and the furniture; it was still completely filled with its overwhelming assortment of material possessions. Yet the townhouse was also filled with something else. He'd felt it before, the quiet, sad pallor that overtakes a home where a murder took place. It was as if the soul of the dead haunted the space, waiting to see if there would be justice, if anyone would care enough to find the truth. Having been in many of these homes over the years, they all had a form of that eeriness of the spirit of the victim, not quite ready to leave.

What he'd also found over the years is that the spirit of the house would speak to you.

He hoped that might be the case today.

Mac dropped his backpack into the light blue plaid chair in the corner of the living room, kept his tall coffee in his right hand and proceeded to slowly and methodically stroll through the house, soaking in the entirety of the home. He started upstairs in the master bedroom, then the guest room and bathrooms, just getting a better feel for Lisa White and how she organized and viewed her life. As on the main level, the walls of the upper level of the townhouse were filled with photos of all sizes and frame types. Some photos were black and white, others color. Interspersed were paintings from artists as well as some of White's own renderings. She was big into painting flowers and he imagined she spent many hours in the back of her home, sitting amongst her gardens, cultivating the subjects of her future images.

The arrangements of the photos and artwork were not what he

would have done from a decorating standpoint. He snorted a small laugh. Mac possessed the Norm Peterson-like gene for taste and decorating, something he really enjoyed doing and was extremely reluctant for others to know about. It just seemed a cop, former college hockey player and all around guy's guy would not be the type to get worked up about paint color, fabric swatches and window treatments. But after he completed the construction portion of remodeling a room, he enjoyed designing what it would then look like in the end.

"If you ever want to stop carrying a gun, there will be women all over town that would hire you in a second to decorate their homes," Sally said in wonder years ago after he remodeled their home in St. Paul.

He even offered up some tips recently to a few of her work friends at the White House, people far away from Minnesota. "As long as you don't tell your husband," he said to Courtney Sanchez, who was an assistant to Judge Dixon. "I'll help, but not a word, NOT A WORD to Dan."

With that discerning eye, he marveled at how Lisa White had organized the hundreds of photos, posters, portraits that adorned and filled every wall of the townhouse. And she had plenty in reserve. In the spare bedroom were more framed posters, paintings and pictures stacked against the walls and stored inside the closet. The sheer volume of it all was rather amazing. Yet despite the mess and the mass, he did detect a method to her madness. On the walls, the pictures, the paintings, the prints were in lined, almost boxy formations. Lisa liked straight lines, which allowed her to maximize the usage of space. She also liked to arrange smaller pictures and photos around singular larger prints, paintings and posters. It wasn't a completely universal approach but it happened often enough that she clearly liked the look.

He spent a good hour sipping from his coffee and just wandering around, taking it all in before he eventually made his way back to the living room and his backpack. He sat down on the floor, crossed his legs and fired up his laptop.

~

Wire sat in one of the soft, comfortable chairs of the conference room and stared at the whiteboards. She'd watched Mac do it a number of times and seen it trigger things in his mind. Besides, she was really waiting on him, ready to do anything he needed were he to find something of interest at Lisa White's.

The ongoing investigation of White's financials from the past several months continued to yield more surveillance footage from stores and museums. Wire, among others, was reviewing it all on the long shot hope that a man would appear onscreen with her and then somehow they could identify the man as Rubens. Of course, to identify him they needed some other variable, some sort of cross reference. Just one image of a man on a surveillance video wouldn't be enough. That was the project she was keeping herself busy with when there was a knock on the door.

"Mind some company?" April Greene asked.

"Not at all," Dara answered and then continued to roll through the surveillance video.

"Where is your partner?" Greene asked.

Wire explained.

"The Walker approach. It's worth a shot."

"On his own, in the quiet, Mac can sometimes see things that others don't," Wire added. "He says it's all part of figuring out Rubens."

They both sat down and watched the surveillance video footage, the snippets of film of White. The techs who put it together didn't think there was much there but a second look was in order. The footage was of Lisa White at various stores, museums and venues for which there was a record, financial or otherwise, of her presence, and video footage. There was footage from gas stations, grocery stores, two museums, a variety of paint supply stores and seven different bookstores in the most recent compilation. It was the book and paint stores that drew most of their attention, under the theory that it was those places where she tended to linger and walk the aisles, where perhaps she could have crossed paths with Rubens. However, after two hours, Dara and Greene had made it through all of the surveillance tape and never saw White approached by a male. With a frustrated sigh, she moaned, "God, I hate sitting around waiting for the next shoe to drop."

"You're not sitting around," Greene replied as she intensely studied the whiteboard.

"I'm not?"

"No," the FBI behaviorist replied. "More than any of the other detectives in Boston, Chicago or LA, you and McRyan are playing the game."

"I'm already getting sick and tired of hearing about the game with this asshole."

"I hear you but like you said earlier, it's all part of learning Rubens. It's like poker. You don't play the cards, you play the player. The cops in Boston, Chicago and Los Angeles for the most part played the cards. To my way of thinking, what Mac has you two doing is playing Rubens. In those other cities, the detectives chased Rubens like a standard murder case. He is anything but standard and the standard methods won't work."

"You sound as if you admire him."

Greene blinked a few times and then slowly smiled. "I don't admire him but I will acknowledge he fascinates me. I respect that the human mind can do amazingly great and amazingly cruel things and that merciless, disturbed people can do complex things. So I respect that and I recognize how hard he is to catch, which again is why I think you're doing the right thing. In the other places, the police spent all their time interviewing witnesses, chasing weak leads, and nobody really sat down and tried to think of how Rubens was going about doing what he was doing. How did he identify his victims? Where did he identify them and what was his motivation? They let the clock dictate their actions. Those detectives never seemed to make a move, try something to smoke Rubens out. I didn't think then and I don't think now that's how you catch him."

"Other jurisdictions did what we're doing. They checked surveillance footage, ran financials, talked to witnesses."

"Yes, they did," Greene answered. "But it was the lead detectives that did all of those things. It's not how you catch him."

"How do you catch him?"

"I'm not sure you can. But if you're going to, I think you do what you are doing. There are plenty of good cops and special agents to run down the normal stuff. That DC detective, Coolidge, is good. Let him talk to people and interview the family. He's smart enough to know if he hears or sees something you need to know about. What you guys need to do is focus on Rubens. Get inside his head. You think the case how he pursues his victims."

"In other words, when Mac said the other day, 'I've got three more women to play with', that's playing Rubens?"

"He said that?" Greene asked in surprise.

"Yes."

"Interesting," Greene answered with a smile.

"My God, you find this stimulating."

"Absolutely," April replied. "Don't you?"

"Not the way you do."

"That I get. Look, from a strictly investigative and behavioral standpoint, I'm absolutely fascinated to see if it works. Mac's trying to figure him out, trying to anticipate his next move and trying to determine how to smoke him out," Greene stated with a tone that said she was extremely interested in hanging around and watching it all play out. "And I think Mr. McRyan has asked a very interesting question up here, in my opinion."

"What's that?"

"Why is Peter Paul Rubens so inspiring to our killer?"

"Why is that? Why Rubens?"

"I don't know," Greene replied. "I've never been able to figure that out. In profiling and studying him, I've never made the connection. It might be that he just likes Rubens and this is his perverted way of honoring him or it could be that Rubens symbolizes something deeper."

"I figure he had some bad experience with a plus-sized woman," Wire suggested.

"Maybe," Greene answered. "But staging them like in the pictures suggests to me there is more at play. The use of Rubens, the intricate staging suggests that there is more than just a bad experience with a voluptuous woman that has influenced him."

"Didn't anyone ever ask?"

"You mean did any of the detectives who've communicated with him, that Rubens has called and tormented—did any of them ask?"

"Yeah."

"Not like that. Not until McRyan did the other night," Greene replied.

"How did you know he asked that question?"

"I read the transcript of the call. He should keep asking that question."

In the late afternoon, Mac continued to study the numerous photos of the Lisa White murder scene lying on the floor and then continually scanned the packed walls and cluttered shelves of the living room.

The clue had to be where the body of Lisa White was staged.

If this was a game, there were rules. And one of the rules, as established by Rubens, was that the clue was always in close proximity to the body, in the room where the body was found. In all of the cases where clues were left behind, whether it was Boston, Chicago or Los Angeles, the clue was in the same room.

Rubens was consistent on that account.

If he was also consistent, it would be a combination of something. If that wasn't a rule, it was certainly a characteristic. The clue would be a name from a painting connected to a book. An obscure reference connected to something in a photograph. Lisa White's living room must have been like a playground for Rubens. There was so much to choose from. There was far too much to choose from.

Mac uttered something to Wire about the Zodiac Killer code and he didn't realize how right that comparison seemed to be until now. That was what made the process seem impossible. It was like solving a Rubik's Cube or one of the *Good Will Hunting* math problems.

But it was there.

Mac worked his way from one wall to the next in the living room. It was a tedious process to come up with possible names. He worked his way through each photo or painting, looking for a name or a reference to a name. If he found a name combination, he would type it into his laptop and send it to Wire who would then have it checked.

Based on previous victims, the name could be the combination of a name and/or an object. The left wall was something of an entertainment wall. It contained a collection of pictures, paintings and three large framed movie posters: *Charade*, *Breakfast at Tiffany's* and *Sabrina*. There were two signed framed pictures, one of Diane Keaton and another of Faye Dunaway, names that had been checked along with a number of black and white as well as color photos of movie marquees from old theatres from around the world.

Since all of the photos and framed movie posters on the left wall rested over a small couch, any first name he came up with was run with couch, sofa, love and seat. Thus far, he had run searches on Michele, Lois, Ronda, Vivian and Muriel Couch, Sofa, Settee, Chaise, Lounge, Daybed, Futon, Love and Seat, among other names. Out of those searches, two Rubenesque women popped, a Faye Couch and Joan Love. However, both women were married with children, not Rubens' type. One would be with her daughter at a swim meet this evening and another was going to be with her husband and son at a track meet.

His most recent searches involved a photo of an alley next to a picture of a flowing river. So he tried all variations of the name Allison along with River, Creek, Stream, Brook, Tributary and Canal but nothing popped. At another point, he picked out a picture of St. Cecilia's Church in Cologne that had a picture of a quiet country road to the right. He tried Cecilia Road, Roads, Rhodes, Street, Broadway, Lane, Avenue, Boulevard, Way, Path, Freeway and Highway. And since a Lisa White painting of a flower was never far away, he tried every first name against Flowers, Plant, Plante, Blossom and any other derivation of the word flower he could think of turning into a last name.

Such was how his day had progressed, going through all of the many objects of the home, trying to find a name combination of some kind, trying to see if he could determine how Rubens might have picked a clue or set it up. On the far wall, opposite of his position, were built-in bookshelves and cabinets. On the shelves were hundreds of books. He'd proceeded to run the book titles, author names and even had run the main characters in those books as names. Seeing where Mac was going, Wire had an FBI tech quickly set up a search program to rapidly run the names. He was getting results almost real time.

The problem was the results weren't leading to any potential matches.

"Maybe this is exactly what he wants me to be doing," Mac mumbled to himself. "Staring at walls, picking out names, hoping one is the right one in a metropolitan area of slightly over six million people." Mac pressed on despite his doubts. At least for today, he was, to use a poker term, pot committed.

Wire and April Greene stopped by in the mid-afternoon to check in on him. They stayed for an hour. It served as a refresher for Wire and gave Greene a real feel for the crime scene as compared to the photographs back in the conference room at the field office. It also gave them an idea of what Mac was trying to do and what he was up against.

"Impossible," Greene remarked as she and Wire began to leave.

"Not impossible," Mac replied, sitting on the floor in front of his laptop. "But I'll admit it here and now to you two and God, it's really, *really* hard."

In the early evening, he'd started working the right wall, which largely consisted of more built-in bookshelves filled with books and photos, not of people, but of famous places in Europe, including the Eiffel Tower, the Louvre, the Vatican, London Bridge, Big Ben and

Parliament. It made him think of Chevy Chase as Clark Griswold from *European Vacation* going crazy as he couldn't turn left out of a roundabout. "Look, kids, Big Ben, Parliament." He then checked all of the actor and character names from the movie particularly if their address put them in nearby Chevy Chase, Maryland.

It was a long and tedious process, but if a name popped, he put it into the program, and in return, he could look at a DMV photo and other information that could be culled. He'd found two other possibilities from that side of the room, but quick checks revealed that the women named Joan Venora and Elizabeth Novel, while Rubenesque, were clearly not targets. One was married and would be spending the evening with her husband and the other was on a trip in Europe.

He'd been going nonstop for hours.

His eyes were tiring and a large yawn emerged. For the first time in hours, he checked his watch and saw it was nearly 7:00 p.m. Two hours to go. He'd fought the impending dread off most of the day but he could feel it coming. "Shit," he sighed, an unsuspecting woman's life a mere two hours from ending.

The front door slowly creaked open. He looked up to his left to see a welcome sight. Sally was standing in the entryway.

"How did you ..."

She waved him off. "Wire and that April Greene told me. She said I should stop by and make sure you're not turning into that guy from *A Beautiful Mind*."

"You mean John Nash."

"Yeah," Sally replied while spinning around, taking in the surroundings. "The good news I guess is I don't see any long yarn strings running wall to wall."

He protested. "Sal, this is an active crime scene. You shouldn't be here."

"And I'm a former prosecutor who's walked hundreds of these and you're the obsessed special agent who needs to eat." Sally held up two Jimmy John's sandwiches. "Nothing but the best for you, buddy."

He didn't argue as he devoured two Italian Night Club sandwiches, two bags of kettle chips, and then washed it all down with a super-sized Diet Coke. While gorging himself, Sally slowly walked around the living room, taking in the surroundings.

"I haven't walked a crime scene in a while," she mused when she finally sat down next to him as he finished his second sandwich.

"Any thoughts?"

"Yeah, what you're trying to do is find a needle in a dumpster full of needles."

"What are you saying?"

"I'm saying I get what you're doing, isolating yourself in here and trying to see what he saw, trying to think how he thought, but this place—" She waved around the living room and shook her head. "How are you supposed to figure it out? It's impossible."

"Not impossible. The clue is here," Mac answered as he wiped his hands with a napkin. "Although right now I'd certainly agree to nearly impossible."

"Yet you're here? Why?"

"Because it's not just about this victim, Sal," he replied, sucking down the last of the Diet Coke.

Sally got it. "No, it's about the victim after that and the victim after that, isn't it?"

Mac tipped his head in acquiescence. "Unfortunately, when I get the name of tonight's victim I'll see the clue he left and—"

"That will tell you something."

Promptly at 8:00 p.m., he knocked lightly on the door.

"Hi!" Audrey greeted with a big smile as she opened the front door. She'd made herself up with lipstick and a sleeveless dress in attractive shades of blue. "Oh, and you brought wine."

"Yes, a nice white," he replied as he leaned in and kissed Audrey on the cheek. "I know how much you liked this one when we dined last week."

"Excellent, would you like me to open it?"

"Oh, no, no, no, I can do that," Rubens replied. "Just show me to the kitchen and a corkscrew, of course."

It was apparent to him that Audrey did not often drink wine at home. There was no wine rack of bottles and it took her a few minutes of rummaging through her kitchen drawers to find the long-lost wine-opening device, an aged corkscrew with flecks of rust on it. He used a knife to cut the seal and then deliberately went about twisting the corkscrew in. It took him a minute to work the bottle but eventually the cork emerged with a muted pop.

"Wine glasses?"

"Up to your right," she replied.

"Ah, yes," he replied as he retrieved two wine glasses. They were really glasses for red wine, but it appeared it was all she had. He wasn't sure she knew the difference.

"Why don't you go into the living room and make yourself comfortable," he suggested. "I'll finish this up and bring the wine in."

"Sounds great." Audrey retreated to the living room.

A half hour later, they were discussing the Women in World War I display at the National Museum of American History when he noticed the first effects. As always, the first sign was the eyes. There was a drowsiness creeping in as her eyelids ever so slowly and almost imperceptibly became heavier. That was a few minutes ago and now her movements were becoming slower and less coordinated and her speech was starting to slur.

Such was the effect of Rohypnol.

While he had no intention of raping Audrey, the effect of a date rape drug served its purpose and was slowly dropping Audrey's defenses.

Audrey was starting to actually feel the effects as well, and the other thing he noticed was she started recognizing she was feeling them and belatedly sensing the danger.

He'd seen that happen before as well.

But it was too late.

They always realized it too late.

Audrey looked to him, looked at herself, and it was as if she recognized exactly what was happening. "You're ... you're ... him, aren't you?" she slurred.

He nodded as he casually set his wine glass down on the coffee table as she made the effort to move off the couch, to try and flee but her body wouldn't respond as she slumped away from him. The mind was still willing but her body wouldn't respond. She couldn't even raise her arms to fight him as he slowly laid her back down onto the couch cushions.

"You see, Audrey," he said as he straddled her, using his legs to lock her arms to the side of her body, "one of the effects of Rohypnol is that it essentially paralyzes you." He pulled rubber gloves out of the inside pocket of his tweed coat and pulled them onto his hands. She was trying to summon the energy to yell but he put his right hand over her mouth and continued. "It's why men use it as a date rape drug. The woman becomes powerless against him and it saps her power to resist."

He reached back with his left arm for the couch pillow.

Rubens took one last look into her soft face. Her body was now essentially paralyzed.

She could still see, though, and her eyes were panicked.

Audrey knew what was coming.

There was nothing she could do to stop it.

He carefully positioned the pillow over her face and slowly pressed down with both hands. With his two hands and all of his weight, he held the pillow firm over her face, slowly increasing the pressure. He grunted as beads of sweat formed on his forehead as he maintained the constant pressure. He held the pillow in position, feeling her body spasm with what little fight it had left against the vise-lock that was his thighs pressed against her body.

After several minutes, he slowly pulled the pillow away and checked for a pulse, first on her neck and then at her wrist. There was nothing. He leaned down to her face and her mouth in particular and listened. There was no breathing. He placed his ear over her heart and there was no beat, not even any fibrillation.

It was time to go to work.

~

A little after midnight, Mac walked wearily into the conference room to find Wire and April Greene staring at the whiteboard with Lisa White crime scene photos spread out on the table and up on one of the boards.

He dropped his backpack onto one of the chairs and dropped himself into the next one in frustrated exhaustion.

"You tried," Wire said, not turning to him. "We all did."

"I know," Mac answered. "It's just—maddening. You know it's there but you can't ..."

"Find it," Greene finished, taking one last sip of coffee. "I know the feeling. Even now, knowing how this always goes, it still gets to me. Maybe even more now than it did ten years ago when he first started. It's an incredibly helpless feeling."

"I don't feel helpless," Mac answered. "I just feel like we're behind at this point."

"Do you feel like you're gaining on him?" Greene asked in almost a clinical tone.

"We'll see. Sometimes you don't know until you catch up," Mac answered, keeping things close to the vest. He had an idea that had been running through his mind for two days now and he was nearly ready to try it out.

"What's your next move?" Greene pressed.

"We wait," Wire replied before Mac could answer. Dara sighed and flopped down face first onto the old orange couch. "We wait for the call," she added with her back to them. Five minutes later she was out and Mac, with his legs up on the long conference table slipped into slumber a few minutes afterward.

They'd all expected Rubens would call in the middle of the night, to both inform and taunt, but by 3:00 a.m., the call had not materialized.

"You two should go home and get some rest," Greene suggested, rousing Mac awake and then Wire. "Sleeping in here won't do you any good. Go get in your own beds. You both need to be fresh."

They didn't argue.

By 3:20 a.m., Mac was in his own bed.

At first, the ringing didn't register with him; it was like something in the distance, like the garbage truck on Wednesdays, but his eyes popped open on the third ring, and he rolled right and grabbed his phone off the nightstand.

It was 8:48 a.m.

The number appeared on the screen, caller unknown.

It was Rubens.

"Mac, did you get enough sleep?"

"I slept like a baby."

"Well, now so does Audrey Ruston," and Rubens clicked off.

Mac googled the name Audrey Ruston.

"Son of a bitch, how was I supposed to see that," he muttered angrily, thinking of the movie posters and Audrey Hepburn, the star of *Sabrina* and *Breakfast at Tiffany's*. "It was staring at me the whole time in Technicolor."

Audrey Hepburn's given name was Audrey Ruston.

10

"IT'S TIME TO MAKE A MOVE."

THURSDAY MORNING, 9:40 A.M.

M ac, with slouched shoulders and his hands in his suit pants pockets, dejectedly looked down at Audrey Ruston.

Audrey was posed as the left Grace in Rubens' *The Three Graces*. Her long light brown hair, in addition to her height and body type, made her a perfect fit on the portrait lying on the floor of the living room on the second story of the duplex. The fine attention to detail was as Mac expected. Audrey's hair was styled identically to that of the portrait. Her body was posed perfectly over the left Grace such that you could hardly see the painted Grace she was staged to look like on the poster underneath her.

Straight ahead, resting on a little round table was the small black timer, counting down: sixty hours, twenty minutes and thirty seconds. Rubens planned to take his next one Saturday night at 9:00 p.m. Mac set the timer on his cell phone.

Blocking out the buzz of activity around him, he stood trance-like in the expanse of the living room, deliberately scanning the room slowly left to right, soaking in the space's details. Mac knew that if they didn't somehow catch a break, in seventy or so hours he would be locked in this room searching for the combination of items that would give him the name of victim number three. So as he took in the surroundings, he made some initial impressions. Unlike the living room of Lisa White, this was a room of neat order, decorated and furnished with far greater care, deliberation and organization. Yet, despite the order, it was still another living room with built-in shelves full of books, walls adorned with what appeared to be a more carefully and less randomly selected collection of pictures, paintings and small mirrors, overstuffed furniture and a coffee table full of coffee table books. Mac wondered if all of Rubens' women had the same decorating taste, if that was part of the profile he searched for. To a certain degree, it was something of a necessity if he were to leave behind obscure clues buried in the décor of the home. The irony was that most artists would prefer a blank canvas, but not Rubens.

Wire snapped him out of his trance.

"This must have taken hours to get right," Wire suggested, standing to the right of the portrait of *The Three Graces* and the body of Audrey Ruston.

"Well, he killed her last night around 9:00 p.m. and we didn't find the body until an hour or so ago," Mac answered. "That left him many hours to intricately stage this and clean up."

"And nobody hears a thing."

"I'm sure Coolidge is checking, but I sensed the first floor of the duplex is uninhabited right now," Mac answered as he turned his attention to the medical examiner.

The doctor was crouched down, examining the body, focusing on the area of Audrey's neck and throat area.

"What do you see?" Mac asked, moving to his left to crouch down to get a better angle.

"Unlike Lisa White, I don't see any bruising, so I don't think he strangled her," the coroner replied. "But ... hmpf."

"But what?" Wire queried, seeing the change in the doctor's expression.

The medical examiner got closer with her flashlight and focused in on the area around the victim's mouth. "See the skin around her mouth and nose?"

"Yeah," Mac replied quietly, leaning in closely, "it's discolored. It's white or whitish as compared to the rest of her skin."

"That's what I see, too," the coroner answered. "Plus in her cheeks there is some evidence of what looks like cyanosis."

"Bruising?" Wire asked.

"Yes," the coroner answered.

"He smothered her?" Mac asked, looking up to the doctor.

"Could be," the coroner responded. "I will know better once I examine her back at the lab, but those signs suggest it's very possible."

Mac and Wire both turned and looked to the couch on the far wall. "There were two wine glasses in the dishwasher," Wire reported. "They are freshly clean."

"So," Mac started, moving over to the couch. "So say this was a date. They're sitting here on the sofa. Audrey and our guy are getting comfortable. She's relaxing, warming to the moment because she and this guy have been getting closer to one another. They have some wine and ..."

"He spiked her wine," Wire followed. "Lisa White had Rohypnol in her system. What do you want to bet Audrey will have it in hers?"

"No bet," the medical examiner replied.

"A glass or two of wine is the perfect delivery vehicle for a roofie," Mac stated. "It's part of what he does to incapacitate the victim. So, let's say she did get roofied." He carefully sat down on the middle of the couch. "They're sitting on the couch. It takes perhaps a half hour for Rohypnol to start taking effect. Eventually, she starts to show the signs—slurred speech, droopy eyes, loss of dexterity, and she starts to become incapacitated and he—" Mac looked to the pillow but didn't touch it. "He grabs that pillow, or that one, and jumps on top of her and smothers her. The drug has largely incapacitated her so it wouldn't be that hard."

"It's possible," Wire mused.

"Indeed," the medical examiner blurted, pointing the light of her flashlight up the nostrils of Audrey's nose. "I think I see some strands of fabric in the nasal cavity." With her gloved hand, the doctor pried open Audrey's mouth and peered closely, using her flashlight. "And in the mouth as well." To the forensic tech, she ordered, "Get pictures, nose and mouth."

There were two couch pillows. Mac directed another forensic tech to bag the pillows.

"But does that get us anywhere?" Wire asked. "I mean, it tells us *how*. Once he's in, he drugs them and then kills the victims, but does that get us anywhere?"

"Maybe not directly," Mac answered. "But everything we learn could pay off somewhere. You just never know. The more information, the better."

Coolidge entered the room and looked to Mac. "What's with the suit?"

Mac was dressed in a sharp dark navy blue pinstripe suit. His cream-colored dress shirt was open at the collar. A sky blue tie was in the car. "It's for later," he answered, a comment that drew an interested look from Wire. To Linc, Mac asked, "So, what do we know about our victim?"

"What I know so far is that she worked at the Sewall-Belmont House and Museum near the Capitol." Coolidge flipped a page on his notebook. "Sewall-Belmont House and Museum is dedicated to ..."

"The women who've worked on Capitol Hill," Mac finished.

Coolidge and Wire gave him a raised eyebrow and even the medical examiner looked up.

"What? Us kept men have a lot—*a lot*—of free time," Mac answered. "I walked through it a few months ago and found it interesting. What else do we know about Audrey?"

"She's worked at the museum for ten years as an administrative assistant in their office," Coolidge continued. "She was a model employee. Superbly reliable, never missed work and had lots of unused vacation time. So it was very surprising when she wasn't at the office at 7:30 as she has been every day for ten years, or so they told me."

"What else?"

Linc knew what Mac's question really was. "Yes, her co-workers thought she was acting *differently* as of late."

"She had someone in her life?" Wire asked.

"Yes," Linc answered. "Or so they thought."

"Where have we heard that before?" Dara added with just a tinge of disgust.

"In any event, they thought she did, which they'd generally thought, good for her. But then they thought of"—he hesitated—"well, they thought of her."

"They thought that their friend perhaps fit the profile of a Rubens victim—" Mac suggested.

"Exactly. So about the time Rubens was dialing you, the people at Ruston's office were calling her home phone and not getting an answer. They tried her cell and came up dry as well. So they went to her employee file and found the emergency contact card, which listed her neighbor two doors down. The neighbor had a key, came over and found what's inside—our second Grace. So about five minutes after Rubens called you, the neighbor was calling us."

"What else do we know about Audrey Ruston?"

"I've been digging on that and I must say, it helps to have Bureau assistance and resources," the MPD detective answered. "She's a native of Washington State but moved here ten years ago, in part to get away from her ex-husband. Apparently, he beat her to a pulp when they were married."

"Did we talk to the ex?" Mac asked.

"Yup, I just did," Linc answered and then shook his head in dismay. "He's a real winner, that one. Dennis Lange, an over-the-road trucker who didn't have anything kind to say about his ex-wife. I believe the phrase 'the bitch probably deserved it' was uttered more than once. He was not exactly distraught at her untimely passing."

"Nice," Wire replied bitterly, shaking her head.

"In any event, he hadn't seen her since she'd left Washington and couldn't have cared less about her, or his current wife, for that matter, whom I heard scream at him in the background. He could provide nothing meaningful about his ex-wife, about any family she may have had or of anyone else who would be worth talking to. If I were to editorialize, I envisioned him looking like one of those drunk and dazed husbands you see in a dirty wife-beater T-shirt sitting on a curb, cuffed in the middle of the night during an episode of *Cops*. He will be of absolutely no help to us."

More forensics people were arriving on the scene and two attendants from the medical examiner's office were coming into the room. It was starting to get crowded. Mac led his group out of the living room and to the stairwell that had led up to the second level of the duplex.

"So what's the plan, boss?" Linc asked.

"We stick to the plan," Mac answered. "Linc, I want your guys working the house here, the neighborhood, talking to anyone and everyone nearby. I also want you going back and really drilling down on her history with everyone she worked with and anyone else you run across, for that matter. Cast a wide net, just like we've already been doing. Also, what did Audrey like to do, where did she spend her free time and what were her interests?"

"In other words," Linc suggested, "where did she meet our guy?"

"Or at least, where *could* she have met our guy? We take her interests, add that to our financial analysis and maybe we get lucky." Mac turned to Galloway, who'd arrived on the scene. "I want our people working Audrey Ruston's financials. With the financials, we do the same thing we've been doing with White, going to every place Audrey Ruston spent money or used her credit card in the last four months. I want any and all surveillance footage. I want it reviewed by multiple people. I want the establishments interviewed—do they remember our victim and was any man ever with her or even talking to her. Coordinate that with Coolidge."

"Done," Galloway answered, jotting down notes.

"And what are you and Wire doing?" Linc asked.

"Along with April Greene, we're still working Rubens. And you asked about the suit, Linc? It's time to make a move. It's time to start taking the game to Rubens and later today that's what we're going to do," Mac answered as he went into the contacts on his cell phone and found his one semi-friend in the national news media.

Once back to the FBI field office, Mac told the group what he wanted to do.

"I like it," Greene answered. "I wish I'd have thought of that twist before. In fact, I should have thought of that twist. How long have you been thinking about it?"

"It wasn't a fully formed thought until yesterday, although it was a question spinning in my head for a few days that eventually turned into an idea that became a move to make."

"I agree with April, Mac," Galloway added. "And while I know the clock is ticking and every second counts, my thought is let's let this simmer for a few hours. I like going before the press later in the afternoon. We'll get maximum media exposure that way, including the evening news, and it'll likely get us some nighttime coverage as well. We need all the coverage we can get."

Five hours later, at precisely 5:00 p.m. Eastern Standard Time, the press conference started outside on the front steps of the FBI field office. Mac didn't want a podium or any formality. He wanted a quick, informal media availability.

Wire needed to get some fresh air and decided to take in the press briefing from one-hundred feet away, sipping a Starbucks while leaning against her Range Rover. As she took a sip from her coffee, a small smile creased her face. She could feel him approaching.

"For someone notoriously media shy, your boy is getting his fill this week," Hugo Ridge noted as he stood close to her, leaning back against the truck, taking in the scene. "He's about to get mobbed."

"I'm a little surprised myself he's doing this," Wire replied, turning toward the tall author. "People like you give him the hives."

"Then why do this?"

"Because he does find you media types to be useful idiots on occasion," Dara answered wryly.

"I'm hurt."

"Poor baby."

"So what you're really telling me is he has an agenda. What might that be?"

Dara explained.

"Interesting," Ridge answered. "I wonder why nobody else ever thought to do this before."

"April Greene said the same thing a few hours ago."

"I imagine she did," the author replied with a snort. "So people like me give McRyan the hives. What about you?"

Rubens had done his research on McRyan and found his foil this time around to be something of a reluctant cop.

The McRyan family of St. Paul was one dedicated to policing and Mac McRyan himself was the son of a revered detective. Yet much of what he'd found on the Internet while conducting his research revolved around McRyan's athletic exploits back in his days as a hockey player in college at the University of Minnesota. After college, he obtained a law degree from the William Mitchell College of Law in St. Paul. It appeared he'd been on another career path but then there was an abrupt change in direction.

While never attributed directly to Michael McKenzie McRyan himself, one article indicated he'd reversed course and pursued a police career after the death of two of his cousins who were St. Paul officers killed in the line of duty. Then there was his rapid rise to detective. In his relatively short time working in St. Paul, Mac McRyan was the lead investigator on a number of high-profile cases. Then he caught the homicide of the political blogger at a seedy St. Paul Hotel, followed it to Washington, and in solving it played an indirect role in Governor James Thomson being elected President.

That case led to the *60 Minutes* segment. McRyan's fiancée worked for Thomson. She followed the governor to DC. McRyan apparently followed her and in taking one look at Sally Kennedy, it wasn't hard to see why.

Rubens found it interesting that McRyan wasn't working regularly. He couldn't believe there weren't opportunities, not for someone with his background and track record. He'd found three Internet articles that reported he'd turned down a position more than once with the FBI. Did he no longer want to be a cop? If so, why did he seem to keep winding up in investigations?

In completing his research on McRyan, one other thing was very clear: the man didn't like the media. He was reluctant to speak, whether in print or on television. In at least three different articles he'd run across, McRyan was described as extremely distrustful of the media. He found a YouTube clip of McRyan outside a St. Paul courthouse, acerbically quipping, "Sorry, no time for gotcha questions today," when a reporter put a microphone in his face. McRyan said it not with a smile and a wink, but with an edge and look of utter disdain for the Fourth Estate.

Yet here he was, for the second time this week on national television.

Why?

Galloway provided some preliminary information regarding the second victim Audrey Ruston, setting the table and then said, "At this time, I'd like to turn this over to Agent McRyan who has some comments to make, and then he will take some questions."

Mac stepped to the stand of microphones. "As you know, the killer we're looking for targets a very specific kind of woman. These are women that have been commonly referred to as Rubenesque. In the day of the painter Peter Paul Rubens, women of this type were described as voluptuous. Today the term people commonly use to describe Rubenesque women is plus-sized. I know some may take offense to the use of that term but please understand that is not my intent. My intent is to alert certain women in the Washington DC area to the absolute fact that a predator is out there and he has already selected his prey. Not just his next victim, but I believe he has selected his last two victims. He has a very specific and intricate plan in mind and wheels for that have already been set in motion. His next victims are identified and he is most likely at this very moment setting them up. He already knows when and where he will kill those women. Let me say that again—there are two more victims and he knows exactly when and where he will kill them."

"Agent McRyan, Heather Foxx, NBC News. How does he identify these women?"

That a girl, Heather, he thought, *the perfect softball to get things started.* "He methodically *hunts* them."

"How? How does he hunt them?" Heather pressed.

Mac liked the follow-up as well. He detested formal press conferences. Informal conversation he much preferred. "Ms. Foxx, we think it's a very involved process, so I ask all of you to please bear with me because this may take some time but I think it's important.

"The killer we know as Rubens didn't just arrive in Washington recently. It is our belief that he has been here for a very long time identifying targets for this sick game he plays. There was nothing random about Lisa White or the victim we found earlier today, Audrey Ruston. They were prey specifically selected by the killer named Rubens only after he conducted thorough research. I have no doubt he followed Ms. White and Ms. Ruston for quite some time before he ever engaged with them."

"Are you saying he spends time with these women, even dates these women before he kills them?" a local television reporter asked.

"We think that's likely, yes."

"How do you know that?" a reporter holding a FOX News microphone interrupted.

"We know it because of what we do know for sure about our victims. The victims all have a certain profile. Now, people tend to focus almost exclusively on the specific body type of the victims, and that's very important, but there is so much more to it than that."

"Like what, Agent McRyan?" This reporter held a CNN microphone.

"Let me start by explaining who he doesn't target. He doesn't target women who are confident and outgoing. He doesn't target women who have had many relationships with men, women who are married and have families. He doesn't target women who work in high-profile or high-pressure environments, whether they be blue collar or white collar. His targets are not doctors, lawyers, saleswomen, waitresses, bartenders, cops or nurses—women who would be likely to smoke out his B.S. in a minute.

"The women I just described are not his targets because they would be women who have a large social circle, close friends and family. Those are women who scare him. Why? Because if he tried to get close to a woman like that she would talk about him with her friends. Not only that, she would *introduce* him to her friends. Friends and family create witnesses, and in all the years of hunting Rubens, there has never been a good description of him. In fact, in many instances with our victims the people who do know them suspect their friend had a new man in their life, yet not once in over ten years and fourteen victims have any of those friends ever met Rubens. Not a one."

"So who does he target?" Heather Foxx asked.

"The exact opposite," Mac answered. "All of his now fourteen victims seem to fit a very specific profile. The women he targets are certainly Rubenesque from a physical standpoint. But it is really the mental aspect that he preys on."

"How does he prey on them mentally?" a local reporter asked.

"As women his victims are not social, outgoing or confident. They are women who are not regularly the targets of male attention or affection. In fact, most victims rarely, if ever, had any relationships with men until the one they may have had at the time of their death. All of his victims are women who were shy, reserved and seemingly had few, if any, close friends or family. For lack of a better term, they were loners.

"They were women who worked lower profile jobs in a support or administrative capacity. Positions for which you can work but you don't have to be assertive, confident or outgoing. These women worked in the background, the shadows, punching the clock and doing their jobs quietly and conscientiously. They were people we don't really notice, yet rely on every day. They had jobs where they could work proficiently but quietly and then they went home to their books, art, gardens, movies, television shows and pets."

"How would he identify these women?" another voice called out.

"We think by trolling bookstores, museums, art galleries, art supply stores, pet stores, arboretums, places where these women went to find the things that interested them but also where they were comfortable, where they felt safe. I think he identifies women who fit the profile at these places, at least in part because those are topics in which he is also truly interested and can speak fluently on. He doesn't fake it."

"So he approaches the women, gives them a line and then he's in?" a reporter blurted.

"Not necessarily. In fact, we think that once he identifies a possible victim, he doesn't approach them immediately. Instead, we think he spends time following, observing, researching and methodically hunting them. He learns about them, what they like, what their interests are, what their life experiences have been and what their dreams are. Then once he's done that, once he's determined a woman is a possibility, then and only then does he make his approach.

"It's probably slow to start because these are women who are naturally suspicious. They wonder why this man is interested in them. They don't have a history of success in this regard, and in many instances, they've had bad experiences. For example, Audrey Ruston was divorced from a husband who was a domestic abuser. She moved here ten years ago from Tacoma, Washington, to get away from him. So the victims are initially wary, but not because they perceive our killer as a physical threat, but because the man is interested when no others have been.

"So we think he takes it slow and easy, a cup of coffee to start, then maybe a lunch, slowly but surely building their trust so that they let him in. So that he can get close. Many of the murders have happened in the victim's homes. In those cases, there is no evidence of forced entry—he's been invited into the woman's home where he then has them at ease and they trust him. They simply don't sense the danger.

"They feel safe, comfortable and maybe even loved. That's when this killer strikes.

"Rubens has the victim completely comfortable. She has these feelings of happiness that a man is interested. The victim, someone like Audrey Ruston last night, thinks he cares for her and maybe even loves her. The victim is completely exposed and open and it's at that very moment, when she is most relaxed, happy and vulnerable that he slips a date rape drug into their glass of wine. The drug incapacitates them. Then, once the woman is incapacitated, he kills them so that he then can, in the safety of the victim's own home, take the time to intricately stage their bodies like the women portrayed in the paintings of Peter Paul Rubens."

"Why does he stage them like the women in the Rubens paintings? What is the significance of that to him?" the CNN reporter asked.

"We don't know that yet," Mac answered. "I do want to know that. It'll be the first question I ask him when we catch him. But today I'm more concerned about the potential victims. So I want to speak to them directly. I want women to be honest with themselves and ask, do I fit this profile I've described?

"Do I look like a voluptuous, Rubenesque woman? Am I a person who typically spends a lot of time alone? Do I enjoy art, painting, books, museums, theatre, the symphony and the like and otherwise live a singular, quiet life? Do I have a poor history with men? Yet, despite that history, has a new man now entered into my life? If so, you need to ask yourself— are you being set-up?" Mac paused. "Because you could very well be the next woman on the news.

"If you find yourself in this situation, *or even think* you could possibly be in this situation, we want you to call us. So that is one kind of woman I want to hear from, but there is also another kind."

"What kind of woman is that?" Heather Foxx asked.

"He chose four victims but I'm betting that he initially identified several more than that. I'm betting there might have been others that he thought were possibilities, that he spent time with before, perhaps deciding not to pursue the relationship. So again, I ask, are you a woman who fits the profile? If so, did a man recently come into your life? And in your case, did he then suddenly, inexplicably disappear? Maybe by chance a friend or family member met him? It could be that someone you know saw him with you. Perhaps someone paid too much attention to him when the two of you were together. Whatever the reason, one day he was there, the next day he was gone. If that sounds like you, I want you to call the FBI field office."

Mac gave out the number.

"I'm not trying to alarm women, but at the same time," Mac sighed for effect, "you need to be vigilant. I beg of you, if what I've described could be you, swallow your pride and call us."

Rubens sat back in the chair.

McRyan had just made a move.

It was a good one.

He was now compelled to counter.

11

"ISN'T IT FUNNY HOW THAT WORKS."

After the press conference, they went about working on another whiteboard for Audrey Ruston. The autopsy was fast-tracked and the read at the scene was correct: she was smothered. While testing was taking place, it was determined that one of the couch pillows was likely used based upon small threads found in Audrey's mouth and nose. A toxicology screen was also being fast-tracked to determine if she was drugged. It was strongly suspected she was.

That information would simply confirm that Rubens continued to use tried and true methods. What it didn't do was tell them anything about who was next.

Coolidge rolled into the conference room a little past 7:00 p.m. and plopped himself down into a chair. "My feet are killing me," he moaned. Coolidge was a snappy dresser: sharp pinstriped suits, bold ties, flashy shoes and the occasional fedora, but a male model he wasn't. The man was carrying significant weight on his short round frame. His legs and feet were bound to give out at some point.

"Anything?" Mac asked.

"Maybe," Coolidge answered as he flexed his legs. "At Ruston's home, we interviewed everyone on the block, and we're spanning out still. At this point, other than the one neighbor who had a key to her place, few people knew who Audrey Ruston was, let alone actually knew her in any meaningful way. And the few that did never recalled her talking about a new man in her life, saw one or even saw evidence of one. Her one neighbor friend said it was rare for her to have company and never recalled seeing any man hanging around, and certainly not one recently."

"Not a surprise, given our victims," Mac answered. "How about her work?"

"I just left there to come here. Now, we might have a little something there. I interviewed all of the employees at the museum and they liked Audrey, thought she was a good employee, but they really knew very little about her."

"Tell me something I don't know," Mac remarked edgily. "I'm still waiting for the little something you teased."

"I'm getting to it," Coolidge smirked. "He's not terribly patient, is he?" he asked Wire with a wink.

"Try spending your entire day with him," she answered with a smile.

"Wow," Mac complained, "harsh."

"Sometimes you have to let the drama build, my boy," Linc suggested. "Audrey's co-workers didn't know her well but they do suffer from a basic human trait."

"Which is?"

"*They're nosey*. Audrey shared an office with two other women. Basically, in this larger interior office, a quad of cubicles was set up. The two ladies, just 'minding their own business', thought they overheard Audrey having recent conversations, excited conversations with someone. The other day they thought they heard something about the Vietnam Memorial."

"The Vietnam Memorial?" Mac asked.

"She apparently had an uncle who was killed over there in 1971 and his name is up on the wall."

"And what day did this call happen?"

"Monday."

"And what did they hear?" Wire asked as she sipped from a Diet Coke.

"I'll meet you there."

"And how did she say it?" Dara pressed. "Was it a bland 'I'll see you there, buddy', or excitedly as in '*I'll see you there*'."

Coolidge smiled. "I asked that very question, my dear Special Agent Wire, and according to her colleagues, it was definitely the latter. That's why they noticed it because it was so out of character."

"They learned all that from minding their own business, huh?" Mac asked, smiling.

"Isn't it funny how that works?" Coolidge quipped in reply.

"She had a date," Wire replied with a grin, looking to Mac.

"And was this conversation on her cell phone or work phone?" Mac asked, also sensing some possible light.

"Work phone," Coolidge answered. "I checked both and I have the printouts here. But on her work records, see these three calls I've circled here?"

"Yeah."

"I've already checked because this last one tracks with the day of the Vietnam Memorial call. It's the number for a burner phone and our guy has a history of that, so that's probably Rubens. I would also note that as far as I can tell he never called her cell phone."

"Because if he did that, she'd turn it into a contact," Wire speculated as they had with Lisa White.

"That's what most people do," replied Coolidge. "Our boy is very careful."

"It's probably one of his rules," Mac stated grumpily as he called Galloway into the conference room. "Let's see what we can do with these phone records, tracking that burner phone number that's circled. Then I need you to have people grab every camera in the vicinity of the Vietnam Memorial and see what turns up." Mac explained to Galloway what they had.

"Linc, did she walk or drive to the Memorial?" Wire asked.

Coolidge flipped into his notes. "They say she was gone at least two hours. That's a fairly long walk from the museum to the Memorial, so maybe that explains the timespan."

"You can do more than that in two hours," Wire answered. "If I'm a woman, I'm not satisfied with a stroll through the Vietnam Memorial. That's a little morbid if you ask me, uncle or no uncle. After that, I want coffee, lunch, something, especially if there is a gentleman caller involved. Especially if this is with a guy who's interested in me, I'm doing everything I can to stretch that out."

"If you're right and they went somewhere, we're probably talking someplace near the Memorial if not perhaps closer to the museum," Coolidge added.

"That's a lot of possibilities," Mac stated, getting out of his chair and going to a large map of Washington DC up on the wall. He ran his finger from the museum to the Memorial. "It's a lot of area to cover."

"We'll just need more guys," Galloway suggested, unconcerned. "I've got a green light for whatever we need. Agents I can get and local cops outside of the district have been volunteering to help. What do we have them do?"

"Get every piece of camera footage from the museum to the Vietnam Memorial. Then we need agents going to every possible coffee shop, restaurant and mobile souvenir, food or drink stand remotely within the area of the Memorial and then between there and the museum."

"It will take some time, but we're on it." Galloway handed Mac a report. "These are the financials on Audrey Ruston, last six months. Credit card report, a Visa, is the first set."

Mac and Wire started working through the credit card report when Galloway stuck his head back in the room and handed Mac a slip of paper. "What's this?" Mac asked.

"A call we received. This woman watched your press conference this afternoon."

"And?"

"She says she might know who Rubens is."

12

"I HAVE A MASTER'S DEGREE IN SCREWING UP MY LIFE."

There had in fact, been a number of calls to the field office following the press conference. After a phone screen, agents were dispatched to learn more. Caution was being exercised and all calls were being followed up on by agents in the field conducting interviews, although Galloway wasn't optimistic on most. "Our people who are screening don't think they're dealing with Rubens or even potentially dealing with Rubens on most of the calls," he explained. "But we're checking each and every one, no exceptions."

"Cover your ass?" Mac asked.

"CYA is one of my specialties," Galloway retorted.

"Okay, but why are *we* following up on this one?" Wire asked.

"She sounded a little more legitimate," Galloway stated. "She seemed to check the boxes based on her picture and the statistics in her DMV file. Plus, I'm a little thin on people right at this moment and you two should get out of here for a bit. Trust me, you'll feel better for it."

A little before 8:00 p.m. Mac and Wire knocked on the apartment door of Priscilla Blumenthal. Priscilla lived in an apartment building in the Michigan Park neighborhood.

Priscilla answered the door and Mac and Wire identified themselves. "I saw you on the television. Heck, they're running it nonstop on the cable news channels." She invited them inside the apartment.

Mac made a quick assessment of Priscilla and he was instantly skeptical. She didn't seem right. Physically she fit the profile, but only kind of. She was taller, five eight maybe and had perhaps wider hips, but as he assessed her she didn't strike him as physically Rubenesque compared to the other victims. There was also an air about her that suggested she wasn't the meek, quiet type that Rubens typically approached. Even as she opened the door, he detected an edge from Priscilla that he suspected would not have attracted Rubens.

That having been said, Mac wasn't taking any chances. Galloway was right. CYA.

"So, Priscilla, tell us about this man," Wire prompted.

"His name is Quentin Hickey," Priscilla replied.

"And how did you meet?"

"I met Quentin two months ago at a benefit for a local private school. My employer is a food ingredient company and we supplied some of our cooking products to be auctioned off in gift baskets. I was one of the people selected, or more like, ordered, to go to the thing. It wasn't an event I'd really want to work, if you know what I mean. Plus, I wasn't getting paid extra."

"Yeah, I hate it when the bosses make you do those things," Wire replied while looking at Mac.

"Right," Priscilla added. "Your partner here makes you do those things, doesn't he?"

"Him?" Wire replied. "*Never.* Anyway, you go to this event and then what?"

"They have this table set up and you talk up your company's products in the hopes that people will bid more for them at the auction. The company gets some good publicity out of it. In any event, Quentin approached to examine our products and struck up a conversation with me."

"And why was Quentin there?"

"He said he had a niece that went to the school and he was there to support her."

"I see," Wire replied with some doubt. "And then what happened?"

"We went out for a drink after the event. Then we went out a few nights later and we seemed to be heading toward something more."

"Yet it didn't?"

"Not after a few weeks, anyway."

"And what happened in those few weeks?"

"We went out, usually at some out of the way place. A couple of times we came back here and you know—"

"What?" Wire asked.

"Had sex."

"Ah, I see," Wire replied and shared a look with Mac. This didn't feel on the level.

"Then what happened?" Mac asked, taking notes.

"He stopped calling, stopped showing up and when I did manage to get a hold of him he wouldn't tell me why."

"Do you have any idea what changed?"

"No, I really don't," Priscilla replied. "Then your partner was on television talking about this Rubens and how he's killing these women and that if you had a relationship with someone and then he up and disappeared, you should call. I started wondering if Quentin fit that profile."

"Describe Quentin for me," Mac requested.

"He's got black hair, wears a beard. He's like six feet tall."

"And do you have his phone number or address?"

"I have his cell number."

Mac wrote it down. "If you'll excuse me." He went into the hallway and called Galloway.

"So what is Priscilla telling you?"

"That she met some guy who she had sex with for a couple of weeks who then stopped calling."

"Oh, so not a lead on Rubens."

"I'm kind of doubting that it is," Mac answered. "But, due to your wise counsel, I'm covering our asses. So run this number for me and we'll find out for sure." Five minutes later Galloway had an address and phone number for Quentin Hickey. Quentin lived up in College Park, which did give Mac a little of tingle of excitement. The other night they'd tracked a call from Rubens up near the University of Maryland.

A little before 10:00 p.m. they knocked on Quentin's door. It was answered by a woman who identified herself as Mrs. Hickey, and Mac and Wire immediately knew it was a dead end. Quentin spelled it out for them while speaking out on the front lawn.

"I knew I shouldn't have taken up with her," he said.

"The affair, you mean?" Wire asked directly and with a hardly disguised tone of disapproval.

Hickey nodded. "The old lady and I have been having issues. We were separated for a time and while we were, I ran into Priscilla."

"Why did you stop seeing her?" Mac asked.

Hickey nodded towards the house. "Luann and I decided to give it another shot. I told Priscilla I didn't want to see her anymore."

"Did you tell her why?"

"No," Quentin replied. "I guess I should have. At this point, she's just trying to make my life miserable. I don't need her help. I have a master's degree in screwing up my life."

As they left Quentin to go back inside and try to explain their visit away, Dara looked over to Mac. "So, Mac, are you sure you want to get married?"

"Like a buddy of mine once said, you only get married twice."

A half-hour later, they pulled back into the parking ramp at the field office.

"You mind if I call it a night?" Wire asked. It was nearly 11:00 p.m.

"No, go ahead," Mac answered, checking his watch, "I'm going to head inside and stare at the whiteboard for a while and then go home myself."

"Don't stay up too late," Wire responded as she walked to her car and Mac strode to the elevator lobby. When he got to the door, he turned around with a big grin and yelled, "Say hi to Ridge for me."

Wire looked up in horror. "How?"

"I have my ways, Dara Wire, I have my ways."

"But—" she started, flabbergasted, heading back toward him.

"I saw you talking to him during the press conference," Mac stated. "I could just tell."

Wire shook her head at him in amazement.

"I don't miss much," Mac added cockily.

"I guess not," she replied, shaking her head, hands on her hips. "I didn't realize you cared," she needled back.

"Someone has to look out for you," he replied and then in a more serious tone added, "Just be careful."

"You don't like him?"

"I don't know him," Mac cautioned. "And neither do you."

"Well, Mac," Wire replied with a big smile, "that's why you go on dates."

"Oh, so it's a date?"

"Well, hold on a second ..."

Gwen watched the press conference on CNN one more time as she finished up the last of her duties at the library. She wondered if she should call. There had only been three times that she had gone out with Louis.

"Are you ready, Gwen?"

"Yes," she replied as she clicked shutdown for her computer. She waited for the computer screen to go black and then joined Melissa at the back door.

"On your way home?" Melissa asked as they walked to their cars.

"That's my plan. I have to stop at the grocery store for some things. I need eggs and milk but otherwise, I have a new book awaiting me at home."

"Good night."

"You too."

Fifteen minutes later Gwen walked into the corner store. She reached inside the cooler for a dozen eggs, opening the container to make sure none were cracked. In the next compartment over, she grabbed a half-gallon of two percent milk and went to the register to wait behind two other customers.

The flat screen television mounted above and to the right of the cash register was tuned to CNN. Once again that FBI agent's press conference was running. The number to call was posted on the screen. She reached for her cell phone, swiped to the second screen and hit the Notes icon and tapped in the number, then put the phone back into her coat pocket.

As she walked out of the store, her favorite little coffee shop was to the left. She deposited the groceries into her car and went back into the coffee shop to get a quick cup of decaf before the shop closed.

Five minutes later, she pulled her car into the garage. Gwen grabbed her cup of coffee out of the cup holder and then set it on the roof of her Camry while she took her groceries out of the back seat. She locked the car and lowered the garage door. She opened the back door of the detached garage and stepped out onto the small sidewalk to the rear of her house.

The thud was sickening as the hammer came thundering down onto the back of her skull.

Gwen instantly collapsed to the ground, her groceries and coffee spilling all over the sidewalk.

She groaned and started to move.

He stepped over her body, kneeled down, placing his left knee on the small of her back and pressed down on her neck with his left hand.

The job had to be finished.

He swung the hammer down viciously again on her skull. Not satisfied, he reached high and way back with the hammer and brought it down with all of his might one more time. This time, the hammer dug deep into her skull, crushing the bone.

Gwen was dead.

He grabbed her purse, ran around the garage and down the alley at a full sprint. He reached his car a block and a half away and quickly sped off.

McRyan had made his move.

He had countered.

But there were two women who concerned him. One more to go.

13

"IT'S A LEVEL OF RUTHLESSNESS THAT BLOWS MY MIND."

As the clock approached midnight and in an effort to avoid drawing any unwanted attention from other media types, Wire met up with Ridge closer to her Alexandra, Virginia home at a small local dive bar. She found the author patiently waiting, reading his phone, perched in a secluded back corner booth. In front of him rested a half-finished pitcher of beer along with two small baskets of popcorn.

"This is as below the radar as I can be in here," he noted upon her arrival. "Shall I pour you a beer?"

"I could use one."

"So what's new?" he asked airily as he poured. "You might as well tell me. I'll find out anyway."

"So you think."

"I'm very good at what I do."

"God, you sound as arrogant as Mac sometimes."

"I'll take that as a compliment ... I guess," Ridge replied with a smile. "So come on, shop talk. What's new?"

She brought him somewhat up to date on the night's activities.

"So this Priscilla pulled the stealth Glenn Close, *Fatal Attraction*, 'I'm not going to be ignored, Dan,' bit?"

"That was kind of our take on it. I almost, *almost* felt bad for him even though he was a cheating scumbag."

"Is it cheating if they were separated?"

"It depends on how separated. I didn't necessarily get the sense it was a lengthy separation. It felt more like the minute he got out of the house he jumped the first thing he could find."

Ridge ordered another pitcher and made it clear one of the reasons he was there. "Look, I'm not really looking for a tip or the next big break in the case, although I'd gladly take anything you'd provide."

"Right."

"Dara, what I am is a writer who is going to be looking to tell a story. A book is going to be written. And this story, like any good story, needs a subject beyond just Rubens."

"No, thanks."

"You sure you don't want to hear the whole pitch? I can be pretty persuasive," the author answered in a tone that said he always ended up getting what he wanted.

"Let's see, all your pitch really means is that instead of getting burned in tomorrow's newspaper, I can get burned a year from now in your next tawdry best seller."

Ridge shook his head in amusement. "You're every bit as cynical as your partner, aren't you?"

"I've been burned before—maybe not by the media, but I've been burned. So let's just say you haven't earned my trust yet."

"Oh, you mean like your partner trusts Heather Foxx."

"I have no idea what you're talking about," Wire lamely replied, sipping her beer.

The author laughed. "*Please.* Let's make a rule, you and I, to not insult each other's intelligence. Other than with Steve Kroft a few Sundays ago, anytime he does cut open a vein, Heather Foxx is involved, whether in Washington or way back when he was in the Twin Cities. I mean, who had the first question at today's press conference?"

"So?"

"So they have a relationship of some kind. I was thinking ..."

"Whatever relationship it is, it's not *that* kind."

"Right," Ridge replied in disbelief. "You've seen Heather Foxx, right?"

"I have and it's not that kind of relationship and if you ever print that, things won't end well for you."

"What, you'll be angry with me?"

"Yes, but even worse for you would be having Mac—or even really worse, Sally Kennedy—angry with you." Wire turned serious. "Word of advice, don't go there."

Ridge took the measure of Wire. "Okay," he answered with some uncertainty.

"Move on, Ridge. Move on."

"Noted," Ridge replied, sufficiently chastised. If he thought he was going to get dirt on McRyan out of Wire, he was sorely mistaken.

He moved onto safer territory.

He talked about himself. It was something he was clearly comfortable doing.

Ridge had written two other non-fiction crime books along with two mysteries, not to mention his job going around the country and writing crime stories for *World News Magazine*. He had a good gig going and was quite impressed with himself, albeit in a completely disarming, if not charming, way. His enthusiasm was authentic, like a little kid in the candy store or on Christmas morning. Ridge clearly enjoyed the stories he got to research and write. His prolific publishing history thoroughly provided, Ridge eventually steered the conversation back to the re-emergence of Rubens.

"Whether you catch him or not, Rubens will give me another book. My publisher already called—the story is just too good. We'll settle on terms here sometime soon."

"Glad we can provide you some entertainment," Wire shot back derisively, leaning back, her arms folded across her chest.

Ridge was unfazed. "Give me a break, Dara. A serial killer who appears then disappears and then reappears every few years, taunting and jeering along the way, setting deadlines, leaving clues, jerking the police's chain and then disappearing without a trace. You can't make it up."

"Who'd want to?"

"Every fiction writer there is," Ridge responded. "Except this one, Rubens, is the gift that keeps on giving. I just have to build some time into my schedule here soon so I can strike while the iron is hot. I'll be burying myself in my home office for a good long while to crank out that puppy after this is all over. The whole thing is just fascinating. I love the adrenaline of it and—"

"And what?"

He leaned in, smiling. "This time I'd love to find a way inside, like April Greene. I want to tell the story more from the police's perspective this time. What the chase is like. What it really does to you."

Wire leaned back, shaking her head and taking a drink of her beer. "I don't think so."

He didn't take no for an answer. "Look, Dara, I've been there from the beginning with Rubens. I mean this, no bullshit—you and McRyan are the best to go after him."

"Flattery will get you more consideration," Dara replied with a smile, but then quickly closed the door again. "But it's Mac's show—you'd have to convince him."

"You're part of it, too," Ridge suggested.

Wire shook her head. "I am, but Mac is the lead. He's the boss, and you can't tell the story without him and you won't truly get inside without him. So on that point, good luck to you. As part of your research, I'm sure you've uncovered that he's not exactly the sharing kind."

"No, I experienced that in person the other night. So if the buck stops with him, what's your role, Dara Wire? Plucky sidekick?"

Wire thought for a quick second. "One part of it is to keep Mac sane and from doing something stupid. He's not just the smartest cop I've run across, but one of the smartest people I've *ever* met. He is wicked smart."

"I sense a 'but' coming."

"A case like this is stressful. I've seen that stress bring out an abrasiveness and hair-trigger temper in Mac that can get him into trouble. He'll just lash out."

"Like outside that abortion clinic on the Reaper case?"

"That would be one example," Dara replied with a nod. "What a shit show that was."

"I remember it well," Ridge replied. "The reporter crossed the line though."

"She did," Wire answered. "And Mac snapped, which you just can't do. Mac," she shook her head and smiled. "The man does not suffer fools gladly. In fact, he doesn't suffer them at all. I can usually help him keep that in check. Plus, I like to think I'm pretty smart and he knows he can trust me. As smart as he is, he needs someone to bounce ideas off of and talk things through with. He feeds off that interaction. So I play devil's advocate to what he's thinking and some-times I'll see something or perceive something differently and we break through." She thought about it for a second longer and then added, "We're a good team."

"Good to know."

"Answer me this," Wire asked, turning things back to the case. "Why Rubens? Why does this guy focus on these women the way he does?"

"The clichéd answer is that it was his mother who didn't love him and she looked like one of the subjects of a Rubens painting. Another dime store theory is that maybe a woman he loved was Rubenesque and she spurned him and as a result, he's taking his revenge on others. That would be the formulaic view of it."

"What's your view?"

Ridge took a sip of his beer and then grabbed a handful of popcorn and tossed two pieces into his mouth. "It's not something quite that easy. For all my witty asides about this case, Rubens is a disturbed man who is pulling his motivation from some very dark place. I mean, to kill for this long? To go away and then come back again and again in some other city? Think about it—there is nothing impulsive about the guy."

"No, he's methodical."

"And careful and selective," Ridge added. "And the way he sets the women up?" He frowned. "It's a level of ruthlessness that blows my mind. Obviously, the guy has some serious issues. But what the origin of that dark place is—" He shrugged. "I don't know. That's an area best reserved for someone like April Greene. That's her bailiwick."

"She's pretty smart," Wire noted. "Mac and I have been reading parts of her books on serial killers. She has some interesting insights."

"Lord knows she's interviewed enough of them," Ridge answered somewhat dismissively.

"Careful, Ridge," Wire needled. "Your competitive chauvinist side is showing."

He laughed. "Dara, honey. I'm no chauvinist. I *love* women."

"I bet you do."

"April's smart, I'll grant you that. She understands the killer's mind, she really does. Now her books on profiling in general, those are the gold standard for that topic. She took what John Douglas did all those years ago and has taken it to a whole new level."

Wire could hear the tone in his voice. "I sense a 'but' coming."

"*But* if we're talking strictly Rubens, her books on that topic are, in my opinion, only just okay. If you're looking for insight on Rubens, you might get as much from the FBI files as from her first book. It was kind of milquetoast, a Joe Friday, 'just the facts, ma'am' approach."

"Too dull for you?"

"*Way* too dull," Ridge replied eagerly. "People want some excitement, some edge of the seat tension. Besides, these cases provide that with this nutjob's clock and Rubens' painting poses. But her first book—" He waved dismissively. "No flair."

"Not everyone wants melodrama, Ridge. Sometimes people just like the truth."

"They want the truth, sure, but not in textbook form. Adults read for entertainment first, knowledge second. A story on a subject like Rubens needs to be engrossing and intense so that it draws you in. It shouldn't be painful, like a reading assignment for a class. People do that at work every day. No, if they go home at night, they want it with some panache, with some excitement. April's books sold well and are required reading for cops and boring people. Mine might not get the seal of approval from law enforcement per se but they show up on the *New York Times* Best Sellers list."

"So did hers, Ridge."

"Her books came out in February and March—that's the easy season for the best seller lists. I made it in the fall, the prime book selling season. I sold more books and held on the lists way longer."

"I suppose you think your dick is bigger too."

"You've spent a lot of time around cops, haven't you?"

"Far too much."

He moved the topic back to Greene's books. "Look, April's works are not as sensationalized, not as salacious. But like I said earlier, where I will give her credit, a ton of credit, is in her other books where she gets into the mind of the killers. She has a PhD in psychology and it gives her insight—insight she's applied to unsolved cases. Her best work is *Inside Disturbed Minds*. You want to learn something, give that one a read. That one was really interesting, the one that really made her. I gained new respect for her on that one. And the one she put out last year was all about unsolved cases. It was what the police should look for and how these killers' minds operate. It wasn't a super long book, but she had seven or eight unsolved cases from around the country over the last ten or so years and picked them apart, picked the killer apart, giving a profile of what the police should look for. That book was fascinating. I read it on a flight from New York to London. It was a really compelling read."

"I suppose she did a hatchet job on the cops?"

"No, not at all," Ridge answered, shaking his head for effect. "The book wasn't about what she thought the cops missed. Instead, she wrote it totally from the killer's point of view—that's what was fascinating about it. I swear I think she's interviewed every jailed serial killer there is. She has a gift to get these guys to open up and spill the details. April really understands the mind of a serial and she applied what she's learned to the unsolved cases. I think the police actually solved one of those cases after April looked at it, just on the basis of the profile and insight she provided. The case had been cold for like five years but they found the guy. In fact, she's been able to write so prolifically and profitably that she now just consults with the FBI whenever she's in the mood. This case undoubtedly has her in the mood."

There was another tone, and Wire followed up. "She ever get you in the mood?"

"April?"

"Yeah, you ever put the moves on her like you're trying with me?"

"I'm trying to put the moves on?"

Wire gave him an eye roll.

Ridge shrugged. "We had a moment or two. There were a couple of nights in Los Angeles four years ago when we were both covering the last Rubens appearance. We talked a little shop one night, had a few drinks and ... well ... you know. One thing led to another. April is not unattractive."

"I never said she was," Wire replied. "She's pretty enough."

"Now who's being catty? That comment was like Obama saying Hillary was likeable enough."

Wire laughed. "Well, as for me, I wouldn't get your hopes up. At least not tonight."

"Fair enough," Ridge replied. "We'll be doing this again."

"Presumptuous much?"

He returned the eye roll.

Dara swerved back to the case. "I've perused both of your books, Ridge, and scanned hers. I think you sell April short on her Rubens books. She isn't completely without flair," she stated.

"No, she's just not as entertaining as me."

"Speaking of entertainment," Wire replied, "you're writing fiction now. Now you just get to make shit up."

"It's amazing what you can come up with when the shackles of facts and truth have been released," Ridge replied with a big smile. "Rubens made me. That first book sprung me forward. Now I've got the gig with the magazine, I write the fiction books, I live in

Manhattan and now my buddy Rubens is back and better than ever. Life is, as they say, really effin' good."

At 1:30 a.m., they walked out of the small pub and to their cars. Ridge played it cool. No moves would be made tonight.

"So I'll see you around?" Ridge asked.

"I imagine you will," Wire replied, having decided he was charming and handsome enough that she wouldn't mind if he did see her around.

Mac turned the chair at the end of the conference table around and stared at the whiteboard, sipping a cup of coffee, engaging in his ritual during cases. From time to time, the board would speak to him, give him an idea, a thread to pull.

His father made an off the cuff remark one time, not long before he was killed, that in murder cases they always had more information than they thought. "Sometimes it's just not in the right context, son. But if you put it in the right order, the right context, the right timeline, suddenly a case could read completely differently."

Mac often thought about that comment when he was a homicide detective. It was often so true. It was why he always put the case up on a whiteboard or a wall. If he could see it all, maybe he could see the answer.

Alas, the board was not talking to him, at least not yet.

He was contemplating calling it a night when he saw the updated paper file that Galloway must have dropped on the table. The updated file had a report on Coolidge's results, or lack thereof, in interviewing Audrey Ruston's friends and neighbors. There were also the financials for Ruston for the last six months.

"I'm disappointed to hear that the woman was a dead end," April Greene offered, leaning against the door frame of the conference room. "That would have been a good break."

"Well, we wouldn't want it to be easy, now would we?" Mac answered as he started perusing the financial records.

"Oh, heavens no," Greene replied. "What would be the fun and challenge in that?"

"Exactly," Mac replied, looking up. "Besides, I don't believe in easy anyway. When it's easy, that's when I get worried. That's when I look for the floor to give way beneath my feet. So, Ms. Greene, what are you still doing hanging around here? I figured consultants keep nine-to-five hours."

"I usually do, but this is Rubens we're talking about. And I liked the move you made at the press conference," Greene stated. "Too bad it didn't pay off."

"It still might," Mac answered more in hope than anything else. "Sometimes these things take time. Investigations are a piece here and a piece there and eventually the puzzle emerges. So this move was a ..."

"Chess move."

"Yes."

"You have vision and the rest of the world wears bifocals, huh?"

Mac laughed at the Butch Cassidy reference, but deflected credit. "It's not about being that clever, really. It's just that I had an idea and the best way to get it out there was to use the newsies. Mostly they're a pain in the ass but they can be useful at times."

"It is the quickest way to get information out there, that's for sure," Greene agreed.

Mac nodded, sat back in his chair, sighed and closed his eyes.

"What are you thinking about?" Greene asked.

"Water," Mac answered, "the deep blue of the Chesapeake Bay."

"Do you have a boat out there?"

Mac smiled and shook his head. "I could. I have a twenty-six-foot speed boat back home in Minnesota. It could handle the Chesapeake, I think. I've thought about bringing it out here but just haven't gotten around to it."

"I have a boat down in the harbor where I live."

"Really."

"Yes," Greene replied. "I grew up in Chicago. My dad's vice, other than running his investment firm, was his forty-foot Trojan Express

Cruiser. He had it docked in a marina by the Navy Pier. We went out every weekend in the summer."

Greene's book *The Homicidal Artist* was on Mac's nightstand. Part of the motivation in Greene coming to the FBI was the murder of her parents during a home invasion twenty years ago. He could see the wistfulness in her eyes at the mere mention of her parents.

"The real reason I was thinking of the Chesapeake is that I'm getting married in a month," Mac stated, veering away from boating. "We're having the reception at the Davidson House and it overlooks ..."

"The Chesapeake," April answered with a little smile. "Very nice, Mac. I've been there and it will be a wonderful place for you. Maybe if we catch Rubens, or even if we don't, maybe the two of you would like to come down and we can cruise the bay and you can check out the view of your reception hall from the water."

"That would be excellent!" Mac replied happily. "Sally would love it."

"Consider it done—we'll do it," April answered and then turned to the television in the corner of the conference room, tuned to CNN. "There you are again."

Snippets of the press conference were being repeated on the cable news channels and were all over the Internet, along with Twitter, Facebook and any other social networking site. It went viral, as intended. If Mac's theory was right, there was someone out there who unwittingly knew who Rubens was.

Greene also saw the deeper element of the move. "You weren't just talking to the women, were you?"

"No. I was talking to him as well. He has my number. His I don't have."

"So this was your what? Bat signal?"

"Something like that," Mac replied, flipping through credit card records for Ruston. "So my hope is I can rattle him a little that way and then through some old-fashioned ... police work we can ... get ... somewhere." He focused in on the middle of a page of Ruston's credit card bills.

"What is it?"

He stood up and found the file on Lisa White, opened up the folder with her financial records, scanned them and stopped with his finger in the middle of a page. "Huh."

"What?" April asked more urgently.

"The financials," Mac replied. "Lisa White and Audrey Ruston have credit card purchases ten minutes apart on the same day at a bookstore called Classic Books. It's a bookstore here in DC."

"I know that store," Greene replied, coming around to his side of the table. "I did a signing there once, maybe twice."

Mac reached for his laptop, made some keystrokes, found the video files for Lisa White and found the surveillance footage for the bookstore the morning of the purchase.

The surveillance system for Classic Books had three camera angles, one focused on the area of the front entrance, a second one positioned over the cash register that also provided a panoramic view of the middle of the store and one focused towards the back half of the store, and the two small, comfortable seating areas situated opposite a stone fireplace.

It took Mac a few minutes, but he eventually maneuvered his way to the right time on the video footage: 11:07 a.m. "Okay, there's White making her purchase, and—" He fast forwarded the video ten minutes to where Ruston appeared, making her purchase at the register. "There's Audrey Ruston ten minutes later."

Mac started scanning back in the video, looking for more glimpses of Ruston. The footage was in black and white but was of decent clarity. As the video played, Audrey Ruston entered the store. She walked inside and slowly walked right to left, checking the aisle markings. She disappeared from view of the first camera. Mac switched to the camera over the cash register. Ruston came into view, still slowly continuing to scan the aisle markings and then she turned to her right into the aisle straight ahead of the cash register. Ruston stopped mid-aisle and took a book off the shelf and started thumbing through it. She'd grabbed a larger book that he could tell contained both text and pictures. Mac couldn't tell what specific book it was, other than it looked like a coffee table book.

As he examined Ruston, Mac found that his attention was slowly drawn away from her. Standing five feet away from Ruston was a man, a man whose face seemed focused not on Ruston as she'd come up the aisle, but instead on the cash register. There was something about how he looked, how he was watching the cash register and his senses told him it wasn't right.

Mac rewound the footage back three minutes and let it run, now focusing solely on the man who was of average height, maybe five-nine or ten with a little weight around his mid-section. April Greene was to his right, watching silently but intently.

"That man?" she asked.

Mac simply nodded. .

The man wore dark-rimmed glasses and had a beard along with a light colored tam hat. Mac ran the footage back and forth three more times before he finally spoke. "April, look at what he's doing *before* Ruston approaches him." Mac pushed play. "Tell me what you see."

Greene moved closer, standing now, leaning down with both of her hands and watching. "Run it back one more time."

Mac did as instructed.

She quietly watched again, moving close to the screen, sliding on her reading glasses that had been hanging around her neck. "Mac, he's watching that cash register—he's zeroed in on it. It's not obvious —he looks very natural, comfortable, but if you're looking close you can tell that he is."

"And who's at the cash register?"

"Lisa White."

"Yes, yes, she is."

Mac let the video run forward. The man continued to eye White. Then Ruston came down the aisle, stopped and took the coffee table book off the shelf. After a brief moment, Audrey Ruston's presence caught the man's attention. In fact, it seemed to have interrupted his concentration. Then the man took another look at the woman and his head snapped up.

"Wait a second," Mac exclaimed and ran the video back, pushed play and watched again. "You saw the head move, right?" Mac asked, pointing, rewinding and then playing the clip yet again. "See how his head snaps there, when he looks over Ruston." He rewound the clip a fourth time. "Look, that head snap right there. You do that when you ..."

"Recognize someone," Greene finished with a hint of excitement. "That moment when you suddenly recognize someone—a friend, an old schoolmate, something like that."

"Yeah, it is like he all of a sudden recognized Ruston, he realized this was ... Audrey Ruston," Mac agreed while lightly shaking his head. Was he seeing things or was this real?

"He seems to recognize her, but does she recognize him?" April asked.

"I can't tell. I can't see Audrey Ruston's facial reaction—her back is to us." Mac rewound the key clip and pushed play again. "As I watch this play out her body language doesn't suggest she recognizes him, especially when he starts talking to her, gesturing at the book and moving a little closer."

"If anything her reaction seems to be one of ... surprise," April stated. "He's the ... aggressor, if that's the right term. Maybe initiator is better."

Mac let the video play out and watched as the two of them started to converse. "He's talking to her about the book."

"He is, like he knows the topic," Greene agreed. "He's in a bookstore, he's talking books. But his focus has been diverted from White to Audrey. In fact, White leaves the store and he hardly seems to notice that."

Mac let the video play out. Over the next five minutes, Ruston and the man talk. As they do, they both seem to become more comfortable, their posture less rigid, more relaxed, as if beginning to feel at ease with each other.

"The flirting has commenced," Mac observed.

"He just made her laugh," April noted as Ruston threw her head back and the man smiled through the beard.

After another few minutes, the man gestured toward the cash register and they both moved forward to the counter. Ruston bought the coffee table book and then the man bought the book he'd been holding in his hand. She paid with a credit card while he paid cash, pulling out a money clip that was thick with bills. "A little walking around money, I'd say," Mac mused.

"More like a pimp roll," Greene quipped, making Mac laugh.

Ruston and the man continued to talk as they both exited the bookstore. "Well, wasn't that all friendly-like," Mac stated. "That was a smooth pickup."

"It certainly seemed that Audrey diverted his attention from White."

"Uh huh," Mac answered. "He had his attention diverted from our first victim... to... no. Come on... no way."

"What?" Greene asked.

"This is a big intuitive leap."

"Go ahead," the FBI behaviorist encouraged. "Intuitive is what I do."

"April, let's stop dancing around this—we're both thinking the same thing here. Let's just say this is Rubens. Did he just get a two for the price of one here? He's watching Lisa White and lo and behold, who walks in, but Audrey Ruston, another woman who perfectly fits his profile."

Greene grimaced and then slowly shook her head. "I see where you're going." April was wary. "What are the odds, Mac? Think about that. I know we're talking Rubens, but do you really think that man is Rubens? *Really?*"

"I've got my two victims in Classic Books. They both loved books, they're both Rubenesque, they both fit the psychological profile of a victim. We have hypothesized—me for only a few days, but you for years—that he methodically hunts these women and finds them in places Rubens and his victims are comfortable. White and Ruston would have felt comfortable in this environment. In the case of White, her financials tell us she went there fairly often and was something of a regular, and this wasn't Ruston's maiden voyage to the store.

If we're right about our killer's education, his love of art, museums, books, his level of education, he too would have been at home in this environment. He would not look or feel out of place."

"So you think he's hunting?" Greene asked.

"If you're a fisherman, you fish where the fish are," Mac answered and then turned back to the screen. "Let's take this video footage all the way back and look at the whole time they're all in the store together."

Mac rewound the footage back to when Lisa White first entered the bookstore, twenty-three minutes before Ruston. She moved from camera one to camera two at the cash register, to camera three and the last row of shelves near the seating area. On all three cameras, she was comfortably and casually perusing the shelves of the store. Two minutes after she'd entered, the man came into the store. He nonchalantly made his way to the middle aisle, the one straight up from the cash register. It was a location that also placed him strategically in the center of the store. He grabbed a book off the shelf and opened it in his hands.

"You're not reading the book," Mac muttered about the man.

"No," Greene shook her head. "He's not, he's faking it."

"He's parked himself. He can see the whole store from that position."

"Maybe," April answered. "I have to admit it, Mac. He sure seems to be watching Lisa White as she takes her time moving around the store. As you flip between the footage for the three cameras, he's clearly pivoting to change his perspective as she moves about the store. If she stops, he stops moving. If she moves, he slowly changes his body orientation with her movements. It's sly—he looks down every so often, turns a page every now and then, turns his back, grabs a different book off the shelf, but he's ... watching her."

"You bet he is," Mac affirmed. "It's like he's evaluating her."

"You can't tell much about him physically," April noted. "Thick rimmed glasses, tam hat and a beard."

"The glasses, beard and hat conveniently hide his face. But I do get approximate height, weight, body type and it gives us a picture to go with," Mac answered, focused on the computer screen. "I know Audrey Ruston was five-seven and she's in flats. That makes our guy two to three inches taller."

"So hypothetically we think this could be Rubens. Is this enough for you to go with?" Greene asked. "I mean, it's a single video clip from a store. He's creepy but this guy wouldn't be the first one to creep around a store staring at women. Heck, I get kooky guys at book signings who stare me down. It gives me the willies but I don't necessarily think they're killers stalking me."

"They could be."

"I've never had an issue. I just thought the men were weird, is all. I was never attacked or stalked or anything like that at all."

"Fine, that was *your* experience," Mac answered, undeterred. "But I don't believe in coincidences in murder investigations. I don't believe it's a coincidence that I have my two victims in a bookstore with a creepy guy giving one of them the eagle eye and then looking like he suddenly recognizes the other and then engages her in conversation."

"So what are you going to do? It's pretty thin."

"We could start by showing it around and seeing what we ..."

"*Mac! Mac!*" Galloway bellowed, jogging into the conference room, an open laptop in his hands. "We have the surveillance footage from the area around the Vietnam Memorial."

"And?"

"We've got something," Galloway answered. "You have to check this out. We have footage of Audrey Ruston with a man at the memorial."

"Is your guy five-ten, Caucasian, with a beard, thick glasses, wearing a hat of some kind? Perhaps a tam hat?"

Galloway looked gobsmacked. "Yeah, how did you—"

"Know?" Mac waved him over and showed him the surveillance footage from Classic Books, explaining the connection he found in the financial records and that both White and Ruston were in store at the same time.

"He's similar, very similar in fact," Galloway stated and made some keystrokes on Mac's computer. "Check out this Vietnam Memorial footage."

The surveillance footage was in black and white of the sidewalk leading away from the Memorial, the panels visible in the distance behind them. "This camera is located near the southern end of the Memorial, by the flag pole," Galloway noted.

Audrey Ruston and the man were walking toward the camera. The man was now maybe an inch taller than Ruston, who now looked to be in heels. The man was bearded, wore dark-rimmed glasses and a tam hat again, along with what looked like grayish or khaki pants and a dark, either black or navy blue sport coat over a whitish dress shirt.

"Is this all you have?" Mac asked.

"So far," Galloway answered. "We're checking for more footage but oddly, cameras are a little scarce in that area so we haven't picked them up yet on other footage. But we're still hunting."

Mac toggled back to the Classic Books video again and then back to the footage at the Vietnam Memorial. The similarities were unmistakable. "There you are, you jackhole," he muttered, but now with a satisfied tone.

"As I said, the guy looks very similar," Galloway mused.

"Screw similar—it's the same guy, Don," Mac replied. "We have our first image of Rubens."

"You don't know that for sure," Greene cautioned.

"There's one way to start finding out."

14

"WEST SIDE, GRAY HOODIE."

W ho was the man in the surveillance video?
Was it Rubens?

Mac was anxious to find out.

In the very early a.m., Galloway and Delmonico began arrangements to release the video of the man at Classic Books and the Vietnam Memorial that they suspected was Rubens.

Just before 4:00 a.m., Mac smiled and then dialed Wire.

"What?" she answered angrily. "It's 3:54 a.m. for crying out loud. You better have Rubens in custody or I'm going to kill you."

"I don't have him in custody," Mac answered. "I have pictures of him though."

"Huh?" she asked, half asleep. "Pictures, what pictures? Pictures of whom?"

"Pictures, more like footage from surveillance cameras from Classic Books and in the vicinity of the Vietnam Memorial." Mac quickly explained, providing a brief description of the man to Wire. "This is the real deal. It's going to be released shortly."

"Okay," Dara groaned, but now fully awake. "I'm on my way."

Wire rolled in at 4:35 a.m., her hair pulled back in a tight ponytail and with a tall gas station coffee in her hand. She found April Greene lying on the dingy orange couch in the conference room. "He even dragged you in this early?"

"I was hanging around late last night when he found the image on the surveillance video at Classic Books and then when Galloway came in with the footage from the Vietnam Memorial. So I never left." She rolled up and stretched her arms and then asked, "Does McRyan ever sleep?"

"Welcome to working a case with Mac," Dara said with a tired smile. "I've seen him go *days* without sleep."

"How?"

"He's wired differently."

Any possible break in the Rubens investigation was of immediate interest to the local television stations, not to mention the networks and cable. Rubens was now receiving nationwide attention. By 6:00 a.m. Eastern Time the video was out everywhere it could be.

After watching the initial wave of coverage, Mac sat back in his chair and said, "Now— we wait."

He was fairly satisfied with himself as he leaned back sipping what seemed like his tenth coffee, rubbing his hand over his nearly two-day-old beard. The closest thing to a shower he had was splashing his face with water. He looked exhausted yet his body said he was anything but.

"You look like a pig in slop," Greene remarked.

"I shouldn't get juice from this," Mac responded.

"But he does," Wire finished with a small yawn then spoke to Greene. "Like I said, he's wired differently."

At 7:30 a.m., Galloway stuck his head into the conference room. "Mac, the owner of Classic Books will be there at 8:00. He has all of his staff coming in. I assume you'd like to greet them."

Mac looked to Wire. "Away we go." To Galloway, he said, "If anything comes of all of this, call me."

"Will do," Galloway answered with a yawn. Mac imagined the man would go to his office and close the door. Agent Galloway was an excellent agent, the true King of Administration. His gift of adminis- tration came from an overabundance of organization. However, people like that needed their eight hours of sleep a night; they needed the consistency of their schedule. A case like this had Galloway's world completely off its axis. Delmonico was an able aid to him. A more traditional agent, she was more used to the varied hours. They worked well together.

Mac and Wire arrived promptly at 8:00 a.m. and the store owner and his staff were waiting. They'd all seen the footage on television, both from their store and the Vietnam Memorial. Every single one knew Lisa White, one of their most dedicated customers. A few recognized Audrey Ruston. She wasn't a regular customer but she'd been in from time to time over the years. These were their people who'd been murdered. They wanted to help, were desperate to help. The problem was the man in the footage didn't register with anyone.

"I know we're a small bookstore but we really do have a lot of people come through here," the store manager said defensively. "Now Lisa White, she came regularly, was a good customer and while she paid that morning, she also had an account that she settled up every so often. I didn't know Ms. Ruston personally, not like my staff and I knew Lisa White, but she'd been in over the years."

"But what about the man?" Mac pressed one more time. "Anything, anything at all helps. If there is anything any of you could remember about that day, about this man, it would help us."

"It would help us find Lisa White's killer," Wire added.

The store owner looked over at the disappointed faces of his staff and shook his head. "I've looked at him here. I looked at him when they played the footage on the morning show." He waved toward his staff. "We all have. He just isn't registering with me, with anyone, Agent McRyan."

Mac wasn't entirely shocked. Rubens was in the store that morning in that disguise. If he'd been in the store other times, he probably looked different.

Mac and Wire left Classic Books and found a small coffee shop. It was a beautiful, warm April morning so they leaned against Mac's X5, sipping coffees and eating egg sandwiches.

"The important thing in one sense," Wire said, "is that they didn't recognize him."

"He's not a regular."

"He isn't even someone who'd been in there occasionally. I watched their expressions, their eyes and he didn't register with any of them in the least."

"Meaning that actually makes it a little more likely he's our guy."

"Not for sure," Wire cautioned. "We can't know that for sure. But my gut tells me—"

"It's him."

"Oh yeah, it's totally him. It's Rubens."

"This is another piece, Dara. With those two slices of footage, we have height, possible weight, mannerisms. And while we don't yet have identification, we have something that we can continue to go with and push. We have him, a picture—nobody has ever had that before. We've made women who fit Rubens profile paranoid, hopefully, and now we have someone for them to be paranoid about."

Mac's cell phone started ringing. "It's Galloway," he reported to Wire and then answered. "Senior Agent Galloway, tell me good news. Uh huh...uh huh... Another one? I don't really... So what makes this one seem on the up and up? Hmm. Okay, yeah, text me the address."

"Another what?"

"Another woman who had a gentlemen caller for a while," Mac explained. "She saw the footage on television this morning and said she thought he looked like a man she was dating who up and disappeared."

"Her name?"

"Martha Schreiber."

Twenty minutes later, having weaved their way through the later morning rush traffic, they pulled up to the townhouse of Martha Schreiber on 8th Street NW between Randolph Street and Shepherd Street NW.

"Look at that, she's a half-block from a Fourth District police station," Mac observed wryly.

"Well, we know who to call for backup," Wire noted.

Martha Schreiber opened the front door before they could knock. "I must have struck a chord if it's you two who showed up."

Martha fit the profile physically. After five minutes of interviewing her, she also seemed to fit the mental and personality profile for a Rubens victim as well.

"So start at the beginning, Martha," Dara started. "Tell us about the first time you met this man."

"Walter," she replied. "Walter Olson."

"Right, so when did you meet Walter?"

"The first time was at the Rogue Art Gallery two months ago at a show for local artists. I like to go to those, I like to support the struggling artists." Martha looked away, as if assessing herself. "I feel like I know what it's like to struggle."

"And what happened?" Mac pressed.

"He struck up a conversation with me. I must have gone to events like that for years and no man ever spoke to me. Heck, no one ever noticed me. But Walter? He did."

"And what did you talk about?"

"Art. Local artists. Famous painters. We certainly were interested in the same kinds of things."

"Did this man, Walter, ever mention the artist Peter Paul Rubens?"

"I thought you might ask that, Agent McRyan. I honestly don't remember Rubens coming up. I remember Van Gogh, Cezanne, Michelangelo, all the famous names and paintings, but I don't think Rubens ever came up."

"And what did Walter look like?" Wire asked.

"He was, I suppose, five ten, probably two-hundred pounds, maybe a little more than that. He was, like me, a little overweight."

"What did his face look like?"

"He wore a small beard. I guess what you would call a Fu man beard. It was just around his mouth."

"How about hair color?"

"Black with some flecks of gray," Martha replied, giving it some thought. "It was as if his hair was turning, you know. I figured he was in his forties age-wise so if he was getting some gray that seemed normal to me. He wore glasses as well."

"And how did he wear his hair?"

"He wore it a little longer—he combed it straight back and it was a little long in the back."

"Like a mullet?" Wire asked, smiling. "Was it business in the front and party in the back?"

"No," Martha replied shaking her head, but with a small smile. "He wasn't some hockey guy. It was just longer, and in the back, it ended at his collar and just seemed to curl up a little. It was a little like Michael Douglas in *Wall Street*. It was a little of the Gordon Gecko look, I guess."

"Okay, I get that description," Dara replied, jotting it down in her notepad.

"So what made you think the guy you saw on television this morning was Walter?"

"He didn't look exactly like Walter, but there were some similarities. What made me think it was him, though, was the way he moved in that video footage. Walter moved with just a slight hunch and a shuffle, like he took short steps. The man in the video walked like that. Then they replayed your press conference from yesterday. I was, as you asked yesterday, Agent McRyan, honest with myself and thought maybe I should call. It is better to be safe than sorry."

"Do you know where Walter lives?" Mac inquired.

"No."

"Did you have a phone number for him?"

"No, I didn't."

"What number did he have for you?"

"He called me at work and he called me here at home."

"On your home line?"

"Yes."

"Do you have a cell?"

"Yes."

"Did he ever call you on that?"

"No. I gave him the number, but he never called on my cell. It seemed odd. Most everyone else calls me on the cell, not that I get a ton of calls."

Mac and Wire shared a knowing look. "Martha, we're going to need to get your home phone records. Are you okay with that?"

"Yes."

"And for your work phone as well."

"I don't want any trouble with my employer."

Wire smiled. "Don't worry about that. We'll handle that and there will be no problems."

"Okay," Mac started. "I want to go back to when you first met Walter. Tell me what happened after you met. Did you go on a date?"

"We went on a few," Martha answered, pulling a pillow up to her chest nervously, the idea, if not the reality that she was a target of Rubens setting in. "After I met him, a week later we had coffee. Then another week or so after that we met at another showing at the Wilson Gallery and then some days later we had dinner at a little out of the way place up in Falls Church. It was after that night I never heard from him again."

"Why do you think that is?"

"I don't know."

"Tell me about the dinner," Mac pressed.

"It seemed totally fine. We were having a nice time discussing an upcoming showing at another art gallery that included a discussion with a professor from James Madison. It was really a lovely night because we were talking about possibly going to the showing. I was so happy as well because a friend of mine who I hadn't seen in a long time was there that night and swung by the table. It was so good to see her and reconnect and it was kind of fun to have someone to introduce Walter to."

"Did you introduce her to Walter?"

"Yes."

"And after that night, you never saw or heard from him again?"

"No."

Mac and Wire shared another knowing look. Walter was Rubens.

"Do you think Walter, or the man I thought was Walter, is really this killer Rubens?"

"We think it's very possible," Mac replied ominously. "You fit the profile to a T of a Rubens victim. We think he follows his possible victims for some time before he approaches them. During that time, he follows, he conducts research to learn as much as he can about the women. Once he approaches them, he goes on quiet dates with them, building up their trust and confidence. And it works because he's done all the leg work, learning what is important to the woman, what her interests are, what she likes, what her history is. However, as part of that, we also think he has certain rules that he follows and one rule is that he never meets family or friends. Not one victim has ever had a friend or family member be able to describe Rubens."

"How come?" Martha asked.

"They never met him because we think he follows this rule. Now this man you call Walter, he disappeared and never contacted you again after he met your friend. No follow-up contact, no explanation. He just up and disappears, cutting you off cold."

Martha simply nodded, now curled up in a ball on her couch, suddenly petrified.

"Martha, it is a good thing you called," Dara said as she moved over to the couch and sat down next to Martha, touching her arm, comforting her. It wasn't hard to see her processing everything, realizing just how close she came to being a victim.

Mac leaned forward in his chair. "Martha, I need you to come with us. We're going to sit you down with an FBI sketch artist," Mac stated. "And I want you to call your friend. I will have a patrol car pick her up and we'll bring her down to the FBI field office to sit down with a sketch artist as well."

"Isn't the footage from the video you already have enough?"

"More is better," Dara answered, looking Martha in the eye. "That footage is from a distance. You were more up close. With a sketch artist, you can provide more fine detail that we can't get from the video. That will help us have a better chance to identify him. The clock is running and he has another victim in his sights."

"He disguises himself," Mac added. "And we think he constantly changes up his look, so the more descriptions, the more details, the better chance we'll have."

"Do you think he'll come after me still?"

Mac nodded. "It's possible, which is why after you're done with the sketch artist, agents are going to come back here with you while you pack a bag. We're going to put you under protection until this is over. So what do you say? Are you ready to come down and describe Walter to our sketch artist?"

"Okay," she nodded. "Let me get my purse."

~

Rubens was drinking a coffee, walking along the sidewalk on the opposite side of the street, observing the front of Martha's town-house, evaluating a potential approach when a black BMW X5 pulled up. Out of the Beamer exited McRyan and Wire.

He froze, looking right at the two of them.

Thankfully, the two special agents were oblivious to his presence, just an anonymous man walking on the sidewalk on the opposite side of the street. But they were going to Schreiber's house.

Forty-five minutes later, he'd walked to the other end of the street to the south. He observed from that comfortable distance when McRyan and Wire walked down the front steps behind Martha.

He was too late.

~

Mac followed Martha and Wire down the steps and the group walked north towards the X5. The two women were talking about jewelry, Dara easing Martha's discomfort by asking about the long necklace she was wearing.

"I get a box once a month from this company," Martha explained eagerly. "It always includes two dresses, two blouses and some jewelry. I keep what I want and send the rest back. This necklace was in last month's box."

"It's really nice. What is the name of this company?" Dara asked. "I should look into it. I never have time to shop."

Mac's phone started ringing. "Excuse me," he said and then answered his phone. "McRyan."

"Nice press conference yesterday," the masked voice greeted.

"I thought I gave it a certain flair," Mac stated, snapping his fingers at Wire. "You disagree, Rubens? I thought I described the current situation, what you do, your potential victims, and how you hunt them quite accurately. It's how we found that video footage of you."

"It was fiction, Mac."

"No, it wasn't, and you know it," Mac replied, putting his hand to his ear so he could hear over the siren of the patrol car passing him. "Otherwise you wouldn't be calling."

"To the contrary. You think you know, but you don't know anything about me," Rubens replied, his voice fading out due to the sound of a siren.

A siren.

Mac slowly spun around.

"Really, you sick son of a bitch? You don't think I know anything about you," Mac continued as he scanned the area southbound on 8th, walking more briskly toward the sound of the siren. "You don't think I'm starting to figure you out? To understand how your mind works?"

"You think one press conference scares me? Do you know how many press conferences have been held about me? That one was no different than any of the others held about me over the last ten years. It won't help you."

"It already has," Mac replied. He started to focus on a man a block and a half down, walking away on the opposite side of the street. The man was of medium height, maybe a little pudgy, wearing a gray hoodie and black baseball cap and moving just a little too quickly to not be noticed. The man was holding a cell phone to his right ear, walking away but then taking a sly look back. "You're absolutely certain it won't help?"

"Absolutely—you've got shit."

"Then how come I'm looking at you walking south on NW 8th Street. Gray hoodie, black ball cap, cell phone to your right ear?"

The man glanced back again and locked eyes with Mac.

Mac took a step toward the man and then he knew for certain it was Rubens.

Rubens took off.

"It's him! It's him!" Mac screamed as he took off at a full sprint. Wire was right behind him, still on the phone, but now calling the MPD.

"Where?" Wire yelled from behind.

"West side, gray hoodie," Mac yelled as he crossed the street, dodging cars.

"I don't see him! I don't see him!"

"He just turned the corner to the right," Mac replied, now across the street and hauling ass down the sidewalk at a full sprint.

Mac veered right around the corner and the street turned southwest and straight ahead was a mass of people at a three-way corner for NW 8th, New Hampshire Avenue and Quincy Street where a multi-vehicle accident had occurred. It was where the patrol unit was heading. It's where other patrol units were arriving.

"Where did he go?" Mac asked out loud as he approached the crowd around the accident, took out his identification and raised his voice. "Listen up! I'm an FBI agent. Did anyone see a man with a gray hoodie and black baseball hat running this direction? Anyone?"

All he got were shakes of the head from the bystanders who'd been more focused on the accident.

"Damn it."

Mac ran across the street to the crowd on the south side of Quincy Avenue, holding up his identification again. "Did anyone see a man in a gray hoodie and black hat running along here? Anyone?"

"Hey, aren't you the guy after that serial killer?"

"Yes, did you see the man I'm describing?"

"I saw a guy in a gray hoodie run cross the street over there." The man pointed west on Quincy. "and then he ran between the buildings. Hey, was that man the—"

Mac didn't wait for the man to finish his question, instead sprinting west to the gap between the buildings, the apartment buildings to the right running southwest on New Hampshire and the buildings to his left running along the east side of Georgia Avenue running south. He pulled out his Sig Sauer as Wire came up behind, gun already drawn. They quickly but cautiously worked their way through the gap, a small, narrowing alley between the buildings.

Mac scanned the right, Wire the left.

They came out of the walkway, which opened out to a large open space filled with people. There was a bus stand to their right, taxis lined up to the left and the Georgia Avenue-Petworth Station for the Metro straight ahead.

They both scanned the area, turning, looking for any sign in the mass of people for the gray hoodie, black baseball cap and sunglasses.

"You've got to be kidding me," Wire growled.

"You take the bus stand," Mac gestured, "I'll try the subway."

"Close the doors, close the doors, close the doors," Rubens kept saying in his head as he anxiously watched the stairway down to the subway platform, his hoodie in his right hand and the black ball cap in the left.

He expected McRyan or Wire to come flying down the steps any second.

Even as the doors closed and the train started pulling away from the platform, he peered nervously at the steps.

He exhaled a sigh of relief and then checked the map for the next station.

He wasn't out of the woods yet.

Mac rushed down the steps and stopped three short of the bottom to scan the crowd. He looked to his left as the train for the northbound track approached.

There was a man with a gray hoodie but he was tall and thin.

He noticed two black baseball caps, but a woman wore one and another was on the head of a man in his early twenties.

Mac pivoted to his right to the emptier platform for the southbound train. There were three people standing on that side. He approached a woman in a stylish dark blue workout suit with a black nylon athletic shoulder bag. "How long ago did the southbound train leave?"

"I don't know, maybe five minutes ago," she replied. "I think I just missed it."

Mac reached for his cell phone.

The doors opened for the Columbia Street Station and Rubens quickly exited the train. The black baseball cap was now rolled into the hoodie that he carried under his right arm. He rapidly ascended the steps up to the street level and immediately started walking east on Irving Street. He'd made it a half block east on Irving when a police patrol unit suddenly turned onto the street and raced by, lights flashing.

He kept walking, increasing his pace.

A few seconds later, he looked back to see that the unit stopped at the station. The two officers exited the vehicle and ran toward the steps down to the Metro station platform.

Mac and Wire braked hard to a stop at the Columbia Street station. There were two patrol units awaiting their arrival.

"I think we missed it," a uniform officer reported. "When we arrived the train had already pulled out of the station."

Wire was already on her phone, having Galloway get the footage for the video cameras for both the Columbia Street station and Georgia-Petworth Station.

"Son of a bitch," Mac muttered. "We had him."

15

"IT'S LIKE A DRUG AND HE'S AN ADDICT."

He was in safe territory now; at least as safe as southeast DC could be.

From the Columbia Street Metro Station, he walked eight blocks east, dumped the gray hoodie and black hat in a random garbage can and two blocks later picked up a cab that dropped him off near the Lincoln Monument. He blended into the midday Saturday tourist crowd and walked as casually as he could along the National Mall toward the Capitol at the other end.

At the Washington Monument, he stopped and purchased a blue sweatshirt, red golf visor and a pair of cheap wrap-around sunglasses. Around the back side of the Capitol, he hailed a cab across the street from the U.S. Supreme Court building. Fifteen minutes later, the taxi dropped him eight blocks from his final destination.

As he made his way back, he continued to check back over his shoulder, walking in a block to block zigzag pattern with the final destination being his small office in Southeast DC. There were no pursuers.

He finally allowed himself to breathe easy when five blocks short of the office a patrol unit rolled by and gave him nary a look. A second patrol unit a few blocks later ignored him as well.

The long trek back gave him the opportunity to reflect on his strategy. Undoubtedly the manhunt would now be heightened with the chase. His obvious play would be to go into hiding and let the heat dissipate.

But with that, his next target could get nervous, could start wondering and having questions.

She could call McRyan. At a minimum, in an abundance of caution, she might cancel.

There were thirty hours left. She needed to be put at ease. The suspicions could not be allowed to creep in.

He entered the dilapidated office building via the narrow rear entrance and went immediately into the back room. In the office, he opened the metal cabinet, began assessing his appearance options and contemplated his look for his next move. He'd spent many hours trying to get a read on Eleanor before he'd approached her. She so loved coffee shops and poetry, so he'd gone with a little more of a beatnik look with her. It was a look that the FBI did not yet have, so that was an element working in his favor.

With first a small dollop of face glue and then his two index fingers, he expertly pasted a small black beard on the bottom of his chin and then a small soul patch underneath his bottom lip. Over his head, he pulled on a black turtleneck and then slipped into some black pants and black loafers. Rather than the beret he'd worn before, he selected a black leather newsboy hat and slipped on some black sunglasses with green tinted lenses. In totality, it was a look entirely different than anything remotely close to what McRyan now had. It was like nothing the FBI was warning women to look out for.

In the mid-afternoon, with the manhunt of the area around Columbia Street station cooling in intensity, Mac and Wire retreated back to the FBI field office and out of the media spotlight. The media monitoring the police scanners heard the Rubens name, heard there was a sighting and where and they descended on the area.

It was good news and bad news. They had another look at Rubens, they would have two new sketches shortly and the day's excitement kept the story front and center; maybe there would be another Martha or two out there that would come forward.

That was the good.

The bad was self-explanatory.

"I can't believe it," Wire groaned, leaning over in her chair, staring down into her coffee. She looked back up to Mac, holding her right index finger and thumb an inch apart. "We were this close, Mac. We were *this* fucking close."

Mac simply nodded, not saying anything, sitting back in his chair staring at the white ceiling tiles, too angry to speak. They were *that* close.

Down the hall, Martha Schreiber was meeting with a sketch artist regarding the man she'd met that went by the name of Walter Olson. Her friend had recently arrived, the one who met Walter up in the restaurant in Falls Church. She was meeting with a separate artist.

An FBI tech stuck his head in the room. "Agent McRyan, I think we have something you should see."

Mac and Wire followed the agent to a small office containing a wall of monitors.

The tech sat down at his desk, his partner to his left. "We're working with a series of cameras for the Georgia-Petworth Metro station. This one to the left is off the stairway down from the street. The other one is for the platform. You said we should be looking for a man with a gray hoodie and black baseball hat. We might have that."

The agent rolled the tape. A medium-height man wearing black sunglasses rushed quickly down the steps, weaving his way through people down to the platform for the southbound train. The man went through the middle door of the train and turned around, intently watching the platform and steps, breathing hard.

"No hat or hoodie," Wire states.

"No, he's holding them," Mac exclaimed, pointing at the screen. "The sweatshirt is rolled up and tucked under his left arm."

"Why not just toss them?" the tech asked.

"DNA!" Mac and Wire exclaimed in unison.

"He couldn't risk it," Wire added.

"So he was as careful here, even under immense strain and pressure, as he was at all of those murder scenes," Mac observed. "He is hardwired to leave nothing behind. Maybe that tells us something, too."

"He's in the system?" the tech asked.

"That's possible," Mac answered. "Although even if he was, we don't have any DNA evidence from any of our murder scenes to tie to him."

"So where did he get off the subway?" Wire asked.

"The next stop south," the tech answered, pulling video up on another screen. "It looks to us like he gets off at the Columbia Street station."

He rolled the footage as the train pulled into the station. Once the doors started opening, the man burst out onto the platform and pushed his way through people to the steps up to the street. "That's our guy," the tech pointed with his finger. "The hoodie is under his right arm."

Rubens quickly made his way up the steps to the street level and disappeared from view.

"Were you able to track him from there?" Mac asked.

"Not yet," the tech answered, shaking his head lightly and then on another screen pulled up a street map of the area around the Columbia Street Metro station. "If he went west, there is a shopping and restaurant area so we might find some security camera and footage that direction. Agents are on the hunt. If he went east," the tech sighed. "Well, if he did that we're probably boned. That's residential and we'd lose him in there. It's all houses. MPD doesn't have any surveillance equipment in there."

The techs ran the tape over and over again with Mac and Wire, looking for any possible additional nuggets. It was surveillance footage, not of terrible quality but it wasn't high definition and their man was disguised. The techs ran the tape slowly; taking stills of the best facial shots of the man they thought was Rubens.

By this time, Galloway and Delmonico had entered, left and re-entered the room. "I've got people going back out and they'll be combing the areas west and east of the station for any other footage we can get our hands on," Galloway reported. "I'm not optimistic, but you never know."

"If nothing else," Mac replied, looking to Wire, "we have these stills."

"And these sketches," Delmonico added, handing them around the room. "From Martha Schreiber and her friend."

The sketch artists came up with two similar sketches. Both sketches displayed a man with a round face and a salt-and-pepper goatee. The only real noticeable difference between the two sketches was that on the one composed with Martha's assistance, the man's nose was bulbous on the end, with one nostril slightly larger and angled up more than the other.

The sketches, however, were different than the man in the video. The Columbia Street station surveillance showed him without the goatee, although the nose seemed somewhat consistent. The sketches, while not a match for the bookstore, nevertheless revealed some common physical features with the facial hair and glasses.

Was it the same guy?

The body shape and height said yes.

The way the man moved, slowly at the bookstore, more rapidly in the chase from the morning, suggested it was. The man's movements were not athletic. He moved with straight arms and almost a shuffle at the store, but that may have been a bit of an act because in the surveillance video when he had to flee, the straight arms were there but the shuffle was gone and while he was no world-class athlete, he moved well and quickly enough to evade them.

"It would be hard to get a conviction with that," Delmonico offered.

"Conviction, hah," Mac answered. Grace was thinking too far ahead. "At this point I just want to identify him. Do that and then I can start worrying about building a case for a prosecution. And on the topic of identifying him, we are getting closer."

"The sketches and the surveillance don't really match," Wire suggested.

"No, they don't," Mac replied as he waved for her to follow him back to the conference room. "And I'm not surprised, by the way. He's always in some sort of a disguise or different look. He's something of a chameleon."

"But we have some commonalities," Wire replied, going along.

"Yes," Mac replied as he stood at the whiteboard and posted the sketches and still photos of the man they thought was Rubens. "There are some things he can't change."

Their subject was Caucasian, approximately five feet ten inches tall and of average build. "I'd estimate between one hundred eighty-five and two hundred pounds," Mac speculated.

If the pictures were of the same man, it was apparent that he was wearing disguises. He had a beard in the sketches and surveillance video from the bookstore and Vietnam Memorial. There was no beard this morning based on the surveillance footage. But there was the noted similarity in movement. They also now knew that their man was approximately 5'10" and of average build.

"He does have a bulbous nose," Wire noted. "Like there's a little ball on the end of it and that left nostril is bigger."

And there was a pattern. "He's using beards, goatees, fu-mans and full beards," Mac noted. "He is always wearing glasses of some kind —sun, tinted or regular, all kinds of different styles. And our man likes hats—baseball and tam caps, it seems."

"You definitely are developing a picture," April Greene added agreeably. "In the last few days you've developed more information on him that anyone has in the last ten years combined." She scanned the whiteboard. "This ... is getting interesting now."

"One lucky break could do it," Mac concurred. "Unless of course, we got our lucky break earlier and completely blew it."

They had a name now as well. Walter Olson.

It was as vanilla a name as there was and undoubtedly not Rubens's real name.

It made Mac think of Minnesota. He wouldn't have been

surprised if there were hundreds of Walter Olsons in Minnesota, Iowa, Wisconsin and North and South Dakota. There were thousands of Norwegian Olsons in Minnesota, along with Andersons, Petersons, Gustafsons, and Johnsons. No matter, if they found a Walter Olson that had some similarity they were checking it out, anywhere in the country.

And the events of the last twelve hours had left them with some-thing of a photo array now.

"We need to get this updated information out," Mac stated. "Let's make these all public."

"I'll take care of it," Galloway stated. "It'll all be out within the hour."

Wire opened the top on a Diet Coke. "I wonder if maybe after today he's spooked. Who knows, maybe he runs away."

"I don't think so," Greene answered, going into profiling mode. "I don't think he'll shrink away. His history says he'll finish what he's started because he's put too much into it. To walk away now, wait a few years until he can come out of hiding is not something I think he'll do. He loves the attention and the danger. I mean, think about it. He gives you clues...he gives you a clock. He called you when he was within a block or two of you today. By doing what you've done, you've *heightened* the experience for him. You've made it an even *bigger* thrill. It's like a drug and he's an addict."

"He's not going to stop, is he?" Mac asked. "He's not going to run now that we're putting on some heat."

"No," Greene answered. "Not in the least. For him the game is on. You two have gotten closer to him than anyone ever has. My read is he'll view this as an even greater challenge and he'll do whatever he has to do to rise up and meet it. It's a game to him and you're only to half-time."

"He's not hiding, is he?" Mac asked, although he knew the answer.

"No," Greene replied. "He's plotting his next move."

Rubens walked into the coffee shop and spied Eleanor sitting at a table in the corner. He ordered a coffee and then made his way to the back table.

"Eleanor, fancy finding you here," he greeted enthusiastically, walking up with his to-go coffee.

"Hi," Eleanor answered brightly, a wide smile of happy surprise. "Do you want to sit down?"

"I only have a few minutes, but I'd love to."

They both sipped their coffees and talked comfortably until he was satisfied she was not at all wary. "I'm so sorry, Eleanor. I'd love to stay but I need to go to meet my friend. I'm already late as it is."

"I'm really looking forward to tomorrow night," Eleanor said with a smile.

"As am I. So 8:00 p.m. tomorrow then?"

"Yes."

"I will see you then."

Eleanor watched with a smile as he walked out the front of the coffee shop and away down the street. A minute later, the barista came over with a big smile.

"Ellie, is that the new guy?"

"Yes. I was so surprised he came in here that I forgot to introduce you."

"He seemed really nice and looked kind of cool and mysterious dressed in all that black. What's his name?"

"Tom. Tom Edwards."

16

"I THINK YOU TWO ARE GOING TO MAKE FINE DETECTIVES."

Mac perused the menu of the Fillmore. He didn't really have a big decision to make; he was having a burger. It was simply a matter of which one. He ultimately decided on the President Taft. The burger was built much like the twenty-seventh president: it was big, two half-pound patties, three kinds of cheese, three bacon slices, an onion ring, an egg, not to mention lettuce and tomato. The burger might as well have been named the Heart Attack. Paddles and a "clear" would probably be needed after he finished it.

The Fillmore had three big-screen televisions. Two of the televisions were set on sports, the other on CNN. Once again, he noticed the still photos from the various surveillance videos and the two sketches were on the screen.

One thing Mac couldn't complain about was a lack of media coverage. The message was getting out. "Problem is, who he was is not who he is going to be," he lamented bitterly.

"And Walter Olson is an alias that will no longer be used," Wire added.

Mac nodded in agreement. "That won't be a problem for him. There is no way he would go through this much planning and preparation and not have worked *that* problem out. I'm sure he has more than a few aliases and I'm sure he doesn't use the same one for multiple women."

"Someone must be making him identifications," Dara replied, looking away in thought. "We could look into people we know who do that."

"But who and where? He could be using anyone, in any city and maybe even someone not in this country. I don't see how we could even begin to investigate that."

"We could at least look into the local people."

"Yeah, we could," Mac answered dismissively.

"Hey, come on. I'm just trying to be helpful."

"I know," he replied with a sigh and a head shake. He took a long pull from his beer glass. "I know you are. Sorry."

Their waiter appeared with two more beers and took their burger orders.

Dara studied her partner and read his anger for something else. "So what's really eating you?"

"I keep going over this morning," Mac muttered. "It was just the two of us. We should have had help ... backup ... resources. Hell, the MPD police station was right there. Right fucking there and yet we went naked." His head slumped down. "What was I thinking?"

"How could we have known he'd be watching?" Dara asked, not agreeing. "How? How could we have known that?"

"Because we had to, Dara. He's calling me. He's obviously researched us. We went public. We tried to draw him and other women out. And what do you know?"

"We actually did," Wire replied with a sigh, shaking her head. "It actually worked. Go figure."

"And we weren't prepared," Mac griped angrily. "We could have that son of a bitch today. This should be over. We could be sitting here celebrating and nobody else would have died." Mac took a long drag from his beer. "We could have had that asshole this morning and he slipped right through our hands. Hell, he can't run for shit and moves like a penguin and we couldn't catch him."

"We did get Martha Schreiber to come forward," Dara stated.

"She gave us a description. Her friend gave us a description. We have a lot more on Rubens now than we did."

"So?"

"So today wasn't a total loss. Quit beating yourself up. And you know what? There might be another Martha or two out there. We just need them to step up."

"Yeah," Mac answered, and then a dark look overtook his face. "They should step up before he gets them."

"What do you mean?"

"I mean Rubens might not have been there following us this morning. He might have been—"

"Re-hunting Martha?"

Mac nodded.

"I wonder if there are others?" Dara asked.

"It's possible."

"So again, maybe after the events of the last couple of days, they'll come forward."

"If they don't, and even if they do, I'm at Ruston's tomorrow. I'm finding that damn clue if it kills me."

Wire looked off in the distance with a slight shake of the head.

It was Mac's turn to scrutinize his partner. "Spit it out."

"What?"

"What do you mean what?"

"Is spending your day locked up in Audrey Ruston's house the best option? Is that the best way to beat this guy?" Dara asked.

"I don't know," Mac replied. "The suggestion box is wide open. I'm all ears—what do you have?"

"We could be out pushing the pictures."

"They are being pushed," Mac countered. "They're on every media outlet available. Galloway is running the photos and sketches through every photo recognition program we have. Uniforms and detectives are out all over town. So that's being done. What can I possibly add to that?" He paused and stared at his beer glass. "Dara, unless we get some new lead to pursue, what else would you have me do?"

"I don't know," Dara replied. "It's just that it feels like sitting around and waiting and you never ..."

"Sit around and wait," Mac finished and took a gulp from his beer. "I agree. Except this really isn't sitting around and waiting. The clue? It's there. The name is there somewhere. Rubens left it behind. He always leaves it behind. I just have to find it. I just have to get inside his mind and figure it out."

"Just don't get too far inside his mind," Dara cautioned.

"Copy that."

An hour later, the burgers and another beer devoured, Mac pushed his way through the back door of the townhouse to find Sally in the kitchen, placing a wine glass into the upper rack of the dishwasher.

"You should check out the living room," she suggested.

In the living room, he found a large stack of wrapped wedding gifts.

"They've started arriving," she reported.

"Wow," Mac answered. "Everyone we invited to the wedding is still coming, aren't they?"

"Yes," Sally answered, slipping her left arm through his right. "But they don't necessarily want to have to bring the gift. So FedEx and UPS it is."

It had been a lousy day but seeing the gifts did make him realize better days, much better days, lay ahead. "It's almost here, isn't it?"

"A month away," Sally replied. "Are you ready?"

"I can't wait," he replied, moving his right arm up around her shoulder and pulling her close. He kissed her lightly. "I can't wait."

"You look tired," she noted, touching his cheek and looking up at his face. She lightly ran her thumb under his jaw. "Your eyes are baggy."

"That happens when you haven't slept for something like forty hours."

"Then let's get you up to bed."

"I need a shower first."

Sally led him up the steps and then went in and started the

shower for him while he slowly got out of his clothes. Mac stepped into the shower, closed his eyes and let the warm water run over his body. While he stood there, he thought back to something Wire had said.

"Just don't get too far inside his head."

As he let the hot water run over his body, his worry was whether Rubens was getting inside his.

Mac could front it all he wanted, but the case was getting to him. One victim he could live with because he wasn't even in the case yet at that point. Then the second victim, he could handle that, but now there would be a third with another in the offing and he couldn't let go of the fact that it should be over. They should have caught him this morning.

He leaned forward, putting his hands on the shower wall, keeping his eyes closed and let the heat of the water and the thickness of the steam work him over.

Mac needed his mind clear.

He needed to keep his cool and not let the clock and the pressure get the best of him. *Keep calm, forget the last play, and make the next play* was something his football coach used to say to him when Mac was quarterback. *If you keep thinking about the last play, you won't make the next one. You can't go back in time so let it go, learn from it and move on.*

That was sage advice. He had to let the morning go and make the next play.

The shower door creaked open behind him.

He turned to see Sally stepping into the shower. His mouth opened but she put her fingers to his lips. "Turn around and just ... breathe. Close your eyes and relax."

He did as ordered. Sally soaped his back with her right hand and lightly rubbed his shoulder muscles with her left. "You need to stop thinking about the case, even for just five minutes. Just let it go."

"I was just thinking the same thing," Mac answered, his eyes closed. He leaned forward, his arms and head resting against the tile of the shower wall. "It's easier said than done."

"Well, maybe what you need then is a distraction," Sally said quietly as her right hand wrapped around to his front and she soaped his stomach. He could feel the softness of her breasts as she leaned into him from behind. Slowly she moved her hand lower.

"Ahh, well now, that is ... distracting."

11:03 p.m. was what his watch read as MPD Detective Lincoln Coolidge slowly made his way into the Homicide Division. He made it to his little cubicle and plopped himself down into his desk chair and went about slipping off his dress shoes. The overtime the Rubens case was providing was an extremely welcome addition to the bank account. There were four mouths at home to feed but the nonstop week was wearing him down. He opened his lower right desk drawer. Inside, he kept a pair of Birkenstock sandals, which he pulled out and slipped onto his round fat feet. The other item inside the drawer was a bottle of bourbon, which he opened and poured some of the contents into his Washington Wizards coffee cup.

"Ahh," he murmured as he kicked his feet up onto the desktop and sipped from his coffee cup.

Then there was a ruckus and a smile washed over Coolidge's face. A minute later two familiar faces were standing in the entrance to his cubicle: Stretch and Hart, both new detectives to homicide. Stretch was six-six and Hart wasn't really named Hart. His name was actually Kenny Smith but they called him Hart after the actor Kevin Hart. The personality, not to mention the shorter stature, made the name fit.

"Linc, ya got that regulatory-violative bourbon bottle around?" Hart asked.

Coolidge nodded to the lower drawer. Hart opened the drawer and proceeded to pour a small amount into his coffee and into the top of the Diet Coke bottle his much taller partner was holding.

"Any progress today?" Stretch asked. Both of them had helped Linc earlier in the week but had been pulled away in the morning to investigate a case of their own.

"Not much. A lot of running around, talking to people who knew the first and second victim, using some video, pictures, sketches and descriptions McRyan and Wire have come up with," Linc replied. "Unfortunately there was no recognition. We struck out."

"The day wasn't a total waste. Did I hear it right that they might have had eyes on the artist earlier today?" Hart asked.

"It's Rubens, Hart," Stretch corrected. "This asshole is called Rubens."

"For some reason, I can't remember that fuckin' name," Hart waved dismissively. "All I know is he's killing big women who look like the bitches some painter painted, so he's the artist."

"You did hear right," Linc noted, pouring just a little more bourbon into his coffee mug. "McRyan and Wire had eyes on him and nearly caught the bastard." He related the events of the morning.

"Too bad," Stretch muttered.

"No kidding," Linc answered as he sat up, crossed his right leg over his left and started massaging his right foot. "Man, my feet are really barking at me with all this street time. So what case has the two of you so occupied at such a late hour on a Saturday night in our fair Capitol?"

"Nothing quite as exciting," Hart answered. "We have a woman who was murdered in her small backyard. She was hit from behind, her purse was taken and her money and credit cards are gone."

"Looks like a mugging gone very, *very* bad," Stretch added.

"Any witnesses?"

"Nada."

"Naturally. So what's the victim's story?" Coolidge asked.

"The vic is a lady named Gwendolyn Waxe," Hart answered. "Worked as a librarian. It appears that she stopped at a local corner store for groceries on her way home. She got home, pulled her car into her small one-car garage, got out and grabbed the grocery bags and when she came out of the back door of the garage to walk to the house—"

"Whammo!" Stretch reported, striking down with his right hand. "She was smashed in the back of the head with a hammer."

"A hammer? That'll do the trick," Linc stated, taking another sip from his coffee cup.

"It did. Killer did it all to get away with a couple of hundred bucks at most," Hart noted glumly. "We have the credit cards on watch but nothing has popped."

"I can't for the life of me figure the motive to kill someone like this for a couple of bucks," Stretch moaned. "It was completely senseless."

"It's DC—people have killed for less," Coolidge stated, having seen plenty of inexplicable crimes in his many years on the job. "Unless it's random, there has to be some reason someone would want her dead."

"Not that we found," Stretch answered, running his hand through his thinning brown hair. "We spoke to her neighbors, people she works with and friends and they couldn't think of anyone who would want to harm her in any way. She was a quiet and private lady, loved books and going to museums. She had a cat and a nice house."

"There must be something else, then," Coolidge replied. "Again, unless it was just random. It could just be random, I suppose. Like I said, it's DC."

"That's what we're thinking, Linc," Hart replied. "But—"

"It doesn't just feel random." Stretch finished. "Something is off. I almost get the feeling like it was *intended* to look random."

"To cover something else?" Coolidge asked and he started to sense that Stretch was leading to something.

Stretch nodded and handed the case file to Coolidge. "Take a look. Tell me what you see."

Coolidge took a drink from his coffee cup and set it on the desk, then opened the homicide file and started thumbing through the pictures, stopping on the victim. First it was her DMV photo and then the photos from the crime scene. "She was a larger woman," Coolidge muttered. "She looks almost..."

"Rubenesque, doesn't she?" Hart noted.

Coolidge snorted, sat back and eyed his two detectives. "You two aren't here just for a drink, are you?"

"No," the young detectives replied in unison.

"McRyan's press conference has been running all day," Coolidge stated, now seeing it. "And then Mac and Wire almost catch the guy this morning."

"Right," Hart answered. "Because the woman McRyan and Wire are interviewing thinks she maybe met the asshole."

"And it looks like in fact she did," Linc reported.

"And lo and behold he's standing outside that house. Why?" Hart asks.

"We were thinking this Rubens character could be cleaning up after McRyan asked these women to be honest with themselves and come forward. Did they meet someone? Did someone come along and then disappear? The woman up in Columbia Heights called to say that might have happened to her. What if there were others?"

"Like Gwen here?" Coolidge asked, nodding in agreement.

"It's a weak tie, but she fits the profile and the way she was killed." Hart shook his head.

"The hammer?" Linc asked, knowing the answer.

"It's too much," Hart finished. "And then there was one other thing we found in the Notes app on her phone."

"Which is what?" Linc asked.

"The Rubens Hotline phone number," Hart replied.

Coolidge whistled. "No shit."

"So Linc, what do you think?" Stretch asked.

Coolidge smiled. "I think you two are going to make fine detectives."

17

"BEATNIKS."

The plan for the day was set early at the FBI field office in a meeting with Wire, Galloway, Delmonico and April Greene, now becoming more of a presence. There had been no new developments overnight on the Walter Olson lead.

"He disappeared," Delmonico reported, going to the map of DC posted on one of the whiteboards. "There is a traffic camera posted a block north on 14th Street, which runs north and south on the east side of the Metro Station. Unfortunately, the camera is not close, a good block away," she noted, running her finger south to north and circling the location of the camera. "We pulled the video for the time around when the train would have arrived at the Columbia Heights Station and we did see this one guy." She pointed on the screen in the distance. "He looks to be carrying something under his arms, he's about the right size, is moving quickly and he crosses 14th Street heading east." She played the video clip back twice. It was hard to make out but the man jogged across the street. Less than a minute later, patrol cars arrived on the scene.

"That's it?" Mac asked.

Delmonico nodded as they all watched the replay again. "If that's him, we missed him by less than a minute, maybe thirty seconds."

"How about the other direction, to the west?" Mac asked. The man he'd seen was probably Rubens, but had they looked everywhere?

"There is the local shopping mall and then a school that way," Galloway added, although not in a hopeful tone. "Surveillance camera coverage is spotty at best. We've been collecting it and still are but we haven't seen anyone fitting our description, at least yet. I'm not optimistic."

"So it looks like he went east on Irving then," Wire speculated.

"That would have been the smart move," Delmonico replied. "It's residential. Houses and apartments for several blocks so given what I see on the tape, we think east was the direction he went."

"I assume we've been conducting a canvas?" Mac asked.

Galloway nodded. "We still are but nobody recalls seeing anyone matching our description. It was mid-morning on a Friday, not a lot of foot traffic in that neighborhood and not a lot of people home."

"Are we checking with buses and taxi companies?"

Delmonico nodded. "Yes, but unfortunately nothing has popped. We checked every taxi with pick-ups within a six block radius and there was nothing. Same with buses, which do have cameras, but again—"

"Nothing," Mac finished bitterly.

"The guy is Houdini," Greene added. "He just doesn't panic."

"Would most serials panic?"

"Many are impulsive so the answer would be yes. However, Rubens is not impulsive. He is strategic," Greene noted.

"Because it's all a game to him," Mac answered, shaking his head in disgust. "Fucking genius whacko is what he is."

"He's not a genius," Wire answered. "He's not. We're gaining on him. We just need to catch him in time."

"So how do you do that?" Greene asked.

"The answer is at Audrey Ruston's," Mac replied. "It's my turn to see if I can figure it out."

Galloway had run special agents through Ruston's home nonstop since she was murdered, seeing if they could discern any pattern, any sign, any hint of what the clue would be. Two cryptanalysts from the FBI, as well as two codebreakers from the CIA, had given it a go with no success. Mac thought it worth a try, although he didn't think it was a code in that kind of sense. It was always the odd collection of items that wouldn't be a code but would have to simply be seen and understood in the proper context.

"Dara, if I need anything to be looked into, you're on it."

"Sounds good."

"I'm locking myself in unless anything comes up worth breaking off for," Mac stated.

"Before you go, I might have something," Coolidge announced as he walked into the room, Hart and Stretch with him. "While you were chasing Rubens over in Columbia Heights yesterday, my two guys found a murder victim who fits the Rubens profile." Linc ran down the background of Gwendolyn Waxe. "The kicker, Mac? She had the hotline number in her phone, typed in the Notes app."

"Seriously?" Mac asked, intrigued, taking a look at the phone. "My gosh, she typed it into her phone at 10:14 p.m."

"And you know what the particularly curious thing is about that, Mac?" Linc replied. "Is that the medical examiner just pegged time of death between 10:00 p.m. and midnight. So she puts this in the phone and perhaps minutes later, she's dead. I don't believe that to be coincidental, especially after your little chase escapade yesterday. Your boy is hunting the women who didn't make the cut to make sure they don't expose him."

"So what are you thinking?" Mac asked.

"I want to take another look at the case of Ms. Waxe here through the lens of our case. I want to go back two to three months and see if there are other facts that fit our profile such as a new guy."

Mac followed with a knowing smile. "And the new guy being a guy who suddenly stopped showing interest for some reason?"

"Exactly, my boy," Linc answered with a nod. "Exactly."

~

Mac pulled up in front of the duplex for Audrey Ruston. A patrol unit was parked in front and Mac dropped off coffee and a box of rolls for the two officers.

"Thanks," one patrol officer stated, digging into the rolls.

"And here I thought this detail would suck," the other officer answered, taking a sip of the warm coffee.

"Mary McRyan didn't raise no fool, boys. Enjoy," Mac stated.

The patrol officers were stationed out front to both keep people away and to be there if he needed anything. Mac hoped he would need something.

Mac had stopped back at Ruston's twice since the murder. They were brief stops, just enough to walk the second floor of the duplex and get a feel for it. He expected he would be back doing this very thing and a little familiarity was good, he thought.

Lisa White's townhouse was a ridiculous collection of books, paintings, pictures, plants and art pieces that made it impossible to find the clue to Audrey Ruston's name. The clue was ultimately Audrey Hepburn and the two movie posters for *Sabrina* and *Breakfast at Tiffany's*. The two movie prints with Audrey Hepburn, whose real last name was Ruston, was impossible, and intentionally so.

"He had to make the first one impossible," Mac said to Wire last night. "You can't make the first one remotely possible or easy. He can't run the risk of the game ending before it starts."

"There's no case, no chase, nothing if he does that," Wire had answered in agreement. "But if he likes the game so much, he has to give you a chance, doesn't he?"

"I think so, at least a small one. I just have to see it."

On that basis, Mac thought the clue to the identity of victim number three would be, relatively speaking, potentially more find-able. However, while Audrey's house was not overflowing with the clutter of Lisa White's, it wasn't without its objects of possibility.

Audrey, like Lisa White, loved her books. She was proud of her collection and took great care in its display throughout the apart-ment. They weren't stacked in corners and on tables. No, instead her hundreds of books were properly stored on the built-in bookshelves, orderly and tastefully placed.

She loved her artistry, with numerous paintings throughout the second level.

Mirrors were also prominent throughout. They were of different shapes and sizes, but she definitely liked mirrors and Mac understood the design thought behind it. "It makes the place seem a little bigger," he mused out loud.

Ruston was also a serious photographer. Her work was prominently displayed throughout the house, including in the living room where her body had been staged.

And then there were the knickknacks and baubles. He wondered if she ever left a small novelty shop without buying something.

"Easier, my ass," Mac mumbled as he set his backpack down onto the floor. He took out his laptop, set it on the floor along with his bag lunch and thermos of coffee. Then he took out the case file and selected the crime scene photos and started setting them onto the floor where the body had been located, settling in for the day.

Coolidge's first stop was the crime scene. "Take me through it again," he said to Stretch and Hart.

As ordered, Stretch and Hart walked Coolidge through the murder. "She pulls into the garage, parks and grabs her groceries," Hart explained, standing next to the car in the garage. Then he went to the back door and walked through. "She comes out this door, probably closes it and then takes maybe a step or two on the sidewalk and then—"

"He jumps from over behind the side of the garage and ... boom," Stretch hypothesized, "he came from the side of the garage over there, stepped behind her and hit her in the head not once, not twice, but three times."

"Brutal," Lincoln answered. "So is he sitting here in wait?"

"I suspect so," Stretch replied.

"How does he know she's coming home?"

"Because he was following her, Linc," Hart replied.

"Exactly," Linc agreed. "That's another reason I think this could be Rubens. The only way he can be there is he knows she's coming home."

Stretch opened his notebook and flipped through some pages. "She worked until 9:30 p.m. the night she was murdered. That was her regular shift at the library."

"And he would know that," Hart added. "Because if it is this artist guy, he's followed her, knows her schedule...the whole nine yards."

Coolidge and Hart let themselves into Gwen's house while Stretch stayed in the car making phone calls to Gwen's coworkers. Coolidge took the home office and rummaged through all the papers and drawers. There was a paper calendar on the desk but there were few notations in it. Her desk was orderly, with some stray papers loosely organized. The drawers were equally tidy, the files well labeled and filled with the usual bills, receipts, insurance policies, investment information, tax returns and a will. It was all standard, common and told Coolidge little.

Hart strolled into the home office. "I see no signs of a man or boyfriend or anything like that."

Stretch came into the room a moment later. "I might have something on that. We need to go see two ladies."

The two ladies were Gwen's coworkers, Leslie and Connie. Twenty minutes later, Hart, Stretch and Linc were sitting in a back office at the library with them.

"Leslie," Stretch started, "I want you to talk about what you mentioned to me on the phone a bit ago."

"You mean the part where Gwen had a boyfriend?"

"Yes, you and Connie thought she had a man in her life recently?"

"Do you think he might have killed her?" Connie asked.

"That's what we're trying to figure out," Linc answered. "So tell me about this man."

"Well, we didn't even think of it yesterday," Leslie stated. "I mean, it was a while ago that this guy was around."

"What is a while ago?" Hart asked.

"Two months, maybe," Connie answered. "Maybe six weeks."

"It was a bit of a blip on the radar," Leslie added. "Men, now that was something Gwen always struggled with."

"Oh yes, that's true," Connie agreed.

"Explain that to me," Linc asked while Hart and Stretch took notes.

"Well," Connie started, "Gwen wanted to have someone, a boyfriend. Unfortunately, what always seemed to happen is that if a man did show interest, she would completely suffocate the guy instead of letting it happen a little more naturally."

"That's so true," Leslie added, jumping in. "But this time she seemed to be letting it happen. She wasn't obsessing on it. She was waiting for him to call instead of forcing the situation. Everything seemed to be going okay."

"Then what happened?" Linc asked.

"He stopped calling," Leslie stated.

"It was like he up and disappeared," Connie added.

"Why?"

"We don't know. It really disappointed Gwen at the time. She liked the guy."

"What was his name?"

Leslie looked to Connie. "What was it, Bob?"

"Ben, I think," Connie answered. "Ben."

"Last name?"

They both shook their heads.

"Did either of you meet him?" Coolidge asked.

"Connie, you did, didn't you?"

"It was just by happenstance."

"What do you mean?" Stretch asked.

"My husband and I were at the Smithsonian, Renwick Gallery, and we saw her and this man as they were walking the exhibits. She loved to go there," Connie explained.

"You know, I remember you talking about that," Leslie supplemented. "It wasn't long after that the man stopped calling."

"And did you meet this Ben?" Coolidge asked.

"I don't know about meeting him," Connie replied. "I gave Gwen a wave and I remember saying something like, 'Is that the guy?'"

"And she said yes?" Stretch asked.

"Yes, and she had a big smile."

"How about the man? What did he look like?"

"Oh gosh, I can't really recall," Connie said. "I mean, he was medium height and did have longer blondish hair. Beyond that, I don't really remember."

"You said blondish hair?" Stretch asked. "You're sure?"

"I'm pretty sure," Connie answered, "and the hair was a little longer."

"Do you remember the date that happened?" Linc asked.

Connie reached inside her purse for her cell phone. She started swiping through screens until she found it. "It was a Saturday, that much I remember. I recall it because then Earl and I went to dinner and my Earl—" She smiled and shook her head. "Well, he's not big on going out. He likes staying in as he's a bit of a homebody. It was Saturday ... February 22nd."

Coolidge looked to Stretch and Hart. "We need to go to the Smithsonian, boys."

An hour later Coolidge and his detectives were at the Renwick Gallery, a place that neither Hart nor Stretch had ever been to.

"What about you, Lincoln?" Hart asked. "Have you ever been here?"

"Twice, in fact. The first time was with my wife many years ago. The other time was a few years ago with my daughter on a school field trip. It's an interesting place."

On the way over, Linc called Mac who put Coolidge with Galloway. Two FBI crime scene techs joined them at the gallery. The detectives and techs were immediately led to the security office and the computer that housed the security surveillance system. The clock was ticking and they needed to get through surveillance video in a hurry. Galloway had also gotten into Gwen's financial records.

"It's amazing how quickly the Bureau can access this shit," Stretch bitched in admiration. "This shit would take us a day, if not days," Hart added.

"It usually should for us as well," the tech answered. "This case is a priority, straight from the director. That has a tendency to make things move *much* faster." Then he said to the security officer for the gallery, "We have our person of interest making a purchase at 3:03 p.m. on February 22nd. Do you have a camera focusing on the cash register area?"

"We do."

It took a few minutes to find the day, and then the footage for the register, but then they rolled the video.

"There is our victim," Stretch pointed. "That is Gwen Waxe."

"And the guy with her...he's staying in the background, or at least trying to," Hart mentioned.

"But not far enough," Coolidge replied. "If it's our guy, this is yet another look." The man was sporting a small beard off the bottom of his chin, lightly shaded glasses and a black leather newsboy cap. That was different, but to Linc, the nose looked right, as did the general shape of the man's body.

"He looks like one of those sixties kind of guys," Stretch stated. "They wear the black, have the little beards. What do they call them?"

"Beatniks," Linc answered. "I better call Mac."

18

"IT MUST ABSOLUTELY KILL YOU KNOWING HOW CLOSE YOU WERE TO CATCHING ME."

The conference call was quick. It included Coolidge, Wire and Galloway.

"Let's go with it, Linc," Mac stated and then turned to Galloway. "Don, put it out now. All the cables, the networks, the local stations, the Internet, everything. Let's get it out. We're running out of time."

"I'm on it. Where are you on your end?"

"I'm working on it," Mac replied with the enthusiasm that suggested he was nowhere.

That's because that was exactly where he was. Nowhere.

Mac spent hours in the townhouse and he had come up dry. He peered through the curtains of the front picture window. The sun was setting and 9:00 p.m. was just an hour away.

As the clock ticked down, he was starting to wonder if Dara was right. The clue was here but was it even possible to find it? Was it only possible to see it after you knew what it was?

He immediately understood the clue at Lisa White's when he first heard Audrey Ruston's name. The two movie prints were in half of the crime scene pictures. They stared at Mac for hours while he locked himself in Lisa White's townhouse. It was just he couldn't make that connection. He wasn't able to make that intuitive leap to put it together.

He pushed himself up off the floor, stretched and even yawned. He was exhausted. The days were getting to him. His ability to endure the long hours of a high-intensity case had always seen him through but he was starting to wonder if he could keep going like this.

Maybe that was part of Rubens' strategy in the game. It was like in football: a strong running team could wear down the defense if they kept giving the ball to the star running back and they kept pounding the defense. In the first and second quarters, the defense could hold. But in the third quarter and then in the fourth the defense would wear down and ultimately break and the running back would get loose for the long touchdown run. This is what it felt like now. Rubens was wearing him down with the constant pressure, the clock and the stress.

"That's how he wins," Mac mumbled and he immediately became angry. "Stop feeling sorry for yourself," he scolded, admonishing himself. "There is still time."

He needed to snap awake, so he went to the bathroom, turned on the cold water and closed the drain, letting the sink fill. Then he went to the kitchen. Luckily in the freezer was a tray of ice cubes, which he took back to the bathroom. He cracked the cubes out of the tray and dumped them into the pooling water and then shut the faucet off. Mac held his breath and dunked his face into the ice-cold water and held it there. After what seemed like thirty seconds, he raised his face out of the water and took in some air and then did it again. The water was invigorating and he leaned back down and splashed some more on his face, then ran some of the cold water through his short blond hair, trying to reactivate it as well. He leaned forward on the sink and looked in the mirror. The water was revitalizing but he still looked tired. The circles under his eyes were prominent, and despite the water he'd run through his scalp, his hair looked lifeless.

"You look ten years older, McRyan," he said quietly to the mirror as he looked beyond his face in the reflection to the shelf on the wall behind him, tilted his head, looked closer and muttered, "Huh."

He turned around and looked at the framed picture on the small white shelf, which had a row of small knobs underneath to hang towels and a robe. The picture was taken in the living room, a room he'd spent the last several hours in but something in the photo was different. In the background was a headshot picture of Eleanor Roosevelt mounted on the wall opposite of the couch. "That picture isn't there now," he muttered.

It had been moved.

Mac, with the bathroom picture in hand, purposefully walked back into the living room and went to where the picture of Eleanor Roosevelt was mounted on the wall in the picture in the bathroom. The lighting was dim so he flipped on the overhead light. With more illumination, he saw what he was looking for. Where the picture of Eleanor Roosevelt had previously been hung there was a slight fade mark around the outside of the replacement picture.

"It doesn't cover the fade mark," he murmured quietly as he ran his fingers over the fade line. Upon further reflection, in a now different context, the replacement picture was wrong for the spot on the wall, he thought. For someone who was so fastidious about her house and how it looked, it was not obviously wrong, just not quite right.

"So where are you now, Eleanor?" Mac asked, looking around the living room. Eleanor had been moved to the wall to his left. Mac moved to the picture and examined it and then reached behind for the wire and lifted it off its nail. Behind the picture was the nail the picture of Eleanor hung on as well as another nail sitting two inches below. "The nail for a smaller picture."

So when did it move? Mac wondered. *Did you move it, you clever son-of-a-bitch?*

"This arrangement isn't right," Mac muttered, standing back away from the picture, his arms folded. "These pictures just don't go together."

Mac took the Lisa White crime scene photos out of his backpack. He focused on the pictures with the movie posters, *Sabrina* and *Breakfast at Tiffany's* and the wall they were mounted on.

With his attention focused on the arrangement, it too took on a different look to him. "This doesn't look right, these two together," he mumbled quietly.

It was harder to tell at Lisa White's because there was just so much displayed. At first blush, it didn't look like she had any rhyme or reason to how she hung the mass of pictures on the walls but if you looked a little closer, there was something of a ... pattern. She organized pictures by having large pictures, painting or framed movie posters surrounded by smaller pictures. It gave off the look of a collage, yet there was a distinct pattern of organization on the other walls of the house. The pictures he peered through and his own memory confirmed it. Yet, despite that seeming organization, there were two large movie prints positioned together on the wall that were the clue for the name of Audrey Ruston.

Did Rubens move them?

He reached for his cell phone.

"Dara, you need to go to Lisa White's right now."

"Lisa White's?"

"Yes."

"To do what?"

"I need you to check the two movie prints that gave us the name Audrey Ruston."

"Check for what?"

"Nail holes behind the prints."

Eleanor was perfect in every way for him.

The only flaw was where she lived.

He preferred houses or townhouses for the privacy they tended to provide. That was an issue with Eleanor. She lived in a turn-of-the-century four-story building that was once apartments and was now converted to condos. And while there wasn't security physically onsite, there were surveillance cameras in the main lobby and the main back entrance, or so he'd learned in researching the building.

So this would be tricky.

Knowing that, a dig was made into the architectural history of the building and the area surrounding it. That had revealed an interesting part of the property's past.

All of that swirled through his mind as he walked up the front walk to the building, his backpack slung over his shoulder, two bottles of wine along with other necessary items inside.

Promptly at 8:00 p.m., he hit the buzzer for Eleanor's condo unit, number 304. The door immediately buzzed and eschewing the steps, he took the elevator up to the third floor, went to unit 304 and knocked.

The door opened immediately.

"Hi, Tom," she said happily.

"Hello, Eleanor," Rubens replied as he took her hands and leaned in and kissed her on the cheek, breathing in her perfume. As he stepped back he took in her appearance. It was an interesting selection, a brown Burberry dress with tiers of suede and he noticed the music playing in the background, Adele, and he recalled having seen a picture of the singer wearing that very kind of dress.

"Please come in."

He stepped inside her condo. Quickly he scanned the area to confirm his recollection of it. It was a nice, open space, with a living room that opened into a dining area. A singular wall divided the kitchen from the living room. Overall, it would provide him with plenty of room to work with later. And then there was one other thing he noticed: her tabby cat lurking near the entry into the kitchen, staring him down for a moment before heading down the back hallway toward the bedroom.

"What's in the backpack?" Eleanor asked, drawing him back to her.

"Wine, of course," he replied. "A nice Pinot Noir and a smooth Cab. What tickles your fancy?"

"Pinot Noir would be great."

"An excellent choice, my dear. Would I find an opener and glasses in the kitchen?"

"Yes, let me show you."

In the small kitchen, Eleanor retrieved two long-stemmed wine glasses and a corkscrew and seal cutter. "Please go make yourself comfortable on the couch," Rubens suggested. "I'll take care of this."

"Mac, I think you're right. The movie posters were moved," Wire reported eagerly over the speaker on his cell phone. "There are a bunch of nail holes behind the *Sabrina* print."

"Where did it come from?"

"If I had to guess, he moved it from the hallway leading from the front door back to the kitchen area. There is a space of pictures that don't necessarily fit but based on my quick measurements, they look like they would have fit where the *Sabrina* poster now rests. What are you looking at?"

"A picture of Eleanor Roosevelt," Mac answered. "It was moved at some point. It used to be to the right of the wall that had the three mirrors with pictures of Amelia Earhart and Rosa Parks, making for a nice little arrangement of famous women. So why move it?"

"If he did," Wire blurted.

"He moved it," Mac replied. "He moved it. I can feel it. The question is why move it here? Why move Eleanor here?" He stepped back from the wall to see what the picture could tie with. There was nothing close to the right of the picture. To the left was a painting of a bald eagle and then a watercolor painting of the sun rising over the horizon. "Left to right I have a painting of the sun and horizon, then a picture of a bald eagle in flight and then Eleanor Roosevelt."

"That doesn't sound like anything," Wire stated after a moment's thought.

"Yeah, if he's giving me a name, Eleanor should be first, not ... last. It's like he's dyslexic, unless ..." Mac wheeled around to look at the other wall, the mirrored wall.

Wire caught the hesitation in his voice, "What, Mac? What do you see?"

"The opposite wall, it has the three mirrors on it," he replied. In the first mirror was the reflection of the picture of Eleanor Roosevelt. To the right is the reflection of the bald eagle in flight and then in the third mirror is the reflection of the painting of the sun coming over the horizon.

"I wonder," he murmured as he went to the picture of the eagle and then the sun. Behind the watercolor of the sun, there were two empty nail holes. He rubbed his index finger over the holes and the sheet rock was puckered enough that it seemed like the nails were recently removed. Of course, maybe he was feeling and seeing things he wanted to see rather than what was actually reality. He next checked to the left under the picture of the eagle and there were no stray nail holes. It most likely hadn't been moved. As he stepped back away to assess the arrangement, he could understand it. It was the biggest piece and was hung at the proper height and centered properly on the wall so it seemed that it had been hung there all along. So if he was right, the Eleanor Roosevelt picture and the sun watercolor were new to this location. "Dara, this is the arrangement. It's in the reflection of the mirrors."

"What is it, Mac?"

"Eleanor Roosevelt, a picture of a bald eagle in flight and then the watercolor of the sun coming up over the horizon."

"It's Eleanor something then," Wire yells excitedly. "Eleanor, Roosevelt, eagle, horizon and sun."

"Eleanor, Roosevelt, eagle, horizon and … sun," Mac says loudly. "The Roosevelt is too easy. If I dump that, I get Eleanor Eagle—"

"Eagleson!" Dara yelped. "Eleanor Eagleson, Mac. Try that name."

"I'm on the laptop," Mac replied excitedly, his fingers flying on the keyboard, typing in the search terms and slamming the enter key with his thumb. "I've got nine options." He started clicking on each link.

"Hurry, Mac! It's 8:53!"

"I'm working on it." He replied as he clicked on the second Eleanor Eagleson. "No, not her."

Then on the third. "No, not Rubenesque, too skinny."

Then on the fourth. "No, she's married. And ... the same on number five."

He clicked on number six. This Eleanor Eagleson was unmarried. Her license photo, two years old, showed a woman with a round face and a shortish pixie haircut, and then he looked at her physical measurements. "Dara, this might be it. This Eleanor is unmarried and is five foot five and 185 pounds."

He checked the last three and none were good options. "I think it's number six, Dara. She looks right for it!"

"That's gotta be her," Dara replied. "It's gotta be."

Mac clicked on an address link. "Jesus, she's just minutes away." He glanced down to his watch. 8:58. "Shit, Dara, it's this Eleanor Eagleson! It's her. We gotta go." He read off the address to Dara as he burst out the front door. "*Let's go! Let's go! Let's go!* We've got the victim," he bellowed to the patrol officers waiting in front, who immediately got down into the patrol car.

"Hang on," the officer driving warned as Mac pulled the back passenger door closed.

The effects were starting on Eleanor. Her eyes were starting to droop just a bit and as always, the speech started to slur, just slightly at the beginning. Not enough that Eleanor was noticing. As far as she knew it was simply the wine. A quick glance down to his watch told him that the drug had not affected her as quickly as he wanted but it wouldn't be long as they continued to talk.

One thing that has always bothered him a little about Eleanor was that she had the annoying habit of keeping her cell phone close. It wasn't as if based upon his observations of her over time she had a large social circle that would be constantly texting her, so it always seemed odd to him. Yet there it was and it was beeping. She had a text. The good news was she seemed to be ignoring it.

"More wine?" he offered.

"Tom, are you trying to get me tipsy?"

He smiled and shrugged. "Maybe."

Eleanor held her glass out. "Yes, please," and then slid a little closer to him and unsteadily leaned into him. He could tell she was feeling a little amorous as she moved her lips close. He kissed her back and then poured more wine into her glass, lightly reaching for and steadying her right hand while he poured.

Her phone beeped again and as he glanced left, this text was in caps and read: *URGENT!*

This time, the phone drew Eleanor's attention and she sloppily reached for it.

He watched as her lips slowly moved while reading the text message: *Urgent! Tom Edwards is on the news! He's Rubens! Get out!*

The change in her expression was immediate, even in her weakened state. She looked to him. "Yoooou're hiiim are ... are... aren't you?" she slurred.

"Who, Eleanor?" he asked in reply, while at the same time he reached into his suit coat pocket, pulling out black leather gloves.

"Ru...Ru...Rubens," she slurred. "Yo...yo...you're ... h...h... him."

Eleanor pushed herself off the couch, scrambling to get away from him. The drug was working on her but she wasn't yet completely immobilized.

He quickly jumped off the couch after her, lunging for her but he was off-balance.

Eleanor pushed him away but as she did, she stumbled backward toward the kitchen, crashing into the wall, but not down to the floor.

Leaning against the wall, trying to steady herself, she reached to the glass and metal bookshelf to her right. She grabbed a snow globe off the shelf and weakly threw it at him, yelping out a half-shouted "Help! Help!"

She reached over for a small statue but it fell out of her hands as Rubens threw his shoulder into her, trying to pin her to the wall. As he wrestled with her, they both fell to the left and into the bookshelf, knocking them both hard down to the floor, with the metal and glass shelf landing on top of them in a loud crash.

"Help!" she yelped, a guttural yelp, not loud enough to be a scream, but too loud nonetheless.

Swiftly he threw the shelving off of them. He rolled on top of Eleanor, straddling her with his legs and frantically grabbing at her throat with both of his hands and squeezing, his thumbs depressing her windpipe while his fingers wrapped around the back of her neck. He shook her head and banged it violently and repeatedly against the floor, grunting as he increased the pressure.

Eleanor weakly flailed away at him, trying to fight him but the drug has taken too much effect. She had no strength and her punches had none.

Anger and rage rising up in him, he tightened his grip on her throat like a vise, strangling her while she gasped for air, her eyes frantically blinking as he drained the life out of her.

He kept pressing on her throat, grunting as he shook her head until the movement underneath him quit. He stopped and felt that her body was still and unmoving beneath him. Breathing heavily, he rolled off of her and leaned into the wall, wiping the sweat off his brow.

There was a heavy knock on the door.

"Eleanor, is everything alright in there?" a man's voice yelled through the door. "Eleanor! Eleanor!"

Then there was a siren and not just one. There were sirens plural and they were closing fast.

This was trouble.

Think quickly, think quickly.

He pushed himself up off the floor and grabbed his wine glass off the coffee table and smashed it on the floor, stomping on it.

The knocking on the door frantically continued, the neighbor sensing something was very wrong. He raised his voice and pounded harder on the door. *"Eleanor! Eleanor!"*

Rubens went to the front door and quickly peered through the peephole to see a small man pounding on the door. *"Eleanor, I heard a yell for help. Eleanor, are you okay? Eleanor!"*

The sirens were getting louder.

There wasn't much time.

He quickly pulled his backpack over his shoulder and then grabbed the nearly empty wine bottle from the coffee table. At the front door, he quickly turned the deadbolt open and pulled the door open to find Eleanor's neighbor in mid-knock.

"What's going on in the—"

Rubens smashed the wine bottle against the right side of the small man's head, sending him instantly down to the floor of the hallway. He kicked the man in the head.

Another woman's head was sticking out of her apartment door to his left. "I'm calling the police!" she screamed.

Rubens heard her slide the deadbolt closed as he ran past her door and to the back hallway of the building.

"We need to set a perimeter! Lock it down, the whole area and send an ambulance!" Mac barked into the police radio.

"Agent McRyan," the patrol officer in the passenger seat reported, "someone called in Eleanor Eagleson's name, saying she was with a man named Tom Edwards who looked like the Rubens pictures from the Renwick Gallery at the Smithsonian."

"This is it, then, for sure," Mac exclaimed. "*We've got to hustle!*"

"Almost there," the officer driving yelled as he turned the patrol unit hard right, fishtailing slightly and then accelerating down the street and screeching to a halt in front of the building mid-block. "This is it!"

Two more patrol units arrived from the west as Mac got out of the back of the patrol car. He could see another set of flashing lights several blocks away approaching the area. More sirens were audible in the distance.

Mac quickly glanced to his watch as he ran up the steps. 9:02 p.m. "Dammit!" He looked to his right and pointed to a senior officer, a sergeant, who was up and out of his patrol car. "Lock the entire area down, expand the perimeter around this building as units arrive and stop everyone and everything, and I mean everything! Nobody moves. Shelter in place!"

"Copy that," the Sergeant yelled back and then reached for his shoulder radio.

"The rest of you are with me!" Mac ordered as he burst through the front door of the building. A resident was holding the interior security door open. "Up on the third floor."

Mac noticed the hallway leading through to the back of the building and another set of steps. He quickly turned, pointed at two officers with two fingers and gestured to the back of the apartment. The two officers, guns drawn, moved past Mac and went to the back.

"Up here! Up here!" a voice yelled down.

Mac started up the steps, taking two at a time.

At the third floor landing, Mac looked left to see a man lying on the floor and what looked like dark green glass lying around him. He was bleeding profusely at his left temple. "I'm not getting much of a pulse," a tenant reported as a uniformed officer kneeled down to help.

"Agent McRyan," another officer yelled pointing toward the open door. "Inside the apartment."

Mac looked to his right and the open door for Unit 304, and inside he saw a pair of legs lying on the floor. He pushed himself up off the floor and went inside, and found Eleanor lying on her back, her arms lying spread away from the sides of her body. Mac leaned down and checked for a pulse at her throat and got nothing, then reached for her wrist. "Shit!"

He put his head down to her chest and listened. Then he felt it, or thought he felt something, maybe the beat of the heart. She was probably fibrillating but there still might be a chance. "Is that ambulance here? Where are the paramedics?"

"Right here," a paramedic replied as he charged into the room and kneeled down.

"I'm not getting a pulse," Mac reported, looking up to the paramedic. "But I thought I felt her heart beat."

The paramedic's partner came into the condo and the two of

them went to work on Eleanor. Mac looked back to his right to see another set of paramedics were arriving and tending to the man in the hallway.

Mac pushed himself up and stepped back into the hallway to find Wire coming up the front steps and checked his watch: 9:06.

"Agent McRyan, you need to hear this," a patrol officer hailed from down the hall to the left.

Mac and Wire hurriedly approached the officer and an older man standing outside the door to his condo. "I saw him," the man reported. "I saw him out the peephole go down the back steps. I did follow and looked down. He went out the back door."

"How long ago?" Wire asked.

"One minute, maybe two," the tenant answered. "We could hear sirens when it was all happening."

Mac went to the stairway and yelled down, "He went out the back! He went out the back!" As he yelled, he could see officers rushing out the back. He reached for his police radio. "This is McRyan—set the perimeter at six blocks. Our man is on the run out the back of the building. He may be hiding. He may have gotten into another building. Again, lock everything down, no vehicles move, shelter in place! Shelter in place!" Then Mac's phone rang.

It was a number he didn't recognize; it wasn't tied to a contact. "I bet this is him," Mac said as he looked to Wire and then swiped the screen to answer. "McRyan."

"You were so close, Mac," the masked voice greeted. "I've never had a call *this* close. So exciting."

He's outside the perimeter, Mac immediately thought as he checked his watch. "I'm on to you."

"Do you really think so?"

"I figured out Eleanor Eagleson, didn't I?"

"Come on, Mac," the voice teased. "I had to keep you in the game a little bit. Eleanor was easy as far as the clues go. I mean, it was right there in the mirrors. How long did you actually have to sit there and stare at it to figure it out? I'm actually kind of disappointed it took you as long as it did."

"Bullshit," Mac answered, having stopped on the main level of the building, looking out the back, seeing patrol units and officers out searching with flashlights. "I'm in your head. I know how you think now. And as for Eleanor ... we're going to save her," he bluffed. "Paramedics are working her now. I heard her heartbeat—*I felt it.* We're going to save her, you piece of shit. The ambulance is leaving right now."

He could tell there was a hesitation, albeit slight, on the other end. "She'll tell you nothing. She'll be able to tell you nothing."

"We'll see, but even worse for you, you sick fuck, you didn't get to make her the third Grace. You didn't get to leave your little clue or set your clock. You didn't get your masterpiece. You failed."

"Did I, Mac? It must absolutely kill you knowing how *close* you were to catching me," Rubens taunted. "Knowing you were within mere minutes, maybe even a minute, maybe even seconds of catching me, and yet *you* failed. You failed another victim, Mac. And Mac, this is not over. We go on. It goes on."

"When? When does it go on?"

"This is the best part, Mac." And even with the voice disguised, he could hear the laugh, the sick laugh. "You have less than two days— you have forty-seven hours until the last one. You get one more chance."

"What? No clue? That's hardly sporting."

"This isn't a sport, it's winner takes all," Rubens replied evilly. "You had your chance and you missed. In fact, you've missed twice. Nobody else ever got one shot at me, let alone two. You've done better than anyone else in the game but still, you failed. And now you will pay the penalty for that failure. Now I'm not telling you who the victim is. You're not going to find *her*—you're going to have to find *me*. And Mac, no matter what you know or even what you think you know about me and how I look and how I operate, you don't know anything. Remember that."

The line went dead. "Jesus."

"Mac, get out here now!" Wire yelled, waving from outside, standing in the driveway leading to the underground parking garage.

Mac pushed the back door open. "What do you have? Do we have him?"

"No, but I think I know where he went. Follow me," Wire replied, leading him across the parking lot into a small grove of trees and brush to find two uniformed officers and a civilian standing around a pipe sticking up a foot above ground. A cover and crowbar lay on the ground to the left. "Mac, this looks like an old sewer line," Wire reported.

"Seriously?" Mac asked in disbelief. "There? He went down there?"

Wire crouched down, aiming her flashlight down the narrow hole. "I think I can see what look like fresh footprints in the dirt at the bottom of the ladder."

"I never even knew this was back here," a tenant reported. "And I've lived here for five years."

"Shit, now this guy is a gopher," Mac bitched, kneeling and looking down into the hole.

"Down we go?" Wire sighed.

"Down we go," Mac answered. He looked to a patrol officer. "Let me borrow your flashlight." The officer handed it over to Mac and Mac pointed it down into the darkness of the hole. There was a narrow ladder leading down the cylinder-like tube. He slipped the flashlight into his jacket pocket and stuffed his Sig Sauer in the front of his jeans. "Cover me."

Wire had her gun in her right hand as she held the flashlight in her left, aiming it down the narrow hole while Mac climbed down as quickly as he dared. The shaft down to the sewer was barely large enough for him to shimmy down the ladder. He kept his focus down while the light from Wire's flashlight was somewhat blocked by his body. Even with the spotty lighting, he could see the fresh footprints in the dirt on the bottom of the old sewer pipe. At the last step, Mac stopped for a brief moment, listened and then held the rung of the ladder with his left hand and pulled his gun from his waistband. Hearing nothing, he jumped down the last step to the floor of the tunnel, crouching down to avoid hitting the top of the pipe with his head. He took out the flashlight and pointed it down the narrow sewer tunnel. There was nobody ahead but he could see footprints leading away.

He looked up and Wire was already making her way down. He moved forward ten feet, dropped down on one knee, pointing the light forward. While doing so, he quickly checked his cell phone and noticed he didn't have a cell signal. No bars.

A minute later Mac, Wire and two officers were with him in the pipe. "Stay on your radios," Mac yelled back up the tunnel. "The footprints lead forward to what I think is the west," Mac reported and then led the group ahead into the darkness of the tunnel.

At six-foot-one, Mac had to crouch down to move through the tunnel, as did the two officers. Even Wire, who was five-nine, had to keep her head down. It made for slow going and then there was the stench. The sewer pipe had likely been out of commission for years but it was still a sewer pipe and there were remnants of sewage in it.

"This is awful," Wire moaned as she coughed, pulling her t-shirt up and over her nose.

"Breathe through your mouth," Mac suggested through a cough.

"Like that ever works."

As they worked their way straight down the tunnel, Mac called back to the officers. "Do your radios work down here?"

One officer called into his radio but only got static. "Negative, sir."

Mac checked his phone again and he continued to have no cell signal.

"Me neither," Wire added, checking hers. "What time do you have, Mac?"

He looked at his phone. "I have 9:09 now."

The group cautiously worked their way forward, moving more quickly as they became more comfortable with the low ceiling height of the pipe.

"He wouldn't have immediately gotten out of the tunnel," Mac surmised. "If he heard us coming, he knows we'd set a perimeter around that building. He had to get outside of that perimeter."

"Mac," Wire asked. "If he knew this was here, if he planned on using this as a possible escape route, he knew where he was probably heading."

"And if he planned to use this tunnel, he wasn't going to get out of it right away," Mac answered. He noticed a gap in the tunnel ahead, what appeared to be a connection, a "T" in the pipe. As he stepped into the junction, the height of the pipe was taller and he could stand up freely.

"This must be more of a main line," a patrol officer stated as he entered. "We were in a branch line."

Mac crouched down and scanned the pipe to the left and could see prints. He turned to his right and didn't necessarily see prints but he also didn't see as much dirt on the bottom of the pipe. "It looks like the prints go left," Mac stated. "Wire and I will go that way. You two go the other for a few blocks, just in case."

Mac and Wire moved forward while the two officers went the other direction. Mac held his gun in his right hand crossed over his left, which held the flashlight. He favored the left side of the tunnel. Dara followed ten feet behind, doing the same shading to the right side of the tunnel.

"How far away are we?" Wire whispered quietly.

"Hard to say," Mac answered quietly, moving forward. "It feels like we've gone blocks, several blocks, just based on my sense of direction," he added and then stopped, going on alert and looking back. "There's a ladder ahead, maybe thirty feet."

Wire nodded.

Mac moved forward quickly and reached the ladder and pointed his light up, following the ladder rungs up the narrow exit tunnel. "The manhole cover looks loose up there. I think he might have gone back up here." He looked back to Wire. "Cover me again."

"I got ya."

Mac stuffed his gun and flashlight in his waistband and started up the ladder rungs.

At the top rung, Mac reached up and slipped his fingers into the sliver of a gap between the cover and the rim edge and pushed the cover off, took out his gun and popped up out of the sewer and into a narrow alley, scanning the area.

It was a dark spot.

There were no street lights near the manhole cover. The closest light was the street lights at either end of the alley. Mac looked down to see Wire making her way up the ladder.

"Where am I?" Mac asked out loud. "I have to be west, a little southwest, but how far? Am I still inside the perimeter?" he muttered as he took his phone back out. He tapped the microphone icon on the screen and spoke into the phone: "Map my current location."

It took a couple of seconds but then his location popped up on the screen and Mac could tell they were several blocks west-south-west of Eleanor Eagleson's apartment building. He ran toward the north end of the alley as he swiped the screen with his fingers left to get the map back to Eleanor's apartment location. It was at least seven blocks back to the east. They were a long way away.

As he reached the end of the alley, Mac stopped, looked back to the east and his shoulders slumped. He pinched the bridge of his nose. "Aw, shit."

There were two patrol units a block and a half east, blocking the intersection, the far edge of the perimeter.

"He's gone," Wire muttered quietly.

19

"IT'S SUDDENLY GOTTEN VERY LATE IN THE GAME."

R ubens paid the cab driver cash and exited the vehicle, then
began the six block walk to his apartment. It was another rule.
If he took a cab, he never let it drop him off where he was living. If he
took a bus, he never got off the bus where he lived. It was always a
stop or two before or after but never where he was living.

The anger had slowly been rising up inside of him as he made his
way back. He didn't get his masterpiece and far worse, Eleanor could
still possibly be alive. He'd been unable to make absolutely sure
before the pounding on the door and the sirens signaling the police's
arrival. He didn't think she would make it. It was highly unlikely but
he also wasn't able to be absolutely certain.

There hadn't been enough time to confirm it.

In fact, the whole night had never happened before. Even in Los
Angeles, when LAPD Detective Walker got somewhat close, he'd still
been able to finish, he'd still been able to leave Rhonda Hollister
posed as he'd desired. He'd been able to tie the bow on that last one
before the police moved in and he narrowly escaped. It had been a
close shave, but he'd gotten it done.

Not tonight.

Once he exited the old sewer system, he set about covering his tracks. From the tunnel exit, he made his way southwest and eventually to the Metro. He took the Orange Line out to East Falls Church. From there, he hailed the cab to drive him back east across DC toward his apartment. Along the way, he'd gotten rid of the salt and pepper wig, matching goatee and the dark-rimmed glasses, which were exchanged for a denim jacket and Washington Redskins baseball cap.

The look of Tom Edwards was gone, never to be used again.

Inside his apartment, he dumped the keys on the kitchen counter, took out a bottle of water and then turned on the television. In all the years, this was always the good part, waiting for the story to break, the chance to revel in the success.

Tonight would be no such night.

The media was all over the story, reporting from outside of Eleanor's condo building. There was an all-out manhunt on for a disguised man and there was more footage now, having been spotted at the Smithsonian as well with Gwendolyn Waxe. The police figured out that he'd been cleaning, especially after the chase from Martha Schreiber's.

That fucking McRyan and Wire, he thought. *They are really good.* But would they be good enough?

For McRyan and Wire didn't have two things.

They didn't have what he really looked like and more importantly, they didn't have what he *would* look like going forward.

CNN had gone with full coverage, it otherwise being a slow Saturday news night, and they had one of the best reporters, Renee Terry, on the story. "The police were just a minute or two behind Rubens, having somehow determined who his victim was and where she lived," Terry reported.

"Renee, do you know how it was the police learned about the victim?"

"The only thing we're hearing," Terry answered, "is that the clue the killer had left behind at the home of the second victim, Audrey Ruston, was actually solved but unfortunately, it appears the identity of the victim was determined just minutes, if not a minute too late. It appears it was literally that close."

"Renee, were the police able to set up roadblocks? Is there a chance he is still in that area?"

"Yes, the police did surround the area. It is very difficult to get in and out of this area right now. Residents were ordered to shelter in place. Every vehicle and person is being stopped and searched. There is also an ongoing building-to-building search. So far, he hasn't been found and we're now just learning why that may be," Terry teased.

"And why is that, Renee?"

"What we've been able to learn is that Rubens may have escaped the immediate area through an old out-of-service sewer line accessible through a manhole cover just outside the back of the condominium building. We are hearing that he may have come out several blocks outside of the perimeter the police set up."

"So they found it," he muttered at the television as he watched the report. "Glad I knew that was there."

"Is the search ongoing?" the CNN anchor continued.

"Yes, it is. The images that the authorities have compiled on Rubens continue to be circulated and the district and multi-state search for him continues, but for now at least it appears that the killer has once again slipped away from the authorities."

"Has the FBI or MPD had anything to say officially?"

"Not as of now. It is expected there will be a press briefing at some point but the situation remains fluid at this point."

"Thank you, Renee," the anchor said and then moved onto another story. Rubens flipped around to both the local and cable channels and the story remained largely the same, and he began to relax.

"Tonight is over," he mumbled to himself. "And you didn't get caught. You didn't get caught and ..." A small smile creased his lips. "The legend is only going to grow."

Convinced that Rubens escaped, Mac went into evidence collection mode.

Grace Delmonico was coordinating the search for any video cameras in the area where Rubens came out of the abandoned sewer line. "Don't get your hopes up," she noted sourly. "This area is almost exclusively residential."

Coolidge was overseeing the building and house searches to see if anyone saw someone come out of the sewer. If so, where did he go? Did he get into a car? A cab? A bus? If he didn't do that, did he get to a Metro line? The closest Metro station was ten blocks west from where Rubens exited the sewer. Given the police in the area and the heightened alert of the neighborhoods in the area it would have been hard to walk ten blocks and go unnoticed, yet so far, nobody had seen anything.

All local cab and car services were being contacted regarding fares and pick-ups in the neighborhood. Bus lines were being checked and Metro station footage was being combed as well.

The problem was, they were looking for a man in a disguise and the get-up Rubens was wearing had undoubtedly long since been discarded, probably before he approached any area where there would be a surveillance camera.

Mac and Wire eventually made their way back to Eleanor's apartment building and up to the third floor. FBI and MPD forensics teams were working the condo in tandem, collecting whatever evidence they could. In the hallway outside of Eleanor Eagleson's condo unit, the group had an informal gathering. Galloway, Delmonico, Coolidge, April Greene and even Hugo Ridge all just shook their heads in dismay.

"Any word on Eleanor?" Wire asked.

"I don't hold out hope," Coolidge stated, a man who'd seen more than one victim fail to be saved.

Ten minutes later, they lost all hope.

"Sorry, guys," Ridge reported. "Eleanor didn't make it. They did everything they could."

214 | ROGER STELLJES

His report drew scorned looks. How could he know before they did?

"What? I have a source at the hospital."

"Of course you do," Wire mocked.

Mac questioned Coolidge. "How did Ridge get in here anyway?"

The MPD detective shrugged. "He wormed his way in. The boys in blue aren't exactly averse to accepting a cash donation to their retirement fund from a reporter. I found him poking around here and I told him to just stay in the hallway. I didn't think you wanted the media seeing him walking out of here. I figured that would be worse."

"He does have a way of inserting himself in, doesn't he?" Mac muttered as he noticed the author making time with Wire. "And a way of distracting my partner," he added with a wry smile that Coolidge returned. Dara was clearly, if not smitten, at least mildly aroused by Ridge's presence and she wasn't hiding it particularly well. There were times when Mac thought she could play just a little harder to get.

"If you want him out, I'll have one of my boys take care of it," Coolidge offered.

"Yeah, do that ..." Then Mac thought for a second. "No, Linc, wait. Let it go for now."

"Really?"

"Yeah, time is getting short, very short and we need all the help we can get. Who knows, he's been chasing this guy for ten years. He might have something to offer."

"So where are we at?" Coolidge asked.

"Good question," Mac answered as he waved the group together. "We had him, we were so damn close. But we missed *again* and now —" Mac paused and exhaled, and then to the group said, "And now he's changed the rules."

"How so?" Wire asked.

"No portrait, no clue and he told me when he called that we had forty-seven hours."

"Forty-seven hours?" Ridge exclaimed in shock.

"No, it's not just forty-seven hours. It's forty-seven hours *and no clue?*" Wire exclaimed.

"He didn't have time. We got here too soon and yet—" Mac shook his head in disgust. "Not soon enough. He told me we'll have to find *him*. By the way, did we ever figure out where Rubens's call to me came from?"

"We pinged the call off a cell tower six blocks over, off of Kansas Avenue," Galloway reported. "Beyond that, we can't tell anything as to where he was when the call came in."

"So now what?" Wire asked, having brought Ridge over to the group.

"We keep doing what we're doing," Mac replied. "The old-school police work has gotten us his description. It prompted a few people to come forward and almost prevented another murder. We have to keep pressing the investigation that way. And—"

"And what?"

"We need a break," Mac stated, sounding as if he was praying. "Good God, do we need a break."

The break would not be the shattered wine glass. It was being recovered but it was essentially reduced to dust on the floor. The pieces were being meticulously retrieved and bagged. "I can't see how it's even remotely possible to put Humpty Dumpty back together," one of the FBI forensic techs stated. "The broken glass from the shelves and wine glass are all mixed together."

The same was true with the wine bottle; it was completely shattered and unfortunately, in all of the commotion of tenants, paramedics and cops arriving on the scene, what might have been retrievable was stepped on and broken further.

The one hope was that in his desperation to flee the scene there would be prints left behind, especially since Eleanor Eagleson maintained her home immaculately. Yet the crime scene tech reported, "I've got just one set of prints in the apartment."

"How is that possible?" Greene complained.

It was actually quite possible for any number of reasons, Mac thought.

"When you have a plan," Mac replied, "you follow it. He didn't touch anything other than the shattered glass on the floor."

"Or he doesn't have prints," Wire suggested.

"Or he has covers over his prints," Ridge piped up.

Mac gave him a look of derision.

"Well, I saw it in a movie once."

"This isn't an episode of *Castle*, Ridge," Mac shot back.

"Hey, I love that show," Ridge replied.

"Of course you do," Mac answered derisively.

"Point is, he could fake his prints," Ridge argued.

"Noted. Now shut up," Mac shot back. Wire rolled her eyes at him and Ridge smothered a little laugh. Mac saw it all but didn't say anything. He'd get Wire back later after whatever it was she and Ridge were working toward fizzled and he went back to New York.

As for Ridge's theory on prints, Mac didn't discount the theory entirely; he was just annoyed it came from the author.

As the group was milling around, starting to lose some steam, Coolidge got a call from the security company. The video footage was sent to his phone and would be forwarded to Mac from there.

"This is the lobby camera," Coolidge reported. "Unfortunately the security cameras only cover the entrances and exits. There's nothing for the hallways." Linc pushed play. "There he is in that damn goatee, just like the description I got."

"I don't think he'll be using that disguise going forward," Mac replied. "It has way too much profile now. A lot of our pictures have him with dark hair, a beard or a goatee of some kind. He's going to have to change that up."

"Unless his plan didn't allow for that," Greene replied. "Everything about this guy says he has a plan and sticks to it."

"I know," Mac answered. "And given how well prepared he was tonight, with that sewer line and all, I'm going to bet that at some point he planned on completely changing up his look just in case, and I wouldn't be surprised if that time was now."

"So how does that help?"

Mac smiled. "We're working with the FBI. I imagine we can come up with all kinds of possible variations of his look that could prove helpful." He looked to Galloway while he said it.

"On it," the senior special agent replied, reaching for his well-used cell phone.

They played the video forward in time to see Rubens exiting the back of the building at 9:01. "So he's in the tunnel maybe thirty seconds, a minute later at most," Mac muttered. The video was played forward and it was nearly another two minutes before officers came out of the back of the building and a patrol unit pulled into the driveway to the parking garage.

It was late, well after midnight and there was nothing left to do at the scene. Coolidge's men and the Bureau were going to continue canvassing the area. With nothing left to do at Eleanor's, they all circled back to the FBI field office to get a better view of the surveillance video.

Greene quietly asked Mac about Ridge's presence. "Do you think it's appropriate?"

"No, not technically and I really didn't like him at the crime scene," Mac answered and then sighed and shook his head. "However, he's a good reporter. He'll get all of this anyway." He figured Wire was already probably giving him some information. "On top of that, April, a little like you, he knows Rubens and may have some insight, and I need all the help I can get. It's suddenly gotten very late in the game. It's all hands on deck at this point—authorities and civilians."

Greene turned the topic back to Rubens. "So do you think he'll change up the disguise?"

"If he planned on it, yes," Mac answered. "If we're right about him and he has a very carefully orchestrated plan, he can't change his look much now unless he planned on doing so. But if you figure the police get onto your look, you have to be ready to change it so I'm betting whatever it was he looked like, that look is no more."

"If he did plan on that, then his last victim won't be as suspicious."

"Perhaps," Mac answered. "He can change hair color, beards, mustaches and all that, but his nose is what it is. His eyes are what they are, his gait is what it is and his height and weight aren't really changeable, so hopefully there would still be some recognition there. We have some good images of him, not to mention the descriptions and sketches. We're continuing to put all of that out there. People, and women in particular, are going to be on guard and looking for him, wary that their new boyfriend is potentially a serial killer. That was part of the reason I spoke the other day, to get women to be honest with themselves and ask is this new man real? If a woman is more on guard, they have a better chance of protecting themselves."

"That's all true," Greene replied agreeably.

Mac broke away from Greene and went to the whiteboard and stood in front of it for several minutes, focusing on the street map of the immediate area around Eleanor Eagleson's apartment building, tracing the route of the sewer tunnel with his finger to where they came up in the alley and then noting the location of the cell phone tower on Kansas Avenue. *Eleanor's condo. The phone call. We go on. Whatever I think I know, Rubens says I don't know. No clue as to the identity of the fourth victim. They had to find him now. The sewer pipe. The cell tower.* He just kept looking at it all, arms folded, quietly taking it all in, starting to slowly shake his head.

Wire approached, took one look at him and said, "What?"

"What do you mean, what?"

"The look on your face," Wire answered knowingly. "I've seen it before. You're staring at this map in a way that says something is bothering you."

Mac nodded. "We're missing something here. I keep running the sequence and elements of tonight's events through my mind. There is something about the call that is eating at me. I keep thinking there is more to this."

"More to what? Is it something at the scene? Was it something on the phone call? Was it something Rubens said?" Wire fired at him rapidly.

"Maybe," Mac answered, but in his mind, something else was getting to him. "Something that happened isn't sitting right with me but I can't for the life of me figure out why I think that right now. It's teasing me like a fly that I can't swat."

"It's late," Coolidge suggested as he approached. "And I know all about your legendary ability to keep going, Mac, both you and Wire, but it's nearly 3:00 a.m. and you two need rest. We all do. Even just a little, a few hours will do wonders."

"Then let's get some," Mac replied. "Let's all go home," he said and led everyone out of the conference room. "Get some rest and we'll get back at it by 7:30."

In the parking garage, Ridge lingered at his car, waiting for the others to pull out. Wire was the last one out of the elevator lobby and he approached as she hit the key fob to unlock her Range Rover.

"Hey, I wanted to say thanks for letting me hang around tonight."

"I'm a little amazed Mac let you do it," she replied with a smile. "He must really be tired."

"Or desperate times call for desperate measures," Ridge replied with a wry smile. "What a night. The rush of it—it's intoxicating."

"The rush of a case can do that."

"In all my time, I've never got to be *that* close to it all. How do you come down from that?"

"You really want to know?"

"Yeah, what do you do?"

"Let's go back to my place and I'll show you."

20

"OH SHIT! SHIT! IF I'M RIGHT…OH MAN, THAT REALLY CHANGES THINGS."

Sally was up and rustling around, getting ready for work and the activity snapped him awake. Mac was a light sleeper, always had been, even as a child. He didn't suffer from insomnia necessarily but he was a fitful sleeper at best and, as Sally frequently warned, around the time he would turn forty he'd probably start snoring like a chainsaw. That day was coming.

"Keep running and keep your weight down and sleep on your side, and *maybe* you'll be okay," she playfully warned one morning.

"And if I don't?" he replied while he poured her a cup of coffee.

"I'll make you wear one of those sleep apnea masks that make you look like a pilot," she snorted. "And then every day I'll ask you how many MIGs you shot down last night."

"I think I need to go out and run. I need to keep my weight down and sleep on my side."

He wanted to sleep more; he probably should sleep more and he really needed to sleep more.

That was not an option.

Rubens gave them forty-seven hours. They were now down to thirty-nine. Mac needed to get moving.

He rolled onto his back, looked into the walk-in closet and saw

Sally's pale, magnificent naked body in the reflection of the wall mirror. Mac smiled, pushed himself out of bed, went to the door of the large closet and leaned against the door frame. His fiancée was a beautiful woman in so many ways. At this moment, he was admiring her physical beauty as she wrapped a long white towel around her curvy body.

She noticed him watching. "What?"

"I could really use a quick fifteen minutes," he said as he flicked his eyebrows.

She glanced furtively at the clock on the vanity and then back to him, thinking and then seductively started biting her left lower lip. "I can give you an enthusiastic ten," she replied as she dropped the towel, rushed him and pushed him into the closet and down to the floor.

"This is new," Mac remarked with a smile as Sally quickly slid off his boxers and jumped back on top of him.

"Did I ever tell you how much I love this closet you built me?" she said in a hushed voice as she kissed his neck.

"No, but I must have done a really good job."

"Oh, you did," Sally replied, her lips a centimeter from his. "You definitely, *definitely* did."

What started and quickly finished in the walk-in closet was then immediately restarted and then refinished again in the shower. In all, Sally gave him a good twenty-five minutes and was scrambling to get out the door as he poured her a coffee and spread cream cheese on a toasted bagel for her.

"I have to say," Sally said, her smile beaming as she came rushing into the kitchen, "that was a heck of a way to start the day."

"What can I say," Mac answered with a grin, still feeling tired but significantly lighter and looser. "You motivate me."

"I'd like to keep on motivating you," she replied as she leaned in to kiss him again, lingering at his mouth. Her right arm curved around his neck and she kissed him again, a slow soft lingering kiss. "We haven't had nearly enough of that lately."

"I agree."

"Then catch this asshole," she ordered, softly pecking his lips one more time.

"I'm working on it," he replied and broke away before he made an attempt at wrestling her back upstairs.

Sally looked at her watch. "Not bad. I should still make it kind of on time."

"In that case," he teased, reaching for her hand.

"Easy, tiger," she laughed, slapping away his hand while she sipped from the coffee mug. "I can't believe we did all of that in twenty-five minutes as it is." A seductive grin spread across her face. "We shouldn't have been able to do it twice in that ..."

"Short of a time frame," Mac finished and was suddenly slack-jawed. "He couldn't have done it in that ... short ... of a time."

"Are we talking about what just happened upstairs or something else?" Sally asked, seeing the sudden change in his expression. "We're not talking about upstairs, are we?"

Mac stared at the ceiling. "If he couldn't have done that—" His voice trailed off and then he wheeled toward Sally, his eyes wide. "Oh shit! Shit! If I'm right...oh man, that really changes things. And that's why he said we go on. That's what he said. I can't believe it! That really, *really* changes things. But I gotta confirm it first."

"What? What are you talking about?"

"You gotta be kidding. You have got to be effin' kidding me," Mac just kept muttering over and over as he paced around the kitchen.

"Mac, what is it? Is it about the case?"

"Yeah? Oh yeah," he finally answered as if just realizing she was still there. He kissed Sally quickly and ran toward the stairs, yelling, "I gotta call Wire. I gotta call Wire right now! This could be huge."

As he sprinted back upstairs, Sally smiled in amusement. "I guess I cleared his mind."

She was deep in sleep, a comfortable, relaxed, exhilarating sleep, so comfortable she ignored the phone and let the call roll to voicemail.

That didn't stop the caller and the phone from immediately ringing again. She rolled over and saw that it was Mac. Of course it was Mac. It was always Mac at times like this. "Yeah?" she answered sleepily.

"Get up and get to Eleanor Eagleson's."

"It's early."

"It's 6:39 a.m. to be exact."

"Right, like I said, *it's early.*"

"But now you're up, so let's go."

She sensed renewed enthusiasm in his voice. "Mac, why?"

"Just be there in fifteen minutes. I'll have coffee. I might have figured something out. It could be big, it could crack this thing wide open, but I need your help to confirm it."

Wire sat up, sensing the excitement in her partner's voice. "Okay, easy there, pal. I need at least a half-hour."

"Okay, okay, just get up and get going, will ya? Time's a-wasting."

She hung up and rolled over to her left to find Ridge, now awake lying flat on his back, staring at the ceiling.

"Good morning," he smirked as she looked down at him.

"Morning."

"Quite the night," he continued.

"It had its moments."

They'd raced to her place and started in the living room before making it up to the bed for round two. Round three occurred a little later, after they'd first raided the refrigerator, emptying her temple of takeout food boxes. She found Ridge to be an energetic lover and then some, and he had a couple of moves she'd never experienced. She had to admit as she stared down at his cheesy grin surrounded by stylish stubble that it left her feeling a little more alive. But she wasn't kidding herself. Ridge lived in New York and wasn't any sort of a long-term option. He was too much of a poser for her, long term. But in the here and now, she could definitely do with a couple of more nights like that one.

"I gotta get going," she said.

"So early?"

"It was Mac. He has something he wants to get after and get after now. When you're on a case with him, you move at his pace, which is generally warp speed." She leaned down, quickly pecked him on the lips and rolled out of bed.

Ridge sat up and admired her naked body, her long legs, toned stomach and smaller but firm breasts as she stumbled across the room to the closet and grabbed a robe. She worked out. Her body was quite feminine but exceedingly taut and, he thought, incredibly sexy.

"It was interesting to be on the inside of the investigation like that last night."

"Don't make too big a habit of it," Dara cautioned with a smile as she started assembling a wardrobe, pulling out a pair of skinny blue jeans. "You don't want to get on Mac's bad side. I've seen people on that. Trust me—you don't ever want to be there."

"Good to know," Ridge answered, not particularly concerned. Then he changed subjects. "Look, at the risk of killing the mood, I do have to ask one question..."

"What's that?"

"You and McRyan, you two ever ... you know?"

Dara put her hands on her hips and her relaxed look suddenly turned dark. "Really? You think that is a wise question to ask right now, Ridge? Do you want me to hurt you?"

"I'm just curious. Have you?"

"*No*, we haven't," she bit out and studied his expression. "You're surprised?"

"Given the night I just had with you, I'm *amazed*."

"Have you seen his wife-to-be, Sally Kennedy? You want to talk about amazing?"

"Yeah, but you aren't exactly bad looking," Ridge answered. "So again, I find it hard to believe ..."

"Not everyone is a walking hard-on like you, Ridge," Dara threw over her shoulder as she turned to open a dresser drawer.

"Maybe not, but come on—you have to have at least thought about it. I'm secure in my masculinity so I can say this: McRyan is a good-looking guy. I mean, he really strikes me as your type and you two have chemistry. I can see it."

Dara thought for a second and then answered honestly. "If Mac wasn't head over heels in love with Sally, I'd have had him in this bed a long time ago. And you know what? I think he'd tell you the same thing."

"Yet you two haven't given into it?"

"No," Dara replied. "Not even close, and there have been plenty of times where we could have."

"And no?" Ridge didn't believe her.

"We're really good friends and occasional partners, and that's as far as it goes. And I count Sally Kennedy as a very good friend of mine. Heck, I'm a bridesmaid in her wedding. So, Mac and I?" She shook her head. "It ain't gonna happen."

"We'll see."

"No," Dara answered sharply. "We won't, and I'm just fine with that. Besides, Mac is not a cheater. He's one of the most loyal people I've ever met. And not just to Sally. If you are one of his friends, one of his good, *good* friends, he'd do just about anything for you."

"Well, good," Ridge answered. "It actually gives me a little more faith in people. And ..."

"And what?"

"And I suppose an angle to cover in my coming book."

In a flash Wire jumped on the bed and was on top of Ridge, forcefully pinning his arms down while squeezing his ribs with her thighs. "Ridge, if you mention this conversation in your book... If you even make a vague reference to it, or to Mac and I..." She moved her face close to his and whispered in her most threatening, gravelly voice, "If you even in the most obscure subtext imaginable allude to it, trust me —you'll need a chapter in that book on the castration of your amazing dick at my hands. Do you understand?"

"You think my dick is amazing?"

"Ridge, don't test me."

"I won't."

She dug her nails deeply into his wrists. "*Ridge*," she warned in a hiss.

"It won't happen. I promise, I promise, I promise!" Ridge pleaded with pain in his voice, but apparently not enough.

Wire twisted even tighter.

"Ow!" he screamed loudly, now in considerable pain. "Dara, I promise. I absolutely, positively, cross my heart and hope to die, promise not a word. Never, *never*."

She looked down into his face. Could she trust him? This *was* important. He must have been able to tell she was suspicious. She was contemplating whether her night was a massive mistake.

"Dara, not a word, I promise," Ridge answered seriously and he could tell she finally started to believe him. Then he lost his somber demeanor. "As long as—you know—maybe me and my amazing dick can keep coming by for a while?" he suggested with a goofy smile.

"I'll think about it," she replied, maintaining her grip.

"So how long until you have to meet McRyan?"

"I said a half-hour," Dara smirked as she released Ridge's arms and slowly lowered herself down on top of him, "but I left some wiggle room."

Wire pulled up and Mac had a tall coffee waiting for her, along with a croissant.

He gave his watch a dramatic stare.

It had been fifty minutes, but she blocked it out, reached for the coffee and took a long drink from the tall, now lukewarm mocha. "So is it just the two of us?"

"Yes," Mac answered. "For now, at least, other than the two uniform cops hanging around and keeping people away, I kind of told them what we'd be doing and bought their silence with supplies from Dunkin' Donuts."

"What *are* we doing?" she asked while drinking her coffee and following Mac back into the woods behind Eleanor Eagleson's condominium building.

"Testing a theory."

"Which is what, exactly?"

"In due time, partner. But first, you're going to time me."

"From where and why?"

"I'm going to start from here. You're timing me from here until I come out the tunnel where Rubens did last night."

"So I start, go to my car and ..."

"Meet me at the manhole cover in the alley."

Mac took out his flashlight and lowered himself down to the floor of the tunnel as he heard Wire yell, "I'll meet you on the street."

He went through the sewer as quickly as he could with the flashlight. The night before he and the others picked their way slowly through the passage, having to crouch and proceed carefully, unsure of what awaited them ahead.

No such caution was now required.

This morning he knew what to expect, not needing to hold his gun. So he jogged slightly hunched. Did Rubens, he wondered? Maybe he didn't have to. Mac was a tall six-one, nearly six-two. Rubens was shorter, five-ten at best. It might have been easier for him. Mac would have to account for that.

The other thing he checked for intermittently was whether there was cell phone reception. There were no bars. At one point, he tried making a call but the phone remained silent.

He reached the "T", turned left and took off at a more rapid sprint. He reached the ladder and climbed his way up and pushed the cover up and off.

Wire was waiting for him. "Eleven minutes, seven seconds," she reported, holding up her cell phone display.

"Okay. I want to take one more run at it."

The second time he really pushed it, now familiar with the tunnel, not checking his phone. Mac just hunched over jogging, and then when he reached the "T" in the tunnel he ran at nearly a full sprint until he reached the ladder up to the street.

He shaved more time.

"Ten minutes, fourteen seconds, Mac," Dara reported, taking the last sip of what was left of her coffee as she sat casually on the back of her Range Rover, the tailgate lifted. "Now will you please tell me what the hell this is all about?"

"You would agree I'm in good shape and a pretty athletic guy?" Mac asked.

"Yes and yes," she replied. "I didn't need you to go through the tunnels to prove it though."

"So how long do you think it takes someone like Rubens to get through that tunnel?"

Dara's eyes narrowed, trying to figure out where Mac was going. "It would have taken him longer. From what I could tell from the video the other day, he is no speedster or athlete, certainly not like you or I. So that works against him. On the other hand, he's shorter than you."

"He wouldn't have had to crouch to the degree I did, especially in the tunnel before the T."

"Right, so that might narrow the gap a little, I suppose, but not nearly to the point of evening it out." She thought for a moment and then shook her head. "It would have to take him longer than you. I bet by a minute, maybe two. Now why is that important?"

"It's all about timing, Dara. Let's go back to last night. I roll up on the scene at 9:02—I know because I checked my watch as I ran up the front steps of the apartment building. I knew I was up against the clock. I raced upstairs into the apartment and found Eleanor there and checked her pulse. That took maybe two minutes, between checking on her and waiting for the paramedic.

"So now it's 9:05.

"I step into the hallway, you arrive, more cops are arriving, and then the neighbor reports Rubens ran out the back door of the building. The neighbor thinks he did so maybe a minute or two at most before we arrived on the scene.

"So he's out the door at 9:01 according to the surveillance footage. If he had pre-opened the manhole cover, he was in that tunnel mere seconds later. If he had to open it, it's more likely thirty or forty seconds later, so that would make it 9:02."

"Which is when you arrived, right?"

"Right. I'm arriving in the front of the building at 9:02 and we rushed in.

"Then Dara, you arrive, and it's 9:05, maybe 9:06 now. Again, I know this because when I started running down the hallway toward the back steps is when I got the call from Rubens, which came in at 9:06:43.

"So if he exits the building at 9:01 and gets down into that tunnel less than a minute later, he's maybe four to five, maybe six to seven minutes ahead of us at best."

"Okay, so?" Dara asked.

"When his call came to me, he'd then be where?"

Wire's eyes lit up, seeing where he was going. "In the tunnel. But he couldn't call you from down there with no cell phone reception. We checked repeatedly and we were getting no signal in that tunnel. The timing must be off somehow."

"I wondered about that, which is why I wanted to run the tunnel this morning and time it. Dara, I don't think we're off. And even if we're off a minute or two here, it still took me a good ten, if not eleven minutes to get through that sewer tunnel. I'm certain I moved quicker through those sewer pipes than Rubens.

"Dara, he couldn't call from the tunnel and he couldn't have made it through in time to call me. It's not possible."

"Soooo ... you're saying he's not the one who called?"

"Nope."

"So who did?"

"I think Rubens has a partner."

21

"MAC, WHO IS RUBENS?"

W ire looked at him slacked jawed. "Partner? You think he has an accomplice? You think he's working with someone?"

"Not quite so loud," Mac replied with a smile, looking around the alley.

"Sorry, but you think he has a partner?"

"Yes. Did you read the transcript of my call with Rubens last night?"

"I did, so?"

"What did he say about going on?"

"He said we go on. He said ... we. You think he meant..."

"I figured he meant the game between you and me and him. I thought that's what he meant by we. But what if he meant something else? What if there was a verbal slip? The call isn't from the killer at the scene, it's from the partner who's distracting us from the chase. Maybe the partner isn't always the one making the call. Or maybe better yet, it was a ..."

"Subtle clue," Dara mused, finishing Mac's thought.

"Who knows," Mac answered. "It's another little wrinkle in the game. He's seeing if we would catch it, pick up on it and figure it out."

"But Mac, a partner?" Dara exclaimed, still not quite believing what she was hearing. "For something as sick as this? Really?"

"Think about it. How else can he be such a Houdini all the time?" Mac replied in a hushed tone. "How does he evade Walker in Los Angeles? His timing was a little like ours last night, not as tight but within minutes. How does he make a phone call from the sewer pipe where you can't get cell service down there? How is it he never gets caught? He's got help. *He*, is a *we*."

The look on Wire's face was one of disbelief that was slowly evolving into comprehension.

"It makes sense when you think about it," Mac added, selling the theory. "And if I'm right, it changes things dramatically for the better."

"How do you figure? Doesn't that double our problem? Isn't that another person to look for? We're no closer to finding the partner than we are to finding Rubens."

"On the contrary," Mac answered. "Now that I know he has a partner I think I know who Rubens is—or at least who one of the people that make up Rubens is."

"You ...know...who Rubens is? *Who*?"

"Let's go back to my place."

Ten minutes later, they were up in Mac's attic office and he was digging through his home file on Rubens, the initial paper copy that Grace Delmonico had given him.

"Mac, who is Rubens?" Wire demanded, the suspense killing her.

"Just one more second," Mac delayed, digging through brown expandable files. "Here it is." He held up a folder marked *Boston*. "So, do you remember back in Boston they arrested a guy, a medical examiner? He had a tie to victim number one and they had him on surveillance video within a block or two of the second victim."

"Sure, I remember spending a minute on that as background information. But Mac, they released him."

"They did so because he was in custody when the third victim was murdered and under surveillance when the fourth victim was murdered."

"Right, so he didn't do it."

"But Dara, if he had a sidekick, doesn't that scenario play a little differently?"

"So you're thinking the partner killed the third and fourth victims?"

"The pieces fit. While the last two victims were staged as Rubens likes to do, the clock and clues were left and those were *new*, so that's different. Those were an add-on, along with a taunt, a message which all served as a diversion away from the man they had in custody."

"And the method was a little different too," Dara added, giving the file a look.

"That's right—that's what I was thinking as well as I ran through that sewer tunnel a second time, giving this theory of mine more analysis. In most of Rubens' murders, the victims were drugged and then strangled."

"But not those last two victims in Boston. They were not killed as cleanly as the others," Dara observed. "The third woman was killed with a baseball bat and the fourth with knitting needles—one stuffed in the victim's ear and the other through her right eye."

"So those two cases feel different when you look back on it now, don't they?" Mac asked as he rummaged through another file.

"They do," Dara agreed. "It's as if someone else killed the first two with one method and someone different with a more brutal method took care of the second two victims. The similarity is they're Rubenesque women who were staged like Rubens paintings."

"Ah, found it," Mac exclaimed as he pulled out a picture and handed it to Dara. It was a mugshot of the man the Boston police arrested ten years ago. "What do you think?"

The photo is of a man in his mid-thirties with dark black hair. There was no facial hair although he did have a five o'clock shadow that made Mac think of Richard Nixon. The man had a bulbous nose and his right nostril looked a little bigger than the left.

Dara set the photo down in the midst of the sketches and surveillance photos they had developed of Rubens over the past couple of days. She studied the pictures for a minute and the similarities were evident. She looked up to Mac with a small smile. "It's possible. You could continue to have sketch artists refine what we have with this photo." She looked back down at the photo array and then back up to Mac again. "What was the medical examiner's name?"

"Munger," Mac replied. "Dr. Maynard Munger."

22

"LIKE ALL GOOD STORIES, YOU HAVE TO START AT THE BEGINNING."

M ac and Wire slid their way quietly into the FBI field office, found Delmonico in her office and discreetly picked her up on their way to Galloway's. Inside Galloway's office, without saying a word, Mac shut the door and along with Wire pulled closed all of the blinds covering the interior office windows.

"What's with all the cloak and dagger?" Galloway inquired with his tie askew, the top button of his dress shirt undone and tufts of his hair jutting out in various directions. The senior agent was working on his third cup of coffee with two other cold half-finished cups sitting amongst the piles of paper on his desk. Then he took quick notice of the sudden liveliness of McRyan and Wire's body language and the excited looks on their faces. "What do you have?" he asked.

"We've been doing a little sleuthing on our own this morning," Mac stated.

"And we figured something out," Wire added.

"Which is?" Galloway inquired, sitting back in his chair, arms folded.

"That Rubens has a partner," Mac answered.

"What?" Delmonico breathed in disbelief.

"A partner?" Galloway huffed.

"Yes, and from that, we think one-half of Rubens is named Maynard Munger."

"Munger? Munger?" Delmonico asked, trying to place the name. "Wait a second. Wasn't he the guy Boston arrested ten years ago?"

"Indeed," Mac confirmed.

"Perhaps you should start from the beginning," Galloway instructed, sitting back with his arms folded. "How do you get there?"

Mac explained what he and Wire had been up to the last few hours. "No way Rubens makes that call last night—no way. Not possible because he's in that sewer tunnel. He had help, someone to call and distract us."

"And told you *we* go on," Delmonico clarified skeptically. "So you hear that and figure there's a partner?"

"I'll admit maybe that's a logical leap on my part," Mac replied, conceding the point slightly. "Maybe I'm hearing something that isn't there. Except I keep going back to the fact that there is no way that Rubens made the call from that sewer pipe. Not with a cheap burner phone. It didn't happen. He has a partner."

"And this person...what?" Galloway asked. "Killed the third and fourth victims in Boston?"

"Yes!" Mac and Wire called out together.

"So it begs the question," Mac asked. "Where is Dr. Maynard Munger?"

"Dead," Delmonico replied, looking up from her laptop. "Maynard Munger is dead."

"What?" Wire yelped, suddenly crushed, looking to Mac in shock.

Mac was not surprised. "Of course he's dead. What I'm curious about is how and when?"

"I'm reading from a story in the *Boston Globe*," Delmonico answered. "About four months after he was arrested he was on a sailing trip in the Atlantic."

"A sailing trip?" Wire asked.

"That's what it says," Grace answered. "A few days after he set sail on his own, Hurricane Ernesto took a more northerly track, although by the time it got farther north it was downgraded to a tropical storm.

After the storm passed, Munger's sailboat was found capsized in the Atlantic south of Long Island. They found the sailboat but no sign of the body."

"That's one way to do it," Mac replied.

"You're not the least bit surprised, are you?" Wire asked Mac, shaking her head at her own sidekick's ability to see three steps ahead.

"No. Think about it. What better way to disappear than to make everyone think you're dead?"

"Let me get this straight," Galloway asked, holding his hands up, still a skeptic. "You're saying that Munger faked his death by capsizing his sailboat in the Atlantic so that he then could come back four years later and murder women in Chicago? Have you two had enough sleep?" he asked incredulously. "That's crazy."

Mac laughed and reached into his pocket and handed a folded ten-dollar bill to Wire. "You were right."

"I told you," Wire replied with a proud smile, waving the bill in her fingers.

"What?" Galloway barked, now holding his arms out.

"I bet ten dollars you wouldn't think this was crazy. Dara said you would. She was right."

"Well, it is," Galloway snorted. "It's damn crazy."

"Is it?" Mac shot back, undeterred. "He disappears for three to four years every time, so why would the first time have been any different? Besides, if he doesn't disappear, every time Rubens came back people would look at Maynard Munger. Or his name would come up and he would be in the spotlight. If he's in Chicago or Los Angeles while Rubens is operating? He'd instantly be a suspect."

"Instead," Wire added, picking up the train of thought, "for the last ten years he's been a mere footnote in books, long forgotten, doing this right under everyone's nose."

"And he's been doing it with help," Mac finished. "It's the only way he can call me and be in that damn sewer tunnel at the same time. For all intents and purposes, Rubens is not one person, but two."

"Okay," Galloway began, the level of skepticism in his tone receding. "Let's just assume for a second that what the two of you say is true. What do you propose to do?"

"Wire and I are going to go to Boston and look into this."

"Hold on," Delmonico interrupted. "We have a little more than thirty hours and you think that the best investigative approach is to go to Boston?"

"Rubens didn't leave a clue behind to work with," Mac answered. "He said we'll have to find him, there will be no clue as to the victim. Well, here all that is left is to keep pushing the pictures, keep encouraging women to call and to keep working the neighborhood around Eagleson's condo to see if anything pops. You don't need us for that. Lincoln Coolidge, his men and the Bureau are already doing that."

"So you're going to Boston to see if you can find the trail for Munger?" Delmonico asked.

"That's the plan," Mac answered. "And given the sensitive nature of this, not a word about it to anyone around here, either of you. Not a single soul other than the two of you is to know about this."

"At least not until we lock this down a little more," Galloway agreed.

"Right," Mac replied and then to Delmonico said, "Grace, I need everything you can find on Munger but again, keep this close. Not a word to anyone else in the investigation, including Coolidge, April Greene, anyone. For now, this stays among the four of us and that's it."

"Even Coolidge?"

"I hate to lock Linc out but he likes talking to the reporters and to just talk in general. It's his affable nature."

"What do you need for Boston?" Galloway asked.

"A plane to take us up there and wait for us," Mac answered, pacing the floor of Galloway's office. "The other thing I want is Gavin Sullivan, the retired detective who had the Rubens case, to meet us at the airport and for you to give the chief a call up there and make whatever we need available to us. Again, he needs to keep it on the down low. We have time yet. If we're right about

Munger, I don't want to spook him. If we're right about a partner, I don't want to spook whoever that is either. This is our last chance to nail their asses before they go back into hiding again for three or four years."

"I'll get the plane ready and take care of that, but Mac, what do you think you can find in Boston?" Galloway pressed. "It's been ten years and you've got little time to work with."

"Like all good stories you have to start at the beginning. Boston is where it started. In the meantime, get everything you can on Munger —I mean back to the day he was born, where he went to elementary school, who he took to prom, his college professors, medical school classmates, jobs, friends, pets, anyone who ever crossed paths with him. Being a partner in an enterprise like this doesn't happen with someone you don't know. You don't walk along the street and find this person. This is someone you know somehow, that he had some sort of relationship with at some point in his past. That's where we'll find that person."

"...Yes, my flight gets into town at 1:30 p.m. tomorrow... Yes, I am so looking forward to getting back to town. A month is just too long to be away... I can't wait to see it as well, and you. I've missed you. It is going to be fantastic. See you tomorrow." Rubens hung up the phone, a satisfied smile on his face.

"So, Maynard, she's set?"

"Yes, enthusiastically so," Rubens answered and then snapped angrily, "and don't call me Maynard. I always hated that name."

"Sorry. Your name changes so often I can't keep track. It's the one I can remember. However, as for your date tomorrow, you're *sure* she's ready to go?"

"I am," Rubens replied edgily. "I don't like how you're questioning me."

"Come on, can you blame me after last night?"

"Last night was not my fault! I didn't choose that location!"

Munger shouted and then pointed out, "You did. That was *your* idea, not mine. I told you it could be problematic."

"But *you* chose her," his partner answered evenly. "When you chose her the condo became the only real play for you, which is why I had you so well prepared. I thought there was a chance that clue would be too damn easy so you're lucky, very lucky that I prepared you for that. I provided you a way out. You're quite fortunate it worked."

Rubens nodded reluctantly. "That's true but the heat is really on now."

"The plot has indeed thickened. It's starting to get really good. This is the fun part, Maynard."

"Quit calling me Maynard."

"Sorry, but this is where the challenge lies. You're not *afraid,* are you?"

"No! No, I'm not afraid. I've never been afraid. But at the same time, we've never had this much heat on us. I mean, did it ever occur to you that if I get caught, *you* could get caught?"

"I'm not the one out killing."

"Ah, but you have," Rubens answered, wagging his finger. "Have you ever thought that maybe it might be good to just walk away now? Give it some time, reassess and maybe reappear a few years down the road again?"

He was pushing back, a rarity in their discussions.

"No. No, no, no. We can't do that, not now. If you shrink away now, it won't be the same. It'll never be the same. When you came out of hiding next time, it would just be sad and pathetic, like a Spice Girls comeback. Your aura would be gone because you didn't finish the job."

"Good thing we've changed up in several ways, then."

"You mean the fact you left without setting a clock or leaving a clue? Without McRyan having a way to find you?"

"No, I mean my look," Maynard answered, holding up the wig of long blond hair and the thick scruffy beard. "And the fact that I'm not Glenda's *new* boyfriend. It's been a slow burn over a longer period of time, which if you will recall, was *my* idea. We've not done that before. I'm not a new guy showing up in a woman's life. There won't be the suspicion from her because as far as she knows—"

"You look nothing like all these Rubens images. And, at least as far as she knows, you've been out of town for a month."

"Exactly. So, McRyan's warnings to women on that front are meaningless. He's dead in the water."

23

"YET YOU WATCHED HIM AFTER YOU RELEASED HIM."

T he FBI plane landed in Boston in the late afternoon. While on the flight, Mac and Wire dug deeper into the Boston murders attributed to Rubens. Like Chicago, Los Angeles and apparently Washington, Rubens stuck to four victims. The women all fit the overall profile of a Rubens victim. They were shy, reserved, had few friends and they all fit the voluptuous physical profile. There was the signature staging of the victims in tribute to famous Rubens paintings, although the setups were cruder and not nearly as detailed or dramatic as his later work.

"He was growing as an artist," Wire remarked.

"Yeah, a homicidal one that kills very specifically."

"God, I'd love to know what it is about these kinds of women that make them attractive to him," Wire remarked. "Why *these* women?"

"Even April Greene doesn't know," Mac replied. "And this is what she does."

"What do you think?"

"Me?"

"Yeah, what do you really think, Mac? Give me your uneducated guess. That's better than most people's educated guesses, even if they're experts like April Greene."

"He had faulty brain wiring to begin with," Mac answered. "Then all it took was some trigger, some life event at just the right time to set him off. You don't wake up one day and decide to kill women in honor of Rubens. You decide to kill women like that and you use the whole Rubens thing to dress it up."

"So Rubens doesn't matter now?"

"Sure it matters, but the more I've thought about it, it doesn't matter as much as whatever event triggered all of this," Mac answered. "I asked Rubens why the tribute to Rubens the artist because I hoped maybe he'd let slip where he became such a fan of Rubens and if he said something, maybe we find him that way. That was the point of the question. I could care less about the artist Rubens. I simply was looking for a way to identify the killer who calls himself Rubens."

"And what about the helper?"

"I didn't know about the accomplice when I asked that question," Mac replied, glancing up from the files. "I suppose it depends if the partner is the alpha or not."

"Is the partner a helper or—"

"The one actually pulling all of the strings," Mac finished. "In a relationship like this there is usually an alpha. One is the dominant and the other submissive."

"It's not *Fifty Shades of Grey*," Wire counseled.

"Isn't it?"

"What, you think Rubens is killing under orders?"

Mac shook his head. "No. I think he would be someone who was predisposed to do it to begin with. The partner, if the partner is the dominant, is the one goading him into it, pushing him to do it or maybe possibly using Rubens the killer to fulfill the wishes the alpha has."

"Why?"

Mac slumped back into his plane seat. "I... I don't know. Maybe they get off on manipulating someone into doing something. Think about it this way—when we interrogate a suspect, we manipulate them, don't we? We maneuver them into telling us things they don't want to tell us and trap them. And when we do it and it works, we—"

"Get something out of it? In some cases, we get off on it."

"Right, we get something ... mental, intellectual, emotional, whatever it is, out of succeeding. It's the same thing with the alpha. The alpha gets something out of manipulating Rubens into doing what he does."

"Or they're the helper."

"Or they're the helper," Mac replied. "But let me tell you something."

"What's that?"

"If it was the partner that was on the line with me last night while Rubens was running through that sewer line, that partner was one hell of an actor. That person was *excited* to be on the line. They were taunting, confident, arrogant and—"

"And what?"

"Having fun."

"Fun? Having fun?" Wire repeated.

"Yes."

"Mac, that voice was masked. How could you tell?"

"I could tell. Sure, the voice was masked so that hides the actual voice but it doesn't necessarily eliminate the other elements like pacing, tone, emphasis and word choice. I could hear it in the voice. The person was having ... fun. They were getting to do something they don't usually get to and they were in the moment."

"Huh," Wire mused, suddenly thinking she should take another listen to the call. "Not the voice of a helper then?"

"I don't think so."

"Could have been acting?"

"Make the voice an Oscar nominee, then."

The plane taxied to a stop as the sun was beginning to work its way down the western horizon. Waiting on the tarmac, leaning against a silver Ford Fusion sedan was a man they recognized from a photograph in the file as retired Boston Police detective Gavin Sullivan.

After quick introductions were exchanged, Sullivan got right to it. "You're really thinking it was Munger? How can that be?"

Mac recounted the events of the prior night and then the intellectual leap to Munger.

"Rubens has help, that's the only way I get the call last night. I'm thinking if he had a partner last night, he could have had one ten years ago and Munger actually disappearing or being thought dead makes me think it is more likely, not less, that it is actually him. If Rubens reappears a few years later, don't you think people would have started looking at Munger again? You don't think people would have made at least a cursory check on him? But if everyone thinks he's dead nobody gives him another thought."

Sullivan considered what Mac had to say. "If you're right, how was I supposed to figure all that out?"

"You weren't," Wire answered, shaking her head. "There is no way you would have known."

"It took them, *assuming it's a them*, making a little timing mistake last night for us to figure it out ten years and fifteen victims later," Mac added. "We got a break. There is no way that call was made by Rubens when it was. He was in that tunnel." Mac switched Munger topics and asked Sullivan, "So you knew Munger, right?"

"Not really well," Sullivan replied, obviously still chewing on Mac's theory. "But I did know him, I suppose, like any homicide detective knows a medical examiner."

"Tell us about him," Mac asked.

"Well, he was a quirky guy for sure." Sullivan told them what he knew of Munger as he drove through the Callahan Tunnel into Boston and then veered to the north to the Zakim Bridge crossing the Charles River. "Maynard Munger, as I recall, was originally from Chicago, although his family moved to Connecticut when he was like fifteen years old. Munger went to school at Providence College where he studied pre-med and one other thing."

"Which was?" Wire asked.

"He majored in pre-med but he had a minor in—get this: art history."

"Art history?" Wire asked, looking incredulously to Mac.

"It's legitimate," Mac replied dryly, quoting the Brad Pitt line from *Mr. & Mrs. Smith*. "So when the bodies were staged like women in the paintings and you saw the art history minor—"

"It was a little nugget that made us think maybe Munger looked good for it all. It's not a huge intuitive leap to think that someone with an interest in art would stage murder victims as a tribute to a famous painter."

Sullivan went on to explain that after college, Munger graduated from the University of Connecticut Medical School. "He performed his residency at Massachusetts General here in Boston."

"Mass General?" Wire asked in surprise. "How does he go from Mass General, the best hospital in the country, to being a medical examiner?"

"I remember asking him that very question ten years ago," Sullivan replied. "He said he liked the science, the unique medical conditions, the interesting diagnostic cases, but not the patients."

"No bedside manner?" Mac asked.

"No," Sullivan replied with a light shake of the head. "He was social enough, but at the same time, he didn't seem to have a lot of warmth to him. Corpses don't engage in conversation and ask if they're going to be okay. They only speak through the evidence and that seemed to work for Munger."

"Did you work with him often?" Wire inquired.

"Often enough," Sullivan answered casually, his right hand draped over the wheel. "He was a pretty decent medical examiner although when I look back on it, I always thought he was just a bit of an odd duck."

"How so?" Mac pressed.

"Two reasons. First, he was always just a bit awkward," Sullivan answered, looking away for a second. "He was just kind of a cold guy. I didn't think much of it at the time. He was a medical examiner—they're all a little off if you ask me. You go to medical school and then you spend all your time with dead bodies figuring out how and why they're dead. I thought you became a doctor to save lives."

"What was the second reason?" Wire asked.

"The one thing that seemed to really animate him was death," Sullivan answered. "He loved murder scenes. Most M.E.s, they want to get the body back to the morgue and examine it. Not Munger."

"He liked the crime scenes?"

Sullivan nodded. "He liked hanging around, overseeing evidence collection, looking at the evidence, offering unsolicited opinions on it, asking questions about it and trying to figure out what happened at the murder scene before he ever got the body back to his examination table. Even there, if you went and saw him, he would get animated, even excited in discussing the details and presenting his theories like he was Quincy M.E. from the old television show. At the time, I thought nothing of it other than he was just into it and had passion for his work, which in general is a good thing. We all like working with people who like their jobs. However, in retrospect, it probably should have been recognized as a sign of some greater interest than normal in death and murder."

Their first stop was Munger's last known residence, a relatively modest apartment building resting on the north side of the Charles River. "Nicole Franzen, the first Rubens victim, lived two floors up from him," Sullivan stated while they stood on the sidewalk looking up at the six-story apartment building. He pointed to the left side of the building. "Munger was on the second floor at the end. Franzen was two floors directly up above Munger's unit."

"I assume you looked at people in the building right away?" Wire asked, walking past Sullivan as he held the front door to the building open.

"We did," Sullivan answered. "And we interviewed Munger. He, like all other building residents who were home at the time, said he hadn't heard or seen a thing. At the scene itself, there was no physical evidence left behind, no forensic evidence that we found. Early on, we really didn't have any leads."

"But then a few weeks later he showed up on surveillance video at 3:00 a.m., walking a few blocks away from the second murder scene," Mac stated, leading Sullivan. "And then you had a lead."

"That's right," the retired detective answered. "We're northeast of downtown right here. Bunker Hill Monument is two blocks east of this building. You could see it as we drove up here. Now the second victim, Paige Wetmore, she lived way over just west of Fenway Park."

Mac had been to Fenway a few years ago to watch the Twins play the Red Sox. "That's gotta be like, what? Four miles from here?"

"A tick over that, *if you're driving*. And walking over there is a whole different story. You can add a good mile to that total just to get there, walking city streets and having to cross the Charles River."

"And he said he was out for a walk five miles from his apartment at 3:00 a.m.? He really said that?" Wire asked Sullivan.

"Yes, ma'am. So, a guy who lives in the building of the first victim shows up on surveillance footage a block from the murder scene at 3:00 a.m., taking a ten-mile round-trip walk? What do you think, Agent Wire?"

"I think that sounds very odd. I think that sounds like a very questionable excuse."

"That's what I thought, too," Sullivan answered. "Now the time of death was pegged between 9:00 and 11:00 p.m. and he claimed he was home at that time and didn't leave for his walk until around midnight."

"Could he prove it?" Mac asked.

Sullivan shook his head. "Nobody could verify that, but if you are home alone, who really could?"

"Someone in the building saw him, perhaps?" Wire asked.

"Nobody came forward to say that and he couldn't give us anyone," Sullivan answered. "So I went along with him and asked him what he was doing at home. That's where it got really hinky because he wasn't really able to give me the kind of answers you'd expect."

"Like what?"

"It was simple stuff, Agent Wire. For example, and I remember asking him—I recall the exchange very clearly. I asked him what he was doing at home.

"He said: I was watching television.

"So then I asked him: Okay, what were you watching?

"He couldn't tell me what he was watching.

"So I sat across the table and was silent, just kind of staring at him in disbelief and he picked up on that. So then he tried to tell me: Well, maybe I was reading."

"So I asked: What were you reading?"

"No specifics?" Wire asked, shaking her head.

"He couldn't remember what he was reading," Sullivan answered. "He couldn't tell me the book he was reading or the television shows he was watching."

Sullivan looked to Mac and then back to Wire. "You two have done this job a while. You just can tell when someone isn't on the level, when they're full of shit."

"For sure," Mac answered with a nod.

"Munger—" Sullivan shook his head at the memory. "When we had him in the room he didn't admit to anything. He didn't crack per se, but you could just tell he wasn't on the level."

"It was hinky?" Wire asked.

"For sure, you get the hit off the guy that he isn't being honest, that he's hiding something," Sullivan answered as he got them admitted to the apartment building. The tenant in Munger's old apartment on the second level let them in to look around. "Thank you," Sullivan said pleasantly to the tenant. "We appreciate your accommodating us and we shouldn't be long."

"No problem. I'll run an errand," the tenant replied, grabbed his spring jacket and car keys and he was off.

After the tenant was gone, Sullivan closed the door and picked the story back up. "So after we found Munger near victim number two, we looked at him much harder for the first victim, Nicole Franzen. Like I said, he told us he was home alone but nobody could confirm it."

"I saw a surveillance camera in the lobby as we came in here," Mac stated. "Am I to presume that was not there ten years ago?"

"Correct," Sullivan answered. "There was nothing of the sort at the time."

"Okay, so how do you think he pulled it off?" Mac asked. "Assuming he did."

Sullivan took them back to the front door of the apartment, opened the door and stepped into the hallway and pointed to the left. "Munger has the end unit here. It's fifteen feet to the end of the hall and there on the right is the entry into the end stairway well. When I was thinking Munger was the guy, I was thinking he went up that way."

They all went up the steps to the fourth floor. The occupant of the apartment was out of town but the building superintendent let them in to look around after seeing their government badges.

"I can't believe a neighbor didn't hear or see anything," Wire suggested, looking around the apartment while scanning the case file.

"I hear you," Sullivan answered. "However, at the time Nicole Franzen was killed, the apartment next door was unoccupied, awaiting rental, so nobody was there to hear anything. Also, conveniently, the tenant across the hall was out of town. So he had an easy way to get up here unseen and—"

"None of the nearby tenants were home," Mac supplied. "So how did he do it?

With our victims in DC, he's using a date rape drug to incapacitate them. I didn't see any evidence of that in the toxicology report on her murder."

"Here's what we thought happened," Sullivan answered and moved toward the front door. "He came up here and knocked on the door and we think she let him in. There was no evidence of forced entry. I'll get to it in a minute, but it turns out they did know each other and had some history. So we thought she let him in the apartment voluntarily."

"And then he did the deed?"

Sullivan nodded. "There was a dating history although it was in the past. So this is total speculation but I thought perhaps he was up here trying to rekindle it and she rebuffed it. At some point, she asks him to leave, turns her back to him and walks over here to the door to open it so he can exit. Now," the retired detective held up a crime scene photo of the interior wall to the left of the front door. "See the indentation into the wall here and the height of it?"

"Yes," Mac answered it immediately. "He came from behind and smashed her head into the wall."

"Right," Sullivan remarked. "At which point she's incapacitated, weakened, disoriented, concussed, whatever. It puts him in the power position and I think he then pushes her down to the floor, gets on top of her and—"

"Strangles her," Wire finished the thought, instinctively reaching for her own throat. "You think it was a crime of passion, spur-of-the-moment kind of thing."

"That was my thought," Sullivan replied.

Mac was taking a closer look at one of the crime scene photos, taken from low to the ground and noticed a picture in the background. "I'll be damned."

"What?" Sullivan asked.

"*The Judgment of Paris*," Mac muttered, holding up the photo. "It's a painting of Rubens'. It's on the wall in the background in Franzen's apartment."

"Yeah, so?" Sullivan asked.

"So maybe that's why he chose Rubens. That's the inspiration."

"What are you getting at, Mac?" Wire asked.

"You and I were talking about it on the flight up. I've asked why Rubens and now maybe I know why," Mac answered. "Detective Sullivan has described a potential crime of passion. Munger comes up here and Franzen rejects him, perhaps not the first time. This time, he gets angry and just snaps. Enraged, he smashes her head into the wall and then strangles her. It's all over in a minute or two. But now he's done the deed. She's lying here on the floor and he's thinking—"

"What the hell do I do now?" Wire finished.

"How do I deflect attention away from me because I had a history with Nicole Franzen?" Sullivan added. "That's what he's thinking. All of that is running through his head now that he's killed her."

"Right, the *oh shit* moment," Mac continued. "But he gets his wits about him. After all, he's been around crime scenes before. He knows how you guys think. So he's thinking that he needs to deflect and fast. So how does he do that?"

"He makes it look like some sort of ritual killing," Sullivan answers. "He makes it look like it might be the start of something."

"Right, so Mr. Art History Minor starts looking around the apartment and he sees *The Judgment of Paris* hanging on the wall and knows that's a painting of the famous artist Peter Paul Rubens. He looks down and it dawns on him that Nicole is very Rubenesque in shape." Mac moved around the apartment, looking through the crime scene photos, visualizing how the furniture and furnishings were laid out ten years ago. "So he sees the portrait and he sees his way to make it look like something other than a spurned lover. So he undresses Franzen and lays her nude in the middle of the floor of the living room here. He poses her body with her arms wrapped above her head and then winds the lacy blanket through her arms and around her body, finishing in the front."

"So when the police do discover her, they immediately start wondering about some sort of ritual, serial kind of killing because her body has been very specifically staged," Wire speculated.

"Which is what we kind of did," Sullivan agreed, nodding. "When I saw her staged like this, with the picture in the background, I thought this might not be a singular event. We were on the phone to the FBI within a day or two asking for their take, so if that was his intent, it worked."

"But Mac," Wire asked, "if this was a crime of passion, how does Munger go from that to wanting to kill again?"

Mac folded his arms and thought for a moment. "I see your point. I guess if April Greene were here, she might speculate that killing once, seeming to get away with it, stirred something in him. That's when the ... transition occurs. He sits for days and obsesses about it, thinks about it more and more and how he got away with it and how he felt after, and he didn't necessarily feel bad. Instead, the more he thinks about it the more he wants to ... do it again. He wants that thrill again. Munger gets a thirst to kill again so he goes about planning and finding another victim."

"Or," Wire offered, "he decided to kill another woman and stage her in a similar Rubens-like way to further deflect attention from himself for the Nicole Franzen murder."

"That's not bad," Mac replied. "That works, too. Might be a little of both."

"But under either of your scenarios he still screws up," Sullivan stated, "because he gets himself caught on that surveillance footage over by Fenway. And once we questioned him and started looking into his history, we learned pretty quickly that he'd actually gone out on a few dates a year before with Nicole Franzen. Before it really got going anywhere, she apparently ended it. After it ended, there were a number of phone calls but those eventually stopped."

"Attempts to rekindle the flame probably," Mac speculated. "Which might have been what he was doing the night of the murder."

"That's what we were thinking. However, by the time he killed Nicole Franzen, assuming he did, Munger hadn't called her in six months."

"So how did you discover that Munger dated her?"

"A neighbor told us, but she didn't mention it until after we'd picked Munger up and we were searching his apartment. That's when she stopped down and dropped that little nugget on us. She said, 'Well, you know Maynard and Nicole did go out on a couple of dates.'"

"And he had failed to mention that, I imagine," Wire suggested.

"It did seem to have slipped his mind," Sullivan answered with a wry smile. "When we were first here interviewing neighbors, he said he hardly knew who she was. Clearly, he lied about it. Why lie?"

"To avoid suspicion, obviously," Mac answered. "Which was really kind of dumb because that only raised suspicion on your part, which was silly because he also probably knew that you had no physical evidence tying him to the scene."

"That's right. No matter our suspicions, we didn't have near enough to charge him," Sullivan answered. "Nobody placed him near this apartment and while it was extremely odd that he would have been out on a long walk at 3:00 a.m. it's not entirely impossible either. People do weird shit sometimes, and Munger was an odd duck, and it was also true that he liked to go on long walks at night. So while it was an awfully incredible coincidence, in the absence of any physical evidence or any witnesses placing him at either scene, all we had was our suspicions."

"Did he ever ask for a lawyer?"

"No, Agent McRyan, he never did, which I always thought was odd. But he admitted nothing and the clock was running. Because he'd hung around murder scenes and the police so much, and because he was a pretty smart guy to begin with, he understood how the process worked. We could only hold him for so long. The problem was that while we had him in custody victim number three went down. I get the phone call from the killer, if that's who it was, telling me where to find the victim, Naomi Ratliff. With her time of death, it clearly happened while Munger was in our custody."

"So you let him go," Mac stated.

"We had to. How could he be the killer of number three if the girl was murdered when he was sitting in our interrogation room?"

"Yet you watched him after you released him," Wire stated.

"Why?" Mac asked. He knew the answer.

"Because he just seemed so right for those two murders," Sullivan replied, shaking his head. "But then we got another call. The caller told us about victim number four, Katrina Wiggins. When the call was made, we had eyes on Munger, sitting in his apartment, casually reading a book. Two detectives were watching him at the time Wiggins was murdered. Heck, we had eight cops in total on him, covering every exit of this apartment building. He did not murder Katrina Wiggins."

"When you watched him, how did you know he never left the apartment?" Mac asked. "It couldn't have been easy to see into his apartment."

"No, you wouldn't think so," Sullivan replied. "He left the curtains wide open and he was visible so there was no question, Mr. McRyan, he didn't do it. And then that was the end of Rubens. I get the call from the killer saying *nice try* and that he was gone, and he was. After that the murders stopped, the calls stopped, *everything* stopped."

"You kept investigating?" Wire asked.

"For some time, but the trail went ice cold. Munger eventually went back to work and actually showed up on one of my murder scenes two months later. He acted as if nothing had ever happened, but it was—"

"Awkward," Wire supplied.

"Weird more than anything else," Sullivan corrected, "because something wasn't right about him. Then a few months later he resigned and was set to take a job somewhere else, which at the time I thought was probably best for all involved. Then another month or so later I saw the article in the *Globe* about him dying at sea and to be honest, until the call earlier today I hadn't thought about him in years."

"Not even when Rubens reappeared in Chicago?"

Sullivan shook his head and exhaled a sigh. "I tried to help those two Chicago detectives as much as I could, but Munger was not someone I thought one second about. I thought Munger was dead—hell, the whole world did. But now you're telling me he isn't."

Mac shook his head. "I don't think he is."

"So what's next?"

"We're meeting with his old boss, the Chief Medical Examiner, first thing in the morning," Mac replied. "Until then, take us around to the other murder scenes."

"And what if all of that doesn't help you?"

"Then we have to think about going public about Munger and turn the heat up that way."

Grace Delmonico worked her computer, continuing to save pieces of information into a separate file labeled *Munger*, which every so often she would forward to McRyan.

At the moment, she was sifting through information the Chicago field office was putting together on Munger when he was a child. He lived in and around Chicago until he was fifteen when his parents then moved to Hartford. The documents included grades, individual pictures and class pictures from his elementary and middle schools. He seemingly was in a new school every couple of years, his parents having moved around a lot. Grace took a look at his fifth grade class picture with Munger wearing a mustard yellow and brown shirt with tufts of hair sticking out. "Your mom didn't give you much of a chance with the girls, did she?"

"Who didn't have much of a chance?" April Greene asked as she knocked on the door.

"Oh, nothing," Grace answered and slyly switched screens on her computer. "What's up?"

"Any updates?"

"Not much," Delmonico answered disappointedly, slowly shaking her head. "Coolidge and his men are continuing to knock on doors and our tech guys are scrubbing video of the area from last night but there haven't been any new developments."

"Where are McRyan and Wire? I haven't seen them around all day."

"They're working on something," Galloway replied blandly as he walked into the office and dropped a note on Delmonico's desk.

"Like what?" Greene asked.

"Mac doesn't always share with us," Galloway answered with a wry smile as he leaned against the wall. "That's how the hierarchy of this thing is structured. He and Wire get free reign to do their thing. All I know is that they were back at Eleanor Eagleson's earlier and they found something interesting to them so they're following up on it. What it is they have not told me. I'm waiting to hear if there is anything they need Grace or me to do."

"And I assume that hasn't happened then?"

"The silence has been deafening," Galloway answered.

"It's weird," Greene noted. "I mean, it seems so quiet around here."

"So?" Grace asked.

"Look, I'm not being critical, but it's almost like we're just waiting for the next victim."

"We're not," Galloway replied with a hint of defensiveness in his voice.

"People are out doing their thing," Delmonico added and then spoke to Galloway. "Do we have updates on our photo array of Rubens?"

"We have some variations with blond hair, without mustaches and a few with longer hair. The local shows are going with it on the ten o'clock news and the cable networks have it and will slide it into their newscasts."

"Can I see?" Greene asked.

"Sure," Galloway replied and handed her a copy.

"How'd you come up with these new looks?"

"It was Mac's idea," Delmonico replied. "Remember, he thought Rubens might change up his look. These are possibilities. I don't know if they help or hurt."

"How so?" Greene asked.

"We're mixing in speculation and pictures we don't have with actual pictures and descriptions we do have," Galloway answered. "There is a risk of diluting people's ability to recognize him. However, as Mac said, we just need to get a break somehow so we put all this out there and maybe somebody calls and maybe that somebody is his fourth victim."

"I rarely say this," Delmonico added with a wry smile, "but I actually feel bad for men tonight. If what we're doing is working, women everywhere in Washington DC are looking at their boyfriends like they could possibly be killers. Suspicion is at an all-time high."

"Most men probably deserve it," Greene replied sarcastically and laughed. "I mean, their lady friends will be looking at them funny and they'll be thinking what does she know?"

"Does she know about the other woman?" Delmonico stated with a laugh.

"Does she know about the money I lost?" Galloway added. "Wives and girlfriends always know those things."

"Does she know about ... whatever," Greene added with a broad smile. "I'm with you, Grace. It can't be a good night for men."

"Like you said," Delmonico replied, smiling at Galloway, "they probably deserve it."

"And I'll be leaving now," Galloway said as he slinked away to the laughter of the two women.

"We shouldn't be laughing," Greene said to Delmonico. "We really shouldn't."

"No, no, we shouldn't but ... sometimes gallows humor is necessary."

"Indeed it is." Greene checked her watch. "With it this quiet I think I may just head home. Call me if anything pops."

"Will do."

As she exited the elevator and moved toward her car in the parking ramp a familiar voice called to April Greene.

"Any insights into the mind of our boy Rubens, Chief Brain Wizard?"

April spun around to find Ridge smiling at her, leaning against the building wall, a can of Diet Coke in his hand. "What's going on, author?"

"Not much, April. It's been quite quiet today."

"Yet you're still hanging around and looking for...let me guess. Dara Wire?"

"Or you."

"*Please,*" April mocked. "Save it, Ridge. Don't try to bullshit the mind reader. Your new girl isn't around here, that I can tell you. In fact, I haven't seen her or McRyan all day."

"Where are they?" Ridge asked, a look of surprise on his face. "Their cars are here but I haven't seen them either." It made him think back to how quickly Wire bolted out of the house in the morning. "Maybe they caught a break of some kind."

"I have no idea—they don't report to me, Ridge. If anything, I suppose I report to them," Greene answered, twirling her keys in her fingers, waiting for it.

"Well, they're not here, nothing seems to be going on and it's getting late. What do you say you and I go get a beer and talk some shop?"

Greene shook her head with a wry and knowing smile. "No, I think I'll pass. I did that once, remember. I didn't like where it ended up."

Ridge laughed, his turn to mock. "Oh come on, April, on those two nights you *very much* liked where it ended up."

"You flatter yourself, Hugo," Greene replied with a smile and then turned to walk away. She looked back over her shoulder. "It wasn't *that* great."

Ridge laughed back. She was mad he left before she woke the last morning, but it was great and she knew it.

As the clock approached midnight, Mac and Wire sat in a booth in the hotel bar having a drink. Not much was said as they both contemplated the case. Whatever momentum they thought they had earlier in the day seemed to dry up upon their arrival in Boston.

"I'm not sure what it was we thought we'd find here," Mac groaned. "We probably could have done all of this from Washington. Maybe we should have."

"Second-guessing yourself?"

"I've been second-guessing what I've been doing every step of the way, Dara. I went home and puked a week ago when I said we had to play the clock, that I had three more bodies to work with. Three are dead and number four might as well be at this point."

"She isn't dead yet," Wire scolded.

"Well, she's not but—"

"And number three almost didn't die, Mac. We were close."

"Close is irrelevant," Mac replied and raised his drink slowly to his mouth, stopped and then threw the whole thing back, grimacing as the bourbon went down and held his glass up for another drink. After the waitress left he said, "I just keep thinking we're onto something here. Maybe it's hoping."

"Well, for what it's worth, after tonight I'm more convinced than ever that your theory he's alive has legs."

"Why?"

"Too much about Maynard Munger, whether it's his background or his behavior fits for the first two murders here in Boston. Think about it, Mac. Munger was a medical examiner, so he'd understand evidence collection, not to mention what might be found during the autopsy. He's extremely intelligent. Shit, he did his residency at Mass General, maybe the best hospital in the country. And talking to Sullivan tonight, speaking with him, I came to the conclusion that he was a solid detective. You can see it in his eyes, Mac. After tonight, working with us, he knows he had the killer in his hands, across the table from him. He had him and he got away. Sullivan knows Munger killed those two women. His belief in that has me convinced." Wire took another drink. "How about you?"

Mac nodded. "I believed coming up here Munger was the guy and Sullivan said nothing tonight to make me think otherwise."

"So tomorrow do we go with Munger?"

"I don't know," Mac answered, swirling his drink in his hand. "Despite what you and I believe, take a step back and think for a minute about how that sounds. Our theory is that the murderer is a supposedly dead medical examiner from Boston who was in police custody when the third victim was killed and under intense police surveillance when the fourth victim was murdered. The proof of an accomplice is my hunch about the timing of that phone call and maybe the use of the word 'we.' I think we're right about the timing on that but it is possible we could be wrong. Now, I don't think so, but it's speculation on our part. And you want speculation? This whole 'we' theory from the phone call is a massive reach. Now, conversely, Maynard Munger disappeared at sea and that's what could have actually happened. There is no evidence he survived, none. There was a tropical storm that would have tossed his sailboat around like a toy boat in the bathtub and we're saying he either lived through it or was off the boat before the storm hit but again, what evidence do we have? It's a story even your boyfriend Ridge wouldn't dare make up."

"He's not my boyfriend."

"Ahh, but you've slept with him, haven't you? I mean, why else would it have taken you nearly an hour to get to Eleanor Eagleson's this morning?"

Wire's jaw dropped just a bit with an incredulous look but she recovered quickly. "What business is that of yours?"

"None," Mac replied lightly with a wiseass grin and then his mood immediately turned dark again as he veered back to the topic of Munger. "It's just that our whole theory sounds desperate."

"It could sound that way but I don't believe that and neither do you," Dara replied. "And I don't give a rip how it sounds, I really don't. I say we go with it and we live with the consequences."

"Fuck it."

"Hell yes. If we're right, maybe you spook him away, maybe he pulls up if he hasn't already. Or maybe you force him into a mistake. Better yet, someone identifies him for us. If we're wrong, we're wrong. If we lose a little face in the process, so what? I can live with that and so can you."

Mac nodded and took one last sip of his drink. "Munger's old boss will be back here in Boston in the morning. Let's meet with him and then get back to DC. Maybe we get lucky."

24

"WE DON'T HAVE TIME FOR A LOT OF BUREAUCRATIC BULLSHIT ON THIS."

Maynard Munger stood in front of the small mirror and began to assemble the look for Gabriel, the former logger, now sport fisherman and art lover. He started with the large, full, bushy beard, the kind that oddly seemed to be in style. It wasn't a long "Duck Dynasty" beard, more of just a full, unkempt one. It was the kind he was seeing with a number of professional athletes and just working people in general. It was a passing fad, he thought, but it worked for the here and now. With the beard secured on with a healthy dose of face glue, he slipped on the wig of long blond hair. Sometimes he'd put it into a ponytail, and other times he let it simply fall to his shoulders.

It was a look tailored specifically for Glenda.

He researched Glenda, had sat at the next booth over listening in as she spoke with two work colleagues and heard of her thing about men with blond hair and beards. There were lots of men like that back in her hometown of Duluth, Minnesota. She liked guys in flannel shirts and jeans who were men of the land. "I can't stand ties," he remembered hearing her say. "Give me a man who works with his hands."

And Glenda had some history with men. She'd been married

briefly ten years ago and unlike most of the women he pursued, she'd been with many men. She said it to her friends, she said it to him, and he believed it. She was the first victim or potential target he'd ever slept with; a date he'd let get out of control. Glenda basically jumped him. But as a result, he knew she was getting too close for his comfort, especially with his plan coming to the point where it was time to start.

He needed time away from her so, as far as she knew, he'd been gone on a long business and fishing trip. He'd kept in phone contact the whole time, calling not daily, but certainly every few days because he knew this time would be coming.

As he worked his disguise, he thought of Glenda. Her voluptuous appearance was a little more recent of a development. Facebook photos from the not too distant past revealed a slimmer look. She walked with a slight limp and she complained a few times about a balky right knee. He suspected the knee hampered her ability to stay as active as she would have liked and that had led to some weight gain. Even now, she wasn't really perfect for him. Glenda was a little slim for it, but she was close enough. She was close enough to the ideal for him but, conveniently, she was not close enough that *she* would actually think of herself in that fashion.

At one point in her life, Glenda ran an art gallery in Duluth, a small city of 85,000 in northeastern Minnesota that rested on the far southwestern shores of Lake Superior.

She loved art, sculptors and especially painters and had a particular passion for Cezanne. It was what animated her and made her alive and, as he'd found out that one night, amorous. And quite conveniently, there was an exhibit opening at the National Gallery of Art today featuring some of Cezanne's finer work.

It was the perfect place for them to reunite after his long time away.

A little before 9:00 a.m., Colin Sullivan turned right off of Albany

Street and into the parking lot for the Office-Chief Medical Examiner for the Commonwealth of Massachusetts.

"Detective Sullivan, it's been awhile," Dr. Reginald Wayne, Chief Medical Examiner, greeted Sullivan as he entered the office.

"It's good to see you, Doc," Sullivan answered and then introduced Mac and Wire.

"I've seen the news accounts of your exploits chasing that killer. I'm sure you've heard of our experiences with that man from Colin here. Now Colin called me yesterday to make sure I would be in here this morning to talk about Rubens and said you also wanted to discuss Maynard Munger."

"That's right," Mac confirmed.

"He was cleared of the murders, as I recall," Dr. Wayne replied. "And he is dead so what could he, and for that matter, I have to do with this?"

"That's the thing, Dr. Wayne, we don't think he is dead," Mac replied. "I think there is a chance, an extremely good chance, that he is very much alive. We think he is in fact the killer people know as Rubens, and we think he has an accomplice."

"A partner?" Dr. Wayne replied, his mouth agape, looking to Sullivan for confirmation. "Colin, is this true?"

"I think based on my discussions with Agents McRyan and Wire that it is possible Munger is alive and has an accomplice. It explains a number of things, especially how he was so perfect for the first two murders and yet didn't commit the last two ten years ago. Having a friend helping him explains how that could have happened."

Mac spent a few minutes walking Dr. Wayne through the theory. "We think there is no way he could have made that call and been in that sewer tunnel."

"So we think he had a partner," Wire added.

"And that got me back to Munger," Mac finished.

"I understand," Dr. Wayne replied. "But how can I help?"

"We're trying to get a handle on Munger, what he did, what his job was, where he went and who his partner was and how he came to meet that person. It all started here in Boston and this is where he worked and obviously what he did as a medical examiner is integral to what he became. So if he has an accomplice, it could have been someone he met here in Boston and perhaps someone he knew on the job here."

"So can you tell us about what he did here, Doctor?" Wire asked.

"He was a medical examiner," Dr. Wayne replied, "an exceedingly good one who took a particularly keen interest in his cases. He worked out of this office here in Boston and the surrounding area. We get many interesting cases."

"What were his duties?" Wire inquired.

"He performed the typical duties of a medical examiner, Agent Wire. He would start at the murder scene and then would return here with the body. He would conduct his examination and determine cause of death. I, myself, like to dictate my reports but as I recall, Maynard liked to type his so he would often dictate his notes but then type his reports. I'm sure as Detective Sullivan will attest, Dr. Munger was very thorough. His reports were well written, insightful and proved quite invaluable as cases proceeded."

"Where would Dr. Munger type his reports?" Mac asked.

"On his office computer."

"Where was that?"

Dr. Wayne waved for them to follow him to an office down the hall. "Maynard had this office back when he worked for me. The examination room is across the hall, so he would conduct his examination in there and then come into his office here to complete his reports."

"Besides his own cases, what else would he have access to?" Mac asked and suddenly a thought came to his mind.

"With his access, certainly any other case on our system," Dr. Wayne answered. "As would any of my other examiners. Why do you ask?"

"What are you thinking, Mac?" Wire queried. She had noticed the change in his expression.

"In a second," he replied. "Dr. Wayne, would the system have identification for the decedents?"

"It would."

"And that identification information would include date of birth, would it not?"

"Yes."

"And social security numbers?"

"Sometimes."

"How about driver's license information?"

"If the person had that with them, it would have been procedure to collect and enter that information."

"Mac, are you thinking what I'm thinking?" Wire asks.

"Yeah, that's the answer to how he goes around undetected."

"Undetected?" Dr. Wayne asked. "I'm sorry, I don't understand."

"Dr. Wayne, one question we've had is how our killer moved from city to city without detection. We surmised that he was using different identities as he moved around. I'm suddenly thinking his position as a medical examiner would have been ideal to steal identities. He undoubtedly would know that the FBI and local police would look for patterns in names and people who relocated."

"But," Wire started, "if you have numerous pieces of identification you can simply move from state to state, no issue, using a new identity or identities each time. How long again was it after his arrest and release until he disappeared?"

"Four months," Dr. Wayne answered. "He resigned, and a month or two later is when we heard he'd been lost at sea."

"Was it he resigned, or was it he resigned before he was going to be fired?" Wire inquired.

"No, he truly resigned," Dr. Wayne replied. "Maynard said he couldn't take the looks, the suspicion. He said people looked at him like he was a pervert."

"Did they?"

Dr. Wayne shrugged. "He wasn't exactly wrong about that but given all that had happened it wasn't that surprising. I thought it best that he move on and I was quite relieved that he saved me the ordeal of having to terminate his services. He told me he planned to take a job down in Miami. I did in fact provide a reference for him as my opposite number down there had some concerns about his involvement in the Rubens matter. I explained that Maynard had been cleared and that while a bit quirky he was eminently qualified and really quite good. As I understand it, he was sailing his boat down there when he disappeared."

"So in those four months, he's planning his disappearance and he starts collecting identities," Mac speculated and then looked to Wire. "God, why didn't this occur to me yesterday? He was in an ideal position to determine which identities to steal. He had access to everything so he could determine whether use of that identity would be detected. He would know if the decedent was homeless, a drug addict, or someone with little or no family so that the use of the identity wouldn't be detected."

"So now what are you going to do?" Sullivan asked.

"How long did Munger work for you, Dr. Wayne?" Mac asked.

Wayne opened the personnel file for Munger that was on his desk. "He was one of my first hires. He worked for me for a little over six years."

"That gives us something of a window. We don't have a lot of time for bureaucratic bullshit on this. Rubens is going to kill his next victim tonight at 8:00 p.m. so we have to move fast. The FBI is going to need to access your system. We are going to run the names, social security numbers, dates of birth and any other identifying information of every autopsy conducted by this office in the ten years before Munger disappeared. Then we are going to cross reference that against identities that surfaced in Chicago, Los Angeles and most importantly, Washington DC and the surrounding area. We'll see what pops."

"I'll do whatever I can to help," Dr. Wayne replied. "Whatever you need, we'll do."

"Excellent," Mac replied as he swiped the screen on his cell phone and placed a call. "Senior Special Agent Galloway, here is your new priority, and on this one, we gotta haul ass." Mac explained what he needed.

Despite the speed required, there were hoops to jump through.

There were phone calls back and forth between Mac and Galloway, Dr. Wayne and his higher-ups with the Commonwealth, and eventually FBI Director Mitchell and the Massachusetts Governor and Attorney General. Two hours later, the go button was ready to be pushed.

"What are you doing in the meantime?" Galloway asked.

Mac looked at his watch, which read 1:45 p.m. "Wire and I are making a beeline to the airport. We're on our way back."

The reporter was resting on the bench in the waiting area for the medical examiner's office, awaiting the confirmation of the identification on a murder victim so he could finish up his report and get his editor off his back.

He saw the double doors open and immediately recognized Mac McRyan and the woman; her name was Wire, he thought. Rubens was a big story in Boston, where the notorious killer got his start. So why were they up here? Before he could get up off the bench and ask that question the two were whisked away in a gray Ford sedan.

The story he was working on was the usual pop and drop murder, probably a mugging gone bad. It would require a paragraph or two at best, well inside the front page of the paper. On the other hand, McRyan and Wire, with the clock ticking on yet another victim, were up in Boston meeting at the medical examiner's office.

The reporter reached into his pocket for his cell phone. He hadn't spoken to Ridge in years and wasn't even sure the number was still good but decided to give it a try.

"Hugo, it's been a while, I know... Yeah, I've been good. Say, I know you're down in Washington covering the reemergence of our old friend Rubens... Yeah, in any event, I just saw the most curious thing. Agents McRyan and Wire just walked out of the office of the Chief Medical Examiner up here in Boston ... Yeah, Dr. Wayne is still the chief. Look, maybe we can help each other. Do you have any idea why they are here?"

25

"YOU ARE A WALKING CONTRADICTION."

The FBI plane was granted priority clearance and landed at Reagan National at 3:33 p.m.

An FBI Suburban and DC patrol car awaited their arrival. They jumped in the Suburban and were quickly whisked away with lights and sirens to the field office. They arrived ten minutes later, greeted by Delmonico.

"Let's go," Grace waved with urgency. "Galloway says we're getting somewhere."

Mac and Wire rushed inside the building. April Greene, Ridge and Coolidge were waiting inside as they came in. Mac was not sure he approved of Ridge's presence.

"A little odd, the two of you standing together," Mac commented, the tone of disapproval obvious.

"We've both been after this guy for ten years and something is going on," Ridge answered and then pointed at Mac and Wire. "And you two were up in Boston."

Mac turned to Wire with an accusatory look.

"I said not a word," Wire replied and then asked Ridge, "How the hell do you know that?"

"A source," Ridge replied. "You both need to learn that I have them everywhere. So what do you have? I'm going to find it out eventually anyway."

"Come on," Mac directed. When they got to the conference room, he turned to Ridge. "Not a word to anyone outside this room. Not a fucking word, do you understand?"

"Maybe you're unclear on how a reporter operates."

"You have been offered a ticket inside," Mac replied. "It has conditions. Accept them or hit the bricks."

"Not a word without you saying so," Ridge acquiesced.

"Okay," Mac replied. "Does the name Maynard Munger mean anything to you?"

"Why have I heard that name?" April Greene asked.

"He was a medical examiner from up in Boston," Ridge supplied quickly. "He was the one BPD thought was the killer of the first two Rubens victims for like ten minutes."

"That's the one," Mac answered. "He's Rubens."

"But Mac, I remember this guy now—I was up in Boston. Munger was in custody when victims three and four were killed," April Greene argued. "How can he possibly be your killer?"

"He has a partner," Wire replied.

"A partner!" Greene and Ridge exclaimed together.

"Yes," Wire confirmed. "We figured it out, or more really, Mac figured it out yesterday." Mac and Wire explained their working theory.

"Wow," Greene replied, amazed.

"Holy shit," Ridge breathed and then went into storyteller mode. "This just keeps getting better."

"Speak for yourself, asshole," Greene growled disapprovingly. "This guy is out killing women." She looked to Mac and Wire. "Are you going to put Munger out there?"

"With his face, we can really make some progress," Coolidge added. "That definitely gives us something to work with. Maybe we could age that picture by ten years and that could help, too."

"We're right there with you, Detective Coolidge," Galloway answered. "We've been working his picture from ten years ago against our sketches and the good pictures from the Metro cameras that day he was chased, and the ones you found on the Waxe case. You can see the similarities between Munger and the man on the surveillance pictures, particularly the nose. That bulbous end of it is somewhat distinctive. You look at the two pictures and there are definite similarities."

"It's the same man," Greene replied and handed a picture to Coolidge. "Don't you agree?"

"Yup."

"Mac," Galloway stated, "we're starting to get some hits. Names from the list in Boston that also appeared in Chicago and Los Angeles."

"Names?" Greene asked. "How?"

"He was a medical examiner," Mac explained. "We think he may have been using identities he stole while working in the Office of the Medical Examiner for Massachusetts. We're running every autopsy for the ten years before he resigned for names, social security numbers and dates of birth against DMV and other records for Illinois, California, DC, Maryland and Virginia."

"And we just got one for here in DC," Galloway reported. "Mac, we've got a hit on a Howard Gilley who Munger conducted the autopsy on up in Boston. That name correlates with an office address over in southeast."

"An office?" Wire asked.

"He has to operate out of somewhere," Mac replied. "Linc, you're with Wire and me." Then, to Galloway, he stated, "Time is running out. Let's get Munger out there. The whole smash, everything."

"It's done."

The date wasn't supposed to start until 5:00.

One rule he had for dates like this was to never be first, to never be the one waiting. He always wanted his lady waiting. So he spent two hours walking the area around the National Art Gallery to see if there was any kind of an unusual police presence. Given what happened at Eleanor's apartment, he was particularly on guard. He had confidence in the disguise and his backstory with Glenda but still, he was taking extra precautions. After two hours, he felt confident that there was no ambush awaiting him.

At 4:57, he watched as Glenda walked up the front steps to the Gallery of National Art. About halfway up the steps, she stopped and rested against the railing, scanning the area for him. It wasn't a nervous or anxious form of scanning but rather an excited one.

That was what he wanted, her in the right frame of mind.

At promptly 5:00 p.m., he crossed the street and walked up the north steps of the National Gallery of Art.

"Gabriel, Gabriel," Glenda waved eagerly.

"Glenda," he replied as she jumped into his arms and hugged him. "I am so happy to see you."

"Yes, me too," she replied.

"You look wonderful," he stated, pulling back and admiring her in a flowery spring dress with which she'd matched a light white sweater.

"And you look very scruffy, in a good way," Glenda said as she stroked his long beard lightly. "I like a scruffy, woolly man."

"Well, this scruffy and woolly man is very much looking forward to walking through the gallery. Are you ready?"

"Yes."

Inside he led Glenda over to the check-in booth and the attendant to get their tickets.

"Here you go, Mr. Ripley. Please enjoy the exhibit," the attendant said pleasantly as she handed the tickets across the counter.

"Let's go see if we can find that Cezanne you were so excited to see."

"Let's," Glenda answered excitedly, squeezing his hand tightly.

"Clear!"

"Clear!"

A few seconds later the SWAT team leader emerged from the office. "Agent McRyan, we have something inside I think you should see."

"What do you have, Sarge?" Mac asked, following the team leader.

"This, sir."

The sergeant pointed to a metal cabinet with the doors opened. Inside were numerous fake beards, mustaches and hairpieces of varying lengths. On the hangers were clothes, his wardrobe. Above the hanger rod was another shelf with hats: three tam hats, four baseball caps and two stocking caps as well as a box of rubber gloves. On the bottom floor of the cabinet, there were also shoes: two pair of tennis, two loafers and a pair of hiking boots.

"This is his place," Mac stated. "No question."

Coolidge burst into the office, dragging another man with him. "Mac, this is the building manager. He says Gilley drives an older model black Honda Civic."

Mac called Galloway. "Don, we're looking for a black Honda Civic registered to anyone on that list of names." Mac hung up and then to the group ordered, "Everyone out, don't touch anything else. Put everything back the way it was. Lock the door to the office. Linc, it's 6:30. We're running out of time. I want your men all over this place. I want men on the front door, the back door and all over this building. When and if he comes back, we take him down."

"Mac! I got Grace on the line," Wire bellowed, holding out her phone.

Mac took it from his partner. "Yeah, Gracie, what do you have?"

"Mac, Galloway says we just got a hit at the National Gallery of Art."

~

"I can't get over how amazing some of those pieces in there were,"

Glenda exclaimed happily. "That was so great, thank you for getting the tickets."

"I enjoyed it, too," Maynard answered, "especially the Cezanne ones. Those paintings were spectacular."

Glenda appraised him. "I guess you are proof that we should never stereotype."

"What do you mean?"

"The beard, the longer hair, the flannel shirt, the sport fishing—none of those say art lover. Yet you know it and you do love it."

"Art is a chance to do and experience something different," he answered. "You know what I would love to do next?"

"What?"

"Go back to your place and open a bottle of wine. I'd be happy to pick up one along the way."

Glenda smiled. "Oh, that is not necessary, Gabriel, I have a couple of bottles. I'll just open one."

"Then let's go," he said, leading her down the steps and across the street. "I'm parked in the ramp just down the street here on the left."

At the car, he opened the door for his Civic and let her slip down inside. As he walked around the back of the car, he made a mental note to wipe it down. Glenda would leave prints inside.

As he dropped himself down into the driver's seat he looked to his right, and Glenda was smiling and shaking her head.

"What?"

"You are a walking contradiction."

"How so?"

"You fish, you hunt and you work in the lumber industry. So I figured I'd be getting into a big pickup truck."

Maynard laughed to cover the inconsistency. "I travel quite a bit and if I need to rent a vehicle I rent a truck to get my fix, but here in Washington with the traffic, the Civic is better for mileage and better for the environment."

He started the car and classical music played over the radio. It caused Glenda to smile and shake her head again.

"And the contradictions continue."

26

"I KNOW YOU HAD HELP."

The name that got a hit was Gabriel Ripley.

"Mac, we're scanning every government computer system and we hit that name as having bought tickets and checked in at the Gallery," Galloway reported over the speaker in Wire's phone. "Munger did the autopsy on a Gabriel Ripley three months before he disappeared. Ripley was a homeless Desert Storm veteran who died from a heroin overdose. No next of kin came forward and he was identified via his military dog tags."

"What time was this show he was seeing?" Wire asked Galloway as Mac swerved through traffic, following two patrol units who were parting the traffic ahead of them on 4th Street Southwest.

"It's been running since 2:00 p.m. and goes until 8:00 tonight so there's a big window for the showing."

"Mac, Munger's picture is appearing on all news outlets, cable and network plus it is all over the Internet. It's not a matter of if we catch him," Delmonico suggested. "It's only a matter of when."

"But do we catch him in time?" Mac replied as he pulled the X5 to a stop on the south side of Constitution Avenue. "It's 7:10. It's getting late early."

"It's not 8:00 yet though," Wire replied. "We've still got time."

Coolidge arrived right behind him. It was all hands on deck now. Three Bureau sedans arrived plus even Greene and Ridge, pulling up in Greene's white Mercedes SUV.

The group quickly ran up the steps and moved inside. Mac showed his identification to the receptionist at the front desk. The security director was on the scene a moment later.

"I need you to lock the museum down," Mac explained. "Nobody leaves unless I say so. And we need to find a man named Gabriel Ripley, if he is still here."

The receptionist checked in her system. "Ripley picked up his tickets from us at 5:02 p.m."

"Where did he pick up them up?" Mac asked.

"There was a reception table set up for the West Building. This was a special exhibit and you had to have advance tickets for the exhibit today so they were checking people in there."

"Come with me," the security director gestured. "Down the hall to where my security system is housed." The director sat down at his desk, made some mouse clicks and pulled up the security camera monitoring the reception table. He started the footage at 5:00 p.m. and ran it through fast forward. He stopped it at 5:02 and let it run normal speed. A man with long blond hair and a long beard walked up to the table with a woman dressed in a floral dress and light sweater. The man moved with just a slight shuffle to his step. He was perhaps two inches taller than the woman, who was in a short pair of heels.

"He's changed up again," Mac noted. "He's got long blond hair now and the big bushy beard."

"Is it him?" Greene asks. "How can you be sure?"

"It is," Mac and Wire answer in unison.

"It's the way he walks," Wire answered. "A little like he has a stick up his ass—we saw it on the Metro video just as he got on the train."

"Is he still here—that's the question," Mac pressed.

The group quickly fanned out into the exhibit, hunting around. Mac approached a security guard walking around the exhibit and described the man.

"I think I know the guy you're talking about," the guard reported after a moment of thought. "I was standing over by the exit out onto Constitution Avenue and saw him."

"He left the building?"

"Yes."

"Where were they going?"

"Out the front door is all I remember," the guard replied. "He and the lady, they left together. They were all friendly-like."

"Where did they exit?"

"The main exit on the north side that leads out onto Constitution Avenue."

"I have a few different bottles in the kitchen," Glenda said as they entered her second-floor apartment. She grabbed two bottles. "Red or white?"

"What would you like?"

"I'm in kind of a white mood," Glenda said.

Maynard took the bottle of white and examined the label. "A Pinot Grigio looks good. Why don't you go into the living room and make yourself comfortable," he suggested. "You can turn on some music if you'd like."

"Sounds terrific."

As he worked the corkscrew, she called from the living room, "How about the Chicago Symphony Orchestra?"

"Sounds good to me," he replied as the cork popped out of the bottle.

"Glasses are right above you in the cupboard."

"Thanks," he answered as he reached inside his pocket. A moment later, he strolled into the living room with the two glasses. Glenda stepped in to accept it. It was an invitation to be close and he took it, leaning in, cupping her face in his right hand and kissing her lightly, a quick soft peck.

"Should we sit down?" she suggested.

"I'd like that," he answered as he quickly glanced down at this watch and his heart skipped a beat. It was twenty to eight. He was behind schedule.

"Agent McRyan, I have him here," the security director reported, pointing at his computer monitor.

"Show me."

The director rolled the video. The camera angle showed the steps down to the sidewalk and then Constitution Avenue to the west. The man and woman walked across the avenue and then continued walking north and out of view.

"And there is no other camera? No other angle out there?"

"Sorry, Agent McRyan, there isn't."

"What street is it that they kept walking north on?"

"That's 6th Street Northwest."

Mac spoke into his phone to Galloway. "I'm sending you some video footage. We have a new emergency project for the tech guys. I need them scrubbing every possible street camera for 6th Street Northwest north of the Gallery for our guy and his date." He hung up and looked to Wire and the others. "Let's get up that direction and see if there are any other surveillance cameras we can access."

Mac and Wire crossed Constitution Avenue and took the west side of 6th Street Northwest with Greene and Ridge in tow. Coolidge and two of his men worked the east side. Mac and Wire ducked inside a flower shop and presented their identification.

"I need your help. Have you seen these two people?" Wire asked, showing the screen on her phone to the woman behind the cash register.

"Let me take a look," the cashier replied, sliding glasses on.

Mac's cell phone rang. It was Galloway.

"Mac, there is a traffic camera pointing south on 6th. It's a little hard to tell but it looks like the man and woman turned into the Colonial Parking Ramp, a block and a half north of the Gallery."

"What time?"

"6:37."

Mac and Wire pushed by Greene and Ridge, rushed out the flower shop front door, turned left and sprinted north to the parking ramp, turned to their left and ran up the exit ramp to the attendant booth. "Where is your office? Where do I find the surveillance system?"

The parking attendant pointed to a set of double doors. "Go through the doors up the steps to the second floor."

Mac took off before the attendant could finish, Wire right behind him. They found the office and barged in, both with their identification out. "I need to see your security cameras. Is there one focused on the exit to the ramp?"

"Yes," the clerk answered, obviously startled. "I'm not sure how to work the system, though."

"Let me," Wire said as she sat down to the computer and started maneuvering the mouse. She found the camera that focused on the ramp exit. At 6:41 p.m., surveillance footage time, they saw it.

"Black Honda Civic," Coolidge pointed out.

"And it turns left onto 6th Street Northwest," Mac added and then barked to Galloway, who was on speaker. "Don, Rubens is driving a black Honda Civic north on 6th Street Northwest. License plate is Maryland, 1-7-3 AET—that's Alex Edward Tango. You got that?"

"Copy."

"Then one more thing: we have surveillance footage and pictures of the woman from the gallery. We need to get that out there. We need to find out who she is."

"We're on it."

Mac and Wire ran back to his X5. Coolidge, Greene, Ridge and the rest were right behind and they all raced north on 6th Street Northwest with lights flashing.

"It's 7:46 p.m." Dara observed. "We have fourteen minutes, give or take."

"There's time. There's still time," Mac muttered as he weaved through traffic, driving north on 6th Street Northwest, scanning for black Honda Civics.

Galloway was back on the line. "Mac, we got sight of the Civic. It stayed north on 6th until it hit Florida Avenue. At Florida, the car turned left and then took an immediate right on Georgia Avenue and continued north."

"Where did it go from there?"

"We tracked it ten blocks north and then we lost it. Georgia Avenue goes residential farther to the north once you get past Howard University."

"Keep looking."

He pulled back from her face, having kissed her for the second time to assess her condition. Glenda was very relaxed and her eyes were drooping just a bit.

It would be five, maybe seven minutes now before the drug took its full effect.

She was still able to move, however, and she was horny. Glenda pulled him back down to her.

"Agent Galloway, you need to hear this," an agent with a phone to her ear bellowed, putting the phone on speaker. "Ma'am, tell Agent Galloway what you told me."

"I think the woman you're looking for is Glenda Richards. I work with her and that looks like her. I never met the man, but I know she's been dating a guy named Gabriel with long blond hair and a bushy beard. She's talked about it nonstop."

Delmonico pulled up the DMV photo of Glenda Richards. "That could be her, Don. That could really be her. Her address is Allison Street NW." Delmonico reached for the phone again. "Mac, where are you?"

~

"I'm waiting just north of Howard University on Georgia."

"Keep going north. We think the woman's name is Glenda Richards." Delmonico reported the address. "That's north on Georgia, a mile and half."

Wire looked at her watch. "8:03."

"Hang on."

~

He could feel her motor skills starting to go now. Her arms were going limper and loosening around him and the kissing was becoming sloppy and wet. Finally, after another long kiss, her face drifted away from him and he could see the look in her eyes, the slow recognition of what was happening.

"What is it?" he asked.

"I don't know. I don't know what's happening," Glenda said. "I ... I ... I feel weak. It's like I can't move."

"I know," he said darkly.

"You ... know?" she slurred.

"Yes, I do," he answered as he pushed himself up off the couch.

Then he quickly spun to the front window.

~

"Hold on!"

Mac hardly eased off the gas as he turned a hard left, fishtailing onto Allison Street.

"There!" Wire pointed to the black Civic parked mid-block. "*There! There! There!*"

~

Maynard rushed to the front window and saw a flashing light turn hard onto the street, coming his way. The BMW skidded to a stop and a woman immediately jumped out of the SUV, running to the front door.

It was Wire and out of the driver's side was McRyan. Two more cars, one with flashing lights, turned down the street.

He backed away from the window.

What to do?

Glenda was lying motionless on the couch, ready to be taken but there wasn't time.

He ran into the kitchen and to the back door. There was a butcher block of knives on the counter. He grabbed a long knife out of the block and exited out the back door onto the small deck. With his right hand on the railing, he threw the knife down to the ground and then threw himself over the railing and jumped down to the ground fifteen feet below, landing hard and then groaning as he rolled over on the ground.

Wire kicked open the front door.

Mac ran past her at a full sprint up the steps two at a time to the front door of the apartment and knocked. "Glenda! Glenda! It's the police, open the door!"

There was no response.

Coolidge and Stretch were coming up behind them.

Mac stepped back and kicked the door just to the right of the knob.

The door shot open.

Wire burst past him and into the apartment. Mac followed her in, covering her right, as did Coolidge and Stretch, moving left to the back of the house.

Mac and Wire immediately saw the body lying on the couch. Glenda's eyes were open but she couldn't move. "Help," she croaked quietly.

"She's alive!" Wire exclaimed.

"Where did he go?" Mac asked Glenda.

Glenda couldn't move, but rolled her eyes to the left.

"He went out the back!" Mac yelled as he moved quickly into the kitchen and found the back door open. He carefully peered out the back and he could see a man running in the distance to the east between the townhouses. Mac yelled back into the apartment as he stepped out onto the deck and saw the man turn left down another alley. "He's on the run out the back, heading east. Call it in. Lock the area down."

Mac threw himself over the railing and jumped down to the ground, dropping and rolling left and coming up quickly to his feet. He ran east in a full sprint.

"Add that we need an ambulance," Wire ordered to Stretch, who was already on the radio. Dara ran back down the front steps to find Greene and Ridge waiting in the street. "Start your car! Start your car! He's on foot heading east."

"Okay! Okay!" Greene replied startled, jumping back inside her Mercedes and fumbling with the keys.

"Where are you going?" Ridge yelled.

"Giving chase with Mac," Wire answered. "Go! Go!"

Munger looked back and saw a man come out the back of the apartment and onto the deck.

Maynard turned left down the narrow alley, running north and saw flashing lights for a patrol car approaching the alley entrance. He moved to the right side of the narrow alley, kept close to the fence and leaned his back against it.

The patrol car pulled to a stop but didn't completely block the alley; only the nose of the car was visible.

He heard the door of the car opening and the officer speaking into a radio.

Maynard jumped from around the corner and lunged with the

knife. The patrol officer, who was distracted and on his radio, reacted too slowly to the attack from the rear.

Munger thrashed at the officer again and again with the knife in a crazed frenzy, his right arm swinging violently, puncturing the officer repeatedly until the officer's arms stopped fighting back and fell to his side.

He grabbed the officer's gun and baton and continued running east.

~

Mac reached the end of the path and peered around the end to the left and saw the patrol unit, a man down and another standing up and then taking off.

"Officer down! Officer down!" Mac hollered as he reached the patrol officer who was gasping for air, covered in blood that oozed from the stab wounds made by the knife lying on the ground to the right.

"Hang on, brother," Mac exclaimed as he reached for the patrol officer's shoulder radio. "This is Agent McRyan with the FBI. I have a ten double zero, officer down, Buchanan Street, east of Georgia. Send an ambulance! *Send an ambulance!*"

"How is he?" Wire asked, gun hanging low in her right hand.

"Not good, but he's alive," Mac answered as he glanced to his right. A block east he could see Munger running with a baton in his left hand and something hanging down in his right. "Shit," Mac muttered as he looked down to see the officer's baton missing, and worse, his gun. "Stay with him."

"Mac, he's gone crazy. We have him," Wire answered, kneeling down. "He's caught. He's not getting out of this."

"He has a gun. He could get a hostage and get inside a house," Mac shot back, pushing himself up and taking off, sprinting east on Georgia.

Mac was quickly closing and as he did, Munger glanced back.

"Munger, give it up!" Mac yelled. "Give it up! There's no way out!"

Munger didn't stop. Instead, he turned left into an alley.

Mac kept after him at a full sprint and at the alley opening stopped against the building on the corner. He pulled out his Sig Sauer and peered left around the corner of a tall fence. The alley was empty and quiet; the only noise the sirens rapidly approaching the area. He did not see Munger running. Mac stepped inside the alley and held close to the fence on the left side while he quickly shuffled his way down, scanning, although it was difficult in the dark as there was no illumination in the alley.

As he stayed close to the fence on the left side, he reached the back end of the building on the right. Behind the apartment building was a large open area with a small playground and swing set.

It was eerily quiet.

"Where are you?" Mac mumbled quietly under his breath as he stepped past the end of the building and more into the open, still stepping sideways to the left, his gun at two o'clock on the back of the apartment building, scanning to the left. At twelve on the clock, he was focused on the swing set, and then sweeping to the left to ten o'clock toward a long building housing single car garages where he zeroed in on an open garage door. "Are you hiding in there?" he muttered in a whisper. Taking a step forward when he heard a slight noise to his right. He pivoted that direction, sensed the movement and danger, and Munger had the drop on him.

Pop! Pop! Pop!

Mac dove and rolled left. There was a dumpster twenty feet away. Mac pushed himself up and scrambled toward it.

Pop! Pop! Pop!

Mac's legs were taken out from under him, sending him down hard on his right side, his gun flying from his grip.

He felt it, the burning sensation in the calf of his right leg.

Ignoring the pain Mac frantically swept with his hands, searching for his gun but couldn't find it. He glanced back to the right and Munger was quickly approaching, the gun drawn, boring right in on him.

He needed to buy time.

"You didn't get her," Mac grunted, pain searing through his right leg. He reached for the wound, or at least wanted Munger to think that was what he was doing. His backup piece was on his lower left ankle and he needed to get his hand down to it. "You didn't kill her."

"But I have you," Munger replied. "I may not make it, I may be a goner, but I beat you."

"Did you?" Mac replied with a grimace, pushing himself up to a sitting position, bringing his left leg closer to his right and reaching with both of his hands to his right leg to the wound, but with the last two fingers of his left hand started pulling up his left pant leg. "You didn't get your four. You didn't get your masterpiece. You only got three women. Glenda is alive. I found you, Maynard. I identified you, Maynard Munger, medical examiner for the Commonwealth of Massachusetts. I exposed you. And I know one other thing, Maynard. You know what that is?"

"What?"

"I know you didn't do it alone. *I know you had help.*"

Mac could see the surprise register on Munger's face.

"Who is it? Who's your partner, Maynard?"

"Don't call me Maynard!" Munger growled.

"Who's your partner? Who put you up to all this?"

"Nobody put me up to it."

"Bullshit, Maynard," Mac answered back, sitting up now, slyly working his left pant leg up. "Someone pushed you, manipulated you. You're caught. No sense being the only one."

"I was *not* manipulated. I did what I did."

"Oh, you were manipulated, weren't you?" Mac laughed. "You were the submissive. Your partner was the alpha, the dominant. You were dominated."

"*No! No! No! No!*" he shouted angrily, pointing with the gun. "I was not the submissive. I did what I wanted to. And you know what I want to do now? I want to kill you."

"But you had a partner, Maynard," Mac replied, his right hand up, pleading. His other hand had the left pant leg up. He was readying to move, to roll left and pull the Glock. "Who was it?"

A white SUV turned hard into the alley.

Munger turned back to see the truck.

The SUV came roaring straight ahead.

Mac threw his body left, rolling twice and reaching for his Glock.

The truck roared down the alley and didn't stop, driving into Munger, sending him flying into the fence.

Mac rolled back right to see April Greene, Ridge and Wire in Greene's Mercedes SUV. April had rammed Munger.

"God, that hurts," Mac grunted as he pushed himself up. Standing now, his Glock 9 out front, Mac limped toward Munger, who'd been thrown into the fence, partially caving it in.

Wire jumped out of the car, picked up the patrol officer's gun as well as Mac's Sig Sauer and stuck them in the waistband of her jeans. As Mac kept his gun trained on Munger, Wire reached down and checked the side of the killer's neck for a pulse. Dara looked back up and shook her head and Mac lowered his gun and stumbled to his left, bracing himself against the fence.

"Jesus," Wire exclaimed, rushing over to him. "You're hit!"

"I'll be okay," Mac bit out through gritted teeth and then looked back to Greene, who seemed to be in total shock. "Thanks, April. I'm glad you didn't stop."

"Y...y...yeah, good," Greene replied, pale and shaking uncontrollably, holding tightly to Ridge's left arm. "Are you...you...hurt?"

"I don't think too badly, although, man, it hurts like a motherfucker."

"I'm not sure about the not too badly part," Dara reported, having knelt down to take a look at his right calf.

Mac looked down as well. His right pant leg was soaked with blood.

"We need to get you to the ER," Dara ordered, taking a hanky out of her coat pocket, tying it around the wound. You're bleeding pretty heavy down here."

"How bad?"

"You're not going to die, unless Sally kills you because you can't dance in a month."

Ridge approached. "He's okay, though?"

"I'm alive. I'll take that," Mac stated, leaning back against the fence, breathing heavily, now realizing he was soaked with sweat. "I don't need to do *that* again."

"Hell of a finish to the story," Ridge muttered, drawing scornful looks from Wire, Greene and a weary shake of the head from Mac. "Sorry, guys, but it is." The author was clearly relishing the thought of writing the story and the financial rewards for doing so.

"Yeah, it is quite the story," Mac replied, but then added with a tinge of disappointment, "You know what would have made it better?"

"What?" Ridge asked.

Mac looked over to the lifeless body of Maynard Munger. "Finding out who his partner was."

27

"WRITERS ARE DANGEROUS."

M ac rubbed his face, exhaled and then looked at the thick bandages on his lower right leg. The emergency room doctor repaired the wound to the back of his right calf. He'd been shot from the side and the bullet clipped the back of his large right calf muscle. The pain from the wound had been searing, and there was a fairly significant amount of blood, as he could now see based on what was left of his pair of khaki pants lying over the chair in the corner. All in all, he was lucky. The patrol officer that was attacked by Munger was still in emergency surgery, having been stabbed several times, most ominously in the neck.

While the wound took out a small hunk of the flesh on the back of the calf, there wasn't much in the way of muscular damage.

"I'm getting married in less than a month, Doc. How mobile will I be?" He was dreading telling Sally about this.

"I take it there's dancing involved?" the doctor asked as Sally tore the partition curtain open to see her fiancé and hear the question.

This was not good.

"This lovely lady must be your fiancée," the doctor smiled, folding his arms across his chest and looking at Sally over the top of his cheater glasses.

"Yeah, Doc, that's her. Isn't she pretty?"

"I imagine, Agent McRyan, you'll want her to be very happy on her wedding day."

Mac took in Sally's worried yet pensive posture and replied, "You have no idea, Doc."

Sally stood looking at him with her hands on her hips. She was fronting disgust but he knew she was both worried and now, it appeared at least a bit relieved. "I heard your question, Doctor. There is in fact dancing. What's his status going to be?"

The doctor looked back to Mac. "Well, what's your pain tolerance, son?"

"It better be pretty damn high," Sally suggested hotly but with a bit of a smile.

"When is the wedding?"

"Four weeks," they answered in unison.

"Can he follow doctor's orders?" the doctor asked Sally.

"From me, yes."

"Good," the doc laughed in reply. "Listen, son. Take it easy for a few weeks. Let it heal up and you should be fine. The wound isn't as bad as it looks—didn't get into the muscle much, but it did some. Use these crutches. Take your pain medication, elevate your leg, ice it and let it heal, and I think you'll make her happy."

The doctor finished up and left them alone.

"Eventful night there, Mac?"

"You could say that."

"Do you want to talk about it?"

"No, not right now."

"Okay. I'm just glad it's over," Sally stated.

"Well," Mac replied with a grimace, "not quite. Rubens had an accomplice."

"So what about this other guy?" Ridge asked, looking at Wire, Greene and Coolidge all sitting on a bench and drinking their non-alcoholic beverage of choice.

"I don't suppose we'll ever know," Greene suggested, not looking up, twisting her Diet Coke in her hands. "Munger is dead. Dead men tell no tales. I mean, we haven't found anything at that office, have we?"

"Not so far," Wire replied as she took a drink from her bottle of water. "I spoke with Galloway a while ago. The FBI forensic team has been in there now for hours. Unfortunately, other than some fingerprints for Munger, they have found little other information and nothing about anyone else, another person who might have been involved. There are some handwritten notes, but they're all about the victims. There was a box of burner phones that the FBI is going to try to figure out where they originated from but I wouldn't hold my breath. They wouldn't lead to a partner, at least most likely not."

"If Munger's buddy has any sense, he's blown town by now," Coolidge stated. "What happened tonight is all over the news. It's over. If that guy has half a brain, he's a thousand miles away by now, making his way to a non-extradition country."

"I guess we may never know, then," Ridge speculated.

"I wouldn't be so sure," Wire replied, shaking her head, a small smile on her face. "You guys don't know *my* partner. Mac is not going to let that rest. If I didn't know any better, he'll be right back at it in the morning, trying to figure it out."

"Really?" Greene asked. "You and Mac have been going days on end without a break and Rubens is put down and done. I think you've both earned some time off. I mean, Mac was shot, for crying out loud —he can't be out there chasing this. I saw all the blood."

"Flesh wound," Wire replied dismissively. "It'll slow him down for a few hours, if at all." She took another sip of her water and offered a small laugh, "You have to understand Mac. He's not the type to let that go. If he has a thread to pull on, he'll keep after it. Besides, he is otherwise not working. He has the time to devote to it."

"But not tonight?" Ridge asked.

Wire smiled and shook her head. "No, not tonight. Sally will be dragging his ass home."

"Maybe his fiancée will shut him down," Ridge suggested.

"Would she do that?" Greene asked. "Can she do that?"

"I kind of doubt it," Wire replied, shaking her head. "She's a former prosecutor and as big a justice junkie as he is, especially for something like this. She'll make him rest, slow him down some, scold him for getting shot, admonish him to be more careful, fret over him, but she *won't* stop him. Heck, she knows she can't. That dogged determination is one of the reasons she loves him so much. Like I said, if I know him, we're not done working this."

"In that case," Coolidge said with a weary smile, "we all best take advantage of the time off we can take before Super Cop puts us back to work."

Ridge laughed. "Super Cop—I like that. I'm going to use it."

"With appropriate attribution, I should hope."

"Detective, you can count on it," Ridge answered with a big smile, patting Coolidge on the back. "You and I are going to have to have a drink here in the next few days."

"If you're buying the bourbon, I can make myself available," the affable MPD detective offered.

"Be careful," Wire warned. "Writers are dangerous."

"You should talk," Ridge snorted. "Last I checked your book is sitting at number one on the *New York Times* Best Sellers list."

"Really?" Wire asked in disbelief. "Honest?"

"Yeah," Greene added. "It's there. Where have you been?"

"Distracted by the case," Dara replied while checking her phone. "I suppose if I had paid attention to all of the calls from our agent I might have found that out."

"Man, what a night," Greene muttered, rubbing her face with her hands. The FBI profiler looked exhausted and just a bit traumatized.

"Are you sure you're okay, April?" Wire asked, placing a hand softly on her shoulder. "You ... killed someone tonight. It was totally justified, completely in the line of duty and I thank you for it, but you did take a life. Do you think maybe you should talk with someone?"

292 | ROGER STELLJES

ROGER STELLJES

Greene smiled and provided a small chuckle. "You mean like a shrink?" The profiler shook her head. "No, I don't think so. I'll be okay— I think. My car is now evidence. There's something I never thought I'd have to say."

"Do you need a ride?" Dara offered.

"Thanks for the offer, but no. I'll call a car service. I'm going to go home, pour myself a very stiff drink and go to bed."

"Come on, I'll walk you out," Coolidge offered.

"Thank you, Detective." She pushed herself up off the bench. "I'll see you guys later."

Ridge and Wire watched as she walked down the hall with Coolidge.

Wire turned to Ridge, who was in turn smiling at her.

"So, Agent Wire, after cracking a big case it seems like a celebration is in order."

"I agree."

"It's late. How about I buy you a burger and a beer?"

Wire nodded. "You know what, Ridge, that's exactly what I need."

"CHECK OUT THE CUTE BLOND GIRL TO HIS RIGHT."

"No, I'm not staying home today," Sally admonished playfully, slapping Mac's hand before leaning down to peck him on the lips. "And don't even try to start anything," she added with a wide smile.

"Come on," Mac begged. "It'll help the healing process."

"Hah," Sally replied and then added with an evil smile, "until that leg heals you aren't getting any there, buddy."

"Oh, that's just cold. That's just so, *so* cold."

"Well then, don't get shot in the calf, dumbass," she counseled as she went into the walk-in closet and started selecting her outfit for the day, choosing a light gray skirt suit.

Mac pushed himself up and rolled his legs over and put weight on his right calf. He grimaced. It was sore, *really* sore. "This is going to suck," he muttered as he reached for his crutches.

Sally stuck her head back out of the closet. "What are you doing?"

"My pain meds are in the kitchen," he replied. "That and I'm going down to make you some breakfast."

"Stay in bed," Sally ordered. "I can take care of myself."

"I know you can," Mac retorted as he pushed forward with the crutches. "But I'm not going to just lie around. I want to get up. I'm not going to sit around and be pathetic."

Twenty minutes later Sally walked into the kitchen. He had coffee, scrambled eggs and sliced strawberries waiting. She sat down on a center island stool while he hopped on one leg around the island to sit down with her.

"You should use your crutches."

"I should do a lot of things," Mac replied as he leaned against the counter and reached for his cup of coffee.

"Yeah, like not get shot," Sally said in a serious tone. "You know, one of these days you're not going to walk away from something like this so easily. Luck runs out."

Mac nodded. It was a thought that popped into his mind more than once and this was a conversation they'd had far more than once. "What I do is not without risk." It was something she'd heard on many occasions.

Sally didn't really want to talk about it any more than he did. He'd survived and was making breakfast. It was time to move on and that was a good thing.

Mac found the remote for the flat screen and turned on the news. They quietly watched CNN for five minutes until the story of Rubens came on.

"Change the channel," Sally asked. "I've heard enough about that asshole."

"I hear that," Mac agreed as he switched to CNBC. At least the stock market was recovering some.

"Your book is doing quite well, by the way," Sally announced. "Top of the best seller list."

Mac nodded, looking at his phone. "That probably explains all the calls from my agent. I should give her a call today."

"Good idea, do something sedentary. I don't want you even thinking of leaving the house today. You need to rest and let that leg heal."

"Rubens has a partner out there," Mac replied. "That jackhole needs to be found. That person is a murderer and has the blood of fifteen, and if I add in Gwendolyn Waxe, sixteen women on his hands."

Sally smiled at him and shook her head. "He won't be found. You have no leads. In fact, you pretty much have nothing to go on."

"You don't know that."

"Yes," Sally nodded, "actually, I do."

"You talked to Wire?"

"Yes, and Galloway, Delmonico and Lincoln Coolidge and so I know, *I know* you have *nothing* to go on. No hot lead, nobody to even talk to. So, just relax today and let them handle it. If they find something, they'll call. Take a break."

Sally left and he occupied himself by watching some Sports-Center and caught up on his hometown teams. The Wild were in the playoffs. Unfortunately, they were once again struggling with their nemesis, the Chicago Blackhawks. The baseball season was in swing and he checked up on the Twins, who were off to a brutal start, and he even scanned an NFL mock draft to see who the Vikings might select.

He couldn't go back to sleep so he crutched his way up to his office and started digging into his file on Rubens. He called in to the office, looking for Grace Delmonico.

"You're late," Grace growled.

"Excuse me?"

"It's 8:45. I had you and your dedicated ass in here by 8:00 a.m. in the office pool. Instead, your lazy ass is at home. You cost me money. So are you coming in or what?"

"Not today," Mac replied.

"We all thought you'd be in for sure."

"And I'd like to be. But I want to get married in a month so I'm going to behave myself, at least for today. But while I'm not coming in that doesn't mean I can't work. Have you still been collecting stuff on Munger?"

"Yes," Delmonico replied. "And you can remote in to it and see it real time. I'll send you the instructions."

"Do that," Mac replied. "Is Wire in?"

"Uh, no," Grace answered.

"Yeah, she's probably with Ridge," Mac replied. "Send me the remote access instructions."

At 11:15, he got a call from Wire. "You want company?" she asked.

"Yeah, stop over, I'll make some lunch."

"No, you'll rest. I'll grab some takeout."

Wire arrived an hour later with Chinese food and they retired back up to his upstairs office.

"How's the leg?"

"It hurts. How's Ridge?"

"Do you want me to answer you or pretend you're Sally?"

"Sally."

"The man is a machine."

Mac cackled and Wire laughed as well. Mac reached down and rubbed his leg as he tried to get comfortable.

"Is Sally pissed about that?" Wire asked, pointing at his leg with her chopsticks.

"More than a little," Mac answered as he fumbled with the chopsticks, trying to eat some noodles. "I told her I was a fast healer."

"You better be," Wire replied. "If for no other reason than that surprise honeymoon you have planned for her."

"I will be ready. There is no way I'm screwing this up."

At 2:00 p.m., they got on the phone with Galloway, Delmonico, Coolidge and even April Greene.

"Mac, Munger's buddy has to have left town, don't you think?" Galloway asked.

"Maybe," Mac answered. "It might depend."

"On what?"

"Whether Munger was the alpha or not," Mac answered. "And I don't think he was the alpha." He related the confrontation. "He was not happy when I said he was the submissive. That's because he was."

"So if he was the submissive, you're saying it's not over?" Galloway asked. "The dominant will what? Just find a new minion?"

"Something like that," April Greene replied. "The dominant will try to find someone to fill that submissive role. People willing to engage in this sort of stuff don't grow on trees. It's not like there's a Rolodex of submissives willing to be a serial killer. It could take years but sooner or later, the dominant person will find a new collaborator."

"So Munger was the submissive?" Coolidge asked.

"Based on what Mac is reporting, it sure sounds like it," Greene answered. "He could have also walked away from this in Boston."

"When he was caught," Coolidge added.

"Right," Greene replied. "Mac thinks, and the more I think about it, I'm inclined to agree, that the accomplice killed the other two women to get him free."

"At which point," Mac stated, "the accomplice owned—"

"His ass," Greene finished the thought. "So the person who killed the last two in Boston became the dominant and manipulated Munger into continuing. I mean, from my perspective it seems as if Munger wanted to kill and had the compunction to do so but from what Mac describes about his talk with Munger in the alley, at gunpoint, I might add, it appears that whoever this other person was, that person perhaps controlled the mental and emotional aspects of their relationship."

"So how do we find this person?" Coolidge asked.

"Munger," Mac answers. "It's all we have to work from. We have to continue digging into his life history. If he did kill all of these women in conjunction with someone else, then that person he partnered with is not some casual acquaintance. It is someone *he knew*. There has to be some evidence somewhere in his history of that relationship."

"You have some information," Galloway suggested. "What we put together when you first suspected it was him."

"We do," Mac replied. "And we'll go through that all again with a different perspective, but I suspect we'll need more. It probably happened in Boston, so we should start there, looking into who he has worked with, lived with, ran with. Then we look at medical school and college. Heck, we go all the way back to his childhood. That connection happened somewhere."

"Mac, I would caution you," Greene warned. "It's not like this person is going to jump out at you."

"Maybe, maybe not," Mac answered, not totally agreeing, "When you start looking at all the people in his life suspiciously, like they're potential partners, when you put everyone in that context you might see something you otherwise wouldn't."

Mac transitioned to a different topic. "We found his office yesterday. My question now is where was he laying his head? We don't have that yet."

"I've just been handed a note, Mac," Galloway stated. "We found it."

～

Wire drove to the apartment, located across the Anacostia River on East Capitol Street. The structure surrounded by squad cars was a faux colonial-looking apartment building, red brick with black shutters around the picture windows, white trim and a white-pillared portico over the main front entrance to the building.

Wire slowly walked with him while Mac crutched his way up the sidewalk.

"This shit is going to get old in a hurry," Mac muttered. "This is embarrassing, hobbling up here like this."

"Quit your whining," Wire countered with a serious tone. "If you want less time on them, use them now, especially if you want your fiancée happy."

Mac stopped and stared down Wire. "Sally called you, didn't she?"

"Well, duh."

"Figures," Mac replied bitterly. "Whose partner are you anyway?"

"I'm looking out for my fellow sister," Dara retorted. "So quit your bitching. You were shot in the line of duty. I don't think anyone around here is thinking any less of you, although you did let Munger get the drop on you."

Mac stopped and turned to Wire. "I'm never going to hear the end of that, am I?"

"Oh hell no," Wire answered with a big smile.

"*Sweet,*" Mac moaned.

Coolidge's men Stretch and Hart met them under the portico. "The building superintendent saw a picture of Munger on the television this morning and he started to see the similarity to a tenant named Robert Stein," Stretch reported. "Mr. Stein was a tenant that drove a black Honda Civic, a factoid that first made the news last night. So the super, being a fine citizen and all, did his civic duty and called it in."

"How long has he been here?" Mac asked.

"Nearly a year," Hart replied. "In fact, the superintendent said he was looking to check in with Stein to see if he was going to renew his lease. It was up at the end of April and Stein, as he knew him, hadn't said anything about renewal."

"Of course not," Mac noted. "He would have been gone."

Mac and Wire slowly made their way up to the apartment on the second floor. It was a standard two-bedroom unit with one bath, a small galley kitchen and family room area. The apartment was spartanly furnished, with rather drab furniture arranged around a thirty-two-inch flat screen television. Sitting on an end table in the family room were books on the Smithsonian, Gallery of National Art, and the Stegall Museum, among other points of interest.

"His research interests," Wire mused.

"His fishing holes," Mac corrected.

One bedroom was completely empty and the other contained a twin bed, a narrow nightstand with a small lamp and alarm clock. In the closet were various clothing options, long and short sleeve dress shirts, jeans and dress slacks. On the shelf above the clothing rod sat five folded white t-shirts, two black t-shirts, a stack of black folded boxer shorts and a small box with colored and white athletic socks. Also hanging in the closet were two golf shirts, yellow and green, along with a red hooded sweatshirt. There were a series of light-colored, button-down collared shirts, all larges. There were six pairs of pants, all thirty-eight-inch waist and thirty-inch inseams; four tan khakis and two pairs of Levi's blue jeans.

"Perfect for someone who was five-foot-ten," Mac noted.

"Shoes are nines," Wire added, picking up a pair of Nike runners. There were also two pairs of penny loafers, one pair black and the other burgundy. "There are not a lot of clothes in here for a guy who lived here nearly a year. What do you make of that?"

"He lived like a monk," Coolidge suggested. "I mean, look at the place, pretty limited existence."

"By design," Mac replied. "If he was changing up his look all the time, why not the clothes as well and why not get rid of any clothes that could incriminate you? Look at all of the empty hangers. He used the clothes, then discarded them as he started killing."

"I suppose we'll never really know," Wire finished. "He's dead. We can't ask him."

They left the bedroom and worked their way back to the kitchen where an FBI tech was working on a laptop computer that had been found in the living room.

"Anything?" Wire asked.

"I've been going through the Internet history," the tech reported, looking up. "There are all kinds of interesting searches on here. In particular, I've found searches on Eleanor Eagleson, Lisa White, Audrey Ruston, Gwendolyn Waxe, Martha Schreiber and Glenda Richards."

"That should confirm it, then," Wire stated. "This was his place."

As they exited the apartment complex, early evening was rolling in and he'd felt his phone buzzing in his pant pocket, undoubtedly Sally. His leg was starting to throb and he was getting tired. "Can you drive me home?" he asked. "In fact, I'll feed you."

Wire looked at her watch.

"I need you to play blocker on Sally from going off on me. I'll get you out in plenty of time so you can catch up with Ridge, if that's what you're worried about."

"Oh, all right."

Wire did come inside and sat down and had dinner with her two friends. Sally served a chicken stir fry and poured Wire and herself a nice white wine.

"None for you there, buster," Sally scolded when Mac held out a wine glass. "Wine doesn't play well with those pain meds."

"This just keeps getting better," he groaned as he reached for his glass of ice water.

The three of them actually enjoyed themselves for an hour talking about politics, the White House, the wedding, anything but the case and Rubens. Mac hung in there until almost 9:00 p.m. Then the nonstop days finally caught up to him. Mac started nodding off at the table.

"We better put sleepyhead to bed," Sally suggested.

"What?" Mac said, popping awake. "I'm good."

The two women laughed uncontrollably.

"You are so not good," Wire mocked. "Go to bed. Call me tomorrow and I'll come pick you up."

"I always wanted a chauffeur."

Wire departed to go find Ridge. Sally guided him upstairs, fed him his pain meds and then tucked him into bed with the remote for the television. He was out in less than five minutes.

He slept.

It was the way it always went on a case like this.

Mac would go full out for days on a case but eventually he would experience the massive crash.

Now was that time.

He slept through Sally watching television, through a thunderstorm, through Sally getting up and getting ready for work. It wasn't until 9:45 a.m. that his ringing phone finally woke him up.

Wire rolled by and picked him up at 10:45, and he was in the FBI field office by eleven feeling more alert and awake. The leg even seemed better, less throbbing and it was more of a minor annoyance. A long slumber would do that.

"Where is everyone?" Mac asked as he hobbled his way into the conference room.

"They're sleeping, too," Wire answered. "Delmonico and Galloway burned the midnight oil last night, along with some others, to collate all of the data on Munger." Dara waved to the table. "We have ten more boxes of documents to sift through. In addition, Grace has created a huge computer database of information on him and there will be more to come."

"Wow!"

"You asked for it," Wire stated dryly. "You better start digging."

"I guess I better do that," Mac stated as he laid his crutches down onto the floor, pulled up a chair to the table and tipped the top off a banker's box.

At 3:30 p.m., they snuck out for a break, going to a coffee shop for an iced coffee and late afternoon snack.

"How many boxes have you gone through?" Wire asked.

"Five so far," Mac answered.

"Anything?"

"He was an outstanding medical student," Mac replied. "Yet it appears during his time in medical school, he didn't make many close friends. Agents have tracked down all of his classmates from his medical school class. As a person, they say he was crazy smart, harmless, nice enough and tried to fit in but apparently had a unique ability to be awkward around crowds and say the wrong thing at the wrong time. The same thing was true at Mass General—people said he was generally nice, but quirky, awkward and a social misfit but universally they all are surprised he was Rubens."

Wire nodded. "Same thing I'm seeing. At Providence, it appears he didn't really have any tight friends although he was remembered. He was the kind of guy who went to a party but nobody really talked to him. His first-year roommate said he and Munger spoke when they lived together, but hardly after. There was one guy from Providence who said he stayed in contact with him after college."

"Any particular reason?"

"He thought Maynard was a guy who needed a friend," Dara answered. "He said Munger was awkward, a little shy but really *wanted* to be liked and tried hard to be liked. He said if you got him out of his shell, got him to feel comfortable and you were open to someone who was a little odd, maybe off-putting, he wasn't a bad guy to know. It was just that most people never seemed to give him that chance."

"Sometimes really brilliant people are a little different."

"That's what this guy said about Munger," Dara replied. "This friend became a doctor as well, practices in Cleveland. He said he also kept in touch for a few years because Munger was so smart but he just couldn't fit with people."

"Like the lead in the television show *House*?"

Wire nodded. "He actually made that reference. Not a massive over-the-top prick like Dr. Gregory House, but every bit as smart."

"You know," Mac asked on the way back, "if he was so socially awkward how did he become such a Don Juan to these women?"

"Maybe he didn't need to be with these women, given their histories and backgrounds."

"The theory being he was hunting people every bit as quirky as he was."

"Yeah."

"Maybe," Mac replied. "Still, he must have developed some game along the way."

"It could be that the partner helped with that. If the partner was the dominant, then maybe he taught the pupil a few things."

At the field office, they got back to work. Mac looked at the boxes and thought about what he'd looked at, which was all from adulthood. Instead, he changed up and first went to a file marked *family*. Munger's father was an insurance salesman of modest success and his mother a homemaker. If mom and dad were modestly successful, their two children were exceptionally bright. Maynard wasn't the only one to go to medical school. Maynard had an older brother named Elston who was many years his senior. Elston, too, was a doctor, who later married and started a medical practice in Portland, Oregon.

Unfortunately for Maynard and his brother, their parents both died young, his father of lung cancer, apparently a heavy smoker, and his mother of breast cancer. Tragically, just a few years later, nearly eleven years ago, Elston took his life as well.

"Talk about a tragic family," Mac murmured.

"What?" Wire asked.

Mac explained what he'd just read. "No wonder Maynard was so screwed up."

All of that might explain some of his odd behavior as an adult. The question Mac now pondered was if Maynard was also an awkward social misfit as a child.

There was a box marked *Chicago Schooling*. Mac flipped off the top of the box, and inside were records sorted by his years in school. "Delmonico is an organizational machine," Mac noted.

"She learned from Yoda Galloway," Wire noted. "You want some coffee?"

"No, thanks," Mac replied, "but I'd love a Diet Coke with ice."

"I'm on it."

Mac started in with Munger's school records, starting in high school and working his way backward. In reading through the documents, it was apparent that Munger moved schools a lot. He went to school in a number of Chicago suburbs: Schaumburg, Wheaton, Aurora, North Aurora, Oakbrook and Lake Forest. As a child, he never got to stay anywhere more than a year at a time. No wonder he became socially awkward. He never seemed to stay in school long enough to make any friends or establish the relationships you need to develop confidence.

From a records standpoint, each year there was a new school, a whole new file with transcripts, report cards, yearbooks, and various other documents. It was tedious work, sifting through his grades, classes, and interviews with his high, middle and elementary school teachers. He kept working his way back, flipping through some pictures. "I got to hand it to Grace—she has his fourth ... grade ... class ... whoa. That can't be."

"What?" Wire asked, as she came back into the room.

"Has anyone seen April today?" Mac asked.

"No, I don't think so," Wire answered, holding Mac's drink. "What? What is it?"

Mac pushed himself out of his chair, limping to the far end of the table.

"Mac, your crutches."

"Screw it," he replied as he dug through the stack of books on Rubens that had been resting on the end of the conference room table, largely ignored.

"What is it, Mac?"

"His fourth grade class," Mac answered, flipping to the back of the book titled *The Homicidal Artist*. "I knew I'd seen this name somewhere else. Unbelievable."

"What?"

Mac handed a picture to her. "This is Munger's fourth grade class picture. He is in the middle row, third in from the left, mustard yellow shirt, hair sticking out in various directions, the typical fourth-grade-boy look. M. Munger."

"Right, so?"

"Check out the cute blonde girl to his right."

"A. Crandall."

"Right."

"Who is A. Crandall?"

Mac opened the book and flipped to the back page and the author biography. "Crandall is the maiden name of one April Greene."

"What?" Wire answered, taking a closer look at the book. "No way."

"She was born and raised in Chicago and North Aurora in particular. She married fourteen years ago and was divorced twelve years ago from a guy named Jason Greene. They were married just a couple of years. Cripes."

"I can't believe it. Are you sure?"

Mac sat down in a chair and put his face in his hands and shook his head. "That was a hell of an act she put on in that alley," he muttered through his hands.

"In the alley...she wasn't driving her SUV into Munger to save you," Dara exclaimed, "She was doing it to—"

"Save herself," Mac answered, completing the thought. "She took out the one person who could name her. And afterwards, the shaking, the shock, the horror on her face—it was all an act."

"My God, it's April," Wire muttered in disbelief.

"We've been played," Mac moaned, reaching for and throwing the book across the room. "We've been played all along."

April Greene lived in Woodbridge, Virginia, south of DC, halfway between the Capitol and Quantico. Mac, Wire, Galloway and Delmonico leaned against a Suburban while an FBI team cleared the house.

The team leader exited the front door. "Agent McRyan, the house is cleared and she is not here. But—"

"But what?"

"There is something for you and Agent Wire inside, in the office upstairs."

The group made their way inside the townhouse. Mac painfully climbed the steps with the crutches, with Wire right behind him. At the top of the steps, the office was to the left. Inside there was an old, immaculately maintained and polished cherry wood writing desk. Sitting in the middle of the otherwise empty desktop was a laptop computer, a flash drive, a pink carnation and a note reading: *Mac and Dara, Play Me. -A.*

Mac inserted the flash drive into the port on the left side of the computer. It was a video. Mac maneuvered the mouse to the play icon. April Greene appeared on the screen, dressed casually in blue jeans, gray top siders, a cream-colored, button-down collar shirt left open and a plain white t-shirt, sitting casually right leg over the left in a desk chair to the left of the sailing photos on the wall opposite of the desk.

"Mac and Dara," she smiled at them, a knowing smile. "I knew the two of you would be my greatest challenge and you two, you did not disappoint. You were more than up to the challenge. When you found Maynard, I knew you'd eventually figure things out, especially you, Mac. When Dara talked about how you'd never let it go, that you would keep pursuing it, I knew my time as April Greene was likely at an end."

Wire shook her head. "Me and my big mouth."

The video continued, "So, how was it that you ultimately found me? I bet it was that fourth grade picture, wasn't it?" Greene smiled and lightly shook her head. "I knew it. That picture, that terrible fourth grade picture was a track I could never completely cover.

"So, I'm sure you're asking how and why?

"I've always been fascinated by the process of manipulating people ever since I was a little girl, even as far back as fourth grade. If Maynard was alive, he'd tell you that.

"Me? I was the original mean girl," April said with an evil grin.

"I played those fourth graders like pawns. Even at that early age, I realized just how easy it was to manipulate people. The mind is *truly* an amazing thing.

"It can be molded and controlled in so many ways. You just have to know which button or buttons to push. Take Maynard, for example. Influencing him wasn't hard. Once he killed and got the high from it, he was addicted to it and I just had to keep feeding him the drug.

"Now, I know one question you must have is why Maynard killed these women? Why these Rubenesque type women? It was pretty simple really. Nicole Franzen, the original Rubenesque type woman, dumped him, which of course you now know. Maynard—" April shook her head. "The poor boy really had it bad for her. But back then Maynard was so inept with women that he couldn't hold onto her and not making it work with her was a huge disappointment for him. She had the hook in him something fierce, and that she eventually rebuffed him only made it worse. He just couldn't get her out of his head. However, at that point, he wasn't thinking of killing her, he was simply obsessed with her. But then, as with so many things in life, there was that triggering event that changed everything for Maynard. The event that ultimately brought Maynard to me. That trigger was his brother, Elston Munger.

"Maynard revered Elston. Elston was his senior by nine years but Maynard loved him very much, idolized him and spent his life trying to be like him. I think it's why Maynard went to medical school, because Elston did.

"Sadly for Maynard, Elston committed suicide eleven years ago after his wife, a very Rubenesque-looking woman named Leslie up and left him for another man. His brother's death, what caused it and who caused it changed something in Maynard. For a month after his brother's suicide he stewed on that loss, on women, on the fact that his brother's wife, that woman, that undeserving, overweight woman left his brother and so devastated him that he killed himself. Maynard knew that Nicole Franzen, failing with her, the same kind of woman as Leslie, was slowly tearing him up inside. She had the hook in him and he couldn't let her go and wasn't going to let her do to him what Elston's wife did to him. Maynard was not going to end up like his brother. So he went to her apartment to give her one last chance. When she wouldn't take him back? When she said there was no way in hell she would ever want to be with him? Well," April shrugged and shook her head, "you know the rest of the story. He snapped and killed Nicole. But then, what he discovered after killing Nicole was that he liked the power of the kill and soon he felt the hunger, the need, the desire to do it again, *and again*.

"I was called up to Boston to consult on the case because of the ritualized nature of the murder, the staging of the body similar to *The Judgment of Paris*. Then Maynard was brought in for questioning. I watched from behind the glass when Detective Sullivan was interviewing him and I knew, *I knew*, Maynard was the killer.

"I could have offered Sullivan my opinion but their evidence was paper thin. They didn't have enough, not near enough. And besides, as I stood behind that mirror, looking in on Maynard, I had an epiphany. What I realized was that the person I really wanted to help was Maynard. I saw in him the perfect research tool. He was a brilliant doctor who also possessed a thirst to kill. So I decided to help Maynard and I killed the last two in Boston.

"After I saved him in Boston, I went to see him. He talked all about how he wanted to put it all behind him, move on with his life and career. Maynard claimed to me that he was innocent and that all he wanted was to get his reputation back." April paused, smiled and lightly shook her head. "It was all a front. It took me two minutes and I could tell he wanted to kill, *to keep killing*. He had the hunger.

"I could see the thirst for it in his eyes. It was a rage that was not satisfied. It took me all of a half-hour to convince him of his need to keep going, that he wouldn't be able to stop and that he would kill again. I told him I could relate to him, the power and satisfaction that killing provided. After all, I'd done it myself. I understood him. I wanted to help him. *I was like him*. When I said that, when I related on his level, when he saw that and understood it, he folded and then he was mine.

"So I wanted to see how far we could take it and how far I could push him. It took a few years but I worked with him on approaching women, so as to wear down those awkward edges and give him some tools with the ladies. Nobody had ever taught him anything along those lines but he was smart, a very quick learner and had a certain air of confidence he'd gained from his two kills. He was strutting a little bit, so to speak. So in addition to teaching him how to approach women, I gave him a little extra flair and panache, a timer and clues to heighten the risk and increase the excitement. I gave him the timing on the phone calls, or on occasion made the call myself, like in Los Angeles or here in DC.

"So for ten years, he played the killing game three more times. And in turn, I studied him for those ten years. What a fascinating subject he was. It was such a pity I ended up having to kill him. I'm sure you can understand that no artist wants to kill their muse."

April crossed her arms and sat back almost studiously. "You know, in many ways, he was the perfect partner because he had enough impulse control that he could stop and then start killing again, much like BTK, Dennis Rader in Wichita. Maynard was able to have that control as long as he had other passions he could pursue, which for him was his art. He loved museums, galleries, libraries and he truly had a passion to paint and travel.

"I was rich and he was making me richer, so I funded his sojourns out of the country, and in turn, he provided me so much insight.

"You see, Mac and Dara, I was every bit as much of a gunner as Maynard was. The difference is I had *all* of the skills. I had the book and street smarts and even more importantly, I had the vision. The rest of the world truly is wearing bifocals.

"Think about it, just think about it," April urged with a wide smile, enthusiastically gesturing to the camera, sitting forward in the chair. "Think about the vision of what I did. To be able to study a serial killer up close in the wild, in his native habitat, planning the killing with him, steering him toward the victims, studying him while he did it, the victims and their interactions together is something nobody has done. It was something nobody else had dreamed of doing.

"So many people would spend their time interviewing captured serial killers to try to understand their mind."

April shook her head and snorted. "*Boring.* What was exciting was studying Maynard while in action? Out in the wild? You have no idea what that meant for me.

"I learned so much more than anyone possibly could about how a mind like that works. And of course, it did allow me to help the FBI catch many killers, to burnish my reputation, to make sick gobs of money and provide me yet greater access to cases and killers around the country. But," she added and a devilish grin swept across her face, "I also used what I learned when it suited *my* needs and *my* desires."

"Oh shit," Mac muttered, understanding where April was going.

"You don't think?" Wire asked, looking to him.

Mac just nodded.

"Oh, I so wish I could see your expressions now," Greene laughed and smiled, sitting back into her chair, right leg back over her left, her hands softly clasped together under her chin, elbows resting on the chair's arms. "I bet you two just thought it was Maynard, didn't you?" She shook her head and smiled. "No, no, no, there have been others I followed, watched, studied, encouraged and even assisted. Many others, and—" She added with a darker expression, "there will be more."

She paused for a moment to let that sink in.

"Unfortunately, your immediate success has meant that I have to go away for some time and make some changes of my own. After all, I can't make the game easy for you. I'm sure you understand. In fact, I'm sure you wouldn't want me to make it easy. Mac, to quote something you like to say— what would be the fun of that?"

"Me and *my* big mouth," Mac muttered, glancing to Wire.

"Mac, I truly hope your wedding is everything you hoped it would be. You are a *very* lucky man. Sally Kennedy is a beautiful and bright woman. Take good care of her."

"Dara," Greene stated with a knowing smile, "enjoy Ridge while it lasts. I did once and have thought of those two nights often. He is a very vigorous lover. Please feel free to tell him that. I'm sure he'd want to know that truth. He'll probably revel in it."

April exhaled and lightly clasped her hands together. "Well, that's it. There is so much more I could say but I think it best for me to just save it until next time. You know, I can hardly wait. We'll have so much to talk about." She leaned forward in the chair. "So, until we meet again, I will simply bid you two *adieu*."

The screen slowly went dark.

The room stood in stunned silence.

"Did I just really watch that?" Wire asked in shock, breaking the silence.

"I guess now we know who the dominant one was."

"She manipulated him, manipulated other killers, manipulated the FBI. Heck, she's manipulated everyone."

"Yes, she did," Mac mused as he picked up the carnation and twisted it with his fingers.

"What do you make of the carnation?"

"It's a calling card," Mac answered, turning to Wire. "Sometime, somewhere, we will find it lying next to a dead body, and when we do, we'll know the game and the manipulation is on again."

"HOW CAN YOU OF ALL PEOPLE LET IT GO?"

The wedding day *was* everything he hoped for.
Dick, Rock and Riles were present and fully tuxedoed, along with Chief Flanagan as well as Mac's family, Uncle Shamus, Paddy and Shawn, and the others. The Kennedy clan was present en masse, always a fun group, livening up the party. Judge Dixon and even President Thomson made an appearance, staying for dinner, offering a hearty toast and taking a brief dance with the bride before duties compelled his departure back to the White House on Marine One.

It was a great party and as they sat at the head table after the dinner, eating their pieces of wedding cake, Mac smiled and turned to his beautiful bride. "I have a surprise for you."

"What's that?"

"You remember Antonin Rahn?"

"The eccentric oil man worth billions? He was the man who helped you on that case up in North Dakota."

"That's him. It turns out he's very appreciative of everything I did for him and it also turns out he owns two private islands in the Caribbean. He's letting us have one for the week." Mac reached into his pocket and pulled out his cell phone. "Let me show you a few pictures." He pulled up the file and started swiping through the pictures and watched as Sally's jaw slowly dropped open in amazement and excitement.

"Oh my God. We have an island in the Caribbean, an actual island all to ourselves. You're serious?"

"Yes, oh, and I forgot. A boat, too."

"A ... boat too. I see."

"It's gonna be great."

"You have no idea," Sally replied and it was her turn to tease. "You should see some of the things I bought to wear." She leaned closer and whispered seductively in his ear, lightly biting his earlobe, "I look really good in all of it. At least what there is of it."

"I'm a lucky man."

"You've no idea."

He leaned in and kissed her. "Oh, yes, I do."

A half-hour later as the sun started setting Mac slipped outside to grab some fresh air and found Wire by herself on the patio, looking out trancelike to the water of Chesapeake Bay, a glass of champagne in her hand.

"Hey."

Dara snapped out of her daze, turned to him and smiled. "A beautiful day, Mac. Congratulations."

"Thank you."

They both stood quietly, leaning against the wood railing and looking out over the ocean, feeling the cooling breeze on their faces.

"What's on your mind, Dara?"

"What makes you think something is on my mind?"

"Oh, I don't know. There is a big party going on inside and you're out here by yourself. In your absence, one of Sally's very buzzed single and aggressive friends from the White House staff is making serious moves on your date."

"Ridge?" Wire answered. "She can have him."

"I see," Mac replied, looking straight ahead out to the stray boats in the distance cruising in the cool blue waters. "So, that video is still eating at you, isn't it?"

"I can't get it out of my mind," Dara answered quietly, looking down. "It comes to me in my sleep, when I'm working, when I'm exercising. Heck, it popped into my head during the ceremony. I see *you* and I think of *her*. Why do you think I've spent more time than I've really wanted to with Ridge?"

"Because he's a machine?"

Wire smiled and nodded. "*That* and he keeps my mind occupied."

Mac figured that was the case.

"What about you? Haven't you thought about it?" she asked.

"Only all the time," Mac replied. "Like you, I've had a distraction. The wedding and all of the stuff leading up to it has served to occupy my mind so it hasn't perhaps been eating at me like it has you, but the thought of April is ever-present and I'm sure will continue to be for some time."

"What do we do?"

"We let the FBI continue to hunt for her, but you and I? You and I? We have to let it go."

"We have to let it go?"

"Yes, we let it go. *For now.*"

Dara was surprised. "How can you of all people let it go? Doesn't it eat at you that she got away? Doesn't it eat at you that she played you, played all of us? She played everyone for years."

"All the time," Mac replied, slowly shaking his head. "It eats at me all of the time."

"So how do you just let it go?"

"Because she's gone and we can't find her, at least not right now. We've hunted for three weeks and there is not a trace of her. Not one trace. She knew the day would come when she was exposed and she was ready for it. Dara, she inherited twenty million from her parents when they died. She's made like another ten million through her books, yet all the FBI can find is $500,000 worth of miscellaneous assets consisting of a townhouse, a boat and a little over twenty-one thousand in a bank account. Why? Because she hid it, knowing she might have to run one day." Mac sipped from his glass of champagne. "The FBI is continuing to search high and low for her. Galloway and

Delmonico are on it and you and I both know how good they are, but I think in the end it will be a waste of extremely valuable manpower better used elsewhere. She's gone and we're not going to find April until she decides it's time to come out and play this wicked little game again."

"So we just wait, then?"

"Unless the FBI miraculously finds her, yes," Mac replied. "We have to live with that because that's just the way it is. You have to be able to rationalize that."

Wire turned to the water and sighed. "I wonder if I can."

"Trust me, you can. Listen, Dara, someday, somewhere, April will be back. That could be six months from now or six years. Who knows when it'll be? I know this much, though: I'm not going to let that dominate my life or my every thought. You know why?"

"Why?"

"Because she'll be back. She won't be able to help herself. But until then, don't let her manipulate you like she manipulated Maynard Munger. Don't let her inside your mind, don't let her control your life. Because if you do that, then she—"

"Wins."

"Don't let her win. Let her take the loss. You know what? We won this round—maybe it wasn't a knockout, but we won. Three women died, not four. Munger, her muse and a psychopath, is dead and will harm nobody else. She's on the run, and is no longer April Greene, the great serial killer profiler. No more best-selling books or inter-views on national television. No more fawning press and cops just begging for her help. She's no longer April Greene, the great serial killer profiler. She's April Greene, the fugitive from justice, currently number one on the FBI's Most Wanted List. So in that sense, we took half of the game she loved to play away from her. So in my mind, that's a win for us, a big win, and while she didn't show it on that video, she knows we were the winners and it's burning up that gunner ego of hers." Mac smiled. "And here is one other thing she should know: when she comes back we'll be ready. We'll understand our opponent, and here's one other thing: I don't like to lose."

"Me neither."

"I know you don't. When she comes back, I promise you, we'll take her down for good. You and me, we will catch her. But in the meantime," Mac grinned, looked back inside and hooked his left arm for Wire to slide her hand through, "I'm throwing a hell of a party inside and you haven't danced with me yet."

"Mac, I got news for you," Wire answered, smiling as they walked back inside.

"What's that?"

"You really can't dance."

"Oh, come on. I thought I gave the lawnmower and sprinkler a lot of flair."

She sat in the chair on the back deck, the boat floating gently in the soft late-day waves of the bay. Through the narrow opening in the bandages covering her face, she was able to use the powerful binoculars and focus in on Wire and McRyan chatting on the patio, looking out over the waters of the bay.

"Talking about me, I'm sure."

April watched the two of them until they turned and went back inside to the reception. She pushed herself up out of the chair, went inside the boat cabin and started the engines, bringing them to life. She pushed the throttle down, felt the roar of the motor and the lift of the boat as she set off for the open waters of the Atlantic Ocean, thinking about how she needed to go away and disappear, to make the trail to her colder still, yet fantasizing of when she could return to start the game. And next time, when she came back to play, when she came back for McRyan and Wire, it would be for keeps.

A note to my readers...

Thank you for reading and I sincerely hope you enjoyed *Next Girl*

On The List. As an independently published author, I rely on each and every reader to help spread the word. If you enjoyed the book please tell your friends and family and I would really appreciate a brief review.

The next standalone thriller in the McRyan Mystery Series is *Fireball.* I've also started a second series called the FBI Agent Tori Hunter Series and the first book is *Silenced Girls.*

Thanks again and I'm always writing a new book so look for Mac in the next mystery! To stay on top of the new releases and new series please join the list at www.RogerStelljes.com and I'll let you know when the next one comes out.

ALSO BY ROGER STELLJES

MCRYAN MYSTERY SERIES

First Case - Murder Alley

The St. Paul Conspiracy

Deadly Stillwater

Electing To Murder

Fatally Bound

Blood Silence

Next Girl On The List

Fireball

The Tangled Web We Weave

Short Stories

Stakeout - A Case From The Dick Files

Boxsets

First Deadly Conspiracy - Books 1-3

Mysteries Thrillers and Killers - Books 4-6

FBI AGENT TORI HUNTER

Silenced Girls

Never miss a new release again join the list at

www.RogerStelljes.com

ABOUT THE AUTHOR

Roger Stelljes is the New York Times and USA Today bestselling author of the McRyan Mystery Series. His books have been downloaded and enjoyed by millions worldwide. He has been the recipient of numerous awards including: The Midwest Book Awards– Genre Fiction, a Merit Award Winner for Commercial Fiction (MIPA), as well as a Minnesota Book Awards Nominee.

Never miss a new release again, join the new release list at www. RogerStelljes.com

Made in the USA
Las Vegas, NV
20 December 2023

83297015R00194